SUGA PUSS PUBLISHING PRESENTS...

THE SUTTER ANGELS

A NOVEL BY:
F. KALIFE & ROSALIND ROBINSON

ISBN: 978-1508831754
ISBN-10:1508831750

Cover designed by F.Kalife Robinson & Rosalind Robinson

This book is dedicated to My Mother, the True Angel of My Life.
Rest In Peace, Ma.

F. Kalife

SHOUTOUTS TO MY PEOPLE

Janice & Karron Robinson, Berlinda McDonald, Althea Idlet, Vicky Davis, Michelle Thompson, Raquel Harris, Matilda (Moe), Paula Lawrence, Magolli, Iqueen, Peaches, Laura, Cleopatra. And to EVERY GANSTA BITCH THAT RAN WITH THE SUTTER ANGELS...This One Is For You All. ENJOY!!!

ACKNOWLEDGEMENTS: Terrance Breazil, Drack, Mark Cross, Cabezza, K.O. Smitty, Poz, Ahmed "Polo" Robinson, Black Face & Bill (from Roosevelt), Big Smoke, Lil Smoke, Rosalind Hewitt and her son, Christopher Moultrie, daughter, Briana Moultrie, Tasha Alexander, Will "Scar" Alexander, Nicole "Soonie" Wilmot and Justina Wilmot (yeah, whose permission do I *really* need?), Sissy, Me-Me, Shabey, J. "Freedom" Mobley, J. "Knowledge Born" Callender, Kev Webb, Big Iraef, Jah, Kilo, Yvette Darden, Shaquana, Aunt Marlene, Tut, O.G. Shabazz, Medina, Justice, Supreme, Big Shakim, Big Elson, Lil Elson, Ayatollah, RayHeem (Radar), Don Stone, MarkFour, Nesto, Sharice Williford, Jamel Holmes, Brandon, Wag, Victor Breland, Johnny Ray, Beautiful Life, Big Spadie, Just God, Lil Boxing Bar, Nuke, Wee Whop, Yogi, Rat, Vick, Nice, Black, Georgie, Shalonda, Nicky, Asia, Snow, Lil Momma, Curly, Clee, Donnell, Annette, A.Z., Clip, K-Born, Precious and Black Kev, Brooklyn (Veer), Ghania "Kool" Miller, Venus Chunga Reyes, and Miz of Pincushion Publishing and author of Hater's Animosity, The Bulldog Crew, G-Banks, Bishop and to my homegirl, Valerie Graham.

ALSO SHOUT OUT TO: Big Ox, B-Original, Giant Cee, Donald "Gotti" Rudd, Ahmad A. Rashid, Yafeu, Richard Labron, Du Right, Born Son, Cream, Wadu, Jungle Brim, Patricia Houchen, Tameko Cook, Chucky Don, Lord Prince (VanDerveer), Intelligent Tareef Allah, Trouble, Lenny, Veenie & Cheryl Portis, Chereda Ivory (from Long Island), My Man Shorty B (from Rochester - G-Boys Poster Child), Mario Machete, Hound Dog, and Trina Alexander, Nugget (from Marcy, stay up!), and Baby Ice (from N.A. Rock), the hat boy B-Real, (585) I see you my nigga...My boy Tiko (Elmira's finest). The legendary Mitchell "Bogart" Harper, Queen Ramsey (from BPT, CT. You're my sister from another Mom & Dad, always), Drip and family. Regina, Zyi'meire, Rhonda Elisicia, Dorian Jr., Eastside Roc Town (Short St.), Shamika Wilkerson, Debbie Nicholson, Mr. Gramont, Iesha Davis, Chris "Unique" Wilmore, Kevin Newell, Ms. Obie (I know if anybody's feeling this book, you are), Ms. Roberts, O.G. Gracie Gowens, Jimmy Ace, Rick Martin, (O.G. Survivor), William I-Khan DeJesus (you opened my eyes to this shit and I'll never forget all the hard work you help put in with Brooklyn's Own). Wesley Watford, Tracey Smith, Juwanna Bellamy, Squirrel, Natoka (Mack Momma), My Sisters in Fayette, Alabama; Jennifer, Nicky, Toya and Pat Watson) and to my Buffalo Niggaz, David "Big Hump" Humphrey and Big Spank, and also Big Peace and his wife Lee, Big Smoke and his wife Tammy, World the Don - E.N.Y, and extra shout out to my Godson out in Bridgeport, CT – Bundlez. Money Green, Co Co, Puba and to **Sleepy Vasquez from Glenwood Projects Brooklyn,** Rap from Ft. Green Projects and I can't forget Puerto Rican Boxing Little of E.N.Y who spent countless hours typing up this manuscript for me.

Last, but definitely not least, for my Brooklyn peeps, my sons Timothy and Prince and my baby girl, Brittany M. Blassingame. My cousin Gracie Babb, my baby sister Jaquana, Lightskin Bar (from Ft. Green), To my Florida Ridaz, West Palm Beaches Top 6, Miami's Zoe Pound (What's up Mac-a-zoe!), Zoe Face, and Redd Eyezz. And out West in California, shoutout to Compton's Sylvia Nunn (Piru Legend), Lawrence L.A. Williams, Haitian Toby, Baby Latrell Handy, Hilda Maria Costa, Dorian Carter aka Big Stone from Faragut Projects and his wife, Jamedra Trotman-Carter. Kush from Brownsville, Kay Slay, Hip Hop Weekly, Tracy Cook (from Rochester), my other babygirl – Shanieka Wilkerson, Big Computer, Big Cuz, Bleu Davinci, Chad "J-bo" Brown, Ooowee, Demetrius "Big Meech" Flenory, Lil C, Bull and the entire **B.M.F.** I can't forget the authors who put it down on paper for real; Kwan, Seth Ferranti, Tha Twinz, Zane, G-Unit Books, Nikki

Turner, Carl Weber, Chunichi, La Jill Scott, Terri Woods, and Wahida Clark, J. Victorious Dodson, author of "Your Mother Should of Crossed Her Legs" and "Jack Frost".

MY PEOPLES OUT IN QUEENS: Big Crush, Corley Wall, Monkey, Rat, Stoney, Bizzy, Moe, Clarence, Clutch, Keith, Big B.I., Chazz, Graph, Grandmaster Vick, Clay, P-Man, Gerald "Prince" Miller, Dave & Nacey McClary, Baby Born, Baby Wise, K. "Supreme" McGriff, Lameen, Robo Just, Eugene & Ty Wells, Lance, David Gotti Rodriguez, Todd, Pretty Tony, Raymond "Rashied" Blair, Jock, Pep, Marty, Keven Gaines, and my cousin Uffy Wood, Tommy Montana Mickens, Sheena Babb, and Black Prince Divine Far Rock...Cassie and Ray Hackworth and Ronnie "Bumps" Bassett. Fly Ty, Nitty, Web and I can't forget Monica Steed from Astoria.

HARLEM STAND UP!!!: Felo (1199), Black Rob, Wally-O, Chick, Randy Love, Skip, Von Zip – R.I.P, Ken Ben, Do-Whop, Big Iz, Lou Diamonds (115th Street), Star Chile, Michelle Benese, Guy Fischer, Poppo Cong, Nyasia, Karlec, Michelle, Jolnette "Pepsi" Duke, and Rondell Wilkins.

BOOGIE DOWN BRONX: F. Gee Heyward, Nicole Johnson, Jose Harris, Peter Rollack, Un Gambino, Linda Gray (50 PLUS AND STILL FABULOUS), J. "Rough Sex" Bezemore, Allah Wise, Bug Out, Rondu Bolden, Tom Cross, Cee-God, Irene "Grandma" Clay, and that Rolling Stone Nigga from Webster Projects, Smurf Stone and Boy George, Chicky, Eddie Ed, Kendu, Infinite, Carlos Garcia, Gilbert Owens and my son, Duquan (from Wagner) and my daughter-in-law, Shielaya Nelson.

ATTICA SHOUTOUT: Big Wise (Mano), Young Blakk (BK), Baby, Carlos (Los), Kool-Aid (E-NY), Charlemagne, Big Snipes (BX)...

From Rochester, NY, I gotta say what's up to Deja Archee, Tameka Avant, Gorilla "L", Darren "Double D" Davis retro. From E.N.Y Brooklyn, I cant forget Viola "Bay Bay" Brown, Eugene "Zair" Murray and his wife, Lee. To my man Ian Finlay from 4 corner hustlers original members – Chris "Noon" Henderson, Richard "Blade" Wilkens, and Fred "Lil Fred" Wallace.

To my boys in Syracuse; Anthony L. Williams and to the god Big Born, Ammo and Candice - 518 Albany...and one final "special" shoutout to my loving sister Alice b.k.a "Susie". If I did not mention your name, it's not that there is no love...I simply forgot (LOL). To those I did not mention, much love and respect.

Peace & Blessings
F. Kalife

My first shoutout goes to my girl Tash. Tash if it were not for you I would not have such a wonderful husband. Bree and Christopher; I can't express how much I love you both and how extremely proud I am of each of you. My sisters; Nicole, Dana, Nana, Shakema, Justina and Cassandra: much love to y'all. Last, but not least, to My Boo . . . You're my inspiration, my motivator, you're the love of my life. Withou you, there's no me. Thank you for giving me the opportunity to work with you on this project. I know it's been a long trek toward the completion, but when you fight a good fight of determination and faith, blessings come your way. Now let's get ready for "Sutter Angels II".

Roz aka Sweetie

Chapter 1

ACE & 5-O

As she sat on the passenger side of a stolen minivan, parked on a dimly lit Van Siclen Avenue, Kacky stared out through the windshield, not lending much attention to her small group of childhood friends; Althea, Goldie and Michelle, who were all sitting in the back row seats. She also paid little attention to her sister Latesha, who sat behind the wheel pulling on what was left of the splendidly rolled blunt of exotic Kali Mist marijuana they all had been sharing.

With a nudge of the elbow, Kacky's focus was interrupted by her sister who was passing her the blunt as she spewed the ganja smoke from her nostrils, forming a huge cloud of smoke in the vehicle. After retrieving the marijuana, Kacky paused for effect, then abruptly stated, "Yo, listen up! From this moment on every time a motherfucker test our gangsta, we're gonna let our tits hang like real bitches up out this mutherfucker! Cause if we don't put in some serious work out this bitch, niggas gonna think they can step on our damn toes and get over on us! And in the future try to use us like doormats, thinking they can do whatever the fuck they want to us on account that we bleed once every month! But..." She went on with a snarled expression, "...fuck that shit! We 'bout to make a fuckin' example tonight and leave it absolutely clear that nobody *and I mean absolutely nobody* betta not dare to cross The Sutter Angels!" She was referring to her friends known by their legendary crew name. A crew founded in the early eighties in the streets of East New York, Brooklyn.

The crew consisted of twelve teenage girls who continuously kicked ass and took names of both males and females alike. They all lived on or around the notorious East

New York Street known as Sutter Avenue. Although half of their crew faded and moved to other places, it remained a truism that once a Sutter Angel always a Sutter Angel. Those that did remain together kept grinding and got rich together and cemented their notoriety in the streets of Brooklyn.

"So, Goldie...," Kacky continued in a calmer tone, making sure she made eye contact with her comrade through the visor mirror, above the passenger's dash board, "...are you sure that busted ass nigga lives in the building next to the train station?"

"Of course I'm sure! Don't you remember the day we chased his sisters' home back when we went to 292?" Goldie asked referring to the junior high school they had all attended as teenagers.

"Remember your brother Polo beat the shit out of him with that baseball bat when he tried to intervene?" Goldie added.

"Oh yeah!" Kacky recalled after flicking ashes from the blunt into the vehicles ashtray. "You talking about that nigga, Anthony. Cookie and Tay Tays' older brother?"

"Exactly!" Goldie answered. "Only that, ever since that nigga came home from lock down last summer he go by the name Ace, now."

"Hold on . . . ain't that . . ." Althea began, leaning forward in her seat, squinting her eyes to get a better view. "Yeah! There go that nigga right there!" She shouted, upon noticing him stepping out the doorway of his apartment building. Her shout caused everyone in the vehicle to key in on the young man who had just stepped out onto the concrete pavement.

Ace was a small time thug who had only a few days earlier pistol whipped one of the Angels' workers, while robbing the teenage girl of $4,500 and 50 capsules of jumbo crack she had been selling for the crew.

"I hope you don't fuck this up, Vicky." Goldie said in a low tone, through the open window of the van, to their comrade whom was standing a few feet away from the vehicle. Vicky was standing in the shadows of trees lined along Van Siclen Avenue. She was draped in an all-black, hooded, sweat suit with matching black Reebok Classic sneakers.

"Aaahh, please bitch, shut the fuck up!" Vicky mouthed off to her friend, adding a wink for emphasis before she turned towards her victim. Steadying a half filled Styrofoam cup containing unleaded gasoline, she quickly but quietly began strutting towards Ace who was by now standing in front of the train station's entrance sipping on a bottle of Heineken beer.

"Damn baby!" Ace exclaimed as Vicky strutted a few paces past him. "I thought dark attire was supposed to conceal all that juiciness you swaying about, back there. But, I guess I thought wrong, huh?" He quipped while biting down on his lip.

"I know damn well that bitch ain't just walk right by that nigga!" Michelle said, as the rest of the Angels looked on inquisitively.

"Oh hell no! She's playing herself! Fly this motherfuckin door!" Goldie snapped at Althea, who was sitting closest to the van's slide door. Reflectively she reached under her seat and retrieved her Walther PPK 380 cal. automatic from her Tory Burch clutch bag.

"Relax Gee!" Latesha commanded. "I don't think the hammer will be necessary. Vicky can handle herself, so just chillout and let's watch the scene play out."

At that very moment, in response to Ace's comment, Vicky came to an abrupt stop. After turning her head and arching her back to examine her butt, she leveled her eyes to meet Ace's. She then began, "If perverts like you can see the outline of my ass in these loose fitting sweatpants, than obviously I need to start wearing a bigger size to keep potential rapos like you from lusting."

"Bitch, what the fu..." Ace never got the chance to finish what he attempted to say. He was cut off in mid-sentence as Vicky splashed him directly in the face with the flammable contents in the cup, sending his brew crashing to the pavement. Ace brought his hands up to his face in a feeble attempt to quench the burning sensation in his eyes. "BITCH IS YOU CRAZY!" he yelled uncontrollably. His query was immediately answered by the striking sound of what he perceived to be matches being ignited.

"Yeah nigga, I'm crazy as hell. You may even say I'm a She-Devil, you bitch ass nigga!" Vicky barked back at him with a devilish laughter. She then swiftly tossed the lit matches on his head and turned on her heels. Then quickly strolled up the block towards Pitkin Avenue where she disappeared.

Having seen enough, the Angels pulled out of their parking spot and sped off. Everyone in the van remained speechless as they recalled, watching through their blunt hazed eyes, how Ace's head transformed into a ball of fire before spreading onto his velour Sean John track suit. They recollected in silence how he began to scream uncontrollably while running in a zigzag fashion, every which-a-way, until finally he tumbled to the ground a few cars in front of the van, consumed by the blaze. Ace had fallen unconscious to the ground as the gas-ignited fire continued to deep fry him from head to toe.

The Angels wanted to stay and continue watching the fireworks, but when they noticed curtains being pulled open and lights coming on throughout the surrounding apartments, they had sped off. Latesha quickly hung a left on Pitkin Avenue, clearly escaping being viewed by any potential witnesses. She double parked at the corner of Miller Avenue, and waited approximately fifteen seconds for Vicky to make her way to the van.

"Damn bitch!" Althea cursed, as she slid the door open for Vicky to get in. "Couldn't you have left that damn cup back there?"

"Bitch please!" Vicky shot back at her as she settled

into the closest seat to the window. "Picture me leaving the evidence at the scene of the crime," she chimed as she pulled the hood back and off her head, shaking out her freshly-done-shoulder-length-jet-black-wash-n-set-hair do.

"Now, how the hell could you be connected to the crime when your prints ain't even on the cup? Especially since you had on those black leather gloves the whole fucking time!" Althea snapped sarcastically rolling her eyes at Vicky in their usual playful manner.

"Oh yeah, well I definitely know I can't be connected to the damn crime if they ain't got no cup to retrieve at all." Vicky shot back waving the cup in Althea's face for emphasis while working her neck sardonically from side to side, equaling Althea's playful gesture in return, causing everyone to erupt in laughter.

"Don't pay her no mind, Vicky." Latesha shouted from the driver seat once the laughter had subsided. "You did a wonderfully professional job back there, Vee." she added, complementing Vicky. "Goldie thought you had froze up back there for a moment. She was about to hop out the fuckin' van and put some lead into that mufucka's ass. Only I suggested she fall the fuck back and watch a bitch, like you, work your magic." Latesha continued.

"I ain't even gonna front," Michelle chimed in. "I thought you had a change of heart too, when I saw your hot ass kept walking pass that nigga like you ain't notice his ass standing right there within striking distance."

"Please," Vicky cut in, "I did it that way cause, when I was approaching that nigga I noticed he had one of those I'll-fuck-the-shit-outta-you looks on his face. So I decided on the spur of the moment to go on and walk past his thirsty ass, knowing full well that he was going to make a comment about my figure that would serve me as further incentive. So, I allowed him to get an eye full before I sent his punk ass off to meet his maker, with nothing on his feeble mind but pussy. However, I would have preferred to send him off via lead poisoning." Vicky added, pulling her two shot .38 cal. Derringer out from her hoodie, and kissing the nickel plated barrel like it was her lover.

"Vicky, how many times do we have to tell you to stop bringing that little ass gun on missions?" Goldie admonished her in a serious tone.

"What!? Don't tell me this bitch brought that shit out tonight?" Kacky said, turning in her seat for confirmation.

"Oh yes she did!" Michelle assured. "She was just back here kissing and sucking on the damn barrel like she was trying to make it cum."

"Fuck you!" Vicky quickly shot back. "And fuck ya yellow ass too, Gee! I'll tell y'all bitches one thing..." she continued, "...this shit here might be a little too small for y'all liking but trust me, this lil' baby will leave a nice ass hole in a mufucka!" she added while admiring her weapon as if it was the first time she'd ever seen it.

"Yeah I hear that." Michelle retorted. "But not like the hole this here baby will leave." Michelle bragged as she pulled out and raised her .410 gauge from her Coach jacket laying on the seat next to her. "This shit right here will blow something up and out of a mufucka." she added, and everyone nodded in agreement.

"Okay, but on the serious side Vee," Althea cut in, "I'm in agreement with the rest of the Angels. This was definitely not an appropriate time for that little ass gat. Cause you know anything could happen that would require heavy artillery."

Sucking on her teeth like a scorned child, Vickie replied, "Well, I can't control how y'all feel cause that's a personal emotion. But personally speaking, I feel like any time anybody violates one of us or violates any of our peoples, that's an appropriate time for them to get it and it shouldn't matter what size the weapon is, so long as it gets the mufuckin' job done."

"Hmm," Althea groaned. "I bet they rather take the two hot rocks from that Derringer than from the big ass boulder that'll come flying up outta that .410. Personally, I'd hate to be on the receiving end of any gun fire, but in particular that huge ass cannon right there." She joked, gesturing with a nod towards the weapon Michelle was still brandishing.

"Ah bitch please." Michelle jokingly interjected, breaking any tension that may have risen. "Althea, I'm pretty damn sure you've been on the receiving end of much bigger shit than this." Michelle playfully wielded the barrel of her gat up and down in her clutched right hand, making sexual gestures which caused the girls to erupt in loud joyful laughter.

"Aha, ha, ha, ha..." Kacky chuckled out loud. "Yeah bitch, don't think we forgot 'bout all those bogus excuses you use to come up with 'bout why you couldn't hang with us back in the days. We knew ya hot ass was in my mom's crib with my brother, with ya mufuckin' knees all up in the air and shit!"

Michelle broke out laughing hysterically before she contained herself and added, "Ah huh. Kacky remember when your grandmother told us that she caught Althea and your brother doing the nasty and thought your brother was fucking her with one of Glenda's baby doll's leg until she said she got close up on them and realized it was all ding-a-ling?"

"Girl please, do I remember?" Kacky cracked back with a mocking wave of her hand. "I remember that shit like it just happened a moment ago. That's how my brother got the nickname King-Ding-A-Ling!"

"Umm umm!" Goldie sighed, fanning her face with her open palm. "I remember when Raquel use to fuck him too. She would always brag about how abnormally big his shit was. I swear I don't know how y'all could have handled some shit like that. Unless, of course, y'all bitches got that one size fits all type coochies," she laughed. "If I even suspected a nigga was holding like that, there would be no way in god's heaven or earth he'd get up in this pussy. I mean, shit, I ain't no damn virgin or anything, but I like to keep my shit nice and tight. I can't be having no horse ding-a-ling holding nigga stretching my coochie all out of contour."

"*Ahh* bitch, stop sitting up in here feeding us that bold face lie!" Michelle barked. "Your coochie's like the hundred yard dash. Mad niggas done ran up in it with all different types, shapes, and sizes. You ain't fooling nobody up in here with that your-coochie-got-contour shit, I bet you your pussy is shallow and deep as all hell."

"Fuck you, Michelle!" Goldie shot back. "You can't name any two niggas from around the way who can honestly say they done been up in this here pussy."

"Oh Goldie, knock it off, already and spare us the bullshit drama. Everybody in the damn whip done had our share of dicks. The only difference is you do all your kinky, nasty, freaky shit outside the East. Talking bout yo shit nice-n-tight. I bet a whole god damn African village would fit up in there and still leave room for it to fart!" She ended with the snapping of her fingers for dramatic effect. All the Angels simultaneously broke out in a chorus of laughter, including Goldie.

Suddenly the laughter came to an abrupt halt as they approached the dark quiet street corner of Blake Avenue, where Latesha spotted a police cruiser coming from their right side. She spontaneously reached and grabbed her .45 automatic which was resting on the seat between her thighs. Kacky, never missing a beat, noticing her big sister's arm shoot up with gat in hand, responded in like manner out of habit. She immediately reached down and took hold of her 9 mil. Beretta that was leaning up against the door panel. Keying in on the patrol car, she got into ready mode.

"Yo! Yo!" Latesha shouted aggressively. "if ya'll don't want to go to jail, I suggest you brace yourselves because we got some unwanted company at three o'clock." With that said the Angels jumped into hight alert, causing the van to reverberate the click-clacking sound of their weapons being cocked in preparation for discharge. Pausing at the stop sign, they watched as the patrol car began to cruise. The shotgun riding officer began to speak into the transmitter while scanning the van with keen eyes. Instantaneously, Latesha cut a sharp left in the middle of the avenue. The patrol car quickly followed pulling parallel to the van at about thirty-five yards apart. As the police car doors flew open, Althea was the first to react. Yanking the slide door open, she pierced the silence with a barrage of shots. "BOOM! BOOM! BOOM!"

"YEAH MOTHERFUCKAS, COME ON!!" She shouted after sending the barrage from her .45 automatic in the officers' direction. The slugs drilled silver dollar size holes into the door of the driver's side. Vicky, who followed Althea's lead, leaned out the open van door and utilizing the overhead handle to brace herself, let loose two shots from her Derringer. The first slug missed its intended target by centimeters, but the second was true, finding its mark. It hit one of the officers under the right armpit sending his body jerking back from the impact precisely as he discharged several rounds in return, which wildly missed their intended target. Kacky by now had exited the vehicle and utilized the door as a shield as she discharged her weapon. "BANG! BANG! BANG!" "IS THIS WHAT YOU MOTHERFUCKERS WANT!" she furiously yelled, as she let loose another volley of shots from her nine. Her shots tore into the hood of the patrol car, causing the car's horn to blare incessantly.

"Yo Gee, let's go out the back and get the drop on these pigs!" Michelle suggested to Goldie. She took the lead, jumping over the back row of seats and dove out the back door in a display of athletic agility. Latesha, sat up on the windowpane with half her body out the vehicle and sent a hail of shots flying over the roof of the van at both officers, expertly managing her weapon with both hands.

Goldie, once out of the van, got low on the ground, clutching her firearm in her right hand and crawled combat style along the driver's side of the van. Making sure to stay out of the view of the officers, particularly, the officer on the passenger side, who had no clue that she was quietly approaching.

Unsuspectingly, the officer came up and dumped two shots in Latesha's direction. The shots shattered the windshield before striking the headrest on the driver's side of the van. Upon impact, the bullets sent cushion and leather particles flying throughout the van's interior. Goldie took aim from her concealed crouched position and fired four rounds at his exposed legs. As the officer, suddenly aware of his danger, attempted to shield himself behind the door of the patrol car, three shots tore apart his left shin. He dove into his patrol car on one leg, screaming in agonizing pain. "Aaahh shit! Sam, my fucking leg is gone! Oh my God! Oh my God! Jesus Christ!!!" He kept screaming, horrified.

Michelle, who was patiently waiting for the perfect opportunity to join in on the bombastic festivities with her comrades, cautiously peeked around the van just in time to see that the slide of the other officer's weapon had suddenly recoiled, indicating that his weapon was on empty. She smiled devilishly to herself before taking perfect aim. "I got ya motherfuckin' ass now," she whispered to herself and squeezed the trigger. BOOM! "Take that you fuckin pig!" She yelled, as the sound echoed throughout the neighborhood. The shot caught the officer in the center of his bullet-proof vest. The cannon-like impact caused the officer to crash to the pavement, knocking the wind out of him. Althea climbed outside of the van and also got down low, crawling combat style. Her breast hugged the pavement as she locked eyes with the fallen devil in blue, and as he gasped for what was to be his last intake of oxygen, she trained her weapon on him, blew him a kiss then squeezed the trigger, discharging a slug into his forehead spilling his last thoughts all over the pavement, creating what would turn out to be a forensic puzzle for his investigating colleagues.

"Yo, we outta here! Get back in the van!" Latesha commanded. Realizing that they were no longer under enemy attack, she placed her weapon back between her thighs and waited for all the Angels to hop back inside the van. Once they were all inside, Goldie, who was still holding on to the slide door, yelled for Latesha to pull over next to the passenger side of the patrol car. Latesha hurriedly swerved hard to the left and came to a complete stop along the police vehicle. Goldie and Althea then carefully extended their weapons and fired two more rounds each into the sulking injured officer, putting him out of his agonizing misery. Latesha immediately thereafter, pressed the peddle-to-the-metal, causing the tires to screech as they stormed down Miller Avenue, listening to the police sirens approaching. She looked into the rear view mirror and noticed what appeared to be an illuminating rainbow of red, white, and blue reflecting off the dark city street. Evidently she knew it was the backup police squad en route to the gruesome scene.

"Ayo, I know y'all got yourgloves on," Latesha yelled over the roar of the engine. "Nevertheless, wipe down those weapons as a precautionary measure before we toss them. I'd rather we all be safe than sorry," she commanded. They all began wiping down their weapons readying them for disposal. Kacky quickly reached over and grabbed her sister's weapon and commenced to wipe it clean, as Latesha continued to maneuver the vehicle.

At Livonia Avenue, Latesha pulled into a vacant lot where she volunteered to torch the van after they all exited the vehicle. She immediately began to douse the interior of the van with gasoline that Vicky had siphoned from the tank. After setting the van ablaze, they all rapidly vacated the premises and made their way to two Ford Taurus rental cars they had awaiting several blocks away on Wyona Street. They began to trash their weapons en route to the cars, breaking their firearms down in parts, discarding the bits and pieces into the numerous street sewers along their path. Once there, Latesha quickly climbed behind the wheel of the black Taurus. Michelle followed, climbing in on the passenger side, and Vicky in the rear seat. Kacky and Goldie rode with Althea in the other car as they made their way towards the Van Wyck Expressway en route to Michelle's house on 118th Avenue, in Jamaica Queens.

Chapter 2

CHEM / THINKING BACK

*T*he Angels sat around in Michelle's king size living room, conversing about their night's event while sharing a half filled bottle of Crown Royal XR whiskey. In the background the song "Hood News" by the underground group known as Dirty Hands was blaring from the speakers. However, Vicky was heard over the music bragging, "Them bitches that played in 'Set It Off' couldn't hold a match up next to the shit we put down in them streets tonight." She was making reference to the block buster movie starring Jada Pinkett and Queen Latifah

"Shit!" Goldie exclaimed, "Them hoes were acting. There was no mufucka' lights and cameras in our movie, just straight up ACTION!"

"I know that's right." Kacky chimed in as everybody began hi-fivin' one another.

"God damn, Michelle!" Latesha barked causing the girls to direct their attention towards her in time to observe how she had withdrew her face from the glass she was drinking from, after having taken a sip of the potent whiskey. "Damn! This fucking Crown Royal is stronger than penitentiary steel!" She managed to say, between bouts of coughs.

"Then stop drinking it, if you can't handle it, bitch!" Michelle playfully shot at her.

"Here…" Althea offered, extending her half-filled glass to Latesha, "pour some in here. I need to get as fucked up as I can, right now! And hopefully, when I wake up from this shit in the morning, I won't have no fucking recollection of what took place tonight!" Latesha dismissed her offer without comment.

"I second that!" Michelle quickly interjected. "Everybody in this room should go ahead and get so fucked up, so as to suffer memory loss regarding the events that unfolded this evening!" Michelle further suggested. Then she followed up, saying, "Let's have a toast. A toast to memory loss of tonight's events on the wakeup!"

The girls then in unison all clinked their glasses sealing their oath and commitment. The crew then shook their heads, acknowledging exactly what their childhood-sister-in-crime meant by her loaded statement.

"Well, now that that's understood," Althea said, piercing the lingering silence, "we can all also agree that tomorrow ain't promised and definitely isn't here yet! So, let's enjoy the moment and let tomorrow take care of itself! And by the way, did y'all bitches see how I gave that pig a third eye?" She continued. "That fou-fif ain't no joke! It put a hole up in his forehead the size of a golf ball. Shit! I seen the swings in Miller Park right through the tunnel I left up in his skull.

"Aha, ha, ha, ha!" The Angels all joined in laughter of her boasting.

Vicky, feeling the mischievous urge to tease her, blurted, "A'ight now bitch! You puttin' too much spin on it now," dismissively waving her off and chuckling.

"Come on, y'all know Althea always gotta be all extra wit' her shit, adding all types of special effects to her movie roles n-shit!" Goldie added, to what was turning into Althea's roast. They all broke out laughing, again. Shaking their heads in confirmation to what Goldie had just said.

Vicky quickly cut back in. Only this time to big up Althea, saying, "Really yo, y'all should've seen dat bitch leaning out the van. Damn near on her stomach to bust that shot! She really fucked me up wit' that shit right there! So, I'm givin that bitch her just due. Don't get me wrong! We all got busy tonight. But, that bitch right there represented!" She added with a slight nod towards Althea.

"A-huh, I know that she represented on her stomach, the bitch always do. Y'all know that's her favorite position." Michelle jumped in on the roast, quickly springing up from her black leather recliner, got down on her Persian rug and began gyrating her lower body, demonstratively to the music, in an erotically sexual fashion, mimicking Althea taking dick. The crew could not contain themselves and broke out laughing, again.

"Ah, fuck you, bitch!" Althea countered, once the laughing had diminished.

"Yeah! I love you too, slut! MUAAH!" Michelle quickly shot back blowing a kiss to her.

That was typically the Angel's normal everyday run-of-the-mill type of behavior amongst themselves, whether or not they were under any stimulation. But, more importantly, was the fact that no matter how much they teased each other or tossed profanity and insults at each other, they always did it in a loving, joking, playful manner, always conscious never to offend one another. The Angels' most sacred and evident truth was that they loved no one in the way that they loved each other. They each had long ago, sacredly vowed to truly be their sister's keeper. And they have all proven to each other to have lived up to that vow and commitment.

"Okay! Later for all that smooching shit! Do anyone of you heifers gotta Philly blunt on y'all?" Latesha asked. "Or, do we have to cast lots up in this bitch to choose which one of us is gonna go to the 24 hour store to get one?" Kacky, Althea, and Vicky all responded "NO" in chorus, while Goldie commenced to search in her Tory Burch bag for a blunt. She came up empty.

"Na! I don't seem to have one either." She finally volunteered.

"A'ight then, pass me the deck of cards, Michelle." Latesha customarily commanded. "Okay, now here's the deal. The lowest card drawer takes her ass to the store." Latesha announced, after Michelle passed her the deck of cards. Once finished with the shuffling of the cards, she proceeded to spread them out on the coffee table, face down. She then drew first and came up with the nine of diamonds, which she held up for all to see. Kacky and Vicky followed respectively. They both came up with face cards and also held them in display for all to see. Althea followed and drew the six of spades. Goldie ensued and she came up with the three of clubs which she quickly tried to conceal, but was obviously busted. Michelle, always conscious of the principle of never breaking their ciphers, drew last and came up with the five of hearts.

"Okay Gee, it's on you. You drew the lowest card, not to mention tried to get shiesty!" Latesha assured her.

"Na! Ain't no 'okay', Gee! It's dark as all hell out there!" Goldie blurted out in defiance. "I ain't steppin' out there on account of no blunt!"

"The store's right on the damn corner, Gee! Wat'chu mean, 'Na!' Damn! You actin' like it's a mile away!" Vicky said, admonishingly.

"If that's the way you see it, then you step on out there and get it!" Goldie retorted, rolling her eyes and mockingly working her neck like a cobra snake, ready to pounce on a prey.

During that entire exchange, unnoticed by all, Michelle had risen from where she had been sitting and headed towards her bedroom. She reappeared moments later wielding a Philly blunt in her hand like a magic wand. Across her lips appeared a mischievous grin. She immediately caught hell from every direction, as she extended the Philly out to Latesha.

"See, you ain't shit! Pullin' that crap on us! You knew you had one up in this piece all this time!" Vicky said, being the first to scold her.

"Fuck all that! Gimme dat shit!" Latesha quickly interjected, snatching the cigar from Michelle's extended hand. "Why you lie? Talking about you ain't have one!"

"I ain't lie! I just never answered ya fishy ass. Besides, you asked if anyone had one *on* 'em. And, as you can see bitch, I didn't have one *on* me. I did, however, have one in my bedroom!" Michelle retorted, sarcastically.

"Oh! Now you got jokes, huh?" Latesha shot back at her, snatching the Philly. "You playing that word semantics shit?" Latesha finally said, as she busted open the cigar with her fingernails and dumped its guts in an ash tray. She then poured the weed along the empty cigar leaf to roll it up.

"Oh hell no! What da' fuck is that shit you puttin' up inside that blunt?" Her sister asked in her usual demanding tone. Everyone looked on with curious eyes as Latesha didn't miss a beat, and continued rolling the blunt.

"Yeah Latesha, what the hell is that shit? You know we don't be experimenting with no foreign shit!" Althea chimed in.

"Calm the fuck down...shit. Y'all know damn good and well I wouldn't lace no dare-gone blunt!"

"Then answer the fuckin' question, bitch! What the fuck is that shit you puttin' up in there?" Vicky interjected, squinting her eyes for a better look at the funny looking herb.

"Yeah! Latesha, what the fuck is that and where you get that shit from?" Goldie joined in.

"Exactly!" Michelle followed up while standing over her in a defiant pose, with her hands on her hips and her eyes on the blunt Latesha was rolling.

"Chill y'all! Ain't no need to worry." Latesha assured them, as she fidgeted with the contents in her jacket pocket, negotiating the retrieval of her lighter. "This here is that new kush. They call it 'Chem Dog' down in Barcelona, where they grow it."

"Where the fuck is Barcelona?" Vicky inquisitively asked, looking from one friend to the next searching for an answer.

"Barcelona is in Spain." Latesha informed her before taking a long pull from the blunt, which instantly caused her to erupt in a bout of uncontrollable coughing.

"Damn! That shit there ain't no mufuckin' joke!" Michelle exclaimed before she and Kacky began patting Latesha on the back with open palms.

"What the fuck y'all call yourselves doin'?" Latesha demanded once the coughing bout subsided. "I ain't choking that damn bad for y'all to be beating down on my fuckin' back, like y'all crazy. Shit! What the fuck y'all expected, for me to spit out a damn dog or something?"

"Na bitch, just some trapped up cum from dogs. Maybe Lassie cause the way you pulling on that blunt looked like you was sucking Chem dog's dick!" Althea shot out, long waiting her opportunity to take a good shot at Latesha.

They all simultaneously burst out laughing. Latesha then extended her hand out and stared at the blunt through tearing eyes, marveled for a few seconds as if it had done something out of character or something it wasn't supposed to do. Suddenly, to the dismay of all the girls, she began talking to the blunt as if it was a true flesh and blood living being. "Chem Dog..." she began. "I'm gonna marry you and be the most loyal, committed, and loving wife whosoever walked on this planet. You have changed my life just now and have captivated my soul like no man have ever..."

"Bitch, shut your crazy ass da fuck up before you cause me to call a mufuckin' ambulance to come get'chu!" Michelle warned, cutting her off in the middle of her crazed spiel. "Well, shit! Pass that mufucka over here!" Goldie snapped. "Let us get a sample of Chem Dog's fine ass before you run off to wonderland wit'em!"

Latesha took another drag before handing her the potent lavender and greenish colored herb filled blunt. Goldie quickly snatched the blunt and took two pulls and passed it on to Althea, who along with the others were eagerly waiting to try the weed. The Chem Dog filled blunt was then passed around in a cipher and each Angel twice managed the blunt until they all experienced a high like none other they had ever experienced in their entire lives.

"Mr. Chem Dog, if you ever decide to divorce Latesha's cheatin' ass, I'll be more than willing to step in and fill that void." Vicky quipped. Picking up on Latesha's weed induced spiel and mimicked her, holding the by-now-half-spent blunt inches from her face, staring at it with glazed eyes. The girls all broke out laughing hysterically.

"Shit! We might have to murder Chem Dog's ass before he have us all up in here psychotic n-shit!" Michelle snapped as she extended her hand for her turn at the weed. She then took her two pulls and passed it on to Althea.

Puff, puff...ffhh... Althea took her pulls and exaggeratedly blew the smoke out.

"Damn Althea..." Goldie blurted out, quickly turning her head away. "I'm high enough already, bitch, without you having to blow smoke all up in my damn face!"

"Shit! Y'all know every time that bitch put something between her lips, something white and nasty come flying up out of it." Kacky jokingly snapped.

"Oh, please!" Althea quickly retorted. "Don't even go there with me! Even your brother could vouch for me on that shit. I ain't never went down on him and he's my baby's Father.

"Yeah! That's cause you was too busy acting all uppity with him, yet sucking on everybody else's dick." Kacky rapidly shot back.

"Now, don't have me blow your fucking spot up, up in here, bitch!" Althea continued with Kacky, shooting back at her gesturing with an icy stare.

"Go ahead, Althea. Blow that ass up!" Michelle urged.

"Yeah Althea, blow that bitch shit up! I wanna hear this shit, cause she think her shit don't stink! Acting like we ain't hip to her sneaky trifling ass n-shit! Goldie jumped in urging Althea on.

"Hol'up! I wanna hear this shit too!" Latesha quickly sat up and shouted from her seat on the couch. "Cause Kacky always poppin' that shit 'bout how she don't be getting' her knees dirty.

"That's cause, I don't." Kacky snapped back at her big sister. "Everybody up in here ain't like you and Al. Some of us are decent chicks." She countered while putting on a display of aristocracy and elegancy. Which all the girls mimicked, laughing their hearts out.

"Aaahh, stop lying, bitch! You know damn well you'll play the hell out of a skin flute, so stop frontin'!" Althea cracked.

"You know that's right!" Latesha added, agreeing with Althea's statement.

"Come on y'all..." Goldie interrupted the bantering. "Enough with all this ding-a-ling shit! You bitches making my coochie thump!"

"Oh yeah? Well take your thirsty hot ass on home so Jungle can cool ya insides da fuck on out!" Michelle sarcastically suggested.

"Oh trust me, Ms. Thing, if I wasn't so twisted I'd be hittin' that Van Wyck on my way to 'em!"

"Na! Baby Girl, if you wasn't so twisted you'd be taking them rentals back to the Avis spot."

"Shit, my bad, Michelle! I completely forgot all about that!" Goldie confided.

"Yeah, well maybe you're suffering from memory loss already! However, don't go forgettin' that shit when your ass wake up in the morning. Cause there's too much at stake! And, besides there's too many fuckin' cars out there blockin' up my damn drive way as it is! So, make sure you and Latesha get your asses up in the mornin' and take them cars back. Afterwards, y'all can catch a cab and get back here...that is, unless y'all want us to follow y'all and drive your high-sidity asses back here. Either way, y'all gotta get them vehicles the fuck up outta my drive way. All their doin' is drawing all types of unnecessary, unneeded, and definitely unwanted attention 'n shit! Particularly, that loud ass red one Gee got out there!" Michelle ranted.

"Yeah, I've been thinking 'bout tradin' it for a darker one or perhaps a black Lincoln Navigator, or that new Caddie that just came out. I haven't made up my mind yet, though."

"Got damn...is it me or do that weed got this room stinkin'?" Vicky suddenly asked while fanning the air with her hand inches from her face.

Sniff...sniff...

"Yeah, it's you! Close your mufuckin' legs!" Althea joked leaning towards her playfully pretending to sniff between her legs.

"Yous a damn lie. Don't fuck wit' me, Bitch! You know damn well this pussy don't stink!"

"The hell if it don't!" Althea retorted. Then quickly said, "Nah Vee. I'm just messin' wit'chu! But you right! That shit got the spot smellin' kinda vile!"

"Well, since you was the first to complain Vee, you can go get the aerosol spray out da hall closet and do your thing." Michelle said.

As Vicky ventured to the hall closet, Goldie said. "So, Latesha what spot pumping that Chem Dog?" With glazed eyes and a smirk on her face, Latesha responded, "Bitch, y'all looking at the spot."

"Say word!" Goldie incredulously blurted.

"If I'm lying, I'm dying!" Latesha said, kissing her hand up to the heavens.

"How much of it did you get?" Goldie asked inquisitively, as Vicky came back into the room spraying air freshener.

"Well I got a little over an ounce on me right now that I'm gonna bust down with y'all in the morning before we break out. But so y'all know, I'm really contemplating 'bout puttin' this shit up in a couple spots. We'll give out some samples to a bunch of bona-fide weed heads out there so we could create a buzz first."

"That shit there's so potent that we could sell what normally would be ten dollar sacks for fifteen dollars a pop. *And* still knock whatever competition out there, on they mufuckin' ass!" Goldie ranted on excitingly.

"Huh!" Latesha groaned. "At $6,500 a pound, this shit better knock the competition dead on they ass."

"Sixty-five hundred!" Vicky exclaimed.

"Yeah, but I'm getting' it for $5,000. There's this girl named Gwen livin' not too far from me whose husband be getting it by the mother loads. I copped from her though. And if we do decide to open up a few herb gates she assured me that we'll be dealing strictly and exclusively wit' her and at bargain price."

"Yeah, that's wa'sup!" Goldie enthusiastically exclaimed, with barely opened eyes.

"You already know, Gee! I can already picture the type of money this bomb ass weed gonna generate for us. Trust me." Latesha said as she slid further and further towards the edge of the sofa, where she then leaned back tilting her head back and closed her eyes, letting the weed take its devastating effects over her.

Latesha suddenly began to reminisce, thinking back to the day she had boarded an Amtrak train in Miami, Florida, several years ago, with four kilos of borderline pure cocaine strapped on her. She recalled being en route back to the Big Apple, after having spent a long exciting, hot ass summer with Poppa Duke and her brother. Her brother and a couple of his comrades had come down to the Sunshine State to lay low after having had a notoriously heated gun battle on the streets of Brooklyn. That gun battle became infamous for having left the entire neighborhood terrified, sizzling hot, and crawling with law enforcement agencies in their stubborn quest to capture them.

Latesha continued recalling how after what seemed a short while, they began networking with a group of very powerful Latino brothers, whom at the time controlled ninety-nine percent of all the cocaine that entered the country and how she was first employed and paid a hefty thousand dollars for each kilo she muled back to New York. She smiled inwardly as she remembered how her brother had no idea, nor the slightest clue whatsoever, about how she enjoyed playing a role within his organization. With each trip she had been learning more and more about the viciousness of the drug game.

She studied the drug game like an A-plus student attending an Ivy League college or university. As a result, it only took her a short seven months of mulling for her brother's organization before she had accumulated enough capital to purchase herself that year's brand new BMW 745i. The very following year she was able to trade it in for the newest model. A tradition she continued to follow every year since.

Latesha had done so well that just last year for her thirty-first birthday, she purchased herself a very elegant four bedroom colonial style home which featured a prominent Olympic sized swimming pool. The house was situated in a quiet suburban area in Beacon, New York. A small city located in the upstate area about an hour and twenty minutes from New York City.

With a slight smile gracing her lovely face, she continued enjoying the stimulated state in which she was in. Suddenly she understood that she had come a long way since the days of riding the trains to high schools in other boroughs accompanied by the same group of 'ride or die' chicks she had just gotten high with. She recalled how they used to go around robbing other females of their most prized possessions. From their bamboo-door-knocker earrings to their Gucci, Fendi and MCM designer handbags and basically anything else of value they may have had on them. They had even bum-rushed quite a few guys taking their belongings, as well.

She and Goldie also had a reputation for stealing automobiles with none other than John "Scooter" Clark, an individual notoriously known throughout the neighborhood for his infamous police car chases. Latesha cringed in her reverie upon recalling the fact that one of those infamous cat and mouse chases ended up being the cause of them having to serve an 18 month stint in a division for youth camp.

Latesha and Goldie had served most of their sentence at the South Lansing Center for Female Youths where they constantly terrorized the other girls. So much that they were assigned extra chores around the compound for disciplinary reasons.

One day with less than ninety days left on their sentence, Latesha tested positive for marijuana on a urine test. As a result she was transferred to the infamous maximum security prison for women known as Bedford Hills Correctional Facility. Once there she was placed in a special housing unit better referred and known by inmates as "the box". She was kept in "the box" until her scheduled release date.

Their separation bored down hard on Goldie, who remained back at the youth camp where she refused to associate with anybody. Instead she stuck to her daily workout routine of half an hour on the treadmill and five sets each of squats and sit ups. Afterwards she had to report to C.O. Walker, a corrections officer, who was responsible for assigning her daily chores.

C.O. Walker had an eerie habit of staring and lusting over her while she performed her routine. On two separate occasions he had left her short perverted notes taped to the front of the utility box, where he knew she would have to venture to retrieve the equipment and supplies necessary to perform her assignment. The notes contained explicit details of how he desired the sensual pleasures of her love, how he constantly claimed to have dreamt of her, and how he always kept her at the forefront of his every waking thought.

Goldie, a light-skinned beauty who stood five foot four inches. She had these pair of mesmerizing almond shaped brown eyes, which often lead people to believe she was of Asian descent. She had a body most women would die for, a firm thirty-six D cup, a twenty-four inch waist and a beautifully pronounced apple shaped derriere which never ceased to call the attention of men and women alike. The truth being she had one of those diva like bodies that appeared perfect in every dimension.

Consequently, one day C.O. Walker lost his scruples after oogling and lusting over her all day and finally succumbed to his perverted and crazed urges. A few weeks before she was scheduled to be released on parole he accosted her and raped her. Needless to say, he was discovered and immediately fired. Goldie had sued the state for negligence and for failure to provide her safety and security. However, the case remains on the court's active docket and is still pending a disposition.

Because of their arrest together, on paper, Goldie became officially Latesha's crimey. But Latesha loved all the Angels equally the same whether they found themselves near or afar. The Sutter Angels remained committed sisters forever fashioning their motto: Death By Any Means Necessary, To All Who Dare Oppose Them.

Latesha's reverie moved her on to think about Althea. Althea was the mother of their brothers' child and well esteemed as their sister-in-law. Although they never married they remained very fond of each other. At five foot two inches, Althea was considered the shorty of the group within the Angels. She too was considered a dime piece. She had beautifully dark skin that always radiated a glossy shine, which mysteriously always reminded one of some exquisitely expensive chocolate. She had these chunky, brown, sexy eyes that men of all races, ages and professions found alluring and irresistible, not to mention a body to die for. She was often teased by her crew with having an ass like a baby Montana Mule.

Althea and Goldie shared similarly well shaped and proportioned body characteristics. However the similarities ended there. Goldie was a light skinned Diva and Althea a darker version. Althea also had silky textured shoulder length hair compared to Goldie's long blonde mane, which she went through lengths in keeping it looking fresh.

The tallest of the crew was the beautifully caramel colored Vicky. She stood at five foot eleven inches with an unusually big bubbled shaped butt although, despite her height, very proportioned. Vicky was a vixen and she didn't mind flaunting her well-proportioned body once in a while. Although she was a feisty, very argumentative woman, who loved and was dearly loved by all her comrades.

Kacky bore a striking resemblance of South Africa's former First Lady, Winnie Mandela. Were as Michelle is a spitting image of the Hollywood actress Vivica Fox who starred in the block buster hit "Set It Off". They both were born with a fire that ran through their veins like hot lava.

The difference between the Angels and your everyday around-the-way girls was the unequivocal fact that they were all financially caked-up and that they would not hesitate to send a motherfucker to the upper room.

Suddenly the smile she sported on her face vanished as Latesha recalled the last run she had done for her brother's organization. The run she recalled...that changed everything. Latesha was made to mule eight kilos along with help she really did not need. She had been paired off with a chick she despised off the bat. Not only because she had cut in on her pay, but more importantly because she didn't appear trustworthy to her.

Annette was an Italian chick out of Dix Hills, Long Island. Latesha's brother had met her at a club out in

Nassau County and to everyone's dismay eventually started fucking with her. Latesha never grew to like her nor trust Annette. She often thought that her brother was slipping, letting his guards down and eventually breaking certain rules of the drug game. Particularly, she resented and detested the fact that Annette was allowed, on several occasions, to be present in the lab and that her brother appeared teaching her how to cut the potent powder. So, Latesha always maintained that she should never had been paired off with anyone. Especially Annette for that matter, and *that* Annette should definitely never had been allowed to meet the "connect" nor conduct business transactions with them.

She recalled the day they had arrived at Penn Station, where she expected to be met by someone from the organization. When she was unable to recognize any familiar faces, she proceeded to use one of the station's pay phones to contact her brother, whom was supposed to be laying up at Althea's crib. As the phone's ringing tone blared."...ring...ring..." Latesha had been praying that someone answered, when suddenly she heard Althea's voice shouting into the phone, "Hello!"

"Yeah! It's me, Al. Can you please put my brother on the phone? I wanna know why no one bothered to be here to pick us up. There should'a been someone here waiting!" Latesha shouted over the phone, obviously angry. She was particularly upset that she was going to have to take a cab back to Brooklyn.

"Yo, you mean to tell me you ain't get the news?"

"Na! I didn't! Wha chu talkin' 'bout? What's going on, Al?"

Althea quickly began filling her comrade in on what had transpired. "Ayo, everybody except Boogs, K-Born and O.G. Bazz got busted while you was gone, and..."

"A'ight! A'ight!" Latesha cut her off before she could finish, "Listen, I want you to call my little sister and round up the rest of the Angels. I want y'all to meet me at

Candy's place. And, oh yeah..." She continued issuing instructions, while cupping the phone to whisper, "tell my sister to grab four geez outta my safe and bring that with y'all. You got that?"

"Yeah! A'ight! I'm on it!" Althea replied and hung up the phone, "click."

"Ayo, Nette!" Latesha angrily turned to Annette. "We gotta travel by cab. My brother and them had a little situation. But, don't panic! My little sister got your half of the money for you when we get back to Brooklyn."

Annette looked at Latesha and pretended concern, then, very proper like, she asked, "He's okay, though? Isn't he?"

Latesha dismissively replied, "Yeah! As far as I know, he is!"

After what seemed to Latesha like a lifetime, the cab finally pulled up in front of Candy's building. The cab driver got out and assisted them by removing their luggage from the trunk of the car. Latesha quickly and aggressively snatched both suitcases from the cab driver, and before walking off into the building, turned and addressed Annette.

"Wait out here. My sister's gonna bring your money out here to you. You might as well take care of the cabbie since he's gotta drop you off at your car." Latesha then proceeded to walk into the building without waiting for a response. She hit the stairs, quickly ascending towards her friends' apartment.

Meanwhile, Annette stood quietly but curiously as she waited. Obviously knowing better than to had questioned Latesha concerning the change of the drop off site. Kacky suddenly appeared from the building and after paying Annette returned and joined the rest of the Angels.

The Angels quickly began to clear the kitchen table where they had been eating breakfast while waiting for Latesha to arrive.

"A'ight!" Latesha began. "I want y'all to pay very close attention while I do this because there might come a time where each of you may have to do this for yourselves." Her command was well heeded as the girls paid close attention as she dumped the eight kilos of cocaine on the kitchen table.

Latesha commenced to gracefully unwrap each key while instructing Candy to pour out a sufficient amount of lactose. Then she began the process of mixing the lactose to cut the coke. Using two old record album covers to mix the substance. She finally produced twelve bricks out of the eight she started with. Then she set out to drop off eight keys at the original drop off site. From there she went on to make drop offs to her own clientele. That clientele would eventually make them all wealthy beyond their wildest dreams.

The regular going price uptown in the Washington Heights section of Manhattan had been $13,500.00 a brick. She decided to give them up at $13,000.00 a pop causing them to go like hot cakes. She then utilized $47,500.00 of the fifty-two grand generated to cop five more keys from the southern connect at $9,500.00 a brick. The more money they made the more bricks they had purchased. Until eventually they each had opened up a few spots of their own. Their spots sold dimes of powder coke and crack and the money started pouring in so abundantly that they began a *'buy two get one free'* sale on Sundays.

That was nine and a half years ago. They are still going strong which enables them to live in very expensive and luxurious homes. With the exception of Kacky, who doesn't know how to drive, they all obtained and maintained mint luxurious automobiles. Kacky, nevertheless, owns a few motor cycles and a couple of big four wheelers.

Their long run in the drug game can be credited to them not having had to resort to violence. However, the no violence run unfortunately one day came to an abrupt end when they received a call that some neighborhood thug robbed one of their female workers on top of that he physically assaulted her. That type of action, the Angels had vowed, could never go unpunished.

"Latesha! Latesha!" Michelle shouted, as the rest of the girls watched silently laughing at the way Latesha appeared with her head thrown back and her eyes shut. The girls were marveling at what appeared to be a smirk on her face.

"What is it, bitch?" Latesha snapped, having been abruptly yanked out of her reverie. After registering that all her comrades were standing around snickering at her, she feigned anger for having been disturbed.

"What da fuck y'all want? Can't you see I'm in a zone here?"

Althea jumped in and replied, "Yeah skank. We see that! But what the hell was you smiling 'bout?"

Latesha promptly replied, "If you must know, I was watching an old movie!"

Althea looked around at the rest of the crew before questioning, "A movie? Bitch, you need to cease 'n' decease fuckin' with dat Chem dog!"

On that note Goldie cut in, "I know dat's right!"

"Ah please! Fuck all y'all! Now move the hell outta my way!" She told Goldie as she brushed her off the sofa and stretched out along it. "It's gettin' late up in this bitch! I gotta get some rest!"

Upon arising from the sofa, Goldie said, "Yeah, I know dat's right. I'm willin' to bet dat Jungle's out there riding around crazy looking for me. That nigga ain't gonna be able to reach me cause I left my phone in my Prada bag. I didn't realize it until I was too far from the crib to wanna turn back.

"Bitch you always thinking 'bout dick!" Michelle blurted out. Anyway, y'all hookers know the sleeping arrangements up in here, so make y'all way to y'all designated sleeping area. Michelle then walked off into her bedroom and shut the door as they all began heading towards their well-known customary sleeping locale.

Chapter 3

STILL DIGGING

*T*he kaleidoscope array of lights Latesha witnessed through the rearview mirror, was accompanied by the blaring sound of sirens racing to the macabre crime scene they had just left behind. By the time Chief of Police, Colin Ferguson arrived at the scene, there were so many police officers there, that it resembled the changing of shifts at the station house. The entire area was crawling with dozens of uniformed police officers, plain clothes homicide detectives, police forensics and ballistics experts and what appeared to be all the top brass of the police department.

Among the chaos, the Chief could be heard shouting..."Where the hell is the god damn Chief Medical Examiner?! Has he even gotten here yet?!"

Lieutenant Jackson interrupted the Chief. "Pardon me Chief. I've just been informed that he's just around the corner examining another potential homicide victim."

The Chief gave him a stunned look and asked, "Is it another one of our men?"

Lieutenant Jackson shook his head. "No Sir. It's not another police officer. After examining our fallen Officers, the Medical Coroner was called away to examine what appears to be the body of a black male."

"I want this whole fucking neighborhood turned inside out and upside down until the killers responsible for this are apprehended!" He shouted in his baritone voice to every officer on the scene. Shifting his head from left to right, he continued, "We're going to fight through tooth and nail to make sure that the sons of bitches responsible for this are apprehended and prosecuted to the fullest extent of the law! And I personally am going to see this through, so help me God! Lieutenant, I want you to assign one of the junior detectives to investigate the body around the corner, cause I want all veteran detectives on this one here!" He said, pointing his index finger at the bullet riddled police car. "Our men get our top priority! Now see that these men are taken out of here!"

Lieutenant Jackson quickly jumped to the Chief's command, firmly stating, "Yes Sir!"

Meanwhile, just a few feet away, Detective Tom Fitzgerald and his longtime partner, Detective John Pollack were busy canvasing the crime scene for clues.

"God damn it John, I haven't seen this many spent shells in a single incident since Billy and George were ambushed by those gangsters up in the Cypress Hills Houses."

"Damn Tom, you took the words right out of my mouth: His partner replied, as he chewed on a stick of gum. He then squatted down and with a pencil lifted an empty shell casing from the ground and closely examined it.

"There's something very familiar about this 45 caliber shell, Tom. I just can't quite put my finger on it at this moment."

While Detective John Pollack was studying the shell casing a rookie officer walked over and addressed his partner, "Hey Tommy! We just got a call that a van meeting the description called in by the guys, before they were ambushed, has been spotted torched about a quarter of a mile from here. The firemen assured our guys that it was burned in an act of arson. No one seems to know what to do with it at this moment. What do you suggest be done?" Officer Walker inquired.

"Okay! Once the firemen finish extinguishing the fire, have it flat-bedded to the station house garage to await inspection." Detective Fitzgerald quickly instructed the rookie.

"Hey, Tom! John! You guys about ready to wrap things up, yet!?" Chief Ferguson yelled over to the two veteran detectives.

"Ah! No! Chief! Not just yet, we're still digging!" Detective Pollack responded.

Chapter 4

GOLDIE & JUNGLE xxx

*L*aying beneath Goldie in the sixty-nine position, Jungle's long slick tongue crept like a cobra snake between her banana colored thighs feeling her pussy lips against his face, as he inserted his tongue deep into her creamy slit. She moved in a swift bump-n-grind motion with her waist, causing her clitoris to bounce off his lips.

"Oooohhhh! Yes! Uumm." she moaned when he flicked his tongue along the length of her left pussy lip and down the other causing her to shiver while her mouth stayed busy washing his long thick penis as it stretched her jaw muscles. While she slurped him down to the root, she could sense that he was trying his best not to nut-off under her oral assault. But it only encouraged her to forcefully suck him that much more, really giving him all she had, each time she buckled into an orgasm of her own.

"Ooooh! Shit." she moaned after briefly drawing her mouth from his dick and lathered his face with a slick coat of girly juice, then continued bobbing up and down on his manhood. At times rolling her tongue across the tip, then the underside humming along as his dick throbbed before he began shooting his cream at the rear of her throat. She swallowed his seed with a wanting cravenness as his dick spiraled around inside her mouth until she released it. Then rolled over onto her stomach so he could give her a dick thrashing from the rear. Jungle entered her inch by inch, real slow until he was all the way inside. Then he began to stroke long and deep into her.

"Aaaahh. Yes Baby." she softly moaned, again, as he

slow grinded into her while running his tongue from her left shoulder blade up her neck and stuck the tip in her ear.

"Whose pussy is this?" He whispered in her ear, between licks.

"Y-yo-yours, Daddy! Oooh! Yes! It's all yours, Daddy!" She answered with a slight jerk as he thrust inside of her, stimulating her adventurous structure to a level that created in her a desire for deeper penetration as she wiggled under him, until she was on her back holding her knees wide apart for full access and more depth. Jungle pistoned his dick inside until they met pelvis to pelvis, grinding down into her as she stared up in his eyes moaning, with her own eyes glazed over until her insides started to boil.

Now holding him by the waist, she pulled him into her as she began thrusting her heated, swollen vagina back to meet his on-strokes. Creating wet slopping sounds as her pussy erupted all over his manhood and he continued long-dicking her like his life depended on it. Cupping her backside, he went for broke.

"Ooh, yes. Yes. Fuck me, Daddy. Fuck me. Fuck this pussy!" She pleaded. He didn't need any coaching as he continued to scrape along her pussy walls until he gushed, flooded her insides and rolled over onto his back, breathless and drenched with sexual satisfaction.

"You still mad at me, Sweetheart?" Goldie asked while rubbing his chest.

"Now don't think cause you put it down on a nigga, real proper, that I'm gonna forget how worried yo ass had me last night. I was all over the motherfuckin east looking for you and you wit'cha lil crew shacked up at Michelle's. The police out there fucking wit' niggaz cause mufuckas laid two of 'em out. But fuck da police. I was worried about you!" He ranted.

"Yeah. I feel wha'chu saying, boo. But if it wasn't for Chem Dog I would've came…"

"Who da'fuck is Chem Dog!?" He interrupted.

"This is Chem Dog!" She said, reaching into her clutch bag and handing him the exotic cannabis.

"Damn! This shit looks funny as hell." He said, closely inspecting the marijuana.

"Yeah, well wait till you hit that motherfucker."

"Shit! I know it won't make me forget that I got somebody to come home to at night...humph! The weed don't control Jungle. Jungle control the mufuckin' weed."

"Alright, if you say so." Goldie said sarcastically, before getting up and heading for the shower, feeling lively after a morning of heart pounding sex, she thought with a smile.

Jungle and Goldie have been sexing each other steady ever since the night they met at the Village Hut Club on Linden Boulevard six and a half months ago. He was from the Penn Worthman Houses in the same East New York neighborhood that she and her crew grew up in. He didn't run the streets trying to be thugged out like most of the guys in the East did. But he had no problem dealing with issues when they landed on his lap. He owned a security firm which he started with money he was awarded from a medical malpractice suit when a doctor at Brookdale Hospital diagnosed him of having asthma and prescribed him medication that was for someone suffering from high blood pressure. He was good to Goldie and that's all that mattered to her.

Chapter 5

PHONE CALL

*L*atesha turned over and looked at the digital clock sitting on the nightstand. It read 5:36 p.m. She quickly crawled out of her heart-shaped, queen sized bed, slid into her three inch mink slippers, stretched and proceeded towards her walk-in closet. Her closet measured seven by five feet and it was replete with various furs of exotic animals all lining the left side. Occupying the opposite side appeared a large collection of designer blouses and sweaters by Alexander McQueen, Diane Von Furstenberg and everyone in between. Along the bottom shelf she had a collection of boots and shoes from all sorts of designers. You name them, she owned them: Chanel, Badgley, Mischka, Prada, Gucci, the list went on.

She stood there contemplating on what outfit she would wear tonight for the grand opening of the club "Crystal Ball". She and her crew had planned almost two weeks ago to attend. Finally, she decided on a lime green Helmut Lang dress which she combined with a pair of Charles Jordan ankle length boots. Laying the outfit out across her bed and setting the boots on the floor, she headed off to take a hot bubble bath in her elaborately spacious bathroom. Forty minutes later she exited her bath and as she commenced to apply a light coat of raspberry scented lotion to her body she was startled by the sudden loud ringing of her telephone.

"Hello!" She yelled into the receiver, upon answering on the third ring.

"Now, is that how you were taught to answer the damn phone?" She heard her mother's voice blare through the receiver.

"Oh. Hi Mommy. I'm sorry. How are you doin'? I haven't heard from you in a couple of days now."

"Yeah, that's because you're too busy jet settin'. Every time I turn around you in a different state. It's hard for me to keep up with you." Her mother complained before continuing, "Ya just like your damn Daddy!"

"Oh Ma please! How many times have I tried to convince you to move into this spacious house with me? I don't know why you don't wanna leave that crime infested area and come up here with me, where it's nice and quiet!"

"Chile please. All my friends are right here in East New York. I don't know a soul up there in Beacon. Besides, why should I have to be the one to up and move? I'm not the problem! These trouble makers need to leave out the neighborhood! Not Me! You know some fool done killed two police officers down by the park on Miller Ave the other night? It's been all over the news and on every station too. Nine, seven, eleven, even on channel..."

Their conversation was momentarily interrupted by the beeping sound of her phone, "Hold on Latesha. Somebody's trying to get through to me on the other line. Don't hang up!" Her mother stated in a demanding tone. Two minutes later she clicked back over, "Latesha?"

Latesha quickly responded, "Yeah I'm still here, Ma."

"Good, I was hoping you didn't hang up. Anyway, that was Linda Kay. She called to inform me that cousin Andrew done passed away in his sleep this morning. I'm gonna have to call you back later Baby, cause she's still on the other line all hysterical."

"Alright Ma. I love you! And make sure to give cousin Linda my condolences."

"Okay Baby. Now you take care! Bye, bye." Her mother replied before she hung up the phone.

Andrew was Latesha's mother's second cousin. They had come to New York together back in the late 60's from Fayette, Alabama, when they were just teenagers, along with two of his sisters. He was the only male of five children. He was a comedian in his own right and always the life of every party he attended. Andrew was very well loved and very much liked even by those that didn't know him well or had just met him. He was a ray of sunshine that would surely be missed, Latesha thought to herself.

Latesha suddenly broke from her reverie and remembered that she and the girls had agreed to roll up to the club in Michelle's Range Rover. She hurried and packed an overnight bag, knowing she'll more than likely end up staying out in Queens after a long night of dancing, drinking and bluntin' it up at the club.

Chapter 6

CLUB CRYSTAL BALL

*W*hile piling into Michelle's truck, Latesha addressed the girls, "I want y'all to know dat one day next week we got a funeral to attend. My mother's cousin passed away in his sleep this morning."

"Yeah, Mommy called me this morning and informed me about it after having reached out to you." Her sister interrupted.

Latesha then continued, "I'm just letting everybody know so y'all don't make any plans until I find out exactly what day the service is gonna be held. I know more than likely it's gonna be held at Crowe's Funeral Home out here in Queens. That's who the family normally deals with. At least as far back as I can remember."

"You said Crowe's?" Michelle asked, while turning the key in the ignition to fire up the engine. "I know exactly where that place is at. In fact, it's not too far from here," she added before pulling out of her driveway. Music by Jodeci started playing and thumping through the sound system as they headed to the club for a night of fun.

"Okay! Y'all know we can't go up in that club without gettin' our damn smoke on first." Vicky stated as she reached into the pocket of her three-quarter onyx colored mink coat and pulled out a pregnant blunt of Kali Mist.

"You can count my ass out. I'm not fucking with no Chem Dog tonight!" Althea stated.

"Me either! That shit have a bitch a little too fucked up." Latesha admitted. "But, I brought a hundred sample joints to give out at the club."

"Well for y'all bitches information this is Kali! I wouldn't fuck with that Chem Dog shit while I'm out here in these streets!" Vicky barked as she fired up the blunt using the vehicle's lighter.

"Shit!" cursed Goldie. "Chem Dog was the damn reason I couldn't take my yellow ass home to my man. I told y'all he was riding around mad as hell looking for me. I know that nigga like a book. He was heated, but I put his mind at ease when I put this coochie on his ass." She continued.

"Did you suck his dick?" Michelle sardonically inquired, maintaining her focus on the road.

"What I do with my man is my motherfuckin' business!" Goldie responded with equal derision.

"Yup, she sucked his dick!" Althea chimed in. "Cause if she hadn't, the bitch would 'a been up in here working her damn neck from side to side like she always do whenever she's right. But the bitch is lying through her teeth right now, talking 'bout how she don't be getting her scared up knees dirty. Yeah, right."

"Yeah, that's right! We know *you* like a motherfuckin' book", Vicky interjected. "But fuck all 'a dat. Did cha swallow?" She further derided her.

"That's none of your business, bitch!" Goldie shot.

"Vicky pass the damn blunt! Shit!" Kacky yelled from where she was sitting directly behind Vicky, who was in the front passenger seat. "I bet cha ass won't hog up Chem Dog like that." Kacky added.

"Humph! I bet you I won't either!" Vicky quickly shot back before handing her the blunt. After taking two long pulls she passed it to Althea, who was very careful not to drop any ashes on her $50,000 full length Russian Lynx fur or on her silk white jumpsuit, for that matter. After taking her two pulls of the Kali Mist filled cigar, Althea commenced bopping her head to the Jodeci song, "Forever My Lady".

"Michelle, turn this damn heat off!" Vicky yelled at her girlfriend over the music. "That shit's burning my coochie out!"

"Bitch please! Your coochie already burnt the hell out!" Goldie rapidly shot at Vicky, as if she had been waiting for the chance to get a snap in on her. Then she quickly added, "Keep your damn legs closed, bitch!"

"The bitch always got her legs gaped open when she got a dress on. So leave her alone, ain't nothing wrong wit' her airing out that fish box!" Joked Althea, causing everyone to erupt in laughter.

"Girl, that's hot air coming outta there blowin' up her coochie. And I'm not trying to be sitting up in this truck if it's gonna be smellin' like a fried sea food restaurant!" Latesha chimmed in, causing the laughter to rise up a few notches in volume.

"Bitch! I got my legs open to keep my hammer from rubbing up against my clit!" Vicky shot back venomously, making reference to the firearm she had tucked under her dress and at the top of her stockings.

"Ah please! I wouldn't be surprised if you had it stashed up inside your coochie!" Goldie said, while extending the weed over to the front drivers' seat to Michelle.

"No thank you! I don't smoke behind blow job Divas!" Michelle shot at her after acknowledging from her peripheral view that she was trying to pass her the blunt.

"That was a good one bitch!" Goldie acknowledged.

"Anyway, Vicky..." Althea started, "On some real shit. You better hope like hell they ain't got metal detectors up in this spot or yo ass gonna be left outside sittin' in the truck."

"Althea, you must 'a really fell and bumped your motherfuckin' head." Vicky said, turning around in her seat to face her.

"The damn club is in East New York. Home of the motherfuckin' Sutter Angels! That means I got a green light to take a rocket launcher in that motherfuckin' club if I want to!"

"She probably did bump her damn head or something, cause that shit she just let flow out of her mouth didn't sound right at all!" Kacky said.

"Well, at least nothing else came flowing outta those prized lips!" Latesha stated while poking her tongue against her cheek, making it appear as though something was really in her mouth. And as she teased her everyone got a good laugh off, including Althea herself.

* * * * *

"Um, um, um! There's some fine ass niggas out here tonight!" Vicky said, scanning the line as they pulled into the parking lot across the street and parked the truck with the nose facing the club.

The clubs' name appeared spelled out in blinking neon lights. There was a line of about 500 snaked from the chained off front of the newly upscale club on Glenmore Avenue to around the middle of Wyona Street on the next corner. There were a lot of major street players, gangsters and well known celebrities there for the grand opening. Females were draped in their most revealing attire with hopes of bagging a hustler or some celebrity.

Security guards stood at the entrance of the double swinging doors with intimidating glares as they admitted six people in at a time. The people would be pat frisked and wand with a hand held metal detector for safety reasons before they were allowed to pay the twenty dollar gate admittance fee. They would then proceed through a turnstile that would keep a tally of patrons attending the venue and which led them into the club and onto the dance floor.

Through squinting eyes, Goldie noticed that one of the security guards was an employee and close friend of Jungle's. So she reached in her Tory Burch clutch bag and retrieved three one hundred dollar bills which she intended to give him so that they wouldn't have to wait on the long line to enter. While making their way across the street, the fellas there stared at the Angels in awe. They always appeared to be the flashiest women in the clubs. The fellas seemed to scan their voluptuous figures from top to bottom. Vicky, who noticed the gawking eyes, hiked her mink up waist length as her ass cheeks danced around under her Tibi chiffon dress with every step she took.

"Truck!" Goldie called out to the security guard, who recognized her immediately as they approached the entrance.

"Hey, lil' Sis!" He greeted her as he leaned in for a peck on the cheek, while the rest of the Angels defiantly stood there in all their glamour.

"Here's a little something for you and your crew so we don't have to stand in this long ass line." Goldie said while trying to slip him the bills without the other patrons noticing.

"Yo, money ain't no good here, Sis!" He replied before removing the chain to allow them through.

They then entered the club strutting with an air of confidence that reflected their style and elegance. They entered onto the large floor of the club which featured a floor to ceiling mirror. Immediately they hit the bar for something to complement the weed that was already flowing through their systems. Once at the bar they bopped their heads to the rhythm of the music, as they sipped on Nuvo with their backs turned to the bar.

Enjoying the music, Latesha scanned the club through her Victoria Beckham shades, as she got her sip on, noticing some familiar faces amongst the sea of patrons throughout the crowded venue. She nodded her head in acknowledgement to Jackson Project's King-Pin, the infamous "Snipes" who sat calmly puffing on an expensive cigar with two scantily dressed females on each side and several of his soldiers standing by at ease watching everything within their radius. A few tables away, in the light blue tinted fiber glass VIP section she noticed her younger cousin, Lil' El. He was sitting with a small crowd of his most loyal and trusted comrades. Each was accompanied by a female. Latesha made a mental note to holla at him later on about acquiring some heavy machinery.

"God damn! If he gonna be rocking the house like this every weekend, I'ma have my black ass up in here every Saturday night!" Althea said, straining her voice over the sounds and referring to the DJ as she swayed her body to the music while sitting on her bar stool.

DJ Duracell worked the crowd into a frenzy chanting in between selections, "Do the ladies run this motherfucker?" He screamed into the mic, halting the music, momentarily.

"Heell!! Yeeaahh!!" The crowd responded back in unison before he hit the play button that sent the old school classic jam "Before I Let Go" by Frankie Beverly and Maze, bleeding through the speakers. Everyone applauded and began putting their moves on their partners. The beat was so intense that it forced you to get on the dance floor whether or not you were familiar with the song.

"Oh shit! That's the mufuckin' jam right there." Vicky yelled as they all, with the exception of Michelle, hit the dance floor.

Althea danced her way up to a broad shouldered brown skinned cat who had the facial features of Tyrese, the popular R&B singer, complete with the low Caesar haircut and all. Althea began working her moves on him, grinding her well-shaped ass up against his groin in a circular motion while bending forward with both hands on her knees, giving him as much as he could handle. A few feet away, swinging her right arm around like she was a cowgirl getting ready to throw a lasso around the neck of a wild bull, Kacky was yelling, "Ho, ho! Party over here!" With one leg up as her partner grinded into her crotch while holding onto her raised leg.

"God damn, Baby!" He yelled into her ear. "You da freak of my desire!"

"It's just a dance. Don't get it twisted, Playboy!" Kacky quickly shot back. Killing any thought he may have had of getting some pussy from her.

"Yeah a'ight!" He replied as he continued to grind into her private parts. Kacky could feel his erection brutalizing her vagina as he bumped and grind against her bare pussy while her sequined Alice and Olivia mesh tube dress rode up her thigh, though not enough to notice she was pantyless.

Meanwhile, a few feet away, Vicky was working her dancing skills on a tall, well-groomed brother in a two piece pony skin suit. With her back facing him, Vicky spread her feet apart and with both hands on her hips she commenced to make her ass cheeks jump one at a time; as if they were trying to out bounce each other.

While dancing, Vicky took notice that Michelle was watching from her seat at the bar with a wrinkled nose expression on her face, as if she smelled a pile of shit. Michelle then shook her head in a gesture of disapproval at the way she was dancing. Vicky rolled her eyes and flipped her middle finger at her childhood partner as she continued her lewd dirty dancing routine.

"Put it on 'em Vee!" Latesha yelled from a few feet away as she two-stepped with a chubby guy who was obviously out of shape giving the fact he was gasping for air. Goldie was nearby pressed up closely to her partner who had his arms draped around her waist swaying every-which-a-way. The friction from his lizard skin sweater caused her nipples to expand to the size of thirty-eight point caliber bullets poking through her satin halter top dress. But she welcomed the feeling as she continued to enjoy herself.

"How da hell you make your bootie move up and down like that?" Latesha asked Vicky while making their way back to their seats, once the song concluded.

"I call it ass confusion." She told Latesha as they hi-fived and continued navigating towards their destination.

"Damn Ma! I bet those juicy legs lead straight to heaven!" Said a well-dressed drunken stranger who stepped into their path, brushing the back of Vicky's thigh.

"Na!" She said, shooting him a cold glare. "But, what's between them could put yo ass right at heaven's gate! Now step the fuck off!" She added before Latesha clutched her by the hand and guided her around him.

"Bitch! Let me find out you were a pole dancer in your past life!" Michelle snapped at Vicky the moment she returned to the bar.

"You want me to teach your tired ass how to do dat shit?" Vicky derisively asked Michelle.

"Hell, mufuckin' na! That shit look all nasty looking!" Michelle fired back cringing her nose.

"Ah please Michelle, ain't no act too nasty!" In fact, there's always something deliciously nasty 'bout acting on raw impulse like that! You should try it sometime!" Vicky told her with a wink of her eye. "You might even like it!" She added.

"Na! I don't think so, hoe! That shit y'all was doing out there wasn't Angel-like!" Michelle said with a hint of a smile on her face. "I should've came out there and tossed around some dollar bills." She continued. "And Kacky, as for you, the way you was letting that nigga grind all into your katt, I thought he was really slipping it to you out there. That is until he put your leg back down and I realized his zipper was still fastened. Y'all too much for me!" She added, shaking her head. "But I love y'all bitches to death!" She concluded.

"We know you do." Althea said, having finally made her way back to the bar.

"Althea! Girl you got a wedgy up in the crotch of your pants!" Goldie snapped.

"Eeeel! Pull that shit outta yo kat!" Latesha commanded after also noticing. All the dancing she had done caused her jumpsuit to bunch up between her legs making it appear to look as though her pussy was trying to swallow up the one peice silk outfit.

"You gonna mess around and catch a yeast infection from all that shit disappearing up into your coochie like that!" Latesha continued while Althea began pulling the material from the crease of her crotch with her right thumb and index finger.

"God damn, Althea, you could've been more discreet 'bout it! One'a us would'a gave your nasty ass a block!" Vicky said with a distorted look on her face.

"Right!" Michelle agreed. "You don't do no shit like that in a room full'a thirsty ass niggaz!" Michelle continued to reprimand her.

"Please! Ain't none of these niggaz tryin' ta get killed up in here tonight!" Althea retorted.

"Oh yeah! What'chu gonna use to do it? Cause Vicky ain't giving you her hammer!"

"Oh yes the hell I will! Let one of these pussy chasing mufuckas play da wrong hand up in here tonight and see what the fuck happens!" Vicky barked before taking a sip from her glass of Nuvo.

"A'ight now, we came here to have a good time! Not to turn the grand opening into a grand closing!" Latesha said, calming her girls down a notch as Goldie trekked in their direction bopping her head to the music and pushing her hands, palms up to the air.

"Oh Lord have mercy! Y'all check Goldie out!" Kacky shouted as they shifted their attention towards the direction she was focusing in on.

"What the hell that nigga was doing to her up in the crowd, that got her nipples all poking out like that, looking like erasers n' shit?" Vicky cracked, causing slight humor.

"What da' fuck are y'all staring at?" A confused Goldie asked turning her head around as she approached to look behind her, unaware that it was she who was the center of attention.

"I don't know what 'chu turning around for. We looking at 'chu, bitch! It ain't even cold up in here, so why the hell are your nipples looking like torpedoes?" Michelle inquired. Goldie tucked her chin for a quick visual inspection. She too became surprised at the expansion of her erect nipples and quickly placed her palms over her breasts.

"Hand me my coat!" she said to no one in particular. Michelle began sifting through their coats until she came up with hers.

"Here..." she said, "cover them baby cannons up!" The girls then began chuckling.

"Shit!" cursed Althea, midway through the humor before she said, "Them things look more like weapons of mass destruction than baby cannons!" Her statement caused a furry of laughter to erupt from the girls.

"Don't turn your head Vee!" Latesha cautioned Vicky, once the humor had subsided, "Here comes that nigga you was giving that nasty ass booty dance to." She warned, putting Vicky on point as she used her glass as camouflage to shield the movement of her lips.

"Excuse me sweetness!" The tall fellow began as he approached Vicky. "The moves you were putting on me back there a while ago had me so joyfully alive that I felt compelled to stroll on over here and formally introduce myself. I'm Don Juan."

"Don Juan, huh?" Vicky repeated. "So, how joyfully alive were you, Mr. Don Juan?" she asked, biting down on her bottom lip while allowing her eyes to briefly focus in on his crotch area.

"What's already understood needs not to be spoken of," he philosophically replied, noticing her brief shift of vision.

"So, I take it that you really enjoyed the dance," she purred, further enticing him.

"Oh, I'm sure any man would have enjoyed the treasured opportunity of not just dancing with you. But of watching the expressive and poetic demonstration you presented. I guess I could consider myself blessed to have witnessed it in its entire glory!" Don smoothly answered while running the tip of his tongue along his top lip. And although it was evident that he was addressing his words to Vicky, the rest of the Angels hung onto his every word.

"Well damn, Don Juan, you gonna be the cause of a bitch like me melting up in this motherfucker!" Vicky responded, fanning her face with her right hand for emphasis.

"Well in that case bitch, you should be fanning your coochie and not'cha face!" Goldie cracked as they all erupted in laughter. Don Juan stood there trying to balance his drink in his right hand while he laughed uncontrollably, clutching his stomach with his other hand.

"God damn! Y'all got me over here blowing my cool!" He finally managed to say.

"Don't pay us no mind Don Juan." Althea said. "This is how we enjoy ourselves." She continued. "By the way, I'm Althea. This is Michelle..."

"Bitch!" Michelle interrupted her. "I know how to introduce myself!" She snapped at her with an icy glare. She then turned her attention back to Don Juan and said, "I'm Michelle." Goldie then introduced herself.

"I'm Goldie."

"And I'm Latesha."

"Shit, my bad! I got so caught up in all yoursmooth ass talking that I didn't even tell you my name. I'm Vicky. That's Vicky wit'a "V" as in vivacious." She said with a

defiant nod of her head.

"And I'm Kacky."

"Well nice to meet ch'all." Don Juan politely said to them.

"Like-wise." Goldie quickly responded.

"So, Don Juan, where are you from?" A curious Latesha asked.

"Oh, I'm from Albany Projects, baby. Everyday. All day!" He answered.

"Ain't that around there by Bergen Street?" She asked.

"Indeed so!"

"Yeah, I'm a little familiar with that area. I use to deal with a dude named Mo'Chedda from down that end of Brooklyn. He used to go to Paul Robeson High back in '93."

"Mo'Chedda?" Don Juan pensively repeated before stating, "I know you ain't talking 'bout my man Donnel Moore?"

"Yeah, that's exactly who I'm talking 'bout!" Latesha excitedly replied.

"Shit! Donnel is a mufuckin' Corrections Officer in that spot out on Staten Island." Don Juan said. "But, don't go getting' it twisted though, that nigga still stay in the hood like government cheese and the streets still got love for'em too!" He assured.

"Okay! That's what's up. And if you run into 'em be sure to let him know that I inquired about him. A'ight?"

"No doubt!" He answered proceeding to take a swig from his champagne glass bubbling with rose', oblivious to the fact that he was all the while rubbing elbows with the most notorious women New York has ever seen.

"Anyway, Don, do you smoke weed by any chance?" Michelle inquired.

"Strictly Sour Diesel or Haze. Why wa'sup? Y'all want some smoke? He asked in return, instantaneously reaching into his front left pocket.

"Oh, no, no! We just thought we'd turn you on to some proper trees. That's all." Michelle said, as Latesha handed him two joints. He placed one in the corner of his mouth as he fumbled around in his pocket for a lighter. After igniting and taking two long drags of the reefer stick, Don Juan was convinced that he was tasting the best weed he had ever had the pleasure or privilege of inhaling. He immediately got a quick rush to the head and began coughing up phlegm.

"God Damn! What the fuck is this shit?" He asked in a surprised tone.

"It's called Chem Dog." Goldie chimed.

"Chem Dog?!" Don Juan repeated. "Well this motherfucker sure nuff got some bark to it! A blunt of this shit will put a nigga out on his mutherfuckin ass. Fa' real!"

"Trust me, we know firsthand!" Latesha grinned.

"Oh, I'm sure y'all do. But, what I wanna know is where y'all copped this bangin' ass shit from?" He inquisitively asked, while holding the reefer stick between his thumb and index finger, inches from his face. "Cause a nigga could really get use to blowing some good ass weed like this here." He added with a nod.

"You're in the company of its primary suppliers!" Vicky said. "And as long as you come correct with that bread, you can have all the weed you want."

"Oh is that right?"

"Yup!" Goldie, Latesha and Michelle all answered in unison.

"As a matter of fact, Latesha" Michelle began, "gimme the rest of the samples. I'ma pass them out in the VIP section, cause I know good and damn well we can get some clientele from some of those niggaz up outta there."

"We can go together." Latesha chimed in. "I gotta holla at my little cousin anyway. We'll be right back, y'all."

All eyes were on the two Angels when they entered the VIP area.

"Wa'sup cuz?" Latesha greeted her cousin who was swigging on a bottle of Moet. She suddenly realized that the females who accompanied him and his comrades earlier were no longer in their midst.

"Ain't nothing, I'm chillin'." He promptly responded after a hard swallow. "But I see you and the girls got the bar on lockdown over there! When you know y'all should be up in here with the rest of us financially equipped hustlers." He playfully added.

"Yeah! I know, but you know how we do! We like to be out in the mix of things." She bragged, before clearing her throat and continuing, "Anyway, Cuz, I really need to holla at 'chu, privately for a second," she added.

"Trust me Latesha, you can speak freely around these niggaz. These here are my most trusted men." He said, sweeping his hand towards his buddies.

Pausing briefly to look each of them in the face, once again Latesha cleared her throat, assured that if they were with her cousin there was no doubt in her mind they were cut from the same cloth. "I hate to present a burden on you." She began, "but I need some heat."

"Damn cuz! You can't be serious! You already got enough shit to go to war wit' a small country!" He shot back at her with a trace of shock and incredulity.

"Yeah, but I need some real heavy machinery!" Latesha assured. The seriousness in her tone was enough for him to oblige.

"A'ight, come through 'bout 6:00 p.m. tomorrow to the old spot Aunt Tee Tee use to have out in Bushwick".

"A'ight! I'll see you then." She stated, then shouted across the VIP area, "Ah! Yo! Michelle! Make sure you hit my cousin and his peeps off too! I'm out! Oh, yeah, cuz, make sure you give Shaquana and lil' Shakim my love!" She yelled over her shoulder before exiting the VIP area.

* * * * *

"Where's Don Juan?" Latesha inquired as she approached the girls.

"He went back over to his table." Vicky answered. "But he gave me his digits for future business."

"Dat's what da'fuck I'm talking 'bout!" Latesha gleefully said.

"Yeah girl, I told him the going price was $6,500 a pound, but that we'll give it to 'em for $6,000."

"Well, you could'a let it fly for him at $5,800 being that you like him so damn much."

"Shit! I don't like him that damn much! Business is business." Vickie responded to Latesha's statement with a smirk. By then Michelle came strolling back to the bar with a smile on her face like somebody had thrown a million dollars on her lap.

"What the hell is so damn funny, Michelle?" Althea curiously asked.

"Um, Latesha's cousin was hollerin' at me in the VIP room. I swear on everything that I love that nigga can quench the fire in my coochie any mufuckin' time!"

"Bitch, that lil nigga is at least three years younger than your old ass!" Goldie joked.

"Just be careful, because the niggas in my family are known to move bitches bladders a few centimeters to the left. Ain't that right, Althea?" Latesha mockingly asked her childhood friend.

"Ah, fuck you, Latesha!" Althea barked.

"Anyway…" Michelle cut in, "I'ma let him take me to the movies out in Long Island the Friday after next."

"Why y'all gotta go way out there in the boon-docks?" Goldie asked.

"Because, Sunrise theatre is the cleanest theatre in the entire city. You should know dat Goldie!" Michelle sarcastically informed her.

"Well, I honestly didn't know that."

"Dat's cause Jungle's ass is too lazy to take your yellow ass out there!" She continued deriding her.

"Anyway y'all," Latesha interjected "we gotta take a ride out to Bushwick tomorrow to see my cousin 'bout some more heat."

"Damn Latesha! Don't you think we got enough heat already? What the hell are you tryin' to stock up for?" Vicky asked.

"I'm not stocking up, I'm upgrading, Bitch. Y'all just have y'all nasty asses up and ready, even though we gotta be there six o'clock in the evening!" Latesha concluded.

The girls were so caught up into themselves that they didn't even notice the nights' feature had begun until the crowd erupted in loud applause.

"Check them niggaz out up there!" Michelle shouted, simultaneously nodding her head towards the stage performance. The rapper, whom refers to himself as the lyrical "Shape Shifta" was spitting the lyrics of "Fury" from his smash single "Let's Get It" as his two partners, "Street Deacon" and "K Desert" ad libbed along, until it was time for their group routines.

The audience was in a crazed frenzy the entire time they were working the stage. Then representing the "Nasty North" movement, came the surprise performance of "Don Stone" the underground sensation. He did the necessary to maintain the momentous atmosphere alive, thereby adding hundreds more to his loyal fan base. He rocked, amazed and pleased the club crowd with his very unusual flow and stage performance. Then, after a long night of pleasure, enjoyment and gratification the Angels said their farewells to those they knew and had met before making their quick exit.

Chapter 7

HEAVY MACHINERY

*T*he Angels, as scheduled, spent most of the day leisurely resting in at Michelle's luxurious house after the previous nights' romp at the club. They quickly entered into their business mode and adorned their no-nonsense attitude after what turned out to be a pleasant evening of clubbing. It was on! The Angels were off to the old house in Bushwick where Latesha's Aunt Tee Tee once lived. It was five o'clock when they again piled into Michelle's truck and headed to Halsey Street in the Bushwick section of Brooklyn. Upon arrival they were greeted by Latesha and Kacky's cousin, Lil' El, who quickly led them into the basement where he kept a cache of arsenal, likened to a military sally port.

The basement was elegantly decorated with red and black checkered floor tiles, oak paneled walls and a drop ceiling. In the center of the basement sat two standard size billiard tables with decorative hanging lamps overhead, brilliantly illuminating the tables. One table was dressed in a rich green felt and the other in an equally rich bright red. Up against one wall there was an erected encased rack of expensively designed cue sticks inscripted with such names as Domino, Gleason and Galgani; all great billiard players. In a corner of the basement stood a few arcade pinball machines and video games, while over in another corner sat a moderate sized beautifully decorated bar, mirrored from the floor to the ceiling and fully equipped with dozens of bottles of liquors; champagne, whisky, brandy, scotch, rum, including an array of different types of beers and sodas.

Latesha gave kudos to her cousin, bigging him up on how well he had the place looking. The Angels joined in the praising, expressing their congratulations to him as they made their way to the bar. Alone the formally long and beautifully laminated Formica surface of the bar, sat a variety of snacks; pretzels, potato chips, salted peanuts, chewing gums, and beef Slim Jims. The Angels all declined his offer of drinks, assuring him that they had had enough on the previous night.

Without further formalities, Lil' El led them into a private room wherein with the touch of a concealed button, a camouflaged paneled door proceeded to swing open. Suddenly a closet came to view and along the mirrored walls that encompassed the enclave, there appeared all sorts and types of weapons and artillery; handguns, automatic assault rifles, howitzers capable of launching small missiles, crossbows and other odd looking types of weapons.

Lil' El called to one of his comrades to bring some duffle bags over to the Angels as they stood there taking a visual inventory of the large collection of semi and fully automatic fire arms he had on display. Lil' El turned to Latesha and with a sweeping motion of his hand he gestured and said, "There you go Cuz. Open house for you and your girls!"

"A'ight Cuz! But first school me right quick on this handsome looking thing right here." Latesha requested as she reached and retrieved a weapon off the arsenals' wall rack and began fidgeting with it and checking out its features.

"Oh, that right there is an HK MP5 submachine gun. But, I can have my man B-Hov convert it to a fully automatic, were it to become one of your choices!" He explained.

"Damn! If I pull that mufucka out in a crowded area, it'll be more screaming goin' on then in a Lil' John song!" Althea chimed in as she scanned the weapon in Lateshas' hands.

"I know that's right!" Vicky quickly agreed, "And what the hell is that right there?" she asked pointing at a handgun strewn on one of the hooks on the mirrored wall.

"That shit looks like a nine millimeter, only the frame is too big to be a nine. And trust me, I done bust off too many forty-fives to know that that ain't one of their models either!" she added.

"Trust me El, I can handle that shit right there and a whole lot more!" Vicky assured him. "As a matter of fact, you can pull two of those babies down for me, while Latesha finishes her shopping!"

"Uh hum, you don't know? She's well known, outta the crew, to handle the bigger ones!" Goldie sarcastically said, as she smirked and shot Vicky a stare through the corner of her eye.

"Fuck you hoe!" Vicky mouth off to her. However, not before Lil' El was able to comment.

"Oh, is that right?" he said while reaching up for an M16 assault rifle from one of the racks. "How 'bout this one here?" he asked displaying the weapon.

"Dat's a small thing to Vicky! Trust me!" Althea chimed in.

"Well, god damn, Vicky! Is there a firearm you can't handle?" he asked, not having a clue that the girls were really just snapping on Vicky. But he finally caught on when all the girls simultaneously broke out laughing in unison, including Vicky herself. "Did I miss something?" he asked perplexed before catching on the basis of the humor. "Oh y'all got jokes! But what y'all need to do is get y'all minds outta da gutter and focus on the business at hand. Now let me know what da'hell y'all lookin'na cop!" he concluded with a business attitude.

"Yeah a'ight Cuz. So, what else you got here?" Latesha cut in.

Leading them around, Lil El pointed to a weapon that the Angels were unfamiliar with. "Damn what da'fuck is dat?" Goldie bellowed as they all stood there in awe of the huge ass firearm.

"This here my dear," Lil' El began, as he brought down the weapon from its rack, "is a fifty cal. Barretta Snipers' rifle. And if y'all take this baby offa my hands, I'll guarantee to throw in a few hand grenades, as well.

"Shit! I bet dat mufucka right there will leave holes up inna mufucka, smoking like incense!" Althea exclaimed.

"A'ight." Latesha began. "Gimme four M-16's, eight 10MM, four HK's, three Mac 10's and that 50cal. Barretta! Oh and make sure B-Hov come see me later so he can alter these HK's like you said!" she concluded.

"You got it Cuz!" he said as he commenced to pull open huge chest drawers loaded with the weapons of their choice and their corresponding ammo.

"Let me say dat it's been a blast doing business wit' y'all!" He added as he and his crew commenced packing the artillery into the large army style duffle bags he had provided for them. "Oh yeah..." he added as an afterthought, "don't y'all go letting nobody get close enough to grab one of these weapons from y'all!" he said in a serious tone.

"Cuz please! Colin Powell nor his entire Joint Chiefs of Staff would be able to disarm us once we set out this bitch!" Latesha assured him. "And I know we over-paying you too! So don't go forgettin' those grenades you promised to throw in!" She added as she dumped thousands of dollars in stacks of fifties, twenties and tens that she extracted from her Marc Jacobs parachute pocket bag, onto a huge conference like table in the office. "Just consider it as an early Christmas present." she said, throwing him a peace sign as she and the Angels snatched up the bags of heavy machinery and made their way out of the basement. The Angels exited the house with enough artillery to take over a small third world country.

Chapter 8

BALLISTICS

The aroma of Maxwell House Coffee invaded the air of the spacious homicide unit's squad room in the East New York Sectors' of the 75th Precinct. Detectives Fitzgerald and Pollack sat sipping coffee at their respective desks, snacking on the proverbial "cop donuts", brainstorming over the tactics and strategies necessitated to capture the "cop killers" responsible for the massacre of their fallen heroes. The commonly normal sounds usually heard in the squad room; the radio, the click-clacking of typewriters and the occasional jesting between colleagues for attention, were all absent from the homicide squad room on this solemn mourning day. They were so quiet one could have heard a rabbit pissing on cotton, despite that it was teeming with detectives.

Chief of Police Colin Ferguson appeared suddenly, directing his attention to Detectives Fitzgerald and Pollack then said, "The Mayor is really up our asses on this one fellas! You guys are aware that this is an election year and that he's planning on running again. So, I really need for you guys to bust your asses on this one. The murder of two on-duty police officers *will not, cannot, and shall not be allowed to go without swift and severe retributions!* More importantly, we cannot tolerate nor allow our officers to be ambushed in our streets! Why they did not receive prompt assistance after their stress call is something for me to get to the bottom of. You guys' job is to go out there and just bust some heads if you have too but find some leads to this case. Call in all your favors, pressure every informant and shut down every illegal establishment operating within the seven-five's jurisdiction!"

The Chief's oration was suddenly interrupted when the door of the room was opened, and in entered an officer with a report in his hand. Officer Juan Medina walked over to Detective Fitzgerald and handed him a document, "Sir, the ballistics report you were waiting for just arrived. Here they go." he said handing Fitzgerald the report.

"Chief!" Fitzgerald said excitedly. "I think we finally have here the lead we have all been expecting! Hey Tom! Get a load of this! Remember I mentioned to you that there was something very peculiar about those 45 cal. shell casings we found at the scene? Well, ballistics has found that they match those found in the Cypress Hills ambush case!"

"Okay!" Chief Ferguson jumped in, "now send somebody down to the chief coroner's office and light a fire under his ass so he hurries and pull those slugs out of the officers' bodies so we can determine whether they match also! And get back to me ASAP! Right now I have a news conference to attend with no developing story to tell."

"Okay Chief. We're on it!" Fitzgerald quickly obeyed, then told his partner, "We'll go to the coroner's office ourselves, Tom. Maybe we can dig out something useful from that Cypress Hills case. Some information that'll help us determine whether there's any other connections to this case."

"John. That case was 10 years ago, but I swear I still remember how those bodies had been riddled with so many slugs that they were practically unidentifiable at first sight," Detective Pollack said, "and I remember that there were so many bodies out there that it looked like a mini-Baghdad! That was our first major case, remember? In fact, it turned out to be our biggest case. Up until now, that is." He said solemnly.

"Yeah, I remember, Tom." But those guys are all locked away and most of them with no chances of parole." John exclaimed to his partner.

"Yeah, I know." His partner replied in a pensive state before adding, "I remember it took us almost two years to bring those bastards down. Those assholes were responsible for so much murder and mayhem throughout this city that we ended up with some outstanding commendation. Including our gold shields."

"Yeah well, we need another break like that." Detective Fitzgerald said.

"Hey Harry! Fitzgerald commanded, "I want you to run some names through the system and find out whether any of these scum-bags are walking the streets! I want to know whether they are still locked up or on parole. Whether they are dead or alive and I want their dossiers, wheresoever they may be found, you got that? Oh and I want it yesterday!"

Harry Blumfeld quickly snapped to attention upon hearing his name called by the veteran detective and after recording his orders, sharply responded, "Yes Sir. I'm on it!"

"That's a good idea John, any of those dirt bags could have gotten out on some technicality. Those types of guys are not the kind we want to go around ignoring or letting our younger guys go around playing cops and robbers with." Tom told his partner.

"Yeah, that may be so. But sooner or later they're gonna have to get their feet wet and their hands dirty. Face it, Tom, we got a dangerous job and they might as well get use to it." His partner replied before he said, "Ok Tom, lets head down to the coroner's office and see what we can dig up. The rest of you get out there and start busting some balls! You all heard the Chief, bring this motherfucking neighborhood to its God Damn Knees!"

Chapter 9

CHEM DOG CONNECT

Latesha drove down a practically desolate North Elm Street road in her Beacon, NY neighborhood, en route to the main highway. There was light traffic and very few pedestrians out. She was enjoying the music of a rap group called "D-Block" which blared through the car's sound system as she navigated the luxurious vehicle. As she approached a red light at the corner of Main Street, she shifted her eyes to her left, that's when she noticed a Burgundy 560 Mercedes Benz pulling out from Louden Drive, heading towards her general direction. She arched her neck to get a better view and noticed that the driver of the elegant vehicle was no other than "Gwen". She immediately began honking the horn to attract Gwen's attention. Finally, having succeeded, she instructed Gwen, gesturing with her hand to pull over.

The light suddenly turned green and Latesha headed towards a spacious parking lot and proceeded to park. She then exited her vehicle and ventured over towards Gwen who was exiting her own vehicle, excited and eager to see Latesha. Latesha took notice of the hip-hugging cream velvet Nicole Miller dress Gwen was draped in, along with an expensive pair of Giuseppe Zanotti suede lace up boots that adorned her toned legs.

"Hey Gwen! You looking real nice in that big money outfit you're wearing." Latesha complemented.

"Thank you. You know I try to do my best!"

"Shit! With those $800 boots, and that $1000 dress, you're sportin' girl, you doing more than just trying! Who do you think you're foolin'?" Latesha jested at her.

"Well, they say it's a man's world but it wouldn't be

shit without us women." Gwen retorted.

Gwen was a beauty of a woman. Although she stood at 5'2", she had a pair of well-defined legs that were to die for. She had such a marvelous physical composition that any man would long for her. She measured 38-27-43 and no one could deny she was a true Diva. She had her shoulder length jet black hair in a puffed out hair style that gave her the appearance of a young version of Chaka Khan; the 1980's sex symbol and R&B singer.

"Yeah, well you ain't' never lied." Latesha said as they joined laughing at their puns.

"Anyway girl," Latesha said once the laughter subsided, "I flagged you down cause I wanna put in an order for five pounds of Chem Dog!"

"How soon do you need them?"

"As soon as you can get them to me!" Latesha replied.

"I'll tell you what," Gwen began, "take a spin around and meet me back here in ten minutes and we'll make the transaction. I'll pull over beside you and we'll make the exchange. A'ight?"

"Yeah! Dat'll work. I'll meet you back here in ten then!" Latesha said as they hugged and headed their separate ways. A little over ten minutes later, they met back at the parking lot and took care of their business without a glitch. Latesha immediately set out on her way to her cousin's funeral with Chem Dog riding shotgun.

Chapter 10

ANDREW'S FUNERAL /
VICKY & RONNIE xxx

*L*atesha pulled up, about ninety minutes after her transaction with Gwen, to the Sutphin Boulevard Funeral Home. She found a parking space a few yards in front of the hearse that was to transport her cousin's body to the Woodlawn Cemetery. She exited her vehicle and proceeded to enter the funeral parlor. She was amazed to see that the parlor was packed beyond its legal capacity so early in the morning. There were an innumerable amount of friends and family members in attendance, many whom had traveled hundreds of miles, some from as far away as Fayette, Alabama, mourning and bidding their beloved relative and friend a farewell departure.

Latesha made her way to a seat next to Vicky, Goldie and her sister, Kacky, as everyone attentively listened to Deacon Wilfred Dale Jr., give his eulogy. She squeezed into the end of a long wooden bench to observe the deacon at the podium, lightly dabbing at his forehead with a silk hanker-chief while fumbling through the New Testament Bible.

"What took you so long to get here?" Kacky asked. "I called you about three hours ago." Kacky went on, leaning in close to whisper in her ear.

"I had to take care of some business. Besides, it's better late than never. Don't you think?"

"Jesus...!" the Deacon shouted, "who is the son of God, came in the form of man! How many of you bare witness to that fact?" He asked. The sea of people in attendance all raised their hands and simultaneously shouted, "Amen!"

"God expects us to be a people of prayer, a people of worship!" the Deacon continued. "Our dearly departed Brother, Andrew, loved God. He worshipped God and he will glorify God as he adorns his long white robe and ascends to dwell in the heavenly mansion that the Lord has prepared for him! Glory be to God!" He shouted as he glanced down at his bible. "Jesus said 'Let not your heart be troubled. Ye believe in God. Believe also in me!' Please excuse me ladies and gentlemen," he said, briefly interrupting the sermon, as he took off his glasses and wiped the sweat from the bridge of his nose, to prevent them from sliding down his face.

"Jesus also said, 'In my father's house there are many mansions, if it were not so I would have told you. I go to prepare a place for you and if I go and prepare a place for you I will come again and receive you unto myself; that where I am there ye may be also.' That's in the gospel of John, chapter fourteen, verse one to three." He said. "So..." he continued, "that is to say that our dearly departed Brother Andrew's work down here has been completed. Now his job is to praise, worship, and glorify God Almighty amid the Angels in heaven. Amen! We were created to glorify God, so he may be glorified for the things he has done! May I get a witness?" He again shouted.

"Amen!" the gatherers shouted.

"The great things He has done is without rival and we all rest our cases in God's hands!" He went on.

"In First Corinthians, chapter fifteen, verses fifty-one to fifty-five, God informs us concerning the mystery that is the death of the body. God tells us, 'Behold, I show you a mystery; we shall not all sleep, but we shall all be changed...in a moment, in the twinkling of an eye, at the last trump. For the trumpet shall sound and the dead shall be raised incorruptible and we shall be changed. For the corruptible must be put on incorruption, and this mortal must put on immortality. So when this corruptible shall have put on incorruption and this mortal shall have put on immorality, then shall be brought to pass the saying that is written: 'Death is swallowed up in victory.' Hence brothers and sisters mourn, if you shall, Brother Andrews' departure. But, more importantly, celebrate Brother Andrews' life, as we join and say, 'O death, where is thy sting? O grave, where is thy victory?' I ask you now, first those seated to the right of the aisle to form a line and come pay your respects and bid our Brother Andrew a farewell. And those to the left of the aisle may proceed to do so after." Deacon Dale Jr. concluded before stepping down from the podium.

"Oh, my God! Kacky, who is that tall light skin guy standing by the casket?" Vicky excitingly asked, whispering into her ear.

"Ah girl, please. That's my cousin Ronnie from Alabama!" Kacky answered cupping her hand over her mouth.

"Well, I want to meet 'em before we roll up outta here!"

"You should be ashamed of yourself." Kacky replied to her. "Trying to give away some coochie at a funeral home!"

"Oh please!" Vicky retorted loudly enough to be heard up in the row where Michelle and Althea sat along with a few church elders.

"Sssshhh!" hissed one of the elders, an aged family member from the South, angrily turning towards them and rolling her eyes before focusing back on the procession. When it came turn for them to pay their respects, Vicky utilized the time as a golden opportunity to get Ronnie's attention, using her flirtatious eyes and swaying her hips as she made her way to the casket. She purposely turned her head and noticed the way he admired the way her dress hugged her curvaceous figure to perfection. She smiled inwardly aware that her silk dress showed no trace or outline of any underwear underneath. When they were done paying their respects at the foot of the casket, the

Sisters strolled over to their Southern relatives, seated in the front row alongside their mother and greeted them expressing their condolences. After acknowledging his two cousins, Ronnie directed his attention back to Vicky. He slightly nodded his head and displayed a look of interest which did not go unnoticed by the rest of the girls as they proceeded out the exit door.

"Damn Vicky! Their cousin was looking at you like he wanted to eat you up in there!" Goldie said as they stood outside following the conclusion of the funeral.

"Yeah! If she would've been standing there another five minutes, that nigga would'a started foaming out the mouth!" Michelle joked.

"Please, I was clocking him way before he knew a bitch like me was up in da building!" Vicky replied.

"You need to cool your hot ass down!" Kacky interjected.

"I just might let cha cousin cool it down for me!", She quickly retorted, placing her left hand on her hip in a defiant stance, while eyeing her with raised eye brows.

Althea said with a snarl, "Bitch you better not give him no pussy. You don't know him like that!"

"Yeah, but I'm about ta' know 'em! So be quiet!" Vicky snapped.

"No, you be quiet!" Althea quickly fired back. "We can't even attend a damn funeral service wit' out cha getting all fired up 'n shit!"

"I swear Vicky," Latesha chimed in, "I don't know what the hell we gone do wit' cha fast ass!"

"Y'all bitches ain't gone do shit but keep on lovin' meee!" She sang out snapping her fingers and working her hips in a circulatory motion, causing her ass cheeks to bounce around like they were rummaging for space. That action caused all the Angels to break out laughing hysterically.

"That girl should be ashamed of herself, out here carrying on like that." An elderly woman said to her female friend standing a few feet away. The elder woman stood there with her hands on her hips shaking her head from side to side.

"Yeah she actin' like she ain't get no home trainin'." The elder woman's friend replied with her hand held up to her mouth, watching in disgust as Vicky carried on.

"Girl, stop dancing like you're a damn slut!" Goldie told her through gritted teeth and an embarrassing expression, "Them old ladies peeking over here, whispering 'n shit to each other!"

"Oh please! Fuck them old ass bitches!" Vicky shot back at her while gyrating her hips to some imaginary music in her head. She then noticed Ronnie comin' down the funeral parlor's steps, headed in their direction. "Kacky don't forget to introduce me." She reminded.

"Long time no see." He said, smiling as he approached Latesha.

"Oh knock it off, Ronnie. You just saw us last summer at the family reunion." Latesha replied.

"You sure did" Kacky agreed. "Anyway, I wanna introduce your to our home-girls." Pointing with her index finger, she began, "This is Michelle, Goldie, Althea, and this one right here has been dying to make your acquaintance. Her name is Vicky."

"Shit..." Ronnie began, "I wasn't gone leave New York until I met bey-bee girl." He said in his deep southern drawl, as he continued, "I was measuring hurr up when she wa' standin' at the casket; all dat rump was cloudin' my dang vision up in thurr."

"Oh, was it really?" Vicky sultrily asked.

"Hell yeah little momma! And you got some powwa in yo wawk too, I see!" He assured her.

"I also got some power in my pu..."

"SHUT UP VICKY!" Althea and Goldie simultaneously yelled.

Latesha used the moment to get into Ronnie's head. She had her mind going on overdrive. Thoughts of expanding their operation abroad occupied her mind. "So..." she began, "Ronnie, who are you staying with while your here in New York?"

"You know good and dang well that I stay at Auntie Linda's whenever I'm in the Big Apple." He told her.

"Yeah, you right! I don't know how that slipped my mind." She said before continuing. "But how long are you going to be here before you head back to Alabama?"

"I'm on the first thing smokin' da marrah mornin'!" he said.

"Why you leaving so soon?" Vicky interjected. Letting her eyes roam down to his crotch, as she bit down on her bottom lip.

"I gotta few thangs to take care of back home." He told her.

"Shit, you could take care of a few things here in New York before you leave, if you want to!" Vicky shot at him, slowly and seductively tracing her lip with the tip of her tongue.

"Excuse me, Vicky. But I'm really trying to holla at my cuz right now. I'm pretty sure he won't have a problem givin' you some undivided attention before he leaves New York, so please let me finish what I got to say to him." Latesha told her obviously displaying some irritation.

"My bad! Y'all know I get a lil crazy sometimes!" Vicky apologetically, shot back.

"I apologize too cuz. It was part my fault as well. Cause it take two to tango!" Ronnie added before winking at Vicky, causing her to blush.

"Y'all give me two minutes. Then y'all could do whatever the hell y'all want." Latesha assured them. "Anyway Ronnie, what kind of work you doin' down there?" She asked him.

"I'm workin' part-time at a Pizza Hut in da town. Why?"

'Why...?" Latesha repeated before she went on, "because I'm thinkin' 'bout pumping some weed down there and I want you to move it for me."

"Hell! Dat'a work cuz!" He excitedly replied. "We gotta travel all da way to Tuscaloosa to get some fire if we wanna get blitzed up!" He continued.

"A'ight then, here's what I'm 'a do. I'm gonna give you 50 sample joints to take back to Alabama with you. You give them out and in a few more days me and the girls are coming down there.

Vicky!" Latesha said directing her attention to her. "Do you still have some Chem left from the other night?"

"Yeah, I gotta hand-full of that shit left!" Vicky replied.

"Good, because I don't have any rolled up right now. Take Ronnie to your crib and give him what you got." She said, mischievously winking at her with a light grin on her face.

"Hold on. I'm gonna go let Auntie Linda know she could ride on without me." He said prior to disappearing into the large crowd that had formed outside the funeral home.

"And bitch," Latesha started on Vicky, "don't come runnin' back to me talkin' 'bout your katt all ripped up! I done warned your ass 'bout the niggaz in my family. But, you wanna be hot all up in da ass 'n shit, then go ahead!"

"Oh tramp be givin' her pussy away like its government cheese!" Goldie blurted out.

"Bitch please! If my shit was cheese, it would be that parmesan shit!" Vicky shot back at her, cupping her crotch.

"Eeel! Come on now, don't be doin' that nasty ass shit out here, and you got a dress on too!" Michelle chimed.

"Aaahhh, fuck you Michelle! You don't tell me what to do." Vicky retorted, sucking her teeth.

"*ANYWAY!* " Latesha cut in, easing the tension between the two. "Do y'all remember that light skin chick with all them damn kids? You know, the one that lived on the first floor of that building on Schenck Street, next to the parking lot!" She asked, no one in particular.

"Yeah, you talkin' 'bout Shaneeda!" Althea answered.

"Anyway..." Latesha continued, "She moved out a few days ago. So I'ma open up a Chem spot in that apartment tonight. What do y'all think about Black Pat from Warwick Avenue workin' up in it?"

"She good money!" Vicky answered.

"Shit, Pat is like family!" Goldie added.

"Yeah and besides, you know Mommy love the hell outta Pat. So we gotta take good care of her!" Kacky chimed in.

"That goes without sayin', Kacky!" Latesha assured her. "Anyway, I'm up outta here. I'll get up with y'all later on. And Vicky, you make sure you bring my cousin back home with his dick still intact!" She joked before making her way to her vehicle. She jumped in her whip and waved to the girls before peeling out of the parking spot, leaving the smell of burnt tires behind.

"What Latesha really meant to say was, don't go biting his dick off, cause we all know you gonna put it in your mouth! That's just the type of bitch you are!" Goldie sardonically stated.

"Yeah, and don't go givin' 'em no rabies either bitch!" Althea added.

"I'ma get the last laugh when one'a them niggaz 'round the way start a vicious rumor 'bout one of y'all bitches getting' drunk 'n baptizing his dick!" Vicky shot back at them.

"And I'll be a sober bitch when his ass gets dealt with and baptized with embalming fluid too! You let'a mufucker put my lips and his dick in the same sentence if you wanna and watch what the fuck happens!" Althea shot back with a menacing snarl.

"Please! Michelle snapped, "them niggaz 'round the way know when the Angels are in the house. "Oh my god!

DANGER!" They all yelled in unison, to their re-mix version of an old rap song by the artist "Blah Zay Blah", whom paid great homage to their East New York neighborhood.

Standing a few yards away with her best friend, Mary Smith, Ms. Desire Robinson screamed, "Cut out all that noise over there!" Ms. Desire was better known in the lower parts of Alabama as "Bladie Mae." She had earned the name because of the way she handled a knife during combat. As kids, her children would often wonder why their southern relatives referred to her by that name. One summer back in 1976 her new boyfriend of two months, "Maurice Herman Babb" was caught with his eyes wandering in the direction of the new neighbor, Susie Rivera. Susie was a well-proportioned caramel complexioned, Latin woman who had recently moved to the country from Ponce, Puerto Rico. The rumor had it that Susie could turn a dick into stone with just one glance.

It was during one of Ms. Desire's many gambling parties where they would play poker, spades, rum, craps, and three card Monty, while drinking Bacardi, Vodka and Brandy, or a variety of different kinds of brew that Maurice's eyes must have wandered a little too far. He probably had had a little too much to drink because he openly began lusting over Susie, looking at her through glazed eyes as he sloppily ran his alcohol laced tongue across her lips. They had all been enjoying themselves listening to all the Motown hits, blasting through the speakers of the component set. But none of Maurice's flirtations went unnoticed by Desire. She sprang into action with the swiftness of a well-trained circus cat. With zero tolerance for suffering disrespect from anyone, let alone her man, whom appeared flirting with another woman in her presence, she grabbed a butcher knife and plunged it deep into the interior of his guts. The blood flowed profusely from his wound, some of the guests stood by in shock while others started trotting towards the door.

"Nigga, don't you ever disrespect me, especially in my own god damn house!" She yelled as he lay motionless on the floor in a pool of his own blood. The kids had come running out of their rooms donning their night clothes and stood there in awe of the scene before their very eyes. Someone had called the cops and the emergency medical service and when they arrived, she was still standing over him ranting with blood still dripping from the tip of the knife.

While he was en route to Kings County Hospital, she was being processed and transported through the system. Family members stood behind mopping up the pool of blood as they had done many times before in the South, conversating around the children as if they weren't there.

"Damn! I guess Bladie Mae ain't gone ne'va put her dang-gon blade to ress." Goobie, her first cousin, stated.

"Shit! Now she done lef'a trail a blood from Berry and Fayette, Alabama all the way ta Brooklyn, New York," said her other cousin Dee-Lord in his southern accent, as he shook his head in disbelief. "Since she luv knives so dang much, why 'n hell she don't just get a job in the butcher shop down da street?" He asked no-one in particular.

"Sheeeit! Hurr havin' a dang knife in hurr han for eight hours is too damn dangerous. Y'all seen whut da' hell hurr crazy behind did wit' one in hurr han' fo eight mufuckin' seconds!" Goobie exclaimed.

* * * * *

"Y'all know better than dat," Desire said with a menacing stare that her daughters knew all so well. Y'all just came out a funeral home." She told them, indicating with her finger over her shoulder in the direction of the funeral parlor.

"You right, Ma. I'm sorry."

"Yeah, I apologize too, Ms. Dee." Althea quickly added.

"Don't sorry me to death. Just tone it down." She demanded. "And Vicky, what the hell is that you wearing on your behind?" This is a funeral home not the Flamingo." she barked, as the girls looked at each other with curious expressions on their faces.

"Flamingo!" Althea repeated before shooting Kacky a quick glance.

"Umm huh…!" Kacky began, eyeing her mother with raised eye brows and her hands on her hips, "So what's the Flamingo, Ma? And I hope it ain't no strip club either!"

"Chile please! You better go on 'head. You don't question me! Last time I checked I was still yo damn Momma! And it ain't been no changes since then." she said. "And if it was, I ain't get the memo, yet!" she sarcastically added before turning her back on them.

"You straightened her behind right on out Des!" Her friend, Ms. Mary said in plain ear shot of the girls.

"Ms. Mary needs to mind her damn business, with her nosey ass self." Agitatedly, Althea said.

"Yeah. I'm surprised nobody ain't put hands and feet on her old grumpy ass yet!" Michelle added.

Mary Smith barely ever left her front window. She knew everything that went on within a ten block radius of the neighborhood, especially on her own block. That was due to the networking of her Christian sisters whom spread news around the neighborhood like wildfire. They knew who was doing what, when and where, including how long they had been doing it. Other than on Sunday mornings when she attended church services, she could be seen sitting by her window chatting away on the phone.

"Ah, fuck Ms. Mary! We're wasting too much time and energy talking 'bout her." Althea spat out.

"Yeah girl, you ain't never lied!" Goldie agreed.

"Anyway, since we ain't going to the burial, what y'all wanna do? Cause it's still early out this bitch!" Michelle exclaimed.

"Humph! I don't know, nor do I care what y'all gonna do. I'm trying to get with Ronnie." Vicky interjected.

"Well here he comes now, Vicky. So hurry up, get on your knees!" Althea cracked, causing the girls to snicker.

"Ah, kiss my ass, Althea!" she shot back before Ronnie approached.

"Sorry it took me so long, but my Auntie was talkin' my ears off. Boy, do she get long winded whenever she get going," he said. "I thought my Momma had a pair of lungs on her, but Auntie Linda got her beat by a long shot!" Grrrr... "Oops! Excuse me y'all," he politely said after his stomach betrayed him and commenced to grumble, causing Goldie and Michelle to jerk back.

"Damn nigga, your stomach growling like that?" Vicky asked with her nose turned up.

"Yeah!" he replied. "I skipped breakfast this morning, so you know I'm hungrier than a runaway slave right now."

"Well let's go grab a bite ta'eat," Vicky suggested, fumbling through her Kate Spade clutch bag for her car keys. "You eat sea food, Ronnie?" She asked him.

"Shit! I love sea food! We don't just eat pork and potatoes in the South." He said in a masculine but sexy tone with a trace of lust in his eyes.

"Mmm, I'll keep that in mind. Let's get outta here. I'll get up with y'all bitches later!" She told the girls before leading the way to her car.

"Vicky really think she slick, with her hot ass self. My cousin gone knock the bottom outta her coochie for being so damn fast!" Kacky said.

"Ah please. Vicky ain't got no bottom to her coochie!" Althea said before taking a drag of her Newport cigarette.

"Her shit is like the solar system, dark and deep, with no beginning and no mufuckin' ending."

"Bitch, you dead wrong for that one right there. You probably be talking about my katt like that when I'm not around too!" Michelle stated as she studied Althea with keen eyes.

"I ain't gotta talk about 'cha tore out cat. Niggaz in da' hood talk about it enough as it is!"

"You a mufuckin' lie, Althea! Don't even try dat shit!" Michelle parried back.

"Listen!" Goldie barked, "I ain't got time to be standing 'round chatting 'bout who coochie is worn da'fuck out! I'm 'bout to peel out and take my ass home! Shit, I got a long ride to Albany tomorrow."

"Oh yeah! I forgot you had to go back to court. That case should'a been over and done wit' years ago," Kacky cut in.

"Yeah Kacky, you right." Michelle added in a much cooler tone. "Them crackaz up there playing 'round wit' dat judgment. They need to stop bull-shittin' and break her off wit' dat bread!"

"Well, whatever they award me is gonna be used to wash our illegal funds. And I know dat after all these years, they probably gonna bless da' hell outta my pockets. So we're gonna be straight!" She continued. "The first thing I'm gonna purchase is dat damn warehouse we've been renting. It's not dat I can't purchase it now, it's just dat I don't wanna raise any eye brows throughout the law enforcement agencies!"

"Please! Just listen to your yellow ass, you wasn't worried 'bout the cee-ciphers for the past nine, almost ten years! Now that we all millionaires you getting shook!" Kacky spat.

"Yeah, we had our run and it has been a long one because we have helped out a lotta mothafuckas financially. We have put mothafuckas through college, paid for mothafuckas vacations and put a lot of food on motherfuckas tables. So the hood love us!" Goldie continued. "That's why we're standing strong. Every move we've made so far, has been well calculated because we've taken the time to plan our moves well before bringing them to fruition." She went on preaching like that for the next ten minutes or so, before they all departed to their respective destinations.

* * * * *

Chang Ling Ho Chinese Restaurant, on Amsterdam Avenue, up in Harlem, was unlike any eatery Ronnie had ever been to. Being from Alabama, he was accustomed to frequenting hole-in-the-wall-greasy-spoon-spots. The kind where they'd have Wild Irish Rose and Thunderbird wines on their menu and everything was strictly takeout. "Wow! This is a real classy restaurant", he thought to himself as they sat at a candle lit table in a corner across from another couple who appeared to be deep in conversation. It didn't take long for them to decide on what dish to have and moments later a waitress approached their table.

"Sir, Ma'am, are you ready to place your orders, yet," the waitress politely asked.

"Yes. Umm, I'll have the Lobster Cantonese wit' the spicy butter sauce," Vicky ordered first, placing her menu on the table.

"Sir," she said, holding her order pad ready to write down his choice.

"Ah, I'll have da' silver salmon and umm," he hesitated for a moment before adding, "A Lobster Fra Diavolo."

"And what, may I ask, will you have for beverages?" the waitress asked.

"I'll have a bottle of water, thank you." Vicky replied.

"And I'll have the same thang." Ronnie said.

"Your orders will be along shortly," the waitress assured them before heading towards the counter.

"So, Ronnie...," Vicky began speaking while applying a light coat of Satinette lip gloss, which Ronnie thought made her already sensuous lips look all the more luscious and inviting, "I'm gonna be straight wit' cha. You caught my attention almost immediately, back at the funeral parlor. And I was automatically attracted to you. You already know dat I'm coming down to Alabama in a few days, wit'cha cousins-n-em and so I want to know if you gotta a girl? Also, if you do, is it serious enuff where as you and I would not be able to create some private time for ourselves?" She interrogatively asked.

"First of all, baby gurl, the feelin' is mutual. You too, not almost immediately, but immediately caught my attention back at the funeral parlor, and I too automatically was attracted to you. Wit' dat said and to answer your question, No! I don't have a steady female, but me being a fella with class and all, and whom maintains high opinions of himself, you must understand that I attract the opposite sex like fashion wear, where ever I go," he told her. "But, I'm gonna be straightfoward and to the point with you. When you show your lovely mocha face in Alabama, I promise you that every thang gonna get shut down. It's your wurl and I'm 'a jus be a squirrel tryin' ta getta nut." He stated while peering into the windows of her soul, wherein she noticed his lustful and yearning desire for her.

"Yeah, that's what's up!" She exclaimed, sinking her teeth gently into her bottom lip.

"Yeah, but I'm tryin' ta see ya before I leave. You unnerstan where I'm coming from, lil momma?"

"Trust me, I read between the lines very well!" She shot back thinking, I'm 'a put this here New York pussy on his country ass so damn good, he gonna start trying to claim it.

"Here's your orders." The waitress said placing their dishes and drinks along with their silverware, which were neatly wrapped in custom designed napkins with the restaurant's name embroidered in gold lettering, on the table. The waitress' arrival caused Vicky to snap out of her naughty reverie in time to thank her.

When they were done devouring their meal, Vicky left the customary ten percent tip for the waitress and suggested they head to her place to better acquaint themselves. Once they arrived at her luxurious brownstone home, situated in the Canarsie section of Brooklyn, Vicky pulled her Volvo into her driveway and proceeded to escort Ronnie into her house. Her crib was decked out. The living room was huge and the floor was adorned from wall to wall with a candy apple red shaggy rug. The walls were entirely mirrored and reflected the butter soft black leather sofas, love chair, and recliner perfectly arranged throughout the room. The ceiling had been dropped and a huge crystal chandelier hung from the center of the room.

Ronnie stood there in awe of the decorative place. Vicky, after instructing him to remove his shoes, walked over to her entertainment system and turned on her Bose stereo. The slow romantic sound of music came pouring from hidden speakers. Vicky smiled as Ronnie stood there attempting to locate the speaker system. She relieved his curiosity when she volunteered that the speakers had been strategically located within the dropped ceiling.

She quickly led him into her bear-skinned floor covered bedroom, and all at once the intoxicating scent of her Narciso Rodriquez perfume flooded the confines of her room and heightened Ronnie's sexual appetite and lust. They quickly began to desperately, yet, lovingly remove each other's clothing. Ronnie took charge and lifted Vicky's Anna Sui mini dress over her shoulders. Vicky then quickly stepped out of her Alexander McQueen leather winged ankle boots. Then Ronnie began to gently but firmly caress her buttocks while driving his tongue into her sensually opened mouth. Vicky responded to his lustful kiss and in turn ran her hands along his chest and down to his groin.

"Oh my god!" she grasped, as she engulfed and felt the size of his manhood. "What in the ...," she began to say, but Ronnie drowned her words in another sensuous kiss which left Vicky moaning as she pressed against his dick. Sensing Vicky's legs becoming weak, he scooped her up and carried her over to her queen sized bed.

He laid her down and whispered, "Damn baby, you sho'nuff is a lovely piece of art work," while gently brushing her hair back from her face. Vicky was at a loss for words as she lay there admiring Ronnie's chiseled body.

"Yeah, and that six pack is a perfect showcase for this thick ass dick," Vicky said, licking her lips as she reached out for his cock. "I heard you were holding, but nothing in the world could have prepared me for this," she said staring admiringly at his penis while stroking it gently.

"Oh, I know you heard I'm a direct descendant of the king ding-a-ling tribe." He said with a sinister grin.

"So I've heard." She replied, still holding a firm yet gentle grip on his penis.

"Well, now you know firsthand that it ain't no myth." He said running his hands over her shoulders and down her back to the crack of her ass. Vicky again moaned and began to bite down gently on his chest and shoulders. Ronnie responded by sensually running his tongue along her body and placing short caressing kisses down along her full breast, stomach and thighs.

Vicky braced herself as she felt him reach for her thighs and part her legs slowly. She looked up into her overhead bedroom mirror and was completely turned on as he licked along the inside of her thighs until he reached her vaginal lips. She shuddered and let out an unexpected gasp as he slowly licked on them. By the time he ventured into her pussy and clung onto her clitoris with his lips, sucking on it and wiggling his tongue against it, Vicky was drenched in pussy juice.

"Oh my god!" She screamed out in pleasure as her pussy glistened with her discharge. Ronnie continued to lick, suck and lap over her pussy, spreading and lifting her legs over his shoulder to better penetrate with his tongue.

Vicky thought she had died and went to heaven, the way Ronnie was eating her out. She began groaning and moaning and thrashing about the bed as he continued his tongue lashing. He was now furiously administering his tongue up and down the entire length of her slit, while slowly but firmly jabbing his middle finger up into her moist but tight vagina. She continued to squirm around in ecstasy and let out a gruesome howl when he suddenly used his thumb to slide back the hood of her clit for full access.

"Ahh, ohh, shit." Vicky moaned as he softly sucked on her exposed clit. He felt an eruption coming from deep within her before he tasted the light dribble from the mouth of her twat, coating his chin. "Fuck!" Vicky screamed out when she felt his tongue enter the depths of her inner core. His tongue went as deep as it possibly could. Extracting what was left of her flowing nectar. She again moaned and groaned in ecstasy as his tongue continued to dance around in the silky confines of her vagina.

Suddenly she couldn't take it any longer and desperately pulled him up and in one swift motion got on all fours. "Hit this pussy, mufucka! Hit it from the back!" Ronnie obligingly positioned himself behind her and drove his cock deep into her crevice. *"Oh god almighty,"* Vicky let out one long moan as she felt his tool invade her inner core. Ronnie held her ass up high and surged in with his pulsating penis. *"Ohhh. Ummm, yeah dig baby, dig!"* Vicky shouted, sinking her teeth into her bottom lip. He must have been an expert at doggie style, she thought, because he connected at just the right angles from the very first stroke. They began to furiously hump each other, back and forth they parried and Vicky whimpered each time his bloated dick head slammed into her hidden G-spot.

"Uhh, uhh, yess, yess, yess," she began climaxing and it felt like she was floating on a cloud. *"Ohh shit! Uhh my god! Long dick me. Aahhh, yeah like that, like that,*

oohh my god!!!" She finally yelled as he excitedly dug deeper into her wet clasping pussy. Enjoying the mixture of pleasure and pain as she bit down on her lip again, she was feeling every thrust, every stroke, and every plunge into her. She was sure that his dick was knocking at the end walls of her love tunnel. Then all of a sudden, when she thought she had felt all of him, he gripped her in an extremely strong embrace and thrust forward and deep into her with such force that he caused her more pain than pleasure.

"Ahh! Shit! Ahh!" She moaned with every thrust. She then swung around shoved him onto his back and straddled him. Then reached between her legs and gripped his penis at the base, and after stroking it up and down a few times, she guided it in and up her. She controlled the amount that entered her while thinking, this nigga shit caught me off guard. But, suddenly, Ronnie lifted his hips up off the mattress, *"Oh my fucking god!"* she screamed as his dick plunged deep up into her juice box, entering all the way to the root, before resting his ass back onto the mattress.

"Relax, Baby, this pussy ain't' goin' nowhere!" She told him as she eased down on him slowly, moaning every inch of the way until his dick finally fitted her snuggly. Her vagina spasmed at the feeling of what seemed like the handle of a little league baseball bat. As she gently and rhythmically bounced her ass up and down the length of his entire shaft, he held onto her butt spreading her ass cheeks wide apart. She began lavishly adding a little more and more hip action to the top ride, squirming on the down stroke, causing a sensational friction to her clitoris from rubbing up against his pubic hairs. Her body twitched, her face twisted up, and her hardened dark luscious nipples poked out like pistons, as a thousand goose bumps invaded them. Her body suddenly began to spasm and jerk as she finally discharged, letting her juices flow like the Nile River all over his dick.

That excited Ronnie all the more and so he flipped her on her back, lifted her legs over his shoulders, spreading them wide, then greedily guided his dick back through the mouth of her waiting vagina and into the depths of her pussy. He rammed his dick to the very depths of her sexual existence, pistoning in and out with abandon. Vicky's pussy continued to erupt with thick coats of girly juices all along the length of his love muscle making it much easier and bearable for her to engulf it.

"Ooooh god! Yes, yes! Ahh yeah Ronnie!!" She cried out in ecstasy as he continued to dig deeper and deeper into her love hole. *"Ahhh, yes! Yeah Ronnie, stroke that dick up in me. Yeah, just like dat! Like dat, yes! Ahhh, stroke it, stroke it baby, sssshhh, uumm."* She egged him on as her pussy spasmed, dripped and flowed with her juices. They came together, both clinging tight to each other and letting their juices flow in torrents.

"LAWD HAVE MERCY!!!" Ronnie yelled in his southern drawl, pulling out of her soppingly wet pussy and rolling onto his back. "You got some good ass box, gurl!" He finally said, exhausted.

"Please!" Vicky responded, and confidently added, "Tell me something I don't know!"

"Now why did I sense a lot'a of conceitedness in that statement?" He asked, admiring her body as though it was designed by the wisdom of time.

"Nah, what you really sensed was a lot'a damn confidence!"

"Oh, is that right?" he asked, watching as she crawled out of the bed and waltzed past him, ass jiggling with every step she took. "God damn!" He further added in a more subtle tone.

"You better believe it!" She barked at him while looking over her shoulder. "Grab that sandwich bag of weed from outta my night stand drawer, on the left side of the bed." She added as she proceeded into the shower.

"That's that Chem Dog Latesha made reference too, but don't go lighting that shit up in here, cause that shit there is powerful than a mufucka and I don't want my place reeking from its smell," she instructed him.

Chapter 11

CHEM SPOT

*T*he Chem spot was doing great. Things had picked up in only three weeks. The clientele was almost unbelievable. Black Pat barely got any sleep. Every time she turned around there would be a knock on the door by another customer wanting to purchase. Business was really booming. There were times when there would be lines of customers from the door all the way back out to the buildings' entrance. She loved her new occupation, it was definitely a far cry from the minimum wage job she had just recently quit. She had been a messenger in Manhattan where she would pick up packages and deliver them to various destinations throughout the Westside of Manhattan.

Black Pat didn't mind working during the summer season where they would issue her a mountain bike to get around from one place to the next, depending on the distance she'd have to travel. But for the measly two hundred dollars she was paid every two weeks, it wasn't worth working during the inclimate season. Especially in the brisky weather that New York was experiencing. She hated the way the wind would blow in her face and cause her eyes to tear up, as she rode the bike in that hawk. So when she was offered the opportunity to run the weed gate she didn't hesitate to jump right on it. She remembered when Latesha approached her and summoned her to her mother's place.

"Pat...," she remembered Latesha saying, "I know you already got a lil job and I'm feeling your independent nature. You're not running around here like these other young chicks who be laying on their backs for a Gucci bag.

I'm opening up a weed spot two blocks from your house and I wanna know if you are interested in workin' for me? It would be worth your while and it'll pay six hundred dollars a week. But, if you unable to work full time you could holla at your friend Tameko and see if she would be willin to come aboard and split shifts wit' you. But you gonna have to pay her half of wha'chu get."

"Hold on, let me get this straight. You willin' to pay me six hundred dollars fa one week, every week?" She excitedly asked. "Cause, if that's the case, I'll work dolo and pocket the whole six hundred fa' my mufuckin' self!"

Even if Latesha's offer was only $300 a week, Pat most likely would have jumped on it. After all, it was almost twice as much as she was earning on her last job.

"Yeah, I'll pay you every Sunday but I'm gonna let you know right now, I don't want nobody coming up in the spot unless it's my girls! But I wouldn't mind if Tameko came and chill with you though. Puerto Rican Nesto is gonna be pickin' up the money from you and supplying you with more work when needed. I'll give you his cell number when I get you settled into the spot." Latesha informed her.

Nesto was a Puerto Rican guy who stood six foot two inches tall and although he was of Latin descent, he could pass for a black brother. He wore his dark curly hair well-trimmed, and his blowout style lended an African-American appearance to his features. He was what the hood considered a pretty-boy. But everyone who knew him knew that he'll mix it up in the streets on any level. Latesha had brought him aboard her crew immediately after he came home in the early nineties from doing a bid. He had served time for a drug case he caught back in the eighties. Nesto was a thorough individual who grew up with her and her siblings and had proved his undying loyalty when he refused to take a lighter sentence in exchange for his testimony against her twin brother BK, who had been facing homicide charges which eventually he got acquitted of.

Nesto was facing ten to twenty years for narcotics related charges. The Brooklyn district attorney had made him an offer which practically would have turned out to be likened to a smack on the wrist, in exchange for his testimony against BK. Nesto did not waste any time in reaching out to the family to inform them of the D.A.'s shenanigans. BK in return for his loyalty and courage ordered his own private attorney and his defense team, who were already being paid a hefty price to represent Nesto. At the time Nesto was being represented by a court appointed attorney from the Legal Aid Society. The private team went to bat for Nesto and got him a lighter sentence without him having to snitch on anyone. Nesto received a four to eight year sentence of which he only served six years and never looked back since.

* * * * *

The Chem spot wasn't your ordinary drug spot, setup in some dilapidated abandoned building. Latesha made sure that whomever worked behind the door for her, did so in a fashionably comfortable environment. And with Pat being like a little sister to the Angels, she felt compelled to fix the place up. She had luxuriously furnished the apartment. Decorating it with the latest entertainment appliances, such as the fifty inch flat screen television, complete with cable and McIntosh MXA 60 Audio system she had installed in the apartment. She had a fine leather sofa bed and recliners in the apartment so her workers could periodically kick back and rest. She always made sure that the refrigerator stood loaded with food and drinks.

Pat felt as though she was getting paid to live and work in her own plushed crib. "What could be better than this?" She often thought to herself. Despite the fact that what she was doing was illegal, the money being generated by the spot and the salary she was pulling was enough to give her such an adrenaline rush that she found all the more inducing and welcoming. The money she was earning allowed her the luxury of draping herself in the latest fashions from Prada, Gucci, Fendi, Cesare Paciotti and Giuseppe Zanotti. The days of her having to save her pay checks for two months, or more in order to purchase name brand outfits, were over. She was now on the express lane, courtesy of the Sutter Angels.

Chapter 12

GOLDIE'S LAWSUIT

*R*ing, ring, ring..., the loud blaring sound of the phone startled Goldie, waking her up and out of her deep sleep. She slightly lifted her head and glanced over in the direction of her indigo colored clock radio sitting atop her night stand by the telephone. It was 6:56 in the morning. "Who da' fuck could this be calling me this early in the morning?" She cursed as she extended her arm and snatched up the receiver. Clearly agitated she spoke into the phone, "Hello!"

"My, my, my, aren't we a little grouchy this morning." The voice on the other end joked.

"Oh, good morning, Mrs. Heyward," Goldie responded, recognizing her attorney's voice. "This better be good, cause not even my mother calls me this early in the morning!" She told her.

"I see why," Mrs. Heyward stated flatly with a hint of sarcasm. "Anyway, I just called to give you some good news. You're now a wealthy woman. Two point five million dollars wealthier. How does that grab you?"

After having spent the last two days holed up in an Albany County court room, impatiently waiting for the judges' well overdue ruling, Goldie had decided to go home and get some well-deserved rest. She knew that her attorney would immediately contact her to inform her of the judges' ruling, once he announced it. However, she was not expecting to hear from her legal representative this early in the day. "Please repeat that again!" she said into the phone, adjusting her tone as she slid up and leaned back against the headboard.

"I asked, how does two point five million grab you?" she repeated.

"Two point five?" Goldie asked after clearing her throat. "Please! I got almost four times that much at my crib stacked neatly up inside my armored safe," she thought to herself.

"Yes. And that'll be after taxes and of course my fee," she added. "How does that make you feel?" she further asked.

"I'm trying to soak it all in. I mean, that's a lotta money! I'm still trying to get over my initial shock!" Goldie proceeded to carry on as if she was trying to win an Oscar for her performance. "Wow! I'm a millionare! I want to thank you for the hard work you dedicated to helping me obtain what was rightfully due to me. May God bless ya!" She finally said.

"You're welcome!" Mrs. Heyward replied before adding, "But it is my job and pleasure to defend the righteous. Now you go ahead and get back to your beauty rest. And since the State does not plan on appealing the Judges' decision, I'll be expecting you this afternoon in my office so that you can pick up your check. And just so you know in advance, the decision will probably come out in today's late edition of the New York Post. There's no need to worry though, your identity would not be revealed. No one else wishes to be sued. So, you may continue to carry on with your normal everyday life, if you so choose to." She concluded gleefully.

"Mrs. Heyward, you couldn't begin to imagine what my normal everyday life is like." She said, trying her best not to break out laughing.

"Well, I could definitely imagine what it could be like now that you're a millionare. So come pick up your check before I spend it."

"A'ight. Bye now." Goldie said laughing before placing the receiver back on its cradle. Just as she was hanging up the phone, she heard the front door open then slammed shut.

"Honey I'm home!" Jungle yelled out altering his voice to sound like some upiddy middle-class American.

"Yeah, I hear you in there trying to sound all proper 'n shit!"

"Well it's a lot better than I sounded the other night, after blowin' dat weed you hit me off with. That shit had a nigga all bent da'fuck up," he said as he made his way to the doorway of the bedroom. "I've been smokin' trees a long time now, since like I was at least fourteen years old. But I have never, in my thirty three years on this earth, been as high as I was after taking a few tokes of that shit you blessed me with! A mufucka should be insane, completely outta his damn mind if he was to blow on dat shit and then tried to get his alcohol drink on too. That shit is too potent by itself and a nigga don't even need to smoke a whole blunt to get fucked up!"

"I'm pretty sure you can do both. After all, you big Jungle, you control the weed, the weed don't control you," She was mocking him for the statement he made the night she tried explaining to him the potent effects of foreign marijuana.

"Oh, so now you got jokes, huh?"

"Nah! You the one that had your chest all poked the hell out that night, trying to be all macho 'n shit when all that shit wasn't necessary. So tell me now Big Jungle." She teased. "Were you in control of that weed after you blew it down?"

"I can't even front yo. That shit was some very impressive shit. Plus, the high lasted a good long while!"

"Humph, just like I thought!" she snapped, rolling her eyes.

"Yeah! Anyway, my man Truck, was telling me how you and your wild ass home girls shut down the Crystal Ball on opening night. Coming through on some real diva like shit."

Jungle knew only half the notoriety of her and her crew. How they were flossers and money getters. But, he was ignorant as to the extent of how much cream they were actually making. Nor did he have the slightest clue about the fact he was bedding down with one of the most ruthless bitches New York has ever bred. And she intended to keep it that way.

"You know we had to step out in style for the grand opening!" she bragged. "Truck let us jump the whole line and a few bitches was mean mugging us, all crazy 'n shit. But chu' know they knew better not to get outta line! Shit...we would'a shut that mufuckin' spot down before it even premiered as the grand opening. It would'a been the grand mufuckin' closing!" She added with a snap of the fingers and a full role of the neck.

"Now that would'na been ladylike of y'all to be all out in da street kickin' and scratchin' up other women just because they said somthin' you and your girls aint like. If y'all gonna call ya'selves Angels than you gotta act accordingly and maintain a sense of humbleness. This aint the eighties when y'all was out there whooping chicks asses all up and down Sutter Avenue. Them days are over with!"

"A'ight, a'ight! You made your point. You aint have to get all long winded with it! Damn!"
"Listen Gee, I'm just trying to hip you to what's really goin' on out in them streets now'a days." He said.

"Nigga please!" She thought to herself. If you really knew the bitch that I turn into once I leave this house, you'd pack ya mufuckin' shit and get da'fuck up outta dodge, quick fast and in a god damn hurry too! "You one hundred percent correct. I can't argue wit'chu 'bout dat!" she said to him. Riiinng, riiinng..., perfect timing she thought as she quickly answered the phone, "Hello!"

"Yeah, you yellow bitch! Why we gotta find out through the grapevine that your pussy done got two point five million dollars richer?" Althea cracked.

"Oh please bitch, spare me the bullshit. I just found out myself, not too long ago!" Sensing gossip in the air, Jungle exited the room closing the door behind him.

"Anyway, we're having a little get together for your worn out ass at the warehouse tonight!"

"That'll work but listen, out of curiosity, did your messenger make mention of my name or did y'all just guess it was me? Cause you know I don't want no thugs comin' outta da'woodwork on me," Goldie asked with a tinge of humor in her voice.

"Bitch please!" Althea barked. "You know we got peoples working up in that courthouse relaying info ta'us! Besides, you know we will backstroke through a sea of mufuckin" thugs! *Are you serious?*"

* * * * *

That night the New York Post's late edition carried the news of the case in the legal section. Althea called Goldie to comment on the article. The Post wrote:

This morning a Federal Judge awarded an unspecified ex-juvenile delinquent from Brooklyn, New York a total of $2.5 Million in damages in a case dating back fourteen years. The case stemmed from the rape of a woman by a Correction Officer while the woman was an inmate at the South Lansing Secure Center for female youths. United States Federal District Judge, Glen White awarded $1.25 million as compensatory damages and another $1.25 million as punitive damages to the woman whom is now 31 years of age.

The case involved, since then fired, ex-Correctional Officer William P. Walker of New Paltz, New York, whom was at the time of the incident working as the young female's supervisor of her assigned work detail at the facility. The ex-correctional officer accosted the female one day and forcefully raped and brutalized her in a closet located in her designated work area. The young woman who has since then become a law abiding citizen and a well-respected figure in her community, was serving a sentence at South Lansing on a grand theft auto charge, stemming from an incident in which she and two other accomplices apparently stole an automobile and were spotted joy riding by police in New York City. A high speed chase ensued involving several police officers.

During the ensuing high speed chase, multiple damages to city property resulted, estimated at $100,000.00. The woman's attorney, Cheryl Heyward, issued a statement to this reporter, wherein she stated; "This case was long overdue, but justice has finally been served. It is impossible to imagine a more despicable and heinous crime than the one suffered by this young woman at the hands of a Corrections Officer employed by the State of New York; as security personnel entrusted with the care, safety and security of young females serving time at a female youth facility. The district attorney's office has assured me that they will not be seeking to appeal Judge Whites's decision and that payment was ordered effective immediately. At last my client can put an end to her 14 year ordeal and finally move on with her life.

The woman testified in court wherin she stated: "I was at the secured facility of South Lansing for approximately 17 ½ months when Walker ordered me to go and clean out parts of a school building on the facilities grounds. And after I arrived, I found Walker there alone," she further testified, "he brutally assaulted me and attempted to force himself on me but was interrupted when another security personnel arrived in the area though he did not witness any wrong doing at the time.

Several weeks later, Walker again ordered me to go to the school area. At the time Walker told me that he planned to have sex with me on top of a table. At first I thought Walker was just trying to intimidate me but he suddenly grabbed me, tore parts of my clothes off and forced himself on me. Although I attempt to ward him off, I was a young fragile girl who was no match for this determined officer. I was hospitalized as a result of the injuries I suffered, was interviewed by state police and reported the incident. Soon thereafter C.O. Walker was arrested and charged with assault and rape."

William P. Walker was fired and arrested at his home in New Paltz. He had been working at the state facility since 1989 and earned $55,895.00 a year. He later pleaded guilty to third degree rape. The young woman sued the state for negligence and after a long battle has today received her well-deserved justice. The woman expressed to the court that she has experienced significant psychological problems and continues up to this date to suffer bouts of depression as a direct consequence of her ordeal.

The woman's attorney also informed this reporter that she also still has a case pending against Mr. Walker, for personal liability.

✳ ✳ ✳ ✳ ✳

"Did you comprehend all dat?" Althea asked her.

"Yeah! Every word of it but lets hope they bless me with a lil more than that on the other one!" Goldie greedily told her.

"Girl stop being so damn greedy. I'll see you later on tonight. Bye!"

"Later!" Goldie shouted back before hanging the phone up.

Chapter 13

WAREHOUSE

After spending most of the afternoon in her lawyer's office taking care of the necessary business concerning her law suit, Goldie decided to pamper herself with a full body massage at one of China Town's finest massage parlors. Then later that night after speaking with Althea on the phone, she headed out to Brooklyn. Pulling up to the warehouse's entrance, she hit their signature tune on her car horn and seconds later the mechanical steel gate rose and she eased her Benz inside. She came to an abrupt stop alongside Kacky's ever present CBR 900 motor cycle and stepped out of her vehicle draped in a red and white silk Roberto Cavalli blouse. And a pair of white Frankie B Jeans that looked as though they were sewn onto her curvaceous body by one of the world's finest tailors. High stepping in her Jimmy Choo pumps, then began greeting her sisters in crime as she approached them. "Hey y'all," she gleefully said, planting pecks on their cheeks.

"Bitch, I said we were having a get together for your nasty ass, not a damn hot pants convention!" Joked Althea, wasting no time getting her snap on.

"Umm huh!" Kacky chimed in.

"And wha' chu mean umm-huh, Kacky?" Goldie barked.

"Well shit, you gotta let 'cha damn coochie breath! Especially, since you be gettin' it all plugged da' fuck up every fuckin' night!" Kacky shot back.

"Please girl!" she responded with both hands on her hips, striking a defiant pose before adding, "Jungle don't be getting' all up in me like dat! Shit, I be rationing this pussy out to 'em!"

"Yeah right, I bet 'chu do!" Michelle interjected. "A little in da mornin', a little in da afternoon and a little in da night wit' some head ta go wit' it!"

"Yeah, probably gave 'em some celebration pussy when she got off da phone wit' Althea!" Latesha said as she rummaged through the trunk of her car, before retrieving a small cardboard box which contained two bottles of sparkling Nuvo Vodka, one pint of Bacardi Dark Rum, one pint of Bacardi Light Rum, a sleeve of Styrofoam cups and a quart of Tropicana Orange Juice.

"Girl please! I sat my yellow ass up in Betty's Beauty Salon almost two hours waiting to get this wash-n-set done! There was no way in hell I was gonna let Jungle sweat this shit out!" Goldie replied, running her left hand through her hair for emphasis.

"So, what took your ass so damn long ta get here then?" Michelle inquired.

"Well, for your info'mation, I had to go handle that business with my lawyer this afternoon, which seemed to take forever! Then I treated myself to a full body massage out in China Town. Shit, I had to do something to clear my mind before I got up wit' cha'll crazy asses! Especially after hearin' Jungle's mouth rantin' on 'bout how we carry ourselves in public." Her last statement cause the Angels to steal glances at each other before returning their gaze and attention back to her.

"What da fuck he meant by 'how we carry ourselves'? Dat nigga don't even know us like dat!" Latesha barked.

"That's right!" Kacky chimed in agreement.

"Dat nigga better stay in his mufuckin' lane and look both damn ways before he cross us!" Michelle shot.

"Please, dat nigga aint crazy!" Kacky chimed back in before sparking up a blunt of Kush weed she had rolled up earlier.

"Nah...," Goldie began, "I was tellin' em how bitches were mean muggin' us when his man Truck let us skip the line at the Crystal Ball Club dat night. And how we dared a bitch ta get outta pocket. Then his ass just completely went off da rocker. Talkin' 'bout how this aint the eighties and how bitches aint kickin' 'n scratchin' no more and that how we're too old to be out there looking for trouble 'n shit!"

"First of all...," Althea interjected, "we gettin' too much money ta be startin' trouble. So he can kill dat shit he's talkin' and even when we was broke, we wasn't instigatin' no bullshit!"

"Yeah, but we sure nuff use ta shut it da fuck down when it did get started!" Michelle shouted and the Angels shook their heads in agreement.

"Ah fuck dat nigga! You should a told his ass dat we're well aware of the fact dat we're not livin' in the eighties and dat we adapt to what's going on in these days n mufuckin' times!" Vicky snapped.

"Yeah! Tell him dat we only kick 'n scratch when we're full 'a ding-a-ling! But if he wanna know how we get down in the streets all he gotta do is put his hands on you!" Althea stated with a cold stare and menacing eyes.

"Ah please, he aint that type a person!" Goldie assured, dismissively waving her hand at Althea.

"I hope not. Cause I aint got *nooo* problem sending somethin' through dat niggaz head! Let 'em play his mufuckin' self."

"Umm huh, you got that shit right, Al!" Kacky agreed after inhaling a healthy cloud of marijuana smoke from the blunt before passing it to Vicky.

"A'ight! Y'all gangsta bitches can help ya'selves to whatever y'all drinking'!" Latesha cut in, transferring the drinks from the box to the top of an old wooden table. The Angels did not waste any time pouring themselves drinks, while the scent of the Kush weed permeated the warehouse.

"Now that – dat's taken care of, let's get some music crackin' up in this bitch!" Latesha barked out as she reached into her car and popped in "Dirty Handz" latest CD and adjusted the volume so they would still be able to hear each other converse.

"Damn! Dat mufuckin' beat is bangin' like hell!" Vicky excitedly yelled out as she bopped her head to the rhythm. She steadied her drink in her left hand as she waved her other hand over her head dangling the blunt between her index and middle fingers. "I aint gon' front," "them niggaz right there is crazy on the mic!" She added before taking another pull from the blunt and extending it out to Althea who immediately took it from her.

"Yeah bitch, we heard you get kinda wild on da mic your damn self!" Michelle cracked before taking a swig from her styrofoam cup.

"Ah shut da fuck up Michelle. You aint hear no shit like that, so don't get me started on your ass!" Vicky barked back with a menacing stare.

"Yeah...!" Althea chimed in, "get on her ass Vee! This bitch thinks she's a damn pre-Madonna any mufuckin' way! And I know she be hiding ding-a-lings in other area codes!"

"You don't know what the hell I do when I'm in other area codes bitch. So don't even go there!"

"Thank you! You just proved my point with that statement!" Althea quickly shot back before exchanging high-fives with Vicky.

"Bitch please! I aint prove a damn thing to you!" Michelle replied, waving Althea off. "And come to think of it...Vicky, didn't you just break Ronnie's country ass off a piece of that stank ass coochie before he went back to Alabama?"

"Yup! I sure the hell did! At least I aint running round the five boroughs handin' out pussy coupons when we all aint together, like you be doing. And I'm willing to bet on everything I love that you're the freakiest bitch outta all of us! And you probably take it up the mud chute too, bitch!" Vicky shot, snapping her fingers three times forming a 'z', while gazing at her with a sly smirk on her face.

"Bitch, you could believe whatever da'hell you want, it don't change nothin'!" Michelle shot back, smirking herself.

"Ahh huh, I can tell by dat smirk on your face and da tone of your deep ass voice, dat I caught your vain bitch!" Vicky teased. "Suck it on up bitch! Like you do everything else!" she added, causing them all to crack up laughing.

"Althea, will you pass the dag gon' blunt! Shit, you aint the only one up in here trying to get a buzz!" Latesha suddenly said once the laughing subsided.

"Oh my god, my bad. I got all caught up in this soap opera shit that's going on up in here, that I honestly forgot that I was still smokin'! Here!" She said, passing Latesha the blunt.

"Bitch, don't beat me in da head with dat bullshit!" Latesha barked before taking a long drag from the blunt.

"Oh please!" Althea quickly snapped back. "If it was dat mufuckin' Chem dog your ass wouldn't be sweatin' it like dat! So spare me the bullshit! Ok?"

"Shit! Speaking of Chem...," Latesha quickly started, directing her attention to Vicky as she blew out a huge cloud of smoke, "Vee did you give my cousin them samples before he left?"

"Oh my god!" Vicky gasped with her hand up to her mouth in an astonishing gesture before stating, "I got so damn caught up on his mufuckin' dick, that I forgot to give him the samples!"

"How could you forget to take care of something that was not only important to us but, simple as hell?" Kacky cut in to ask.

"Easy bitch!" Vicky responded, grinding her lower body in an explicit manner to the music. "Cause Ronnie was slippin' it ta me real nice like! Nah! I'm just bull shittin'! I gave it to him right after I put this coochie on his ass!" she said with a lustful gaze in her eyes as she continued swaying seductively to the music.

"Eeel! Stop dancing all nasty like dat!" Althea said, feinting a disgusted expression on her face.

"Right!" Kacky agreed. "Don't tell me my lil cousin's dick done caused your ass to lose your god damn mind? Calm your hot ass down!"

"Little cousin!?" Vicky shouted in a high pitch. "Please! He aint little! Trust me on dat one, huh! As a matter of fact, dat nigga got the kinda' dick dat'a fuck up a bitch's insides! He damn sure puta' black eye on my coochie and dat's an understatement! So Michelle, make sure ya pussy is nice 'n moist before lil El get up in you! Cause I know you gonna give him some when y'all go out! And I swear to god, I hope he knock the bottom outta your pussy!" Vicky teased.

"Shiiit! Aint no bottom in her pussy! So stop giving that bitch credit!" Goldie yelled out.

"Oh Goldie, please...!" Michelle shot back with a snarl, "Shut da fuck up! Cause I'm hip to your lil sneaky yellow behind! You might got the resta' the crew fooled but I'm on ta ya ass! So don't get it twisted!"

"Don't get what twisted? What da fuck you talkin' 'bout now?" Goldie asked with a serious expression on her face.

"How she got us fooled?" Kacky quickly inquired.

"Yeah Michelle..." Althea chimed. "What da fuck she do?"

"Hold da fuck up...!" Vicky cut in. "I'm a turn the music down, so I don't miss a word of this shit!" After killing the music, she said, "A'ight, bitch, spill da mufuckin' beans!" Then on que, pointing directly at Goldie, Michelle began, "This sneaky ass troll right here, slipped B-Hov her cell number dat day he came through, to convert those H.K. MP5's!"

"Ahh bitch, we thought you had some juicy shit to tell us!" Latesha said in a disappointed tone. "Shit, if she wanna deal wit' B-Hov's lil fine ass, dat's on her! But, if her ass get caught, I'm tellin you now…," she continued, pointing her index finger at Goldie, "if something pops off, you already know that – that's Lil El's comrade and they won't hesitate to slump Jungle's god damn ass!"

"Yeah…!" Kacky quickly interjected, "and if them fake ass security mufuckas' that work for him get involved, you already know how ugly the shit gonna get!" she continued. "Lil El is family and his drama is our mufuckin' drama too! So, if you gonna be creepin' with B-Hov, you best-be extra and I mean extra sneaky about it!" she advised her with concern.

"Please…!" Althea interrupted pointing her index finger at Goldie, "this bitch right here invented the word 'sneaky'. I tried to tell y'all way back when we were going to P.S. 72, dat she gonna turn out to be a damn alley cat! Remember when she got caught by the principle humping on dat nigga Sedrick McNeill in the coat closet across from Mr. Bernstein's class? Oh, but cha'll bitches wasn't try'na hear me though!"

"Sedrick!" Michelle yelled out, diverting her attention towards Goldie. "Bitch, I thought dat boy's name was Jamel Holmes you got caught in the closet with?"

"Hell no! Jamel was supposed to had been her boyfriend at the time her ass got caught!" Vicky volunteered excitedly. Goldie just stood there with her drink in hand, staring Althea down with a menacing look in her eyes for bringing back to light an old embarrassing moment from back when they were kids in public school.

"Umm uh…," Althea began, returning the evil stare wit one of her own, "this bitch's pussy always been hotta than a Jamaican Beef Patty! And she aint gon' nev'a change!" Unphased by her returned stare, Goldie flipped her middle finger at her and mouthed the words, "Fuck you!"

"Yo Gee…," Latesha began, causing Goldie to divert her attention from Vicky towards her, "fuck what da hell they talkin' 'bout right now, just remember what I said earlier! Cause I don't want Lil El or B-Hov to be put in a position where they might hav'ta body dat nigga Jungle on'na count of your carelessness! A'ight?"

"I got chu!" she replied.

"No, you mean on'na count of her hotness!" Althea continued to crack before taking a long pull from the half of blunt Latesha passed her for Vicky. Because of his blood relation to her two comrades, Lil El was indirectly family to her as well. And B-Hov was Lil El's most trusted comrade, one he whole-heartedly loved like a brother, which meant that he too was family. Although she held feelings for Jungle, the fact of the matter was that he was just a steady fuck partner. And six and a half months of dick could never be compared to the sunshine and stormy weathered relationship she shared with her crew. The love and loyalty that she possessed for her comrades were much deeper than anything she could ever feel for anyone outside of their circle. This was her family and to her no matter how good, bad, or indifferent their side may be, it would forever be the correct side for her to stand on.

"I'm feeling everything you sayin', Latesha. But it aint like me and Jungle got strings attached. He's free to do him, like I'm free to do me, as long as we practice safe sex outside our relationship."

"Yeah, but don't dat nigga got the keys to your crib, though?" Michelle inquired.

"Yeah! Dat's cause he's da only nigga dat comes in my house and ninety-nine percent of da time I know when he's comin'."

"But, Gee, how you know if he's really using protection when he's dealin' wit' other bitches?" Kacky curiously asked.

"To be honest wit'chu Kacky, I'm not even really sure if he does or not. I use Reality when we be sexin' anyway. So it doesn't matter to me one way or the other!" she said.

"Reality?" Vicky asked, confused.

"Yeah! That's what they call a female condom and you can still feel the warmth of the dick," she added with a mischievous smirk. "It's a contraceptive. It is so damn thin, yet strong as hell and you can even walk around with it up in your coochie with no bother too!" she added.

"Well, make sure you pack a few for our trip to Alabama." Vicky suggested.

"For what? I aint giving none of 'them country niggaz no mufuckin' pussy!" Goldie shouted.

"Shit!" Vicky snapped, nodding her head towards the others, "one of us might decide to give one of them niggaz some pussy!" You ne'va know. Anything's possible." She added with a wink of the eye.

"A'ight bitch, I'll bring a few just in case!" She conceded, knowing Vicky's wink was a sign that she wanted one for her next romp with Ronnie.

"Speakin' of our trip..." Latesha suddenly interjected, "we gonna go down there on some real Angel shit, stylin' on them southern mufuckas! Plus I'm takin' two pounds of a dat Chem wit' us!" She added.

"I might as well rent a stretch limo to pick us up at the Amtrak station when we get there. *Shiiit* if we gon' stunt, then let's do it all the way big!" Goldie suggested.

"Yeah, dat'a work!" Latesha agreed.

"A'ight, I'll make the necessary reservations for the hotel suite and the limo right before we leave. And by the way," Goldie continued, "when we get back I'm writin' all y'all stink bitches a check for $200,000 so y'all can camouflage some of that dirty ass money."

"Well in that case, when we get back, I'ma get up wit' my moms landlord 'bout buyin' that brownstone. Cause she ain't try'na let me buy her a house outta the hood. So, I figure if she's gonna stay there she might as well own the da'mufucka!" Latesha exclaimed.

"Don't get your hopes up too high though, cause he might not want to sell it!" Althea said.

"Well, if he don't accept my kind offer, I guess we'll have to force him to sell it! Then we can get rid of his damn ass!"

"Yeah! I like how that last part sounds!" Michelle said smiling.

"Uhh huh! Me too!" Vicky agreed.

"Y'all bitches done lost y'all god damn minds!" Goldie shot. "That's how that man feeds his mufuckin' family. Besides, we getting major paper out here in these streets. Spots all over Brooklyn, plushed out cribs," she continued. "And y'all willing to jeopardize what we've grinded so hard for all these years and accomplished for a measly ass brownstone? I mean, it ain't like your moms is personally coming up outta her pockets to make sure her rent gets paid every month." She paused to catch her breath before continuing, "Now, if he's willing to sell on his own free will, that's one thang. But to force da'man to sell, then getting rid of him is a whole nother story! Come one now, y'all wake da'fuck up!" She concluded.

"Nah bitch!" Michelle cursed, "You wake da'fuck up and be more realistic 'bout the damn situation. With the amount of money her daughters are making, ain't no way in hell she should be renting! And since she ain't trying to move, I think buying the Brownstone would be the best thing to do, whether it's voluntarily or not!" Directing her attention to Latesha, she added, "However you decide to obtain that mufuckin' building for your moms, you got my support!" Then slurring her words from the results of drinking a little too much alcohol, she continued saying, "I support you because you the reason why the rest of us bitches is livin' all high and mighty and with out a care in the world and I wanna let you know that I really appreciate everything you done for me! And I say we have a toast to our sister Latesha, for putting us in our positions!" She added slurring her words as she reached for the bottle of Bacardi.

"Nah!" Kacky yelled before snatching up the bottle, "Y'all have enough damn alcohol in your systems already! Y'all don't need no more to drink! Especially this slurring ass bitch!" She added pointing to Michelle.

"Bitch! I'm grown. You don't dictate how much alcohol I consume! Now, gimme da'damn bottle and stop fuckin' playin'!" She commanded, while trying to reach around Kacky to grab the bottle. Kacky kept turning her body and swaying to and fro to keep her from getting at it.

"Come on now, Kacky! Stop bullshittin' 'n give her the dag-gon' bottle! You fuckin' up everybody else's vibe!" Latesha snapped.

"Yeah! But look at her Latesha! She's pissy god damn drunk right now! How the hell is she supposed to drive home tonight!?" Kacky said.

"You don't worry 'bout that! Just give her the fuckin' bottle!" Latesha barked.

"Here hoe!" She said, shoving the bottle of liquor into Michelle's chest plate area.

"Thank you sooo very much!" Michelle said, winking in a drunken stupor. Then, as she twisted the top off the bottle, she added in an equally drunken slur. "Your such a gracious bitch!" She then helped herself to a shot and passed the bottle to Althea, who happened to be the closest one to her.

* * * * *

"Oh my fuckin' god!" Pat said to her friend Tee, "I can't believe she's actually lettin' em do that to her!" Pat and her friend Tee sat in the Chem spot in recliner seats, watching a porno movie on the flat screen television.

"Dat's dat bitch Pinky right there." Tee replied, "She does it all. Ain't nothin' off limits to her and I mean *nothing!*" Tee went on putting emphasis on the word nothing. "Shit! Lil Kim use ta talk dat talk back in da' days, like she was really 'bout it, but this bitch," she continued nodding towards the TV screen, "she walk dat mufuckin' walk for real!"

"Yeah well, more power to her then! But, a bitch like me ain't never gonna take no dick up in my ass, shoot! My ass is an exit, not a mufuckin' entrance hole!" Pat barked as she continued viewing the screen, slightly squinting her eyes.

Tee looked over to her with one of those "yeah right" expressions on her face before stating, "Stop lyin' bitch! You'd do it if they was paying your ass the same amount of money that that bitch is getting to do it!"

"Oh no! Da' hell I wont either! And that's on everything I love!" Pat said, pausing for a second before she added a "humph" and said, "I wish a mufucker would approach me 'bout some shit like that. I'll hawk spit right in his damn face!"

"Umm huh! I hear you girl! But, you got bitches runnin' 'round here doin it for Gucci, Prada and Tory Burch bags 'n' shit like it aint nothing. At least she get close to ten g's to do..."

Pat cut her off before she could finish her sentence, "TEN THOUSAND DOLLARS!" she excitedly exclaimed. "And how long do she gotta let them fuck her for?"

"Oh now all of a sudden you got a change of heart, huh!?" Tee quickly stated, sliding to the edge of the seat as she grilled her friend through investigative eyes. "I see the gleam all up in your mufuckin' face, too. So don't even try to front, bitch."

"Nah! I'm just sayin' though, ten grand ain't no mufuckin" chump change!"

"Yeah and the only difference is that Pinky get paid to do it in front of cameras 'n' videos 'n' shit!"

"Huuhh, I ain't getting' my ass hole dug da'fuck out in front of no damn video camera. That shit just ain't happening!" Pat reassured, shaking her head no.

"Oh, so you sayin' you'd do it fa 'da ten g's, but they can't video record it?"

"On camera or off, either way dat shit gonna hurt, shit!" Pat confided, declining to answer the question.

"Nah, not if the nigga put some K-Y Jelly on his dick before he penetrate you."

"BITCH!!! What da'fuck is K-Y Jelly?" Pat asked, looking Tee up and down with a shitty smirk on her face.

"I don't know! I just heard from somebody that – that's what they call anal lubrication!" she replied, just as they heard a knock on the door. Pat abruptly stopped her conversation with Tee and yelled out, "How many you want?"

"Me wan ya to move ya ras clot gonja some place else! Now cum da blood clot out, fa' me torch da muddafucka 'n bun it down in'a heep'a fire!" The voice behind the door announced. And when the peephole slot slide open, Mikey Dread flicked a lighter inches from the Molotov cocktail he was holding to let whomever was on the other side of the door know that he meant business.

Mikey Dread was a slightly muscular built Jamaican with a heavy West Indian accent. He was of medium height and had dreadlocks running down his back. He stood there with the Molotov in his hand, flicking the lighter on and off as he rapped on the door incessantly with his foot. For the past three years Mikey Dread's weed spot, which was located directly around the corner from the Chem spot, was the number one go to spot for some real good top grade weed. His spot generated anywhere from eight to ten thousand dollars a week in sales, until word spread around like wild fire about the new spot around the corner. The word was that they had a much more potent marijuana that was sure to give a stronger stimulating effect to the user. Mikey Dread's spot began to tumble dramatically in sales.

Once Mikey Dread got wind of the new weed spot and its location, he set out to do something about it. Latesha's idea of giving out samples was the beginning of his downfall.

"Oh my god, Tee, he got a fire bomb or something in his hand and he getting' ready to light that mufucka up!" Pat nervously told her friend, as she scrambled to retrieve her cell phone from the coffee table.

"Ya got ten bumba clot secon's ta fly da'fuckin' bumba clot door 'n begone!" He warned them in a frantic tone as he stood outside the door waiting for it to open.

"A'ight, a'ight! We coming out! Just lem'me get some clothes on!" Pat yelled out, hoping to buy some additional time. "Tee, grab the weed and the money, while I call Nesto!" She quickly instructed before hearing Mikey Dread beginning to count.

"Won, tu, tree, four..., the door shot open before he was finished with his count and Pat and Tee exited as Mikey Dread peered at them, letting his crazed gaze wonder up and down their body. He sucked on his teeth before he began, "A whoo da'fucka disrespect a yodd man and fly a gonja spot 'rounda'blood clot conna frum my gates 'dem?" He questioned in his thick native accent, as he watched Pat lock the door.

Pat and Tee proceeded to evacuate the premises as they continued down the narrow hallway in a hurry and exited the building, nervously looking over their shoulder to assure themselves that Mikey Dread was not planning to douse them with the Molotov cocktail. Instead, Mikey Dread stood there and watched as they scampered away and yelled out, "And don't cum bocc, cause de next time a pussy hole a fly a gates open 'round'eer me gun gon rinse, ya uner'stan!? I mon run dis!" He ranted on as he walked just a few paces behind them. As he cleared the corner he tossed the unlit Molotov cocktail into a nearby garbage can, then pulled out a fat spliff from his jacket pocket and lit it. He then climbed into his midnight black BMW 325i and blew a cloud of smoke out the drivers window as he peeled off, leaving the stench of burning tires behind.

Before Pat and Tee reached the end of the block, Nesto spun around the corner in his dark blue Chevy

Suburban. He came to a screeching halt when he noticed Pat and Tee flagging him. Pat and Tee quickly pointed in unison down the block, where Mikey Dread's Beamer was stationed at a stop sign at the corner of Blake Avenue signaling to make a left turn. "Dat's him down there!" They yelled simultaneously. Nesto quickly peeled off, tires screeching as he raced to tail Mikey Dread.

Ten minutes later, under the guise of the dark night he parked his car on a quiet East New York block. Three cars behind, Nesto sat incognito punching numbers into his cell phone and on the third ring the voice on the other end asked, "Yeah, what's up?". Nesto immediately responded, "It's me Kacky!" He said excitedly, "Can you talk right now?"

"Why? Your fine Boriqua ass wonna have phone sex with me?" Kacky jokingly asked in a seductive tone.

"Come on now, you know we can't be mixing business with pleasure! Besides, you ain't ready for this Latin snake I'm holding!"

"Oh nigga please! I was born ready! You better ask somebody!" She shot back before they joined in laughter.

"You ain't change not one bit, Kacky!" He said once their laughter subsided.

"Yeah, and neither have you!" She shot back, making reference to the many years the two of them spent playfully flirting with each other.

"Anyway..." he began, maintaining his focus on the Beamer, "we got ourselves a little issue. Some Rasta mufucker ran Pat and Tee up outta da'spot! The nigga showed up wit' a molotov cocktail bomb and threatened to burn the joint down. I could literally hear the lame ranting and raving in the hall, while I was on the jack talking with Pat, who called me immediately. I got around there as he was pulling off!" He told Kacky.

"Why you ain't follow his ass?" She quickly interjected in a disappointing tone, interrupting his spiel before he could finish.

"Relax lil sis!" he quickly said, calming Kacky down. "I got this, I'm sitting here watching this lame as we speak! Da nigga in his Beamer blowin on a blunt like he aint got a worry in the world!" He went on telling her. "As soon as his ass is done, I'm'a send his ass to meet Bob Marley!"

"Where y'all at?" Kacky quickly asked.

"We right here on Hendrix and Dumont." He responded.

"OK! Just keep an eye on'em 'til we get there! If he moves, you follow him and keep us posted! But, if he's still there when we arrive on the set, then you break out and we'll handle it from there!" She instructed.

"A'ight! One!" He said into the phone. "Bye!" was all he heard in return before hanging up.

Kacky hung up the phone and immediately shouted out, "Angels, we got drama! A problem just arose!" She told the girls as she calmly clipped her cell phone to the waist of her Apple Bottom Jeans.

"Yeah, we we're trying to listen. So, what the hell was that all about?" Vicky quickly inquired.

"That was my fantasy ding-a-ling on the phone!", Kacky said.

"Bitch, cut the bullshit! We know it was Nesto! Now tell us what da' fuck happened. And stop playin' 'round!" Latesha seriously commanded.

"Well, it seems as though you done pissed off some Rastafarian mufucka, by opening up that damn Chem spot. He threatened to burn the spot down and ran Pat 'n' them outta there! Pat immediately called Nesto and explained the situation to him!" She related to the Angels displaying anger with her every word.

"Well, lets' go see Pat so we can find out how this mufucka look!" Goldie boldly stated while fumbling through her carryon bag for her car keys.

"That won't be necessary." Kacky quickly interjected. "Nesto is already watching that nigga until we get there! They're on Hendrix and Dumont as we speak."

She assured them. "The nigga parked on the block smokin' weed in his fuckin'ride."

"So, why da' fuck Nesto ain't just walk up to da' whip and slump his ass?" Vicky asked.

"He offered to, but I told him to wait and watch him until we got there! Now are we gonna keep standing and debating about this shit or we gon' go handle this mufuckin' business?" Kacky asked, obviously irritated.

"Nah! I gotta better idea! Call Nesto back and tell him to bring that coconut mufucka back to the warehouse!" Latesha commanded her sister, then strolled off toward another area of the spacious building. "We gonna have ourselves a little fun with him before we do what we do!" She added, speaking over her shoulder as she disappeared into a nearby room. Latesha than came out moments later carrying a small canvas shoulder bag and a wooden chair.

"Vicky, go in that room and to the right you gon' see a can wit' kerosene behind the love seat. Bring it to me." She ordered. "We gon' show Mr. Rasta man that we like to play with fire too!" She said with an evil snarl.

"Yeah! I wanna see if he's a real baaad boy when his ass gets here!" Vicky gleefully announced.

"Yeah, we gon' fuck wit' his ass for a while. Then we gon' make him whimper in pain! You know how them damn West Indians are, they think they're the baddest mufuckers on the planet, when they got their damn gun in their hand!" Latesha continued. "We gon' do'em dirty before we send him to meet JAH RASTAFARI! Or whatever the mufuckaz name is. Them dread niggaz be bowing down to! A'ight, now y'all dig in this bag and grab a gat!" she concluded.

"Yeah, we gon' do'em foul! Don't nobody disrespect the Angels!!!" Goldie shouted.

"Ya got that shit right, Gee!" Althea agreed.

Chapter 14

HOSPITAL RUN

Mikey Dread parlayed in his BMW oblivious to his surroundings and to the eminent death that lurked in the air. He sat there enjoying himself, smoking some good cannabis and listening to the latest CD by reggae superstar "Beanie Man". Meanwhile, Nesto sat in his Chevy Suburban elated to have gotten a return call from Kacky, telling him that he was to participate in the Angels next escapade. He pushed in the vechicle's lighter and maneuvered the steering wheel upward to reveal his secret compartment. He reached in and removed the hidden nine 9mm Browning from its stash compartment. After inspecting it to make sure everything was in working order, he reached down under the passenger side seat and retrieved a pair of handcuffs he kept there specifically for moments like this.

This should be quick and simple, as easy as one, two, three, he thought to himself, while chambering a round into the barrel of his nine. He then eased out of the truck with the firearm clutched closely to his right thigh as he scanned the circumference of the block for potential witnesses. As he crept towards the Beamer, he thought - "DAMN!" and told himself – "I wish she would've given me the green light to push this mufucka's wig da'fuck back! Look at this nigga lamping with confidence, like his earlier violation would go without retribution!" He reveled, lost in his thoughts, until he approached the rear end of Mikey Dread's vehicle. He noticed that the driver's side window was slightly ajarred, so he gave the area one more scan to assure himself that there were no witnesses. Then he extended the neck of his nine into the window, inches from the West Indian's temple. Mikey Dread was immediately startled. He flinched and eased his head back ever so slightly and said, "Ayo rude bwoy, wah g'on?"

"Shut da'fuck up Pop-I!" Nesto interrupted as he reached into his back pocket with his left hand for the handcuffs. "Take the key outta the mufuckin' ingnition!" He commanded. "And don't make me tell you again or I'ma start exercising my index finger!" Nesto warned him, only this time cocking back the hammer on his gun. Immmediately recognizing the seriousness of the situation, having taken a glance and noticing the coldness in Nesto's eyes, Mikey Dread thought it wise to comply. Mikey Dread reasoned that if it had been a hit, it would have already been done and over with by now. So, he carefully fastened the cuffs around his wrist.

After placing the restraints around his wrists, Nesto stood there blankly staring down into Mikey's eyes. Mikey Dread returned his icy glare as if studying his features for future reference, unbeknownst that he was on his way to meet some devilish ass Angels. Nesto yanked the car door open and snatched Mikey Dread by his long dreadlocks and pulled him out of the vehicle. "Walk mutha'fucka!" He instructed him as he directed him toward his truck.

Nesto then shoved the Rasta into his truck and instantaneously delivered a crushing blow to his head with the butt of his gun. The blow landed with tremendous impact directly on the Rasta's occipital lobe, immediately rendering him unconscious. Nesto then situated him on the floor of the front passenger side of the truck, in a fetal position. Then ran around the vehicle and climbed in and sped off. Moments later, when he was clear of the crime scene, he slowed to a cruising speed, not wanting to attract any unnecessary and most definitely unwanted attention from the boys in blue, who lately seemed to be a perpetual presence in the neighborhood after the assasinations of their colleagues.

Nesto was cruising towards the warehouse, where Kacky had instructed him to bring the rasta, when all of a sudden Mikey Dread awoke from his slumber and despite his excruciating headache managed to say, "A'mon, if money ya snatch me fa', jus name de'price 'n I'mon'a get it fa' ya, seen? We can reason mon ta'mon, deer's na need ta'go tru all'a dis'ear!" He desperately pleaded in his crackling West Indian accent.

"Do I look stupid to you mufucka! Huh?" Nesto angrily replied. "This ain't 'bout ya money! It's 'bout ya punk ass throwing ya weight 'round, try'na stop other mufuckas from making money! So, don't be actin' like ya don't know what this is about! Now shut da'fuck up!" He continued to bark at Mikey Dread, before coming to a halt at a red light on the corner of Stanley Avenue. "I was really hopin' like hell dat ya tried som'a dat bad boy shit ya peoples be chattin' 'bout on them reggae songs mufucka, so I could'a left ya coconut ass slumped da'fuck over in dat pretty ass Beamer back there! But, I see you'a smart ass mufuckin' coconut." Nesto taunted him.

* * * * *

"Vicky, now I'm a need you and Goldie to get another van..." Latesha began, "so when we're done with dat mufucka we can dispose of him!" Latesha checked the time on her diamond encrusted Arctic watch and said, "Nesto should'a been here by now, so y'all hurry up and get back here with dat van!"

Vicky and Goldie quickly rushed and hopped into Vicky's Volvo just as Nesto was pulling up to the warehouse. The Angels suddenly heard the blaring of a horn just as the mechanical gate was elevating to allow Vicky and Goldie to exit, enroute to complete their mission. As they drove out of the spacious architectural structure, Nesto nodded at them as they passed him at the entrance.

Once the gate came down again, Nesto quickly shouted out, "A'ight now, somebody come get this fake ass Bob Marley ass nigga outta my whip before I decide ta' empty my nine into his mufuckin' scalp!" Nesto then glanced over at Kacky and smiled, displaying his pearly white teeth.

"Whats up handsome?" Kacky immediately complemented him, as she approached his vehicle. Her expression immediately changed once she noticed the captured West Indian in an uncompromising position. "Oh shit!" She exclaimed, motioning to her partners to approach, "Y'all come look at this mufucka all curled da'fuck up like a cheese doodle under the dash board!"

"Ahh, look at'em, he look so calm 'n' peaceful down there!" Michelle purred, extending her neck to look through the passenger side window.

"A'ight cha'll, he aint no god damn exhibit and this damn sure aint no god damn museum!" Latesha shouted in a venomous tone then commanded, "Now take him outta the truck and sit his ass down in that chair!"

"Psss..." Mikey Dread hissed as he was being extracted from the truck. "So ya snatched up a bod bwoy fa' a heep'a pussy clot American women dem?" he ranted trying to look over his shoulder back at Nesto as he was being hustled towards the chair.

"Oh! So he's a bad boy, huh?" Kacky sarcastically asked Althea, who was on the opposite side as they escorted Mikey Dread a few feet to the chair where they shoved him down onto it.

"Ness, are you gonna stay 'n watch how we dismantle this Shabba Ranks lookin' mufucka?" Latesha asked, walking behind Mikey Dread and violently shoving his head forward. Nesto smirked and nodded his head up and down, indicating that he was there for the show, before heading to sit on the hood of his truck. Suddenly the sound of Vicky's car horn interrupted the momentary silence and they all shifted their attention towards the gate. Kacky casually strolled over and flipped the switch which elevated the mechanical gate and they waited for Vicky and Goldie to enter the warehouse.

"Now I just know y'all bitches aint start the party wit'out me! Goldie barked out in a pernicious tone as she exited the black minivan she and Vicky had stolen and noticing the captive stranger confined to the chair. Goldie did not wait for an answer. Instead, she strolled right up to Mikey Dread, pulling on her butter soft leather gloves for a more snug fit. She then cold cocked Mikey Dread in the mouth with a right cross that would have caused the great Muhammad Ali to blush with admiration. The West Indian's head violently jerked back from the impact as Goldie said, "Take that ya sugar cane pickin' mufucka! You thought you could just violate us and go without retribution?" She indignantly asked him before delivering another devastating blow to his face which caused blood to run from the corner of his mouth. A venomous look came over Mikey Dread's face and his eyes gleemed with hatred as he lunged up out of the chair in an attempt to retaliate. However, he was suddenly frozen in his track at the sight of the 10mm Sig Sauer Althea pulled from the small of her back faster than the speed of sound. "SIT DA' FUCK DOWN!!" Althea shouted, smacking the West Indian clear across the face with the butt of the gun, knocking him back into his seat.

"GOD DAMN AL!!" Nesto screamed, excited *and* impressed. "WHAT DA'FUCK IS DAT?" He asked in the same tone, while squinting his eyes in an attempt to indentify the unique features of the weapon in Althea's hand.

"It's a little sumthin' sumthin' that's gonna leave this mu'fucka frozen inside of a body bag if he don't stay his dumplin' eatin' ass seated in that damn chair!" She replied, pressing the weapon between Mikey Dread's eyes as he coughed up bloody spittle and teeth. "Now don't make me speed up this execution!" She told Mikey Dread through gritted teeth, as she cocked back the hammer on the Sig Sauer.

"Oh, he definitely got your message!" Nesto said, smiling. "I can also tell he has the utmost respect for that cocked gat!" he added.

"So you like playing with fire, huh mufucka?" She asked the self proclaimed rude boy as she shoved the nozzle of the gun recklessly into his forehead. Mikey Dread instinctively pulled back from the assault attempting to suck on teeth that were no longer there, as a speed knot the size of a walnut slowly appeared on his forehead.

Finally, Mikey Dread found the courage to say, "Do ya know wha' blood clot posse me deal wit' hea'?" Then defiantly glaring into Althea's eyes with a murderous expression, he added. "An'ya just disrespect I mon, like ya nah care or fear bad bwoy bizness!"

"FEAR!!! FEAR!!!" Kacky repeatedly screamed, pulling out a 10mm of her own, from under her waist length leather jacket and smacking him with all her might right between the eyes, "that shit aint even in our mufuckin vocabulary mutha'fucka!" She yelled in his face as a stream of blood gushed out from his forehead.

"Ahhh!" Mikey Dread screamed out. Then despite his excruciating pain, he turned towards Nesto, whom remained sitting atop his vehicle and with a grin on his lips and blood running down his face said, "So ya sit up lik'a king an' have ya yankee gals'a 'dem do ya durty work!"

Nesto snapped out of his calm state and then pointed at him with his index finger and uttered, "Shut da'fuck up nigga, before I come over there and finish your ass off!"

"Suck ya muddah's cunt!" Mikey Dread retorted back before Althea back handed him across the mouth sending three more teeth air-bourn proceeded by a thick glob of blood which drooled onto his lap.

Vicky stood close by watching the scenario play out

until she decided it was time to participate. She began to rain blows all over Mikey Dread's face. Her leather fisted hands floated through the air, landing on his face with the lightening speed of Muhammad Ali's hands and the vicious power of Mike Tyson's punches. "Umm! Umm! Umm! Take that mu'fucka. Un! Un!" She growled with every punch she landed until finally she became exhausted and stopped.

"Well, god damn bitch! Shiiitt!! I think your ass need some anger management!" Michelle commented in a drunken slur. She then tugged at Mikey Dread's zipper, reached inside his trousers and in a vise-like grip grabbed his testicles and squeezed. "Ahhh!! Oh lawd, nooo!" He screamed at the top of his lungs, in obvious agonizing pain. "Shut da'fuck up Rasta man!" She commanded before palming his nuts and violently twisting them.

"Ohhh, please gaaal!" Mikey Dread begged, throwing his head back and tightly closing his eyes.

"A'ight Michelle, it's my turn now!" Said an overly excited Latesha, while brandishing a straight razor she had retrieved from her Victoria Secret pushup bra.

"Wait! Shit! I'm almost done!" Michelle frantically replied. Then with an evil expression painted on her face, she extracted his penis from the confines of his trousers.

"Oh, my god!" Althea yelped, "He got a big ass dick!"

"Umm, umm, umm, tell me about it!" Goldie sighed, fanning herself with her left hand as they all looked on, transfixed on the enormous size of his member.

"Yeah well, y'all lusting ass bitches bet'ta put this in y'all memory bank, cause this shit aint gonna be big fa'long!" Michelle deviously assured them, stroking Mikey Dread's dick up and down.

"Bitch! What da'fuck is your crazy ass doing? We're s'pose to be torturing this mu'fucka, not pleasing him!" Latesha barked.

"Yeah!" Vicky agreed. "You acting like you gonna suck that shit or something!"

"Not quite." Michelle replied with a mischievous grin. Then turning towards the Angels, she licked her lips and dove her face straight into Mickey Dread's lap. The Angels heard a horrifying scream as she clamped onto his dick and bit down into its bulbous head. They stood there transfixed as she began to vigorously swerve her head from side to side until finally she detached the crown of his dick completely, leaving Mikey Dread hollering, screamin and squirming in excruciating pain with a headless penis. Michelle ascended with blood gushing from her mouth spat out the mushroom shaped head of his dick, wiped the blood from her mouth with the back of her hand and with an eerie venomous look in her eyes turned towards Latesha and said, "Now its your turn."

Nesto seemed to go into a state of shock. Horrified, he clutched his crotch and uncontrollably yelped, "GOD DAMN!" while grimacing and whimpering as if he too actually experienced and suffered the horrific severance of his own dick. Then after composing himself he managed to say "DAMN! Y'all got a nigga scared ta' death ta'get'a blow job now! WORD!!"

Vicky jabbed Michelle in the gut with her index finger before she said, "You know you done lost your mu'fuckin mind, right?"

Michelle looked at her with a sinister smile and said, "Ahh girl, you just mad cause you aint get to wrap those prized lips of yours around that king sized dick."

"You can say what da'fuck you want! But, just know that a bitch like me would neva do no animalistic shit like that!"

"Yeah, I know, bitch! You would have just taken it to the back of your mufuckin' throat 'til it erupted like a damn volcano all down into your internal organs! You can't fool me! I know you like a book!"

"Ahh, Michelle shut your drunk ass up!" Vicky retored, flipping her the middle finger.

"No! You shut the fuck up!" She shot back, snapping her fingers before walking off. While Mikey Dread continued whimpering, squirming and shaking like a pair of Las Vegas craps. Blood flowing profusely and incessantly from what was left of his penis. Suddenly he began to cry out, "PLEASE!!" he begged, in a more slurred West Indian accent, struggling to keep from gagging on the blood that oozed out of his swollen mouth and trickled down onto his shirt. "I mon ah pay fa' me transgression, or fa' wha'eva trouble me cause ya!"

"Nah nigga! It's way too late for that shit!" Latesha remarked. "You should'a never fucked with our weed spot in the first place!"

Sensing he was going to bleed to death, he began pleading even harder, hoping to be released in time to reach a hospital. "Come naw, ya reason wit' I mon! Ya ne'va lose nuttin' pon de'spot dem! So let meh go right naw, 'n we let by gon's be by gon's!" He continued pleading in a lamenting tone and half dazed from the loss of blood and many blows he took to the head.

"Oh, you think you dealin' with some bird brain ass bitches, huh?" Latesha angrily told him, grabbing a handful of dreadlocks and jerking his head back, placing the straight razor inches from his neck. "I should slit 'cha mufuckin' throat right now, for try'na insult my damn intelligence muthafucka! But I got something a lil' more interesting and agonizingly painful in mind for your ass! Cause I wonna see your bitch ass squirm some more!" She then called out, "Yo Vicky! Come do your thing!" She commanded nodding towards the kerosene can.

"My pleasure!" Vicky quickly replied in an excitedly devilish tone.

Mikey Dread knew then and there that his chances of walking away from this situation was heavily clouded as he felt himself being doused down with what he perceived to be a flammable substance. "OH LAWD NO!" He pleadingly yelled, "Please don't dead meh! Jah no! Meh haf nuf gonja 'n money, jus...!'"

"SHUT DA'FUCK UP MU'FUCKA!" Vicky yelled at him, slapping him across the face, interrupting his spiel. "It aint 'bout your money mu'fucka! It's 'bout you disrespectin' us!"

"Baby gal, please!" He wailed as he watched astonishingly terrified as Vicky pulled out a book of matches from the inside pocket of her jacket. "Jah no! Meh sorry fa'disrespectin' da program dem!" He continued to plead.

"Nah nigga! Fuck you" She said. Then lit a match and without any remorse or apprehension, tossed it between his legs. Instantly his body turned into a human torch as they all stood there watching and listening as Mikey Dread jumped up from the chair, tumbled to the ground and screamed his lungs out writhing, squirming and thrashing about as he burned for almost thirty seconds. Latesha then decided to extinguish the flames. She tossed a bucket of water on him and amazingly noticed that he was still breathing. So she waited for him to literally cool off, then wrapped a dog chain around his neck, applying pressure by placing her knee in his back until he stopped struggling and fighting for oxygen. Once she convinced herself that he was dead, she instructed Nesto to un-cuff him.

"Kacky, I'm gonna need you and Althea to clean up this mess while Goldie and Michelle help me dispose of the body." Latesha commanded. "And, since y'all still here," directing her attention to Nesto, "you can follow us to our destination and give us a ride back here."

Nesto immediately replied, "Dat'a work!"

"Well I'ma ride with you Ness." Vicky quickly told him, strolling around to the passender side of his truck. "And don't worry, I won't be up in your truck try'na bite your mufuckin" dick off." She sardonically added, displaying a smirk on her face as she connivingly glanced over at Michelle.

"Fuck you!" Michelle promptly retorted with a smirk of her own. "Vicky! Y'all just make sure you bring me back something to eat, cause I'm still hungry as hell!" Kacky said. "Yeah, Vicky, bring me something too!" Althea added.

"Well, aint noboby got cha'll bitches tied da'fuck up!" Latesha snapped, "when y'all get done cleaning up this mess, y'all can go get'cha own damn food!"

"Okaaay, then! Whatever!" Michelle quickly conceded.

"Ah Michelle, be quiet! Aint nobody even talking to your man eating ass!" Althea jokingly blurted, causing everyone to erupt in laughter.

"Oh you mad cause I beat you to it, huh?" She slurred back with a wink of her eye, when the laughter subsided.

After they laid his body face down across the rear floor of the stolen van, Latesha hopped in behind the wheel and with Goldie riding shotgun and Michelle in a back row seat, they exited the warehouse, tailed by Nesto and Vicky. About a minute into their journey, unbeknownst to them, Mikey Dread suddenly came to and grabbed onto the handle of the rear door for balance, before getting to his feet. Nesto, never missing a beat, began blaring his car horn causing Michelle to spin around and direct her attention to the rear of the vehicle.

Mickey Dread was about halfway out of the vehicle when Michelle suddenly drew her gun and discharged a single shot hitting him right behind his left ear. Mikey Dread tumbled to the pavement, "Take dat on the way out, mu'fucka!" She barked.

Latesha, looking through the rear view mirror, saw Mikey Dread sprawled out on the pavement. She reacted with the speed of light, quickly stepping on the breaks, coming to a halt before rapidly shifting gears and sending the van into reverse. She then quickly accelerated and ran over Mikey Dread's body, as it lay in the middle of the road. Again reacting quickly, she shifted gears and sped off looking into the rearview mirror and witnessed Nesto followup and also run over Mikey Dread's torso. Michelle, looking out the rear window suddenly exclaimed, "I bet his ass won't resurrect from dat shit right there! I hit dat nigga right in the back of his mufuckin"g head!" She bragged.

"Shit! I fucked up!" Latesha admitted with a trace of regret and disappointment in her voice.

"You should'a slit his mufuckin throat like you wanted to in the first place!" Goldie said, without recrimination towards Latesha.

"Well, it's taken care of now!" Michelle interjected. "So, aint no need for y'all bitches to be crying over spilt milk!" She added.

"Yeah you right!" Latesha dismally said.

"I know I'm right." Michelle jokingly responded, breaking the melancholic mood Latesha seemed to be falling into. "Now, let's dump this hot ass van before we run into five-O!" She added.

Goldie quickly told Latesha, "Hit a left turn right here and head towards the school yard on the next corner. We can pull up there!"

Meanwhile, as he tailed behind Latesha, Nesto was telling Vicky, "Yo, straight up, y'all the most vicious, heartless and ruthless broads I have ever had the pleasure of knowin'! I mean, dat was some real crazy ass shit Michelle did back there!" and pulling up into a parking space. He let the engine rev while he waited for the three Angels to set the van ablaze and make their way back to his truck. "Who would ever think dat the notoriously known Sutter Avenue Angels would do some bugged out shit like dat!" He continued. "Shit! I cringed and had ta' grab a hol' of my dick when I saw her bite down into dat niggaz joint like dat!" he stated, displaying a gruesome grimacing look on his face as if reliving the entire incident. "Shit! I'd be terrified! Nah!, I'd be scared ta'death ta'even hand feed one'a y'all bitches for fear dat I might lose a few fingers in the process!" He un-bashfully admitted.

Vicky suddenly interrupted him and holding the palm of her hand up to his face said, "Wait! Hold on! Hol'da fuck up! You putting a lil too much on that shit now! Don't be sittin' up in here judging da'rest of us by dat bitches' standards! Shit! Her actions are her actions!" She told him, working her neck left to right. "Shit! Dat was some real Pit Bull type of shit dat bitch don' did! And just so ya know, my teeth don't make no contact at all!" She paused to emphasize the 'at all' part before she continued, "with da'dick! Shoot! A bitch like me is a mu'fuckin professional!" She confidently assured him.

"Oh, trust me, I believe you sweetheart!" He warmly told her, as he secretly admired her beautifully formed lips.

* * * * *

After cleaning up the crime scene, Kacky and Althea decided to go grab themselves a bite to eat. They hopped on Kacky's CBR 900 motorcycle and headed to 24 hour eatery famously known as White Castle. Althea rode on the back of the bike straddling onto Kacky's waist. A short while into their ride they noticed a small crowd of people gathered two blocks ahead. The crowd was in the middle of the street and suddenly they notice an ambulance peeling off with its lights dancing in the darkness of the night, and its siren blaring.

Curiously, they advanced towards the crowd, navigating between the hoards of people in the middle of the street. Suddenly their attention focused on an elderly woman nearby, draped in a raggedy house coat and worned out slippers, commenting. They listened attentively as the elderly woman was speaking in a southern drawl while adjusting her wig.

"Oh lord have mercy on dat po'chile!" She said. "I had just gotten up to let my cat back into the house when the 'ole thang happen right in front ah my eyes. Some guys shot him in the head like he was some kinda wile animal or sumpthin'! Then they tossed him outta a moving van and ran him over. Twice!" She continued ranting. "You would'a thought dat da people in da truck behind them woulda gotten out ta help da poor man! But nah! They just run him over, *too*! Like he was a rag doll!" She then paused to catch her breath, before continuing, "I'm tellin' y'all this neighborhood done took a turn for da' worst! I prayed da ole time fo'dat po'chile, as I called the paramedics! Thank God he's still alive!" She said adjusting her bifocals.

That was all Kacky and Althea needed to hear. Kacky immediately hit the throttle on the bike - Broom! Broom! Broom! - revving the bike before she gunned down Vermont Street in the hopes of catching the fast moving ambulance. Althea clung firmly to Kacky's waist as she raced down Vermont until she hit Linden Boulevard, where she cut a sharp left, leaving behind the skids of her screeching tires. Running through red lights, cutting through traffic and swerving through the lanes on the boulevard as she sped past the corner of Georgia Avenue. Finally Kacky caught an open lane and shifted gears. She hit the throttle and the bike kicked up to a speed of 100 miles per hour. Broooom! Broooom! Broooom! The engine roared as she raced after the ambulance, eating the boulevard up.

Suddenly they came upon the EMS vehicle and with her arms draped around Kacky's waist, unable to reach her own gun at her waist side, Althea reached into Kacky's waist and extracted the ten millimeter Sig Sauer from underneath her leather jacket. Then holding onto Kacky's waist with her left hand, she trained the firearm on the driver and without warning squeezed the trigger, sending four rapid shots into the moving vehicle. The first two shots tore into the driver's neck, instantly severing his windpipe before exiting and entering into the left side of the face of the paramedic who was riding shotgun. The impact of the bullets blew his cheekbone and left eye completely away.

The third shot lodged into the vehicle's metal window frame while the final slug tore into the driver's skull, drilling straight into his cranium. The ambulance swerved out of control, tires screeching and horn blaring incessantly, as it jumped the curb and violently crashed into the front window of a nearby hardware store. The sound of shattering glass was heard crashing down as the windows came down in a heep and glass flew every-which-a-way.

Kacky brought the motor bike to a creeping halt and Althea quickly leaped off. She trotted the few yards back to the imbedded ambulance and yanked open the rear door. Immediately she heard a female medical attendant's voice yell, "Oh my god!" Althea wasted no time discharging two well placed slugs into the Rasta's forehead and watched how his brain's gray matter mixed with his blood as it decorated the interior of the ambulance.

"Oh God, please! Please don't!" She heard the female attendant plead. Althea turned to her, irritated by the whimpering sound of the woman whining. The attendant looked at Althea in horror and managed to querulously utter, "Your not gonna shoot me too, are you?" as she held her left arm, nursing an injury she suffered as a result of the crash.

"Bitch!" Althea angrily replied, displaying a deviously menacing snarl on her face as she trained the weapon on the horrified attendant. "Unfortunately for you this gun right here is bisexual!" then she squeezed the trigger several times. Boom! Boom! Boom! The sound of the blasting Sig Sauer reverberated throughout the dark East New York Street. She suddenly heard Kacky calling out to her. Althea then turned and quickly leaped on the back of the bike, then Kacky peeled off leaving the stench of burnt rubber behind.

* * * * *

Moments later, back at the warehouse, Kacky was saying, "Yo the next mufuckin' time y'all go to dispose of som'thin' dat's 'pose to be dead, please make certain that da' damn thing aint breathing no more!" She sarcastically suggested when she and Althea rolled into the warehouse and the crew was preparing to leave. Unaware of what had just transpired out on the boulevard, the Angels stared at them as they climbed off the motor bike with a blank look on their faces. "What the hell are you talkin' 'bout?" Latesha asked. "Michelle sent that nigga on his way!"

"I sure 'nuff did!"

"Oh yeah! So why the fuck Althea and I had ta' run down an ambulance carrying that dumpling eatin' son-of-a-bitch and clean up y'all mess! Y'all mean ta' tell me that, that mu'fucka resurrected faster than Jesus himself? Or perhaps y'all mean to say that nigga had nine lives? Cause he sure as hell was alive when I got ta'em!" Althea sarcastically ranted as they all stood there with dumbfounded expressions on their faces.

"Well, if big sis would have given me da green light from the jump, I would have been left that bitch ass nigga riddled da'fuck up with bullets, up inside of his whip and we wouldn't be havin' this conversation right now! Now would we?" Nesto exclaimed as he shot Latesha a quick glance.

"Right!" Michelle agreed. Obviously glad that someone threw her a life line, sparing her further embarrassment.

"Right my ass!" Latesha shot back. "Next time don't be so damn stingy on da trigger!"

"Humph! If her ass wasn't so damn drunk...!"

"It's over now! So kill it and lets be out!" Latesha shot, interrupting Vicky's spiel. "And, since you aint in any condition to be driving, you ride with Vicky. I'm out!" She said before hopping into her Beamer.

"Shit! I gotta get rid of this hot ass hammer I just finished using." Althea said, pulling the weapon out of her waist band.

"Oh nah! You don't gotta get rid'a dat!" Vicky chimed. "The ten millimeters came with black rhino shells. They are specifically designed to explode upon impact so ballistics can't trace whatever is left of the slugs back to the gun." Vicky assured her.

"Dat's good enough for me!" Kacky interjected. "Now gimme back my heater and let's get up outta here!" She concluded.

"I'ma go pick up Pat and drop her off back at the spot. And I'm expecting one'a y'all to get at me wit' one a' dem ten millimeter joints too!" Nesto said before pulling out.

Chapter 15

ALTHEA xxx

*A*lthea awoke the following afternoon to a day of peace and quiet. She was looking forward to seeing her ten year old son, Duquan, who was due back home in an hour, after having spent a week on a class trip at some upstate New York campsite. His incarcerated father, the nortorious BK, who along with his imprisoned crew, had controlled the crack –cocaine drug trade for over a decade in the same East New York neighborhood that was now under the Angels stronghold.

BK was currently serving 18 years to life at the infamous Attica Correctional Facility, entrenched far up in North Western New York for, according to court documents, having participated in a drug related robbery that turned fatal for all participants, respectively.

Duquan was a splitting image of his father. Both were dark and handsome with keen and intelligent eyes that always seemed to be looking into ones very soul. Even after his father's incarceration, Duquan never wanted for anything in his life, except to be with his Dad. He loved his mother more than he knew but he longingly missed his father.

Althea being the thoroughbred that she is, always made sure that Duquan had everything and anything he ever needed or reasonable wanted. She also made sure that BK was relatively comfortable throughout his bid. She kept his books fat with regular money orders and made sure that the subscriptions of his favorite magazines never ran out. She also had one of the best lawyers in NY State retained to represent him on his appeal. The lawyer had just informed her several weeks ago that BK had a good chance of getting out on a legal technicality. Although they were no longer an item, she did make her occasional visits.

Althea finally arose from her bed, drew the curtains back a few inches to allow some sunrays to cascade into her bedroom, then headed to the washroom. After she brushed her teeth, rinsed her mouth and relieved her bladder, she washed her hands then proceeded to her kitchen, where she prepared herself a small health drink. She then headed to her fully equipped gym where she commenced a brief version of her ritual stretching and strength exercise routine. When she was done she headed to her luxurious bathroom and prepared herself a raspberry scented hot bubble bath.

She removed her silk Victoria Secret lingerie, flipped a switch on the wall then stepped into her huge sauna like bathtub. The hot bubbly water immediately caressed her goddess like brown toned skin as it wonderfully soothed her body. She did the "lean back" and closed her eyes. Suddenly her mind was invaded by memories of she and her son's dad, then she allowed herself to lustfully reminisce as her hand quickly seemed to take on a life of its' own.

Her hand dove into the water found her vagina and began to caress and massage it, then allowed her fingers to run up and down the stretch of her slit, she sighed then squealed, "Aahhh...! Aahheee...!", as her body began to deliciously respond to her probing fingers. They had finally penetrated her pussy lips and seemed to be swimming in the sea of pussy juice deep within her. "Aahhh....Oh god!" she sighed.

Althea was recalling the first Valentine's Day right after the birth of their son. She and BK had been celebrating at home sharing a chilled bottle of Moet and feasting on a dozen or more of steamed clams and smoked oysters. Afterwards, they sat in their dim lit living room enjoying the sweet sounds of slow jams late into the night.

Suddenly the sea food must have kicked in and arisen BK's libidinous urges because one minute they were lounging back on the sofa listening to the sultry sounds of the Whispers and the next he was looking deep into her eyes with what appeared to be more than just lust in them. She had gasped as she peered into his eyes and noticed how they seemed to be peering deeper as if into her very soul. He seemed to be looking at her with a lustful desire and determination to please not only her physical body but her very soul.

Althea's pussy dripped with girly juices as she remembered that specific moment. She instantly felt her pussy all wet and knew that it was not just from soaking in the bath water. She recalled how his sparkling brown eyes had amazingly peered into her's with so much sexuality just as he placed a warm and tasteful kiss on her mouth and sucked on her sensual full lips. Suddenly her coochie discharged. "Aahhh...! Uummm...!" she sighed as she remembered how she had lustfully opened her mouth and fervently sucked on his tongue with wanting desire. Althea lit up as if on fire as his hands had softly yet firmly caressed her full breasts through the sheer silk dress she had worn.

Althea had quickly reached for her dress hem and pulled the garment off. She had not been wearing a bra so she immediately cupped her breasts and offered them up to BK who had immediately licked then sucked on her poking nipples. She had let out a sigh, "Aahhh...!" then moaned as he hungrily sucked on her breasts, yet sensually licking at her nipples and their surrounding dark areolas while occasionally licking her all the way up to her full sensual mouth.

"Uummm, uummmm..." Althea moaned as she took pleasure in the way he licked, sucked and kissed on her. He then reached down and cupped her crotch in his hand and commenced to massage her pussy through her sheer

thong. Althea gasped, sighed, cooed and moaned, "Uhhh...,
Ahhh...Sssss....Ummm....Oooh" as BK wrapped his fingers
around the band of her thong and tugged. She immediately
responded raising her ass and hips up off the sofa. He
pulled her thong off and ran a finger up her slit. He then
quickly dove in and commenced to lightly lick at her pussy
lips and lap her juices up. Althea's pussy again discharged
and she squealed, "Aheee...! Aheee! Yes baby! Yes!" She
cried out, as he continued to lap at her coochie. "Oh my god
baby...! Oooohh... you just lapped my pussy juice up like
you was a cat and I was milk. Oh my god, that feels
delicious!"

"Well, I'm no cat baby, but you sure got some sweet
tasting milk up in this pussy of yours." He told her. "And I
aim to drink and lap up as much of it as I can." He assured
her in a sexually charged raspy voice. Then he dove back
into her pussy and commenced sucking, licking and
lapping. Althea again sighed, "Aahhh..." Then released a
strong moan as she felt him suck in her clit, "Uummm... Oh
yes baby, suck it! Suck my pussy! Oh god yes! Ahhhh....!"

Althea's body began to shake, shudder and thrash
about in her bath as her orgasm hit her and shook her out
of her lustful reverie. "Oh shit!" She said. "I was actually
beating this coochie up! Damn...! Woooh!... What a fucking
cum! My god!" She gasped as her pussy juices continued to
flow and cascade down her fingers to mix with the bath
water. "Wow! Oh lord, dat was so fucking good! Wooooh!"

She leaned back to compose herself and again closed
her eyes. Then continued caressing and massaging her
pussy lightly when suddenly as if on cue, her lustful
thoughts returned and took her back into that lustful night.
She licked at her lips as she recalled how BK had kept
coming up from sucking and licking her pussy to place
warm wet and hungry kisses on her fully opened mouth as
if he wanted to make her taste her own nectar.

Althea began working her fingers brutally into her

pussy again, with delirious gusto. "Ahhh...! Ahhh...!" She sighed, kicking up the bubbly water as she repeatedly stabbed and pumped more and more fingers into her hungry vagina. Suddenly, she shuddered and her body spasmed then suddenly she let out a glob of pussy juice and recalled how BK use to love to thirstily lick and lap at her dripping pussy. She squealed, "Aheee...!" as her body involuntarily jerked from remembering the sensations of shock and ecstasy that ran through her entire core that day his tongue slipped from her pussy lips to brush her anal rim.

"Oh my god!" She had exclaimed. "Oooohh...! Oooh daddy! God damn baby! Ahhh...! Ahhh!... Wha...what the fuck you doing to me? Oh my god! Ahhh....." The first time she felt his tongue slip and brush her anal rim, her body involuntarily stiffended then it shuddered and finally it went into spasms. But as she continued feeling BK's tongue licking at her ass rim she completely lost all control of her emotions.

"Oh my goodness daddy! Ooooh...! Aheee...! Baby that's so nasty." She kept saying. "But, oh how so deliciously good it feels. Ahhh...! My god, please don't stop baby! Ohhh...! Yes! Ahhh shit, baby! I'm cumming! Yes, yes! I'm cumming again! My god! Ahhh...!" BK kept licking her ass rim and lapping at her fuck juices then rose from between her legs and made her taste herself in his mouth, again. He pushed his tongue into her awaiting opened mouth and she sucked on it with lustful desperation. Althea briefly said, *"Oooh baby. . . that's. . . so nasty!"* BK smiled before he responded, "Nah baby, you know the saying 'the ass aint but a slip of the tongue away from the coochie!"

Althea sucked on his tongue with the same deliciously nasty thought on her mind. *"Uummm..."* She groaned. Suddenly she let out a gasp as she felt him sweep her up in his muscular arms and headed towards the bedroom. "Ahhh...! Yes baby! You gon' fuck me now! Fuck me now! Take me baby!" She ranted all the way to the bedroom. "Oh my god. I'm so fucking hot! My body feels like its on fire!" She cried.

BK placed her on the edge of the bed and when he turned her on all fours, she said, while wiggling her ass, "Oohh baby you gonna hit me from the back?" As her juices flowed in anticipation of all the dick she knew was soon to fill her pussy. BK positioned himself behind her but only teased her by placing the head of his dick at the sheer entrance of her crevice. And brushed her pussy slit up and down. "*Aahhh. . . .Eeee. . . .Ooohhh*! Come on don't tease me Daddy. Stick it in me!" She squealed.

BK would not fuck into her. Instead he occasionally dipped the helmet shaped dick head into her pussy only to quickly withdraw it. Althea seemed to go crazy from wanton desire. She bucked back hard attempting to impale herself with the entire shaft of his dick, but he would pull back and deny her the instant gratification. "*Aahhh...Baby pleeeaassee...!* Don't be like that. Come on, give me that dick baby! *Please!*" She pleaded and begged.

Finally, he took a strong grip around her slim waist then raised her to him and shoved his dick into the mouth of her pussy, inch by inch he fed her more and more dick until he was all the way in to the hilt. "*Aahhh...! Oohhh...Baby yes! All of it! All of it! Yes!*" Althea cried, "*I want all of it!*" She then reached around and spread her ass cheeks wide to give him more access and leverage into her pussy. "***Aarrrgh! Arrrgh...!***" He groaned, as he pistoned his entire dick in and out of her fuck hole. Althea began to buck her ass back wildly and then grinded as he continued to pump, thrust and shove his dick into her.

"Aahhh...!" Ohhh..., my god! I feel it all in my stomach! Yeah right there! Right there! Hit it right there, baby! Oh my god! Yes, fuck it in just like that! Mmmm...yes, that's my spot right there! Oohh my fuckin, god. . .yes, yes." She wildly cried, shouted and moaned. Then her body went into convulsions as she erupted like a volcano with pussy juice. BK didn't wait for her spasms to end. He turned her on her back and raised her legs high up in the air and stabbed more dick into her. Althea opened her mouth wide and gasped as she felt all of his dick again descending into the depths of her pussy. "Ooww...!" She screamed as she felt his entire shaft slice through her pussy lips and bore deep within her coochie. BK continued to heave and plunge his dick deeper and deeper into her then groaned like an animal.

"Arrrgh...! Arrgh...!", as he continued feeding and furiously pumping dick into her. Althea wrapped and locked her legs around him and began to match his stroke. "Uuggghh...! Uuggghh...! Aaieee...! Ohhhh, ohhhh...yes daddy! Fuck this pussy! Fuck that big dick in! Oh shit! Here I go again, baby! Here I go again! Aahhhh...! Uummm...! Ssss...Yes! Oh my god!" Althea suddenly broke out of her reverie thrashing about in her bath as torrents of girly cum spilt all down her fingers and mixed with the bath water, again.

She waited to catch her breath, after having been gasping desperately. She calmed herself down then heavily sighed, "Wooooh...! What a fucking nut!" She said. "My god, that shit felt so damn good!" She admitted to herself before letting out another sigh, "Wooooh!"

After treating herself to that nerve wrecking orgasm, Althea heard her son yelling for her throughout the house, once he let himself in. "I hear you, boy!" She yelled out. "Stop that damn screaming! I'm in the tub! I'll be out in a minute!" And climbed out of the tub. She snatched up a huge terry cloth towel from the towel rack and commenced to dry herself. She then applied some Palmer's Cocoa Butter lotion all over her silky coco brown skin, stepped into a fresh pair of silk thongs and matching bra. Althea admired her reflection in the floor to ceiling bathroom

Mirror and felt extremely sexy. She also loved her glossy well-toned chocolate skin and approved of the way the sexy lingerie set clung to her body like a second skin. Satisfied, she quickly grabbed and wrapped her satin Anna Sui robe around her body and walked out of the bathroom.

When she saw Duquan he was on his cell phone but still said, "Du! What I tell you 'bout yelling all through the house like that?" Duquan pretended to be wrapped up in some deep conversation over the phone, so she barked at him, "Boy you hear me talkin' to you?" Duquan quickly snapped out of his role play, covered the mouth piece on the phone and answered her.

"I know Ma, I know! 'If it ain't no fire up in here, it shouldn't be no yelling!" He quoted her. "I'm sorry Ma!" He sincerely pleaded.

"That's right!" She quickly confirmed. "Apology accepted!" She told him, giving him a loving smile. "Who's that on the phone that got my baby's ear so bent, that he pretends not to hear his Momma?"

Duquan broke out in a mischievous smile and said, "Its Shalaya, Ma." Shalaya was his girlfriend.

"Oh!" Althea said, as she remembered catching them in his bedroom one day, dry humping each other, when they were supposed to have been studying for an upcoming exam. She had chastised both of them and barred Shalaya from coming to the house altogether.

"Humph. That lil' hot ass girl gon' end up pregnant with a little Duquan before her fast tail ass outta junior high school, if her momma don't keep'a foot on her damn neck. But at least it won't happen in this house." She thought. "Shit, now'a days these damn kids are just too damn grown for their own good."

"By the way, she said to tell you 'hi' ma!" He told her.

"Oh yeah." Althea's lips commenced distorting themselves into a snarl as she said, "tell her I said hi back." Then turned and headed to her bedroom. Althea felt the warmth of cascading sunrays creeping through her slightly drawn curtains. They flooded her bedroom and she seemed drawned to them, so she walked over and peered out the window.

She stood there a moment admiring how the sunlight glistened off her milk white CLK 450 Mercedes Benz. She had that baby sitting up elegantly on a set of twenty-two inch Gloss Black Allusion Rims. The interior was laced with custom made Sherling car seats and all the latest accessories, including a hidden stash compartment for weapons or other illegal contraptions. Althea felt a sense of pride as she retreated from the window and began to dress.

Chapter 16

VICKY'S TRANSMISSION

Vicky sat comfortably in the confines of her vehicle as it cruised at a respectable speed limit down Elton Street. She approached the corner of Sutter Avenue, which was swarming with young Sutter Angel Soldiers as well as their workers. While the pitchers sold crack and cocaine, the security stood guard armed to the teeth. With the early Spring weather manifesting itself, the Angels thought it would be a great idea to have the workers peddle their narcotics on the outside as opposed to being behind the doors of the drug dens. Especially with police raiding all known crack, heroin and cocaine operations.

In Brooklyn, pitching drugs out in the open was unfamiliar to law enforcement. As far as they were concerned, those kinds of deals only went down in the boroughs of Queens and Manhattan. So the Angels took advantage of that fact as well as a few other local king pens.

She blew her horn and waved outside of her open window towards them in acknowledgement as they either nodded or waved back in response. She also took notice to Nesto, who stood quite a few yards away from all the illegal activities. Caught in deep conversation as he chatted with two of his most trusted henchmen as he took his final drag from a Newport cigarette before flicking the butt of the stogie to the concrete. After lowering the volumn of Don Stone's hit single "Taking Broads Home" which pounded from the four twelve inch woofers of her wood grain Pioneer sound system. She then eased her Volvo into a parking spot directly in front of Mark Four's auto repair shop and pulled down her sunvisor mirror for a quick check of her hair and lip gloss before stepping out. Draped in a skin tight money green cat suit that hugged her curves to perfection, her ass cheeks naturally demonstrating it's own version of the thunder clap with every step she took in her six inch suede Madeline Reba pumps. On lookers were in awe of her well- proportioned physical composition, even those who knew her for many years. Just before entering the shop she was startled by the clanking sound of a metal object, which caused her to divert her attention towards her right where she noticed "Faby", a longtime employee of Mark Four's, two car lengths away administering some kind of repair to the driver's door of a yellowish/mustard colored Audi. "Hey Faby!" She yelled out. He began shaking his head from side to side with a sly grin roaming his eyes up and down her vivacious figure before responding "What's up, Vic?" She smirked knowing she was the center of attraction and continued sashsaying into the shop.

"Mm, mm, mm! Y'all look at what the Spring breeze done blew up in here!" Mark Four stated to his two employees who were busy doing inventory when Vicky strolled in.

"Lord have mercy!" Said the elderly man of about fifty-ish as he briefly scanned her body. The younger of the two just stood there gawking with his mouth open until Mark commanded him to get back to work.

"Heyyy, Mark-Four!" She greeted, approaching him for a hug and a peck on the cheek.

"Whats up Babygirl?! Long time, no see!" He said, releasing her from his embrace. "So what the hell can I do for yo fine ass?"

"I don't know. I think my transmission needs to be fixed, cause something is always squeaking everytime I start the mufucker up."

"Shit!" He cursed, leaning into her ear for a whisper, "If I was certain that you would not give my ass a god dam heart attack, I'd be more than happy to lubricate that transmission for you!"

"Yeah, well, I am glad ya old ass recognize!" She shot back with a defiant pose, both hands on her hips.

Mark Four, who was almost two decades older than she, was an old school gangster who was highly respected where ever he went. Back in the late seventies to mid-eighties he had the hood on lockdown when it came to selling weed. Rumor has it that he became millionaire status just off marijuana alone, back then. In the late eighties he retired and used his ill gotten funds to open up a auto shop and a few hair salons. But he was notoriously known for his infamous shootout in 1977 with the local precinct, where he sustained eleven gunshot wounds during the heated exchange of gunfire, then smiled into the Channel 7 Eyewitness news camera with his middle finger in the air, bleeding profusely as he was being lifted into an ambulance.

"Yo Tank!" He yelled out to the young employee, "Stop what you're doing for a few moments and go take a look at my lil' Homegirl's transmission." As Tank and Vicky headed for the exit, Mark could not help but to feast his eyes on her backside, watching as her butt cheeks played a rough game of 'move over' with one another, as she lively stepped out of the establishment.

"There aint no way in hell Pop, that I'm gonna believe that girl ain't get in line more than once when God Almighty was giving out ass. Um um, no, Sir!" He said to the elderly employee, shaking his head and watching Vicky's behind until it was no longer in his view.

"Yeah, Lord knows I wouldn't mine dropping some Johnson off in her drawz!" The old man stated, rubber necking his head in hope for one last look.

"Pop, you crazy as hell, nigga! That pussy right there will put yo old ass in a wheel chair!" Mark Four joked, shaking his head from side to side.

"Oh yeah, then I'll be rolling around with a big ass smile too mufucker." He shot back as they broke into laughter.

* * * * *

"God damn! This is a pretty ass mufuckin' ride you got here!" Tank complemented while nodding his head. He stood at the curb briefly admiring the grey Volvo with the black piping, sitting on twenty-two inch black and chrome joker rims, complete with the spoke inserts and just like the rest of her crew, the interior of her vehicle was equipped with all the latest features.

"Thank you." She replied.

"Alright now sweetie, you can pop the hood for me and lem'me see what the problem is, cause this ride is too damn expensive to be acting up on you."

"Yeah, tell me about it." She said, climbing into the vehicle.

"Ok, start it up now and lets see what happens!" He said after spending a little over ten minutes under the hood.

"Ahh, I see you got the magic touch." She said with enthusiastic sincerity and a smile after starting her engine, which was now free of the squeaking sound. "Alright Tank I really appreciate you taking care of this for me." She thanked. Than reached under the driver seat for her Kate Spade bag and asked, "Now how much do I owe you?"

"Nah, Babygirl, you gotta go inside and handle that with the Boss." He replied, wiping his hands with a cloth before securing the hood. Stealing a peek at her backside as she strolled off.

* * * * *

"Girl you know your damn money aint no good up in my place of business!" Mark said while brushing his hand dismissively towards her after coming back into the shop attempting to pay for their services. "Besides it ain't too often that you walk up in here blessing us with your heavenly beauty!"

"Aahh nigga, listen to you with that old school charm!" Vicky blushed, obviously flattered by his statement with the look of excitement in her eyes. "I never heard that line before. You keep talking like that and you might get something that'll give you a mass heart attack!" She added with a wink before turning on her heels and exiting the shop.

"I'm gonna hold you to that too!" Mark yelled out.

"Yeah you do that!" She shot back before clearing the door.

While opening her car door, Vicky was caught off guard by an individual she did not know and who was a little too close for comfort. "What's up?" He said, aggressively grabbing her by the arm.

"What's up?" She echoed, angrily, snatching away in a defensive stance. "Da' fuck you mean, 'what's up'? Don't be grabbing on me like that. You must be outta ya fucking mind!" She ranted. "Do you know where the fuck you at right now?!"

"I'm in America, standing on the corner of Sutter and mufuckin' Elton!" He sarcastically shot.

"Yeah! Exactly!" She fired back, making eye contact with one of the guys conversating with Nesto in the distance.

"Ah fuck you then, bitch!"

"Nah! Fuck you, mufucker." She barked through gritted teeth rolling her neck.

Nesto's henchman that noticed the commotion from yonder tapped him as he maintained his focus in Vicky's direction. Nesto turned to see what grabbed his comrades' attention, after taking notice and without hesitation, they headed in that direction. With his 9mm concealed in his waistband, he couldn't' believe that someone would be crazy enough to disrespect a Sutter Angel right on the mufuckin' avenue, itself.

Some of the security guys caught on as well and began moving in toward them. Some with their hands underneath their shirts, obviously clutching their firearms until Nesto waved them off.

"Bitch! I will smack da' shit!"

"Oh, no the fuck you won't!" Nesto interjected as he and his two homies approached from his blindside.

"And who the fuck y'all niggaz spose'ta be? Her mufuckin' soldiers or sumthin'?"

"Yeah something like that!" Nesto answered, lifting his shirt to expose the handle of his automatic weapon. "Now I would advise you to move da'fuck on or get moved da'fuck outta existence. The choice is yours, nigga. So make up your mind. Quick!" Nesto demanded as he and his cronies venomously stared him down.

The man cut his eyes towards Vicky with a menacing scowl as he nodded up and down, "Nigga don't be staring at me like you're possessed by the devil. Unless you wanna wake up with wings on your back." She threatened. Sensing that he was in the presence of three killers, he made up his mind almost immediately.

"Y'all got this one bruh!" He stated after diverting his attention back to the fellas, then back peddled.

"Gimme the green light. I'll have him done da'fuck off before his ass reach Belmont Avenue." Nesto begged through gritted teeth, as the violator hopped into his Audi and pulled out of his parking spot.

"Nah, fuck him! That won't be necessary." She replied, easing into her vehicle. "As a matter of fact, hop in for a minute. I got something for you." After entering the vehicle, she popped open her secret compartment and gave him a brand new ten millimeter Sig Sauer and two clips. "I saw that lust in your eyes when you where at the warehouse and thought I'd bring you one, since I was coming through anyway!"

"Good looking!" He thanked her, tucking the weapon in the small of his back before exiting the vehicle. Right before she pulled out of her spot "Faby" leaned into the driver's window and handed her a small plastic card.

"I took that outta his wallet when I noticed the altercation. Dumb mufucker left it in the front seat." He stated while she viewed the card.

"Good looking out!" She said, then tossed the New York State identification card into her stash spot before peeling out. 'Kashawn Green, today wasn't your day to die!' she thought to herself and replaying the incident in her head. "Maybe next time I see you. . . maybe next time."

Chapter 17

SOME GOOD SHIT

*I*t was a seasonably warm dark night in Fayette, Alabama. Ronnie sat comfortable in his mother's Chevy Cutlass Supreme, parked on South West 21st Street, conversing with two of his childhood friends, Sparky and Smokey. They each had a stick of Chem dog ablazed.

Two days earlier, Ronnie had handed out approximately seventy-five sample joints of the weed Latesha had ordered Vicky to give him and take back to Alabama. The Chem dog's effects had the potheads in the small southern town, in a crazed frenzy from the effects of the most highest grade marijuana their lungs had ever had the pleasure of inhaling. Never before had they been blessed with the opportunity to puff on weed of such high potency. And in just a few more days the streets of Fayette, Alabama will be flooded with the herb, courtesy of the Sutter Angels.

"Man! This shit hurr is the bomb diggidy!" Sparky assured Ronnie from the passenger seat, where he sat staring blankly at the joint in his left hand, while pounding his chest with his right before exhaling a thick cloud of smoke, which permeated throughout the vehicle.

"Hell! I wouldn't be surprised if Snoop Dogg and Dr. Dre aint yet get they hands on this brand'a weed, down in California." Smokey chimed in before taking a long toke from the reefer stick that had his chest feeling like his internal organs were of fire.

"Ah nigga, please! This shit was probably grown in Cali!" Sparky said after plucking ashes from the joints tip, into the vehicle's ash tray.

"Oh yeah! So why aint non'a dem niggaz on da' West

Coast rappin' 'bout it, then?" Smokey retorted.

"Now Smokey, that was da' stupidest shit I've heard you say all year!" Ronnie exclaimed, interjecting to snap out of his quiet, nonchalant mood.

"Man, dem niggaz ain't gotta make a rap record 'bout eh'y damn brand'a weed they be out thurr blowin' on!" Sparky added in his deep southern drawl.

"Y'all know what," Smokey interjected, "fuck Snoop Dogg and Dr. Dre, mufuckin' ass!"

"Dat's what da'fuck I'm talkin' 'bout, shit! I can't wait until my cousins 'n'em get da' hell on down hurr, so we can start thickening our goddamn pockets! We gon' shut dis town down for'sho!" Ronnie ranted.

"So, when exactly are they coming down hurr?" Sparky excitedly asked.

"Damn nigga! Calm da'fuck on down! I just spoke ta' Latesha yesterday! And she said dey'a be hurr before da weekend fo'sho mu'fucker! Ya'up in hurr ac'ing mo'impatient then I am!" Ronnie chastised him.

"Man, shit! I'm try'na see yo cuz, ya know I been wa'nin' ta put a dent up in 'ur cat fa' years! Know wa'um talkin' 'bout." Sparky said, clutching his crotch.

"Yeah! And I'm try'na plant sum'mo dis dick up in 'ur friend Vicky! Man I was gon'fo broke, try'na knock a crater in dat gurl's cat! Dat bitch got sum'good ass pussy!" Ronnie bragged.

"Nigga, I don't know no dag'gon Vicky!" Smokey cut in after finishing off his joint. "Nor do I know if'n 'ur coochie good as ya claimin' it to be! But, I do know one thang fo' sho, and dat is, dat – dat damn weed is sum'good shit!" Smokey said as they sat there in the car twisted off the Chem dog.

Chapter 18

CINEMA xxx

Michelle and Lil El sat inside his black Cadillac Escalade sharing a laced pronto leaf blunt of Chem dog, parked in a dark corner of the Sunrise movie theatre's parting lot. They had a little over twenty minutes to kill before the screening, so they sat in his ride enjoying the low sounds of an old Prince CD, spilling over the Pioneer sound system.

"So, El...," Michelle began, twisiting her body around in the passenger seat to face him, "what would your girlfriend say if she knew you were out on a date with the next bitch?"

El paused before answering to take a swig from his Heineken brew. He knew full well that was her way of inquiring whether or not he had a girlfriend. Sardonically looking around his truck as if searching for an imaginary female, he asked her, "Where's da 'mufuckin' bitch I'm 'pose to be out on a date with? Cause I don't see no bitch up in here and neither should you. So, don't ever refer to yourself as a female dog while you're in my presence!" He told her with a stern expression on his face.

"Ah, look at 'chu getting' all righteous on me 'n shit, like you don't be referring to us women as bitches. I'm pretty sure when you, Quannie, B-Hov and Puzzle an'em be kickin' it, y'all be callin' us ehy'thing but our damn names!" Michelle told him.

"Nah Baby!" He said, shaking his head from side to side, "that's where ya wrong sweetheart. First of all, I'm'a gangsta to the bone marrow and I don't have any problems callin' a spade a spade. Second of all, I've been feeling you for quite some time now," he paused to clear his throat before he continued, "in fact, I'm'a keep it a hunnit wit'chu. I've actually been obsessed wit'chu. I've had an insatiable desire ta have you ever since I was 'bout fifteen years old. But, my respect for you has always been absolute! So, I would ne'va disrespect you by referring to you as a bitch. And that's real mufuckin' talk!"

"Word? So, why you ain't never holla at me, back then?" Michelle curiously inquired as she thought to herself, 'this nigga must don't know I got him by a few years in age.'

"Well," he responded, "because at dat stage of my life, when it came to steppin' ta honeys, not only was I shy, but also a little insecure 'bout myself. Besides I didn't know how to handle rejection. Back then, if you would'a shut me down for try'na get at 'chu. I wouldn't have known how to handle it. I use ta really have a hard time expressin' myself. . .back in those days. But I'm blessed and grateful now that those days are long gone, cause a nigga's confidence now is way up to the mufuckin' moon! Anyway, ever since that night at the club, I've been feelin' that obsessive and insatiable urge, again, to give you a'lota this love a nigga been saving up for you on the low." He said, unconsciously groping himself.

Michelle had been looking at him intensively and noticed the fervent look in his eyes as he was confessing his long held secret to her. She allowed her eyes to wander down to his crotch where his dick imprint was so outstandingly impressed on his jeans that she instantly felt a pang in her pussy as she told herself, 'Damn! This nigga got'a big ass dick!' Michelle allowed her eyes to linger at his crotch longer than she intended to, as she continued in her personal thoughts . . . "Its been almost nine months since I last had some dick up in this hot ass coochie of mine." So she took the initiative and extinguished the blunt she had been puffing on. Let out a cloud of smoke and squirmed over closer to Lil El. Then looking into his eyes, she leaned in with her sensual mouth and licked at his full lips

"Uummm..!" Lil El moaned, opening his mouth to permit her snaking tongue to enter. Immediately pulling her closer he began lustfully sucking on her tongue as his hands wondered. Cupping her breasts and tugging at her erect nipples. Michelle shuddered and moaned in his mouth, "Uummm...". Lil El continued to lightly caress her breasts through the sheer silk blouse she wore. She wasn't wearing a bra so the friction was making her hot as hell. Michelle immediately became turned on as she felt Lil El's muscular arms embracing her and his strong hands gently massaging her breast and nipples. She desperately fumbled with his Evisu jeans, as Lil El began lifting her matching silk skirt. When she felt his hands caressing her ass cheeks, she immediately reached in and grabbed hold of his dick. Upon feeling its length and girth she gasped and loudly exclaimed, "Oh my god! Its so fucking huge!", then began to stroke up and down its long shaft. Lil El suddenly said, let's skip this movie shit and go to a hotel."

But Michelle lustfully said, "Oh no, let's do this right here! Shit, aint no shame in my mufuckin' game, Baby. We can get it in right here." Lil El quickly pushed the seat back and adjusted the steering wheel, then told her, "Okay Baby, grab one of them condoms outta da glove compartment!"

"Nah, its cool Baby, I already got a female version up in me!" Michelle quickly replied in a sexually charged and raspy voice. Lil El wasted no more unnecessary time. He pulled his jeans and underwear down below his knees and Michelle gasped as she finally got a brief glimpse of his dick. "Damn nigga!" she exclaimed. Panting for breath he grabbed her around the waist, heaved her up and lowered her onto his erected dick.

Michelle, still gasping, said, "Yeah Baby, my pussy getting wet already." Spasming, she felt his dick head penetrating the threshold of her pussy lips. *"OH MY GOD! Oohhh...! Its so fucking biii... Ahhh..."* she uttered. Words cut short, as she felt the bulbous dick head entering the depth of her pussy.

"Aggghh...!" Lil El groaned as he pulled her down onto him and simultaneously lunged up to meet her descending pussy.

"Ahhh... Oh god, yes! Fuck that dick in me!" She began encouraging him, becoming inflamed with passion. She started bouncing up and down on his dick, grinding on it with every downstroke.

"Ahhh yeah, baby bounce dat pussy on it like that!" He encouraged her back. That made Michelle wild as she began bouncing harder, groaned and moaned. Feeling his dick all the way up to her belly.

"Oh my god! I...I knew it. I knew this fuckin' dick was gon' be good! *Ahhh...Yes! Ahh..."* Michelle whimpered.

Lil El was firmly gripping her by the waist to make sure she wouldn't hit her head on the interior roof of the truck as he bucked up hard off the seat plunging himself deep up into her vagina.

"Arrrggh...! Arrrgh!" He groaned as he pumped in and out *"Yeah baby, take this dick!* **Arrrgh! Uummm...! Ssss...god damn,** *you got sum' good fuckin' pussy! I feel you dripping all on my lap!"* He said, as Michelle leaned down and licked at his mouth and hungrily sucked his tongue into her own, once he parted his lips.

"Mmm.... Uummm..." She moaned. That shit sent Michelle over the top. She started cumming profusely, then suddenly withdrew her mouth from his and uttered, *"Oh, my fuckin' god! Aaaahhh.... I'm cumming. Oh god! Ahh, aaahhhh, mmm...! Yes!* **Oh YES! YES!"** She wailed as she slammed down on his dick and started grinding her pelvis wildly and shuddering from the spasms that took hold of her body.

"Aahhh...! Uummm...! Arrrggh!" Lil El groaned

too. Michelle suddenly stopped quivering, rose off his dick and immediately inserted it into her mouth. *"Aahhh...! Aahhh...! Uummm...! Yeah baby...!"* He moaned as he felt her warm lips engulf his dick. *"Aahhh...! Yeah baby! Suck that dick! Yeah....Ssss, yeah...Babygirl, just like that..."* He said as she sucked and licked at his penis with a crazed passion.

Michelle slurped on his dick as she took more into her mouth and becoming more enraptured as she attempted to deep throat him entirely. She had about two thirds of his dick in her jaws when she realized she couldn't fit anymore of it into her mouth. So she ascended and began bopping her head up and down the long shaft. Then when she felt his dick suddenly becoming thicker, sensing he was about to erupt, she pulled it out of her mouth, causing a popping sound upon release. She then immediately mounted back onto his lap and quickly shoved his dick inside of her, impaling herself with it and commenced riding him like a horse.

"Aahhh...! Yeah! Give it to me baby! Give me that nut!" She cried out as Lil El began thrusting harder and harder. *"Arrrgh... Arrrgh...!"* They both groaned simultaneously as they erupted and exchanged cum juices, holding onto each other tightly.

"Wheeew...!" They both jointly said as they gasped for air. They kissed passionately before Michelle finally rose up off his limp dick. A glob of cum juice seeped out of her pussy and she looked down upon it and marveled at how big his dick remained even when limp.

"Shit nigga!" She exclaimed, "You sure know how to make a bitch feel you in her damn gut!"

Lil El looked at her and instantly became aroused again and said, "Oh you aint felt nothing yet Baby!" He then pulled her closer and kissed her fully on the lips. Then aggressively spun her around doggie-style and for a moment Michelle felt violated. But that feeling quickly disappeared when she felt him lift her skirt exposing her swollen pussy lips and quickly commenced to lick and suck at her pussy.

"*Oooohh...! Oh sssshiiit! Aahhh..., yeah eat this pussy, baby! Yeah...! Mmmm... that feels SSOOO....damn...good...*" She cooed.

Lil El licked at her clit and opened the flood gates again and Michelle cried out, "*Ahhh...! Ahhh...!*" as gushes of her girly juice poured out of her pussy. "*Oh my god!*" She exclaimed.

Lil El arose and said, "Dat shit was delicious Boo!" Michelle felt another slight spasm as she felt appreciated and tremendously desirable.

"Thank you." She gratefully said, while still assuming the position.

Lil El then grasped her tight around the waist and sent his bloated dick head and shaft plunging deep into the opening crevice of her pussy. Feeling the fire in her, he eased himself halfway out then thrusted back in. Michelle's body jerked as she screamed out, "Oh shit, mufucka!" Looking over her shoulder at him with trepidation yet, with such wanton lust in her eyes that Lil El thought he would instantly cum. Instead, he became inflamed and pumped more dick into her.

Michelle squirmed, trying desparately to escape his deep plunges. As she incredibly felt more and more of his dick entering deeper and deeper into her, she cried out, "Aahhh...! Shiiit! No! Aahhhh...Baby! It's too much! *Ooowww...!* I...ah, I can't Baby, *please! Aahhh...!* I can't take all of it! Aahhh...!" She pleaded out, trying harder and harder to evade his thrusting plunges.

But Lil El held onto her tiny waist in a vice grip and said, "Girl, stop all of that damn jerkin' and whinnin' n' shit. You acting like a nigga moving your fuckin' bladder or sumthin'." He then smoothly withdrew part of his dick and slowly began to feed it into her pussy while encouraging her..."Relax Baby. Just let it sink into ya...nice and easy. Yeah, just like dat. *Ahhh...yes, like dat! Uummm...!"*

Michelle couldn't believe what she was experiencing. Thinking...'*Damn! This nigga got a whole lot'a dick!'*...it suddenly began feeling sensationally good to her as she relaxed and allowed him to take control. Lil El kept feeding dick into her with expert caution. Then when she thought he had all of it in her pussy, he thrust forward and sent more dick into her and she thought she would faint.

"OOOoohhh...Oohh...!" Michelle moaned as she felt her pussy filling up with dick. This time, however, she did not squirm, jerk or tried to struggle to escape the dick, especially since Lil El did not ram it in and out. Rather he let it marinate deep inside her pussy, grinding his hip slowly, making circular motions. She felt his dick hit the bottom of her pussy and lovingly settle there. *"Aahh...Yeah Baby*, leave it right there for a moment." She begged him. When Lil El felt her pussy grip to his penis, he slowly began to pump it in and out of her. *"Oh fuck! Yeah, Baby! Now that's it, right there! Fuck it in like that Baby! Aahhh...! Shit! Yes, yes! You, hitting my fuckin' spot now! Aahhh...!"* She uncontrollabley moaned, as she began to throw her ass back at him with lustful desire. Lil El, as if on cue, began to thrust more and more dick up into her. Michelle was going wild with pleasure. *"OOOHHH! MY GOD!! WHAT THE FUCK YOU DOIN' TO ME!! OOOH...! YESS...! OH BABY! MMMMM.... THIS PUSSY'S ALL YOURS NOW! FUCK IT LIKE IT IS, BABY!!! FUCK IT LIKE IT'S YOURS!! FUCK THIS PUSSY LIKE YOU **OWN** IT!!*

Lil El went buck wild himself. He commenced to slam his dick into her as she pleasurably screamed and hollered. He became so enrapt in Michelle's pleasurable screams, that he began asking her, *"WHO'S PUSSY IS THIS? TELL ME? WHO'S PUSSY IS THIS? **WHO THIS PUSSY BELONG TO?**"*

Michelle wasted no time in telling him, *"AAHH! BABY THIS IS YOUR PUSSY! THIS YOUR PUSSY, DADDY! OOOHH GOD, THIS IS YOUR PUSSY! THIS PUSSY BELONGS TO YOU, DADDY!!"*

As he pumped more dick further into her, he told her, *" I WANT YOU TO TELL ME WHO'S **FUCKIN'** PUSSY IS THIS? **SAY MY NAME!!"*** He continued, making her scream, shout, and holler from the sensational pleasure she was experiencing.

Michelle was going out of her mind and yelled out, *"OH MY GOD, EL! YOU'RE A FUCKIN' BEAST! AAAHH...!! SHIT!! YOU **STILL** GOT MORE DICK! AAAHH....! YOU GOIN' RIP MY INSIDES BABY! AAAAHH!!...OH SSHIIT!!"* She cried out. *"OOH YES DADDY!! THIS BIG DICK LIL EL'S PUSSY, BABY! OH YES...THIS BIG DICK LIL EL'S PUSSY!!!"*

"OKAY, DAT'S WAH I'M TALKIN' 'BOUT. HERE BABY, **TAKE THIS DICK! TAKE ALL THIS DICK. TAKE. AALLL THIS DICK! AARRGGH... AARRRGGHH!!! FUCK!!!"** Lil El groaned and growled, stroking deep, just as Michelle began announcing the coming of the waters.

"Oooo-OOOOhhh...! Baby, I....I'm ah....cu... cu...cumming again! Oh my god! I'm cumming baby! Aahhh...! Oohhh...! Oohhh...! Ooooooohhh! Yes! Yes! Ah...ssshhhiiit!" She finally gasped as she felt Lil El also erupt into her pussy.

As they regained their composure, Lil El reached over into his glove compartment and extracted some handy wipes before pulling his dick out of Michelle's pussy hole. Then to her amazement he began wiping her coochie clean. She looked back at him with sincere appreciation and respect in her heart, as she thought 'this a mufuckin''-gangsta-ass-nigga for *real.*'

Once Lil El and Michelle composed themselves, they exited the vehichle and with the scent of sex still lingering on them, they clasped hands and strolled into the six-screen Long Island Theatre and enjoyed an action packed movie wrapped in each other's arms.

Chapter 19

FAYETTE ALABAMA / COPPIN

*T*he Angels were ripping around Brooklyn, during the pre-dawn hours, taking care of their business in preparation for their planned trip down South. Latesha stopped at one of the Angel's stash cribs with her I.B.M. digital money counting machine. She was accumulating $140,000 needed to cop the ten kilos of cocaine from her Florida connect. Latesha intended to re-up while on their trip down South and although the price of the product had risen throughout the years, the Angels didn't have a problem with that, because they intended to double their purchase and almost triple their profit by blessing the product with their magic cut.

While Latesha was out tying up loose ends, she dropped $50,000 on Gwen for ten pounds of Chem. She decided that instead of the two pounds she intended to drop off in Alabama, she would unload five and the remainder would go to "Black Pat" to sell in quarters and twenties. She also supplied Nesto with more than enough weight to last until they returned.

After parking her Beamer in front of her mother's crib she hopped a cab and met up with her girls at the Port Authority. They each carried their suit cases packed with a wide variety of designer wear – from Gucci to Casare Paciotti and everything in between. For safety measures, their luggage also contained some heat. The Angels intended to make a serious statement in Alabama and leave a lasting impression in the southern state long after they're gone.

"Shit! I didn't know Amtrak had reclining seats and

carpeting in their trains." Althea confessed, scanning the train car's interior as they boarded.

"Well you aint seen nothing yet! Just wait 'til you see the last car, that shit is off the chain!" Latesha told her.

"Can we go back there now?" I wanna see what it look like!"

"Althea, please! Let's get our seating arrangements in order first, before we go doin' anything else!" Latesha barked before adding, "Besides, ain't nothing gon' be popping off back there until night fall, anyway! So just relax awhile!"

"Yeah Althea, calm da'fuck down! They ain't sellin no dag –gon sex toys back there anyway! I can assure you of dat, so you can get that thought outta your mind!" Goldie cracked, snickering at her.

"Yeah, I bet'chu can!" She shot back, winking at her while placing her luggage in the overhead compartment before flopping down on the seat closest to the window. Latesha and Goldie slid in next to her and the other girls sat directly in front of them and began conversing as the train pulled out of the station.

Several hours later after blazing a "Sess" blunt in the train's floor to ceiling mirrored bathroom, they headed to the restaurant which was situated in the last car. Althea stood in awe as she observed the luxurious restaurant on wheels. "Oh my God! This shit is hot right here!" She excitedly said. "Shit! I'm 'bout to get my munch on up in this mufucker!" She added in a tone that caused the other passengers to divert their attention from their meals towards their direction.

"Bitch! Your ass aint starving like dat, so stop acting Somalian. You're embarrassing us up in here!" Vicky snapped at her with an evil glare. Althea stared back at her running her eyes up and down before replyin, "Girl, please! Fuck what 'chu talking 'bout. I'm hungry. Shit!"

Goldie, becoming irritated, looked over her shoulder at her friends as they approached the counter and quickly interjected. "A'ight! Come on now, Althea. You got all these damn people staring at us 'n shit."

"Ah fuck these mufuckas! They don't know us!" She replied, waving her hand dismissively at the onlookers.

They then proceeded to order pastrami, turkey and cheese heros, cold beverages and potato chips, then went and sat at the last table. Across from them was a well-dressed couple gazing into each other's eyes and in deep conversation. Goldie and Althea happened to find the male strikingly handsome.

"Ooww girl, dat nigga in front of us is fine as hell!" Goldie stated, suggestiviely nodding towards the individual she was referring to, as she tapped Althea's leg under the table, causing the other Angels to steal guick glances.

"Uumm, he damn sure is!" Althea replied in agreement with a trace of lust in her eyes as she paused with her pastrami sandwich in hand before sinking her teeth in for a bite. Feeling the energy coming from their table, the guy looked over his mates shoulder and briefly made eye contact with Althea who quickly and very openly commenced to flirt with him, seductively licking her lips after taking a sip from her Sprite soda pop.

"Honey, pardon me for a few moments while I go to the ladies room." His well-dressed petite female companion said, as she eased out of her seat.

"Sure thing baby. I'll be right here when you get back." He replied before dipping into a small Tupperware bowl of smoked oysters that his female companion had prepared for their trip.

"You better be!" She replied before sashaying off.

'Humph...bitch try'na work something she aint got enough of...wit' her lil-boney-ass self!' Althea thought before shifting her attention back to Mr. Handsome, who was stuffing his face. "Um, excuse me, Boo, if you don't mind me asking...what is that you're eating?" She inquired, wrinkling her nose as if she was smelling some vile odor.

Looking over his shoulder to make sure his girlfriend was out of hearing range before answering, he replied, "Whatever you want me to eat, Ma," winking at her.

"Oh yeah..." Althea began, raising from her seat and spinning around making a 360° turn. "From the looks of your date, your appetite ain't big enough for all a'dis."

"God daayum!", was all he could muster to say after noticing her shapely figure as she stood there with her hands on her hips, wearing a dark gray, crushed velvet jumpsuit that adorned her perfectly sculped ass and a pair of six inch matching Jimmy Choo pumps that seductively lifted her derrier up in the air a few centimeters.

"I get dat kind'a reaction a lot, Mr. Fly-guy!" She boasted confidently, as she struck another pose for him, with both hands still on her hips, she shifted her weight from one side to the other.

"Girl, sit yo hot ass down!" Goldie barked at her, pulling her down onto the seat by the arm.

"Don't pay her no mind, she's a little crazy!" She turned and said to him with a look of embarrassment on her face.

"Yeah well, I'm'a lil looney tunes myself, at times." He admitted, gazing into Althea's captivating eyes.

"Here comes your girl, playboy!" Goldie warned, placing her hands over her mouth as his date came strutting down the isle drying her hands with paper towels.

"Did you miss me sweetie?" She asked him in a loud enough tone for the Angels to hear, as she approached.

"Humph! I know this bag-a-bones-ass-bitch aint try'na get ragged on in this mufuckin' train." Althea mumbled to no one in particular.

"Althea, you need to stop. That's dat woman's man."
"*And?* What's your point, *Michelle?*" She fired,

snapping her head back.

"What's my point, huh? You would'a saw my point if homegirl had'a caught cha fast ass givin' her man dat little booty show and jumped all over your damn ass!"

"Sh*it*!" Althea rapidly fired back, then curled her lips up before adding, "Dat'a be a good ass way to get her damn family all together..." then paused a second before continuing, "all dressed in mu'fucking black!"

"See Latesha, I told you this bitch was good n' crazy." Michelle said, while pointing her index finger towards Althea.

"Yeah, I know. That's why her ass coming wit' me to Miami, so she don't kill none'a them Fayette bitches over their own man's dick!"

"I aint got no problem goin' wit'chu to Miami." Althea barked.

"Good. Kacky, you take my J. Crew tote bag wit' the Chem in it and give Ronnie four and a half bags. Cause me and Althea ain't getting off wit' y'all. As for the rest of my luggage, we'll use that as camouflage." She said.

"I got chu!" Her sister assured her.

"Do we gotta purchase new tickets?" Althea inquired.

"Nah!" Latesha answered. "Our tickets were for Miami from the get go! Oh yeah Kacky, make sure you have a rental on deck too. Cause we ain't try'na tear that lil ass town up every night in no damn limo! But, keep the limo on reserve, so you can pick me and Al up when we get back." She instructed.

"Consider it done!" Kacky snapped.

* * * * *

Pulling up to the Tuscaloosa Train Station, in Alabama, Kacky, Goldie, Michelle and Vicky made their way to the black stretch Hummer Limousine parked about thirty yards from the tracks. And their middle aged

African-American male chauffeur commenced to placing their luggage into the vehicle and the girls turned and acknowledged Latesha and Althea waving goodbye to them through the train's window. They all quickly waved back then climbed into the limo and proceeded on their twenty minute drive to the small Alabama town.

Cruising down highway 171 North they passed the "Welcome To Fayette" sign and knew they were almost there. When they finally arrived at their destination, they eased into a parking spot, unloaded their gear, squared away their business at the front desk of the hotel and headed to their spacious suite to freshen up.

"A'ight Kacky, you can call your cousin and let'em know we here." Vicky said, while stepping out of the shower, wrapped in a beach size towel.

"Girl please! You late like yesterday! I called him already. He should be here any minute now." Kacky replied.

"Damn Vee, we just got da'fuck in town and already you try'na jump on his bones!" Michelle snapped with a disgusting expression on her face.

"Michelle, why don't you just shut your cock hole up! Every time I turn around you got it open, try'na voice your opinion 'bout somebody else's business! And I know ya mufuckin" tongue got Lil El's dick print all on it. So don't even go there wit' me, wit'cha hoochie-ass-self!" Vicky shot back at her, causing everyone, including Michelle, to break out laughing.

"Ha, ha, ha! I ain't gonna front, you got that one!" Michelle managed to say, as she clutched her stomach in between bouts of laughter.

"Kacky, you better call Lil El and make sure his dick is still attached to his body 'n shit! You seen what this bitch did to the last fuckin dick she had in her mouth!" Goldie added, pointing towards Michelle with her thumb. Instantly, the room became silent.

"Goldie, you know we don't discuss our past business, especially if it ended in someone's demise!" Kacky reprimanded her in a serious tone.

"You right Kacky, my bad." She replied. Suddenly a rap was heard at the door.

"That gotta be my cousin right there." Kacky said, strolling towards the door. She pulled the curtain on the window next to the door and peered out. She saw her cousin Ronnie and noticed he had brought a friend along. Quickly she turned towards Vicky before opening the door and said, "Vicky go put some clothes on, he got somebody with him!" Kacky then opened the door.

"Cuz, what it do?" Ronnie said, then introduced his friend, "This is my main nigga Smokey, right here. Smokey, this is my cousin Kacky from New York, I was telling you about."

"How you doing? And, please don't believe anything Ronnie tells you about me!" She told Smokey, as she greeted her cousin with a hug before stepping aside to allow them in. "Y'all, this is Smokey!" She said as she secured the door shut.

"Hi Smokey!" The girls greeted him in unison before introducing themselves individually.

"Vicky's in the back. Oh yeah Ronnie I got something for you. I'll be right back!" Kacky then added before heading into an adjorning room where Vicky was preparing herself after her shower. She closed the door behind her and while scanning the large room asked her, "Where da' hell did you put that J. Crew tote bag?"

"Girl, you need to stop smoking weed. That damn bag is sitting right next to you!" Vicky answered, nodding towards the bag as she sat at the edge of the bed applying Cantu Shea Butter on her body and face.

Following her sister's instructions, Kacky broke down one bag, halfway. She then placed hundreds of tiny manila and plastic bags that the product was to be packaged and sold in, inside a brown paper bag, along with the four and a half pounds of exotic weed. She then made her way back to the front room with Vicky trailing her, draped in a black and pink satin pajama set and extending the bag saying, "Here you go, Cuz."

"Whats up Lil Momma?" Ronnie said, greeting Vicky over Kacky's shoulder. He then introduced his friend who was mesmerized by Vicky's beauty.

"Aint nothing." Vicky replied to him after acknowledging the introduction of his friend.

"I see you dressed for bed kind'a early!" He said, eyeing her from head to toes.

"Yeah! Aint nothing going on in this town tonight. We noticed how deserted the streets were when we pulled in." She said.

"They got a football game at the high school, if y'all wanna head out somewhere. That's basically where everybody gon'be." Ronnie informed them generally.

"Nah! We good. We ain't really trying to hangout until Latesha and Althea gets here." Kacky chimed in.

"Well, why they ain't come down with y'all?" He asked Kacky.

"Cause they had to make a very important business trip. They'll be joining us tomorrow night." She informed him

"That's good. Cause the Zodiac Club is gon' be juking Friday and Saturday night!" Ronnie said enthusiastically.

"Oh don't worry, we gonna definitely make our presence known tomorrow night! You can believe dat' shit!" Michelle interjected.

"A'ight! Well I'm'a go ahead on home and bag this stuff up. I'll see y'all tomorrow night then!" He said before hugging Kacky and giving Vicky a peck on the lips.

* * * * *

Just like every other trip to Miami, the smell of saltwater had Latesha and Althea slightly nauseous as they stood on Biscayne Boulevard flagging down a cab. A passerby, driving a candy red Porcshe Carrera, blared his horn as he shot them a lustful stare.

Ten minutes later they arrived at the quiet Miami waterfront, where they would conduct their business with the Spanish Mafia's own, Felix Gonzalez. The cold as ice drug kingpin was reclining in a beach chair off in a shaded area with his legs casually crossed, as he puffed on an expensive Cuban cigar. Acknowledging them as they approached, a smile painted his face as he stood up and extended his hand for a shake. "Mami!" He greeted Latesha. "I'm glad you made the trip!"

"Ah come on, you know it's always a great pleasure doing business with you Felo!" She replied, using the short Spanish version of his name.

"I'm sure it is!" He replied, diverting his eyes and attention towards Althea. "And you, my love..." He added, extending his hand to shake Althea's. "I've never seen a star this close to the earth before!" He flatteringly told her.

Althea could not help but blush from his wise and lovely choice of words. She secretly admired the handsome Latino, who was draped in a two piece eggshell colored linen suit. Then the glare from the sun, off his platinum diamond encrusted Patek-Philippe watch, momentarily attracted her attention and she noticed it was a perfect match to his 2.5 carat platinum marquise shaped diamond pinky ring. Finally she said, "Ahh! You probably run that line on all the women you meet!"

"No, no mamacita!" He assured her in a deep latin accent, shaking his head left to right. "Every woman don't shine like a diamond and you're a rare cut!" He added while gawking at her bodacious body before taking another puff from his cigar.

"Ok Playboy..." Latesha interjected before adding,

"we're here strictly on business. And I'd appreciate it if we can take care of it now. I wouldn't want our cab getting too impatient and driving off with our luggage!" She added, nodding in the cab's direction. Latesha then scanned the area looking for Julio and Jose, his two henchmen and when she only seen a crowd of fishermen and sun bathers, she asked him, "Where are your buddies?"

"I gave them the day off. Besides, you're my only customer today. And I have a big proposition for you." He said before pausing.

"Ga' head, I'm listening." Latesha coldly stated, placing her hands on her hips, shifting her weight one side to the other.

"Well. . ." he began, "due to major issues over seas, I ended up with more product than you could ever imagine in your wildest dreams! And I need to start moving it. Fast!" he said before adding, "I know you only want ten blocks, but I'm willing to give you another 20."

"What's the catch?" She suspectingly inquired in her defiant pose.

"I see you haven't changed a bit. Nothing seems to go above your head, huh?" He asked in a rhetorical manner, not expecting an answer.

"Nah, not much." She replied.

"Well, the catch, as you put it, is that you move eighty for me at seventeen a pop."

Maintaining her composure as the wheel in her mind turned, quickly thinking about how much richer she and her crew would become with that much cocaine on their hand to move, she finally said, "So, when do you expect this new business extension to commence?"

"Oh, right away Mami! I got the one-hundred blocks packed in duffle bags in the trunk of that green Chevy parked next to your cab. You say the word. We do the transaction."

"Let's go!" She quickly answered. Her mind clouded by dollar signs, as they made their way to the Chevy. She tossed the small bag of re-up money into the trunk and with his and Althea's help, they placed the duffle bags into the trunk of the cab and headed back to the train station with a hundred and ten bricks.

Chapter 20

PRESSURE

*T*he 75th precinct in the East New York section of Brooklyn was teeming with tension as Desk Sergeant Sullivan stood at the podium addressing the morning shift at rollcall.

"I want a lot more pressure applied to this jurisdiction." The desk sergeant said in a tenacious tone, as he scanned the line up of police officers. "I want every gun totting thug and every crack/cocaine dealer in cuffs and brought back here to be thoroughly questioned with regards to the homicides of our fellow brothers. I also want you guys to take a hold of all the ears and eyes of every known informant out there and to rain down on all barber shops, hip hop venues, fastfood restaurants and street corners until somebody starts talking...and I mean talking loud!"

The sergeant paused to allow his words to take effect, then continued, "I just recently learned through the law enforcement grapevine that the Feds were about to commence a major investigation into this case. That is very puzzling to me because this is our backyard. So I question, why would the Feds want to probe into something that is clearly out of their jurisdiction and clearly does not appear to be connected to the Bureau?" The sergeant meant the question to be rhetorical since he neither expected nor required it to be answered by any of the officers in the room.

"If we do not unrelentlessly press down hard on this case and resolve the brutal execution style murders of our colleagues, then that will leave a black eye not only on this department, but on every law enforcement agency in this city. And I'm not willing to live with that on my conscience and neither should you guys!" He said, vivaciously sweeping his right hand across the room for emphasis. "The N.Y.P.D is culturally accustomed to solve murder cases, especially when it pertains to the brutal assissinations of our own fellow officers! So, let's not be the ones to change that tradition. But, rather let us be the ones to hold that tradition in perpetuity."

Again, Sergeant Sullivan paused to allow his words to sink into the minds of his officers. He cleared his throat before continuing, "As of now, we don't have much to go on. Except the fact that the fourty-five caliber shell casings that were recovered from the scene of this tragic incident are particularly the same as those recovered at the scene of a serial homicide case that occurred almost a decade ago down in the Cypress Hills housing complex. And although I have recently received confirmation that the individuals responsible for that massacre are still Wards of the State and are serving their well deserved terms of incarceration, I still want unrelentless pressure applied to that locale!"

Sergeant Sullivan paused again and allowed his icy blue eyes to roam throughout the sea of police officers in the room. Then leaning forward so everyone was sure to hear his final statement loud and clear, he raised his voice a pitch higher and said, "I want to strongly advise you all to proceed with extreme caution and to remain highly alert out there! Remember...we are dealing with some extremely dangerous people who obviously have no regard or respect for law enforcement!" Finally, Sergeant Sullivan said, "Okay guys, that is all for now. You are dismissed."

As the large crowd of officers began filling out of the lineup squad room, two young homicide detectives whom had been assigned to the homicide case of Anthony McCutchen, made their way towards the sergeant, who was stepping off the podium. They weaved their way through the crowd of Officers exiting the room and waved at the sergeant. "Hey, Sergeant!" One of the young Officers shouted, "You got a minute?!"

"Yeah! What can I do for you boys?" Sergeant Sullivan replied, brushing a strand of his fire red hair from his forehead with his index and middle fingers, as the two detectives approached.

"Well, Sir..." the shorter of the two Caucasian detectives began, "we just got our hands on a video tape that we're quite sure will be of great interest to you in our quest to solve the Miller Avenue ambush of our fellow officers, and..."

"Well, what are we waiting for?!" Sergeant Sullivan frantically asked, interrupting the young detective in mid sentence. "Let's get to the projection room and see what we got!" He told him. The three then hurried off to the station's second floor projection room to view, what could turn out to be the biggest lead into solving the highly publicized case.

"Alright, it's now time!" Detective O'Keefe the shorter of the two young detectives said after inserting the tape into the VHS player and pushing the play button. They sat there and attentively watched the screen for a few minutes as vehicle after vehicle passed through a dim lit block.

"Okay now, one'a you guys please tell me what am I missing here? For christ sake!" The Sergeant asked, frantically looking from Detective O'Keefe to his partner, Detective Donnelly, obviously awaiting an answer.

"Just gimme a second, Boss." Detective O'Keefe anxiously replied as he fast forwarded the tape about twenty seconds.

"Oh my!" The Sergeant sighed with a slight nod of his head, "Very nice!" He said as he lustfully keyed in on the statuesque derriere of a woman draped in an all black sweat suit.

"Yeah Boss, I feel your energy!" Detective Donnelly said in agreement. "Even in those baggy trousers the outline of her shapely figure is apparent." He added with a conspiratorial smirk.

"What the hell!" The Sergeant suddenly shouted, witnessing how the female in the video had doused the young man she had approached with a liquid substance, causing him to react frantically. "Holyshit!" He then added, grimacing as if he himself actually felt the pain when the female lit a book of matches and tossed it onto the young man. He continued to watch as he saw the female calmly stroll away and the victim run in a zig zag fashion, consumed in flames.

"Fellas, although this video graphically depicts the horrible crime perpetrated on the young man, Anthony McCutchen, I'm afraid it's not enough. It would not be enough to proceed with a case in court, even if we do come up with the perpetrator of this horrendous crime. This video does not show a clear visual image of the woman's facial features. Any seasoned attorney would have a field day with this video, if it were to be presented at a trail!" He said, turning to the two detectives. "Okay guy." The sergeant then said, diverting his attention from the screen to look at the two young detectives. "You guys caught my attention with this showing, I need you guys to get out there and bring me back something we can take to court!"

"Wait Boss! Just watch closely!" Detective O'Keefe said with a smirk as he rewinded the tape back to the frame where Vicky had turned to walk away after setting her victim a blaze. "Get a load of this here, Boss!" He enthusiastically told him, pointing his index finger at a van that appeared cruising on the video. "That vehicle matches the description of the stolen van that our guys called in right before they were ambushed! Look at this..." he added, pointing to the bottom of the screen, "the time of this recording is only twenty-nine seconds prior to the actual ambush of our collegues, which took place just around the very next corner!"

"I tell you guys what..." the Sergeant began, "I want every collar that comes through this station house to be drilled for information! I don't give a rat's ass if it's just a purse snatching! You hear! I want'em promised a deal if they could provide information on the identity of this female. Maybe she saw the shooter's faces as they passed her by. You guys did very well!" He told them, extending his hand for them to shake. "You guys keep up the pressure!" He said with a vitalized expression across his face.

* * * * *

SHEFFIELD & HEGEMAN

The corner of Sheffield and Hegeman was sweltering with a group of guys shooting dice as customers brought drugs from Pop and his sidekick, Black Dee. Pop and Black Dee were two low level street dealers who decided to come from behind the door of their crack den to mingle with friends and enjoy the beautiful weather while they pitched their product to the local fiends.

Unbeknownst to them, three undercover surveillance vehicles sat along Hedgman Avenue occupied by two teams of narcotics officers from different branches of law enforcement agencies. They had merged together with hopes of crumbling the drug trade, at least in that area once and for all. A drug trade that was responsible for breeding cop killers in East New York.

After making a few direct undercover transactions, the narcotics officers monitored the corner of Sheffield Avenue, a well known red zone area for illegal narcotics, patiently waiting for the right moment in which to swoop down on the dealers, their steerers and lookouts. They sat in unmarked vehicles photographing and recording as swarms of fiends approached and purchased crack-cocaine.

After servicing the last customer, Pop pulled his cell phone from his front pocket and punched in some digits. A few seconds later he commenced talking into the phone, "Yeah K.G! It's me, Pop! We outta work and..."

"Nigga!" The voice on the other end interrupted, "I know who da'fuck you are! And what da'fuck did I tell your dumb ass about mentioning my mufuckin' name over the damn jack?!" K.G. admonished, barking at Pop over the line.

"You right, Homie. That's my bad." Pop softly replied.

"Just don't let dat shit happen again!" K.G. warned. "I'll be right there in five minutes!" He added before disconnecting himself.

Minutes later the narcotics Commanding Officer directed his attention to the two other law officials who occupied the unmarked police vehicles. "Alright you guys, I've seen enough! Let's get these scum bags off the streets." As he yanked the transmitting walkie talkie from his hip and gave his assisting backup team the green light to move in. The moment he had brought the communicator to his mouth he noticed a dark yellowish luxury automobile pull up along side the curb, directly in front of the two dealers. The driver of the vehicle motioned for a peddler to approach. The same peddler he had just chastised on the phone, moments ago.

"1-Charlie-9...1, Charlie-9..." The Commanding Officer repeated into his walkie talkie.

"Yeah! 1-Charlie-9, copy!" The voice on the other end replied.

"Are you guys getting this?" He asked his backup unit who were only about thirty yards away as he peered throught the dark tinted windows of the surveillance vehicle.

"Roger that!" responded the voice through the small speaker as their communication concluded.

"Okay, Joe. I want you to take a few photographs of that vehicle as well!" the Commanding Operation Officer instructed before pausing. "I got a good feeling that we might be onto something big here!" He concluded.

* * * * *

"Yo, K.G.! I wanna apologize once again for making mention of your handle over da'jack like that!" Pop said as he approached. Pop then bent at the waist and removed two large wads of ten and twenty dollar bills from the inside pocket of his butter soft leather jacket then tossed them into his boss's lap. "On e'rything I love bruh. Dat shit won't happen again!" He said.

Staring blankly ahead, maintaining his composure, K.G. responded, "Listen man, that's over with! Just be a little more mindful of how you conduct business over the phone! Especially, when you're talking to me and you'a be a'ight!" He warned him before reaching under the driver's seat to retrieve the ziplock bag of narcotics. "Here." He said, handing him the package. "I'll be back through this way in about two hours or so. You should be done movin' that by then."

"A'ight, one." Pop said, lightly bumping his fist against his boss' fist. As K.G. was leisurely pulling away from the curb, his path was cut off by one of the unmarked police vehicles occupied by the undercover cops. The vehicle came to a brusque stop in front of K.G.'s automobile, parallel with the automobile's front end, impeding forward mobility. At that precise moment the corner had been swamped by a small army of aggressive undercover officers.

A few guys took off in different directions, but the majority were not so lucky. With their guns drawn, the officers ordered them to freeze, raise their arms high and in clear view and to comply with the search procedure.

During the sweep the undercover officers seized four semi-automatic weapons, four ounces of crack-cocaine, and $16,704 in cash.   K.G., who had a slight problem with alcohol, wasn't under the influence at the time of his arrest. But, he was in possession of a bottle of Hennessy, $11,704 in cash and a small quanity of marijuana, which obviously was for personal use.   The eighteen apprehended individuals were immediately placed under arrest, read their rights and transported to the 75th precinct.

* * * * *

3015 LIBERTY AVENUE

A joint police task force was out executing search warrants all over East New York, well into the wee hours of the morning. This particular police mission was organized to apprehend suspected drug dealers belonging to a group infamously known in the neighborhood as "The Hardy Boys."

The Hardy Boys was a Latin gang who were known for pushing LSD, heroin and crack-cocaine and generating millions of dollars annually. They were known to wire the proceeds to Ponce, a major city in the western coast of their native country of Puerto Rico. Their relatives then would purchase automobiles, expensive jewelry and luxurious homes for them.

After having conducted a successful undercover transaction, authorities knocked down the steel door of their enclave and arrested two individuals who had lengthy criminal records. They were in possession of 1,300 vials of crack-cocaine, 200 tabs of acid (LSD), 47 wax envelopes containing heroin, 3 large brown bags filled with an unsubstantiated amount of U.S. currency, including the three marked $20 bills the undercover narcotics agents had used to purchase two vials of crack and four bags of heroin.

Also seized and confiscated were two illegal semi-automatic weapons and a large collection of pornography.

* * * * *

700 EUCLID AVENUE, 7:40AM

     The task force next mission was to execute a warrant at the Cypress Hills Houses. The task force raided a well known drug locale in the apartment complex ran by a gang known as "Still Notorious". The Still Notorious drug gang was a splinter group of the infamous A-Team, a viciously violent gang that terrorized the East New York neighborhood during the Eighties. The gang's members were known for driving around in flashy expensive vehicles and sporting expensive custom-made jewelry. Their criminal tentacles were said to have reached beyond the East New York neighborhood. They had a base in a twelve unit apartment complex located at 73 Broadway Avenue in the Bushwick section of Brooklyn. They were known to have seized the place from a rival drug dealer whom they had murdered after torturing him for several hours with a curling iron and sex objects.

     The crew was known to hire female couriers to transport their crack-cocaine to the upstate town of Auburn, in western New York, where their workers would sell the product out of various apartments and alleyways. The workers would then wire the proceeds back to the gang in Brooklyn. The profits from the upstate sales would range from $20,000 to $25,000 a day. The Still Notorious gang was controlled by the iron fists of four joint leaders. One of the accused ring leaders of the gang, Ernest "B-Hov" Jones, age 26, had been arrested in the Forrest Housing Projects in the Bronx, where he had been running a second drug ring. Three of the other ring leaders were being sought. They were known as Elson "Lil El" Richards, age

27, Naquan "Quannie" Russell, age 28 and Trevor "Puzzle" Nixon, age 28. Each had criminal records and their rap sheets read like a menu at the fastfood restaurants, long and extensive, including the shootings of seven undercover narcotics officers on two seperate occasions. One of the two shootings involved three undercover narcotics officers out of the 75th Precinct in 1990 and another in 1997, where they shot it out with four undercover narcotics officers out of the 73rd Precinct.

Since 1990, the notorious gang and others had organized and managed a profitable interstate crack-cocaine distribution ring that law enforcement agencies set out to crush once and for all. But, things would not go as planned, and huge horrific exchanges of gunfire battles had ensued.

"NEWS FLASH: CHANNEL 6 EYEWITNESS NEWS"

"Good morning. I'm Sharice Williford reporting to you live from the station. A police sergeant and two detectives were wounded during a gun battle with drug dealers in a buy and bust operation in the Cypress Hills Houses in the East New York section of Brookyn.

Authories said, Detectives John Shaw, Barry Wiggins and Sergeant Gregory Shwartz were shot during a fierce gun battle with five suspected drug dealers early this morning inside of a hallway in the housing complex, located on Euclid Avenue. Three of the suspects were wanted in connection with a drug related homicide which occurred in the neighboring Bushwick section. They have been identified as Elson Richards, Naquan Russell and Trevon Nixon. One suspect was shot and killed by an undercover narcotics officer.

The shooting occurred after undercover narcotics officers bought two ounces of crack-cocaine from the suspects. Then

Sergeant Scwartz and his eight man backup team moved in to make the arrests. The buy and bust operation did not go as originally planned and the officers were forced to adapt to the fast moving change of events that transpired. Detective Shaw fired eleven rounds from his service weapon and Detective Wiggins and Sergeant Shwartz each discharged seven rounds before they were overwhelmed by simultaneous barrages of gunfire.

Two bullets struck Detective Shaw in the torso after having penetrated through his service issued bullet proof vest. Detective Wiggins was shot twice in the left thigh and once in the right side of his hip. They both remain in stable condition at Kings County Hospital. Sergeant Shwartz was instantly paralyzed after suffering three gun shot wounds to his lower back, which severed four inches of his spinal column.

A spokesperson for the police department said, that the fatally wounded suspect had a lengthy criminal record that included arrests for gun possession, attempted murder, menacing with a deadly weapon and possession of a controlled substance. The other four suspects connected to the shooting all fled the scene and are still at large. Sending you now to Bob Cheyney. Once again, I'm Sharice Williford, reporting live from Channel 6, Eyewitness News."

"Thank you Sharice. Good morning. I'm Bob Cheyney, reporting live from Kings County Hospital here in Brooklyn. With me here is Detective Wiggins from the Tactical Narcotics Squad and who was wounded during the buy and bust operation. His team came under fire several hours ago in a Brooklyn housing complex, where two other officers were also seriously wounded as well. "Detective, if you may, could you please briefly explain what went wrong during the undercover operation?" The reporter asked the wounded officer before directing his hand-held microphone towards him.

With glassy eyes that seemed unfocused and his gaze appearing to be thousands of miles away, the officer spoke into the microphone. "Well..." he said, pausing to gulp, "me and my partner, Detective Bowen, were assigned to effect the arrest of two men who had just sold drugs to another undercover officer in the foyer of the building. My partner acted a bit hasty and drew his weapon before signaling me, which by the way is standard procedure. When all of a sudden, one of the suspects over powered him and was able to disarm him of his weapon. As I went for my own weapon, I noticed, out of the corner of my eye, three men trotting down the narrow hallway with machine gun type weapons.

At that point, my partner ran out of the building, so I pursued ~ dashing behind him and alerted the backup squad. All of a sudden gunfire erupted seemingly from everywhere," the detective again paused a moment, grimacing in pain, before he continued. "I will find it very difficult to go back to work for the police department again. This incident has caused me a great deal of pain and a terrible amount of emotional stress." He said from his hospital bed. Then he seemed to finally find his focus and said, "I'll tell you something, those dealers moved with the swiftness and proficiency of military trained combatants in the heat of war. And you know combat can be really traumatic. So, it's gonna be a long and slow recovery for me and I don't know if I'll ever be able to get over the trauma I experienced today."

"Alright, Sir," a nurse interjected, "he needs to get some rest now." She said concluding the interview.

"Okay. There you have it." The reporter said into the camera, "A brief statement of the events as they transpired from one of the officers wounded by dealers during an undercover police drug sting...that went bad. I'm Bob Cheyney from Channel 6 Eyewitness News. Back to you guys at the studio..."

Chapter 21

BACK FROM COPPIN xxx

*T*he limo was waiting for them, just like clock work, when they pulled into the station in Fayette, Alabama. And to their surprise, the rest of the Angels hopped out and helped with the luggage.

"God damn, y'all must'a tore the mufuckin' mall down before y'all left Miami!" Vicky exclaimed when she noticed all the extra suitcases.

"Yeah well, I hope they brought something back for a bitch like me!" Michelle chimed as they loaded the luggage into the limo.

"Oh, trust me..." Latesha began, "there's something in all six of these bags for everyone'a you motherfucking bitches!"

"Oh yeah! What?" inquired Goldie, as they slid into their seats.

"A hundred and ten bricks!" She shot back with a serious expression on her face, which caused the Angels to fall completely silent.

Feeling jubilant about the weight she was in possession of, Latesha fell back, closed her eyes, and immediately slipped into deep thought, until they reached the hotel. After taking hot showers, the Angels got all dolled up, hopped back into the limo and headed to the club to treat themselves to a night of enjoyment out in the lime light of the South. They each packed firearms which they snugged into their clutch bags.

Once they made their entrance into the club, they strolled to the bar with pure confidence. They ordered six bottles of Corona beer then headed to a booth along the wall. Sitting at the table, they blazed a blunt and took in the surroundings, enjoying the blaring music coming from the club's sound system. The DJ, Sly Williams was spinning the latest jams and had the whole club jumping. What seemed like a short time later, Ronnie entered the club with his boys, Sparky and Smokey closely following. They navigated through the crowded establishment until they spotted Latesha waving them towards her table.

"Sparky!" She squealed affectionately when they approached. They shared a long effectionate embrace which with the exception of Kacky, who knew Sparky for years, caused the other Angels to curiously peer at each other.

"Y'all, this is Sparky!" She said before adding, "Every time our family reunion is held down here, he always be try'na holla at a bitch!"

"Yeah!" he agreed, as they broke their embrace. "And she always shut'a country boy on down, too!" He added in his southern drawl, before greeting Kacky with a hug and a peck on the cheek. He then went down the line shaking hands with the rest of the Angels, as he took in their names.

"Oh shit!" The girls yelled out in unison when they heard the DJ play the old hit song, 'I Wanna Thank You' by Alicia Myers. Latesha hurriedly grabbed Sparky by the hand and hit the dance floor, pursued by Vicky and Ronnie.

"Here Smokey, kill it!" Kacky said, swaying to the music as she passed what was left of the blunt to Smokey, just before he trekked toward the bar.

"Put it on'em Vicky!" Goldie yelled out over the music causing the girls to take notice of Vicky as she swayed and shasayed seductively to the music, pressing her ass firmly against Ronnie's dick.

"A'ight now..." Ronnie whispered into her ear, "don't start nothing you aint' gon' let me finish."

Glancing over her right shoulder, she looked at him with gleaming, lustful eyes, that were stimulated by the weed and said, "Why wouldn't I let'chu finish?"

"I'm just making sure we're still on the same page, Babygirl, that's all!" Ronnie quickly shot back, grinding even harder into her backside.

"Calm that dick down, big guy! We got all night!" She purred at him upon feeling the erection through his jeans.

A few feet away, Latesha was waving her hands through the air as if she was signaling to an airplane, obviously enjoying the music. By the way she was gyrating her body up against Sparky one could have been lead to believe that they were actually screwing on the dance floor. Their bodies were rubbing up on each other in sync, as Sparky clutched her tightly around her slim waist.

"So what it do, Shawty? I'm try'na get in'ta sum'thin' ta'night. You know what I'm tawkin' 'bout?" He asked her in his deep southern drawl.

"Please Sparky, what the hell you gonna do with this here, huh?" She said as she grind then dipped on his dick, stimulating her clit on his seemingly long erection.

"I can give it a lot'a pleasure, passion, and make you speak in tongues, if you come on and get wit' me and allow me to!" He answered as he lightly caressed her ass.

Her body quickly responded to his light caress, as goose bumps formed all over her body, causing her to shiver. Suddenly, she felt a light stream of girly juice damp her Victoria Secret underwear. She didn't need any further convincing when she felt strong sexual urges engulfing her. She immediately took his hand and lead him towards the exit.

"Where y'all going?" Althea asked, crossing their paths upon returning from the ladies room. Although she asked the question in a general sense, her focus was upon Latesha.

"Um...we're just gonna go sit in the limo for a little while. We'll be right back." She quickly answered. "Y'all just try not to tear nothing up in here while I'm gone!" She added.

"Humph! Nah bitch. . .Y'all just try not ta' tear nothing up in da'back of da' limo!" Althea sarcastically snapped back taking puffs of her Newport cigarette, striking a defiant pose and diverted her eyes back and forth between the two, than sashaying off with a smirk. As she walked away, Sparky could not help but admire how her ass gracefully swayed in her skin-tight alligator leather jeans that she had tucked into her matching four inch cowgirl boots, which Sparky thought complimented her elegant style.

He quickly dismissed his thoughts of Althea and concentrated back on Latesha who was determinately leading him towards the exit and to the limo parked outside the club. Upon entering the limo, Latesha handed the chauffeur a CD of mixed slow jams that she had brought with her from New York and instructed him to keep the tinted divider up. She then turned towards Sparky and in a seductive raspy voice said, "Now...what was that you were saying inside?"

"I... I..." Sparky began, unable to get another word out. He was completely mesmerized as she seductively stared deep into his eyes and sensually licked her beautiful full lips. Latesha immediately took the initiative as she slowly leaned in and kissed him, drowning any further words he may have attempted to utter. She lustfully opened her mouth and passionately kissed him and Sparky quickly responded. He strongly embraced her and pulled her closer towards him as he allowed her tongue to deliciously swim in his mouth.

"Mmm...!" Latesha sensually moaned as Sparky commenced to suck on her tongue with wanton lust. He allowed his hands to worm down her back until they reached her thigh, then raised her silk Gucci dress over her head and relieved her of it. Latesha wasn't wearing a bra so he quickly began to gently yet firmly caress her volumptuous breasts, lightly tugging at her nipples with his fingers. He then massaged her ass, cupping her buttocks with his strong hands.

"Ahhh...!" Latesha lightly moaned as she felt his strong hands on her ass. Instinctively, she allowed her hands to wander down to his pelvic area and when she felt his immensive hard on, she gasped. "Oh my, god!" She exclaimed as she felt Sparky's dick growing inside his trousers. She grasped a hold of it and felt along its huge size. Again, she gasped, "Aahhh," as she massaged it through his trousers and sucked on his tongue more vigorously. She began getting more and more excited, desparately fumbling with the zipper of his trousers, until she finally unzipped him and reached in with a firm grip on his penis and tugged it out of its' confines. Instantly she broke off their kiss in order to look down at the package she had just retrieved from his pants. "God damn, mufucka!" She exclaimed, "You packin' for real!"

Openly admiring his protruding member with wanton lust and through glossy eyes. Sparky immediately unbuckled his belt, raised up from the seat, tugged at his pants and underwear, bringing them down around his knees and fully exposed himself. Latesha gulped and bit down into her bottom lip, completely mesmerized by the tremendous size of his organ. Still looking down at his dick, she said, "Oh my god, nigga! This is a fucking anaconda you got attached to you." Then she instinctively licked her lips and dove down and kissed the crown of his massive dick before proceeding to lick down the entire shaft. "Mmm..." She sighed, as though she had just tasted candy. Then greedily opened her mouth wide, wrapped her full lips around it and sucked in his dick, desperately attempting to engulf it all at once.

"Aarrrgh!... Oh shit Baby! Yeah!" Sparky exclaimed as he felt her warm sensual lips wrap around his penis.

"Oh yeah! Suck this dick Baby. Aarrrgh!!..." He cried out, as Latesha began making slurping noises as she sucked his tool, bobbing her head up and down with gusto.

"Uummm. . . ", moaning, she raised her head on occasion to suck at the swollen head, before gulping its' stem back into her mouth. Sparky was going wild with pleasure gripping a handful of hair as her lips slid up and down his dick with lustful desire. He then reached over her back with his free hand and through the slit of her thong inserted his finger into her wet pussy.

Latesha moaned and began to suck on his dick vigorously and with great fervor as if determined to take it all into her mouth, but found it difficult to swallow when she felt the crown of his organ at the back of her throat. She was forced to ease up on her desperate attempt and settled for what she already had in her mouth as she continued to administer an impeccable blow job.

"Uuhhh...Uhhh..." She managed to moan, despite having a mouthful of cock. When she felt Sparky's finger exit her soaked pussy and brush the rim of her ass, she squirmed. His finger found the delicate entrance of her asshole. "Oooohh...!" She squealed and her lips locked down on his dick. Sparky felt as though a suction cup had suddenly clamped on his penis.

"Arrrgghh...! Arrrgghh!!" He cried out, as she sucked on his dick like a baby on its' mother's breast. He felt he was about to bust off, so he pulled her reluctant head up. Her mouth released his dick with a pop sound and she looked at him with wild lustful eyes as if disturbed that she was interrupted from her dick sucking. Sparky quickly leaned in and kissed her in the mouth then began to suck on her neck.

"Ooooh..." She purred as Sparky removed her thong and gently pushed her down on the car seat. She immediately spread her legs wide open and Sparky dove in to eat her pussy.

He placed his hands under her ass cheeks and raised her vagina up to him. "Ahhh..." Latesha cried out, as she felt his tongue lick along the slit of her pussy than commenced to suck on her pussy lips. Latesha desperately lunged forward and fed him more pussy. She anticipated the penetration of his tongue into her coochie and began to squirm and gyrate attempting to accelerate the process. She even desperating grabbed his head harder against her pussy. His lips pressed hard against her coochie but he only kept licking at the surface.

"Aarrrgghh...! Shit...! Come on Baby! Eat it! Eat my pussy!" She sighed and begged in desperation. "Eat it...mmm...yeeaahhh...mu'fucka! Ee...eeat my fuckin' pu...pussy!" She cried out, pressing his face harder and harder onto her crotch. Sparky finally inserted his tongue into her pussy and Latesha thought she would die.

"Oooohh...! Ooooh....! Ye...yes! Yes! Baby, yes! Aarrrgh...! Oh my god! Oh my fuckin' god! Yes muthafucka! Yes! Aahhh...!" She yelled in ecstasy, as she felt Sparky clinging onto her clit and sucking on it like it was a cherry. Her juices came flowing out like a river as she heard and viewed Sparky slurping up her essence. She began coming again and uncontrollably screamed out. "Aahhh...! Shit! OOOooh my god!! You're drinkin' my fuckin' juices! Oh shit! YES!! YES!! Drink it! Ahhh...! Shhiit YES!!!" Latesha cried out, squirming and thrashing about as Sparky held on tight and lapped up her out flowings.

"God, damn Momma, you sho' got some pretty good ass tastin' pussy!" Sparky told her as he rose up his head from her coochie, licking his pussy soaked lips while holding her legs open and lovingly staring down into her pussy.

Latesha felt so appreciated that she lustfully kissed him on the mouth. She immediately tasted herself in his mouth and instantly squirted a stream of girly juice again.

Then stared into his eyes and hungrily said, "Fuck me Sparky! Please fuck me now!"

"Oh I intend to pretty Momma!" He said as he placed his bloated dick head on the opening crevice of her pussy, brushed his dick along the slit then plunged inside of her. Latesha's mouth flew open as if the endowed cock was going to come out through it. She gasped as she felt his dick penetrate through her pussy lips. She held onto him and wrapped her legs around him and pushed him further into her.

"Oh my god! Yes!!" She exclaimed with her mouth wide open as she felt his dick rip through the foyer of her vagina and sink deep into her pussy. "AAHH FFUCK! YES! YES!!" She loudly moaned. "AArrrgh! Mothafucka! Yes! Fuck that dick into me!" She kept encouraging as Sparky plunged into her. "Arrrgh! Yeah! Oh my fuckin' god! Give it to me! Aahhh! Shit mufucka! YES! AAHHH...!!" She cried.

Sparky was plunging dick into her with gusto. As he pumped into her with savage thrusts, he groaned, "Aarrrgh! Aarrgghh! Here Momma, take this!" He told her as he fed her more and more dick. Latesha was rising up to meet his every thrust, when suddenly Sparky seemed to thrust her legs further back and plunged his dick further into her.

"Ahhh! Ahhh!" Latesha screamed as she felt impaled by the massive cock. "Oh my god!" She cried out, as she thought she had taken all of his dick into her, but more and more just kept entering her pussy. "Aahhh! Fuck! Aahhh! Oh sss...shiiit! Oooo! Yes!" She wildly screamed and yelled, as she began cumming again with tremendous intensity. Sparky did not let up. He quickly swung her legs and spun her around doggie style.

"Aahhh!" Latesha was sighing when all of a sudden she felt his dick invade her pussy and plunge deep into her again. "Arrrgh! Aahhh! Ssss! Aah, ah. Yes. Yes." She managed to gasp as she felt his dick ramming into her love tunnel and slamming against her inner walls.

"Yeah! Yeah! Oh my god! I feel it so deep inside'a me! Oh shit! Ooooww...oooo! Ahh! Yes! I'm cumming again! Ahhh! Sssss!" She hissed as she began discharging more pussy juice. "Oh my god! Fuck! Let me get on top!" She quickly told him as she squirmed away from his dick. Sparky layed on his back and she mounted him, grabbed his dick at the base and sank down onto it. She instantly gasped, "Aahh!" and began to bounce and grind on his dick, taking the entire length deep inside of her.

"Arrrgh! Shit! Yes Momma! Ride this dick!" Sparky encouraged her. Latesha was lost in lustful desire as she continued to viciously bounce up and down, at times stopping at the base to gyrate and grind her pelvis against his. Suddenly she stiffened and her body began to spasm, "Ah shit! Fuck! Ahhh!" She groaned and moaned, as she released a torrent of girly juices onto his pubic hairs.

Sparky reached and cupped her breast as he bucked, sending more dick into her. Then in one swift motion, he sat up and began to suck on her breasts and Latesha began to bounce down harder onto his dick. He then spun her and again placed her in the doggie style position. She arched her ass invitingly and sighed. Sparky rose on the ball of his feet hovered over her then stabbed down with his dick sending it into her in one long thrust. Latesha groaned as she felt the huge cock entering her. Sparky continued to stab his dick straight down into her pussy with deep vicious strokes. He placed his palms on top of her ass, elevated himself and plunged deep down into her. Latesha stiffened up momentarily as she felt his entire dick inside of her, then she let out a gasp as Sparky seemed to go buck wild.

He began to thrust, pump, and plunge his dick into her from so many angles that Latesha thought she would pass out from the pleasure. "OOHHHH! YES! Bury that dick in meeee! Yes, yes! Fuck!" She cried out. Suddenly

Sparky gripped onto her tight and let out a vicious animal growl as he plunged in hard one last time then pulled out and spent his cum on her ass cheeks.

"Mmmm...." Latesha moaned, when she felt the hot sperm on her ass. As they laid there spent from their wild sex, she thought she heard Sparky still sighing and smiled as she realized that the sound was coming from the front of the limo. "Sshh... Listen." She quietly told Sparky as they heard the chauffeur unable to surpress his moans. They laughed, realizing that he must have been jerking off to the sounds of their love making.

Latesha quickly cleaned up and got dressed. Before exiting the limo, Sparky reached into his pocket, extracted the keys to the rented Ford Taurus he had picked up earlier for Kacky and handed them to Latesha. Then they climbed out of the limo and headed back into the club.

From the entrance they could see that all the girls, except Vicky, were now at the bar enjoying their second round of Coronas.

"I'm'a run to the men's room right quick. I'll get up wit'chu in a minute!" Sparky told her, as Latesha continued to make her way towards the bar.

"Where's Vicky?" She asked once she approached the girls.

"Humph!" Goldie sighed. She then nodded her head gesturing towards Vicky, who was on the dance floor bumping and grinding with Ronnie. Latesha followed her eyes and locked in on Vicky.

"Yeah, look at her, grinding up on your cousins' dick like'a thirsty heifer in heat!" Michelle said before taking a sip of her drink.

"Bitch! I know damn well you ain't up in here talking 'bout somebody grinding on one'a they cousin's dick? Didn't Lil El send your ass back to us a couple'a days ago after giving you a serious dick lashing!" Goldie joked causing the girls to burst into laughter.

"I don't know what the hell you laughing at Latesha, with ya slick ass! Didn't you just get off something stiff?" Althea remarked.

"Oh Al, please! We all peeped her sneaky ass! She wasn't that damn slick!" Kacky chimed.

There humorous moment was interrupted when two well dressed guys rolled in and caught their attention.

"Give everybody a round on me!" Shouted T-Bird, a well known baller from the neighboring State of Mississippi, which was less than an hour from Fayette. T-Bird always came to the Zodiac stuntin' like that nigga "Baby" from Cash Money Records. He was accompanied by his ever present partner, "Bobby Lee". After making his way to the bar, the bartender handed T-Bird a chilled bottle of Moet. Sparky merged from the restroom with squinting eyes and rubber-necking around the party people and hollered, "T-Bird! Is dat you nigga!?" causing the tall carmel complexioned brother, donned in a burgundy two piece linen suit and a diamond encrusted medallion hanging from a platinum necklace, to turn towards him.

"Who else could it be, Playboy!" He replied, extending his hand to give Sparky a pound. Sparky then reached in and gave him a masculine hug and said, "I see you making your presence known!"

"Yeah! You know how I put it down! But, look here, get with me later on, before I head back down bottom. I'm'a go holla at an old buddy of mine!"

"A'ight player! You go do yo thang!" Sparky replied, as the baller slid off to a booth table that was occupied by another individual.

Every time T-Bird came through Fayette, he always showed a lot of love to the people. Each time he stepped foot into the club he always bought a round for every individual in attendance. He was definitely a people person.

'Yo Sparky!" Kacky called, motioning with her head for him to approach. When he got close, she whispered and asked, "Who's dat cat you were just hollering at?"

"Oh, that was T-Bird and his pot'na, Bobby Lee." He replied. "They'a couple'a ballers from outta Mississippi. They always come through here from time to time, showin' a lil love."

"Oh yeah? So what they moving?" A very curious Latesha chimed.

"Ah, you aint got'ta worry 'bout nuttin' shawty. He aint moving that fire!" Sparky assured her, referring to weed. "They strictly move china white." He added, unaware that he was in the presence of the biggest cocaine dealers and distributers his country ass would ever lay eyes on in this life time.

Latesha intended to keep it that way and so she made a mental note to have Ronnie slide the Mississippians a sample of the product she brought with her to the club in the hopes of reeling in some clientele.

"Is that right?" Goldie interjected, as she spun, turning left to right on her bar stool.

"Oh yeah! They definitely on'a come up!" He said.

Vicky and Ronnie, who were by now drenched in sweat from all the dancing, joined them at the bar, once the song ended.

"Shit! Y'all must'a got in a serious cardio workout over in that damn, hot ass corner!" Althea sarcastically said, looking from one to the other with a smirk.

Latesha took the opportunity to lay down the ground work to make an investment for future profits. Because Sparky happened to be amongst their small group, she chose to talk to her cousin privately and out of his homeboy's ear range.

"Yo, Cuz...!" She hollered, shooting off the bar stool. "Let me holla at chu for a minute!" She pulled Ronnie off a few feet away and said, "Listen, there's a couple'a cats who rolled up in the club not too long ago. Sparky said they are ballers from Mississippi. Anyway..."

"I know exactly who you're talking 'bout." He interrupted.

"Well..., I'm quite sure you do. Now let me finish." Latesha snapped, looking from side to side, making sure no one was within hearing distance. She then sarcastically said, "Thank you!" and continued with her intended spiel. "Now here's the deal. First of all, your man Sparky got diarrhea of the mouth and that's bad for business. So, whatever goes on between you and us girls, stays between us. I understand that he's gonna be assisting you with moving the Chem and I'm cool with that. But, that's not what I want to discuss. The main reason I pulled you over is because I'm try'na get in that nigga, T-Bird's pockets. And I'm'a need you to giv'em this." She said, handing him a tiny plastic bag of cocaine she had pulled out from her clutch purse. "Tell'em that if he likes the product, there's plenty more where it came from and that I'm open for negotiation."

"Is that it?"

"Yeah, that's all."

"A'ight! I'm'a get on that right now, Cuz!" He assured her, than navigated his way between the hoards of party people and headed towards T-Bird's booth.

Latesha went and joined her clique and positioned herself at the bar where she would still be in range to view Ronnie as he took care of business. She was suddenly startled by the high pitch voice of Sparky shouting.

"Ah, Latesha, what'chu won't ta' drink?" He asked her, motioning for the female bartender.

"Just get me whatever they're drinking!" She said over her shoulder, not wanting to take her eyes off her potential future customers. At that moment she noticed T-Bird open the small baggie Ronnie had handed him and dip his index finger in it for a taste of the product. Almost suddenly he pulled his head back and looked amazed as the cocaine instantly froze the tip of his tongue.

"Yeah! That's what the fuck I'm talking 'bout!" She thought to herself before Ronnie turned and nodded in her direction. T-Bird then waved her over. Latesha approached the booth and two minutes later she returned to the bar.

"Shit...!" Goldie cursed, "What kind'a business meeting was that? You didn't even holla at him that long!"

"Well, like I told you before, Gee, when you got coke as potent as ours, the product speaks for itself. Shit, the nigga's tongue is frost bit right now! You better ask some mufuckin' body!" She bragged, snapping her fingers.

"So, what's the verdict, then?" Althea inquired.

"The verdict is that the nigga was coppin' his shit at twenty-two grand a brick, from up in Mobile, Alabama!"

"Say word!" Her sister chimed in.

"Word! And from what he told me, that shit ain't nowhere near as frosty as our shit! So, he gonna cop five bricks at nineteen geez a brick. His people should be here shortly to drop him the bread!" She said. "And being that there's too many people mingling outside, were gonna make the transaction in the Terrace Park's parking lot. So, Althea, you and Kacky take the rental. Here take these." She said, fumbling through her clutch bag and handing her the keys to the car.

EXACTLY FOURTY SEVEN MINUTES LATER. . .

Althea eased in next to the complex's community mail boxes situated at the parking lot's entrance and killed the engine. She and Kacky then pulled out their matching ten millimeters, checked to make sure they had full magazines and a slug in the chamber, then slid low into their seats. They sat there literally unnoticed by T-Bird, who was at the wheel of a cream colored Lexus GS400. The ride was equipped with Peanut Butter colored interior seating and twenty four inch rims. His partner, Bobby Lee, was riding shotgun as they swerved into the parking lot. Peering first left then right, they cruised slowly through the spacious landscape until they noticed Latesha, who was parked in a space reserved for the handicapped and waving them over. T-Bird backed into a space two car lengths away from her, exited his vehicle, leaving the engine running and casually strolled over in her direction clutching a black plastic handbag, half filled with the buy money. T-Bird handed her the bag through the drivers' side window and she clicked on the vehicle's interior lights. Then fiddled through each stack of bills until she was satisfied that the entire $95,000 was all there, before signaling the girls who then exited the rental with the five kilos in tow, cautiously watching for anything suspicious; as they made strides towards the drop point.

After the transaction, the girls stalled a moment, as they stood there in the parking lot, in order to put some distance between them and their new customer before they climbed back into their respective vehicles.

"I'm'a take this bread back to the Telly." Latesha said, before pulling out of the condominium complex's parking lot with her sister and Althea closely following behind. They merged onto S.W. 5th Street and headed towards Knight Avenue.

* * * * *

"Look at that motherfucker. He can't handle that shit!" Vicky exclaimed when she and the girls noticed the chauffeur as they were exiting the club. Ronnie had only a few moments ago given him a sample joint and he was bent over coughing his lungs out.

"Are you a'ight?" Goldie asked him, concerned while Michelle and Vicky found it humorous.

"Lawd ha' mercy! Guh..., guhh..., guhh..., dis dat shit right here! God dammit!" He managed to force out in between bouts of coughs. "Um, um, um...dats'a mufuckin' lung assassinator right thurr!" He continued, in his southern accent, extending the joint out in front of him and studying it through glazed eyes.

"So I guess you like it then?" She asked, smiling at him as he struggled to catch his breath. But all he could do was nod his head in approval. Suddenly Vicky's cell phone began blaring in her purse. She answered it on the third ring, once her laughter subsided. "Holla at 'cha, girl!" She said into the phone.

"Yeah. This your boy from New Yiddy." Said the voice on the other end. She immediately recognized Nesto's voice.

"What's up?" She asked. Knowing something had to be wrong for Nesto to be calling while they were out of town.

"The blue coats are forcing unemployment out here. And it's damn near dry!" He told her. "Almost everybody has taken a heavy hit." Nesto was speaking in codes as he made reference to all the sweeps by law enforcement which was causing a lot of dealers to take major losses, creating a demand for product to reach an all time high.

"A'ight. Say no more! I guess we're gonna have to cut our lil vacation short!" She replied, before concluding their conversation.

As she was putting her cell phone back into her purse, she noticed Althea and Kacky easing up the block in the rental and heading in their direction. Then all of a sudden, her attention diverted to an old-timer, who had just exited the club ranting and raving while focusing on her and the other Angels.

"Somebody better let these bitch ass hoes know...this hood belongs to Bobby McCloud!" The old-timer was saying, shifting his head left and right, sweeping the sweltering crowd that was loitering outside the club. "And they outta god damn pocket, puttin' they shit out on my motherfuckin' streets!" He added with a menancing snarl across his face as he glared at them up and down, while walking towards his souped-up money green Chevy pickup.

Bobby McCloud was feared more than loved in Fayette. He controlled the entire town when it came to supplying weed. But his product wasn't of high grade. Most weed-heads only purchased from him to save a thirty minute ride down to Tuscaloosa. He had the town on lockdown and the Angels were now conquering his territory to the extent that his product began, practically over night to move at a snail's pace. Kacky and Althea took the whole scene in as they shot Vicky a knowing stare.

"Ah, fuck him!" Vicky barked, waving her hand dismissively at the old-timer. "Everybody back inside, the drinks are on me!" She yelled to the gathered crowd, who she had moments earlier instructed Ronnie to pass out sample joints to.

Bobby McCloud climbed into his car and drove off without a worry in the world. Unbeknownst to him, Kacky and Althea had been tailing him for about a mile and a half. Then, pulling along side of him, on a quiet dirt road, Kacky leaned out her passenger window, extended her ten millimeter and pinched the trigger twice. The shots hit him directly in the face just as he turned his head towards her, instantly killing him sending his truck swerving into a light pole, causing his body to eject through the windshield, leaving him sprawled out on the hood of his vehicle with three-quarters of his face gone.

"No more Bobby McCloud." Althea mumbled, looking into the rearview mirrow as she sped off at sixty-five miles per hour, down the deserted road. When they reached Third Way, S.W., Kacky shouted, "When motherfuckers sleep on these Angles, they wake the fuck up in hell!"

Chapter 22

LET'S MAKE A DEAL

The raid was a partial success for the Narcotics Division of the 75th Precinct. The undercover officers made dozens of arrests among which appeared KG who was uncooperatively before the desk sergeant in handcuffs, complaining about the illegality of his arrest and requesting to speak with his attorney.

"What's your name?" Asked the desk sergeant as KG stood there before him in the company of the arresting officer.

"*Maan*, I ain't telling you shit! I know my god damn rights, too!" He angrily responded. "I know I have the right to remain silent and to consult with an attorney before I am subjected to any questioning! So, the only thing I have to say to you is that I wonna call my mufuckin' lawyer and not now, but *right* now!"

KG always had the bad habit of misplacing his wallet but this happened to be the one time he was glad that the item which contained his identification documents was no where to be found. He had a good reason for not wanting to reveal his identity.

"I'm gonna ask you again, Boy!" Sergeant Sullivan told him, leaning over the precinct's arrest processing desk, while pointing his index finger inches from his face. "Now...what is your name, young man?" KG remained adamant and refused to answer him.

"He wants to be a real hard ass, Boss!" The arresting officer told the desk sergeant, while clutching the handcuffed KG hard by the arm.

"Alright big shot, we'll know who the hell you are soon enough!" The sergeant said.

KG had been serving a lengthy prison term while the world of technology had been rapidly advancing. He had no idea how advanced the world of technology had become. The days of waiting over 72 hours for the processing of fingerprints and to discover the identity of perpetrators were long gone. Also over, were the days when fugitives could make bail before their true identity were positively confirmed. New technology relied on a digital identification system which took only seconds to reveal the identity of any person processed through the criminal justice system.

The new ID system only required a prisoner to place his palm on the surface of the computer screen and it would automatically process the fingerprints. KG was ordered to place his hand on the screen. As his palm was being scanned, he was mentally scheming about ways to get around the arrest. KG's true identity along with his entire crimnal history was coming across a fifty inch screen right in front of the sergeant.

"Well, well, well!" Sergeant Sullivan repeated, as he viewed the screen before him. "Now that we know who you are, let's get down to business! From what I can see here..." He said, while viewing the screen's contents, "It seems that you're on parole and owe the state another three and a half years. And that does not include the time you are facing on the current charges. Which I can guarantee would run consecutive to your parole time! Now do you *still* want to play hardball? Let me make it more clearer to you! You are facing charges for criminal possession of a control substance, driving under the influence of drugs and alcohol and driving without a license. And I'm quite sure that if we continue to dig, we will come up with a slew of other charges we can make stick! So tell me tough guy, you want to take your chances and continue to play hardball with us or are you willing to cooperate?"

Thinking to himself, KG began to weigh his options and decided to inquire. "What kind'a cooperation are we talking about here?" Knowing full well that he was expected to give someone up.

"Well, I'm willing to make a deal with you if you can help us out with something!" The sergeant told him.

KG again took a moment to consider. He thought about all the money he was making out in the streets and about how much money he would lose if he were to go back to jail. So he decisively snapped out of his reverie and said, "Okay! What do I have to do?"

"Hey, Johnny!" The sergeant called to a fellow officer, "Escort this guy up to the projection room then page Detectives O'Keefe and Donnelly so they can debrief him!" Sergeant Sullivan commanded.

"Sure thing, Boss!" The officer responded.

Chapter 23

CAPTURED

After a few nights of enjoyment in the South, it felt great to be back in New York, Goldie thought, as the song, "Your Precious Love" by the late songstress, Linda Jones played low throughout her spacious condo. She was comfortably laying back on her living room sofa with her head propped up against cushiony pillows and reading "The Ultimate Sacrifice" a best selling book by Anthony Fields , it was one of, if not the hottest novel in book stores today. Her thoughts were startled by the ringing of her phone. Placing the book on the coffee table, she answered just as the second ring was subsiding.

"Yeah! What's up?" She said as she adjusted the receiver on her shoulder with her head cocked to the side.

"Yeah. It's me, Althea!" The speaker on the other end of the phone announced.

"Bitch! I know who it is! I got caller I.D.! And why the hell are you calling me so damn early for!?" Goldie playfully barked.

"Shit! I've been trying to reach Latesha for the last ten minutes now. She ain't answering her cell phone. The bitch probably bouncing up and down on some young nigga'z ding-a-ling, this early in the morning, with her cougar ass." Althea chuckled.

"Girl shut up! Latesha is at the health spa, steam bathing like she always do on Thursday morning. Now if you were doing more thinking and less drinking this early in the morning, you would have remembered that." Goldie sarcastically said before adding, "Why, what's going on?"

"Our good friend got captured!" Althea replied with sadness in her voice.

"Who?!!" Shouted Goldie.

"Just get today's Post and flip to page four and if you hear from Latesha before I holla at her, make sure you give her the same message. I'm out." Althea said, before the line went dead.

Goldie was caught off guard by Althea's early morning phone call, but hearing that a good friend was caught made her rush to buy a New York Post newspaper to read what was going on.

* * * * *

THE NEW YORK POST

New York - Police in Costa Rica have captured an alleged drug Kingpin who was indicted in Miami Beach on charges that he distributed thousands of kilograms of cocaine throughout the Eastern part of the United States.

Costa Rica authorities state that Fernando Gaston, 57 years old, was placed on the F.B.I's Ten Most Wanted list a decade ago. Mr. Gaston was a major player in the Spanish Mafia Cartel and who in the 1980's supplied thousands of kilograms of cocaine to the now defunked notorious A-Team drug gang that terrorized the East New York section of Brooklyn. Helping them build their sophisticated million dollar a month enterprise.

Mr. Gatson is also suspected in supplying the now imprisoned murderous Dominican Wild Cowboys gang, who controlled the cocaine distribution among other illegal narcotics throughout the boroughs of Manhattan and the Bronx during the early to mid 1990's.

According to published reports, the cartel is suspected of the growing gangland violence including the beheadings of rival cartels in Costa Rica.

Mr. Gaston, a U.S. citizen who grew up in Miami Beach, Florida has been called "Cabeza" by his most trusted soldiers because of his large head. In November of last year, a Federal Grand Jury in New York indicted Gaston and eleven other men on drug distribution, money laundering and other charges that included the apprehension of his nephew, Felix "Felo" Gonzalez, yesterday in South Beach Miami. The U.S. Government has offered a four million dollar reward for information leading to his capture and conviction. The indictment was unsealed in July.

It is unclear whether Mr. Gaston will be tried first in Costa Rica or extradited back to New York for prosecution in U.S. District courts.

* * * * *

After getting the news of Felo's arrest, Latesha made preparations to wire his relatives here in the US his share of the money. Then she began searching for a new connect.

Chapter 24

POLICE BRUTALITY

*W*aking up to a spinning room, Vicky reached for the small garbage pail next to her bed and vomited. She was constantly feeling nauseated with morning sickness for the past three days.

After brushing her teeth and taking a quick shower, she dolled herself in a hip hugging burgundy Vivian Tam mini dress and stepped into a pair of matching Gucci wedged heels. After checking herself twice and making sure all was well, she drove to the local drug store to purchase a home pregnancy test kit. Once back home she rushed to the bathroom, opened the small package, bunched her dress up around her waist, squatted over the commode, urinated on the test stick and waited for the results to reveal itself.

After a few minutes two blue strips appeared. It was then that she knew for certain what she had figured all along. She was knocked-up with Ronnie's seed. It had to have been conceived during their first session, the day of Andrew's funeral, since they wore protection during their marathon romp in the South, she thought, with a warm smile spreading across her face. She wiped herself with a handi-wipe, smoothed her dress down and headed for the door. She was on her way to surprise her clique with the good news.

* * * * *

Driving up Sutter Avenue at a respectable speed, Vicky noticed, from her rearview mirror, an unmarked Chevy Impala tailing her. The car was occupied by two Caucasians. "Damn, why da'fuck Po-Po flaggin' me down for?!" She angrily shouted to herself when they signaled for her to pull over.

She followed the Detectives direction and came to an abrupt stop directly in front of Ruby's Candy Store and waited as they approached her car at both sides. Watching them like a hawk, she slightly cracked her driver window and asked, "Umm, what's the problem Officer?" She spoke to the first Detective who approached the driver side of her car.

"Step out of the car, Ma'am!" He commanded in a tone she did not appreciate.

"Why the hell are you pulling me over for in first place?" She snapped back in the same tone of voice he had just used towards her. Before she knew what was happening, the Detectives' partner rushed from the passenger side of her car over to the drivers' side and started yanking on her door handle. Realizing it was locked, he ordered her to open it.

The first Detective, seeing the reaction of his partner, joined in by smashing her car window with his walkie-talkie and snatched her through the broken car window. Causing several cuts and bruises along her shoulder, neck and breasts, as he threw her to the concrete and proceeded to read her her Miranda rights.

"You have the right to remain silent, anything you sa..." His spiel was cut short when she interjected.

"Fuck you! You cracka' mutha'fucka!" She spat through a badly busted bottom lip that was the result of her trip to the pavement.

The detectives were placing her in the rear of their car when Nesto, who was just exiting his mother's deli, directly across the street, noticed Vicky being handcuffed. He immediately flipped open his cell phone and dialed Goldie's number. After a few rings the answering machine picked up. "Yeah, you've reached the residence of Ms. McDonald. I'm sorry I'm unavailable at the moment. But please feel free to leave a message and a number and I'll get up with you at my earliest convenience." The machine beeped at the conclusion of the recording and Nesto spoke into his cellular, "A-yo Gee!! Five -O just bagged our girl, Vicky on the ave.!" Was all he said before killing the line.

Figuring Vicky had contraband in her secret compartment, he knew an N.Y.P.D tow truck would be coming to impound her vehicle, so he waited until they drove off. Then he hopped into her car and made his way to Goldie's place to park the vehicle in her driveway before giving Kacky a call.

* * * * *

Police officers and prisoners alike openly gawked at her bodacious figure as Vicky was being escorted through the police station in handcuffs. After being told what she was arrested for, Vicky knew she had to expect the worse and hope for the best. Her mind kept replaying the events of the night over and over. The longer she sat and thought, the angrier she became.

The question of how they come to find out about Ace's murder lingered in her head as she pulled on a Newport cigarette that another female prisoner gave her, 'I'm sure somebody on the ave got word to the crew' she thought to herself as a slew of questions rushed to her head as she stood up staring at the cell bars while blowing smoke from the nicotine stick throughout the air.

Then she strolled over to the cell gate to steady her nerves. She was so caught up in her thoughts that she hadn't realized her cigarette had burned through the filter, until it burned her finger. She jumped as the sharp pain caused her to drop what was left of the cigarette and started sucking her finger. 'I guess this is my life story, one burn after another.' She thought, as she checked her finger and listened to the loud noise within the cell block.

Kacky was enjoying her morning breakfast when she got the call from Nesto. She immediately informed the rest of the Angels. Then got in contact with their lawyer and commanded her to get down to the station house A.S.A.P...

Alice Kennerly, who was one of New York's top three attorneys had a 98% acquittal resume and worked extra hard for her salary. After returning from the precinct with the particulars pertaining to Vicky's arrest and how badly beaten their comrade looked by the hands of law enforcement, the attorney began preparing a defense.

The Angels would witness their battered and bruised childhood friend's features up close and personal when they attended the arraignment proceedings the following morning. They also found out that she was bearing a child. The courtroom was packed to capacity with media personnel and supporters of Vicky.

* * * * *

The Day After Arraignment . . .

THE AMSTERDAM NEWS

A Brooklyn woman who allegedly killed a man late last month by splashing a flammable liquid on him then setting him on fire on an East New York street, was arrested yesterday and held without bail.

Vicky Davis, 31, of Brooklyn, pleaded not guilty to First Degree Manslaughter in Kings County court. According to Authories, a surveillance camera from a nearby 24 hour store captured Davis splashing the liquid from a styrofoam cup at least twice as she walked towards the man. He tried to fend off the attack. In the video a woman could be seen reaching into her clothing with her left hand for what appeared to be a book of matches that she lit before tossing atop of the victims head, setting him ablaze.

If convicted, Davis could face a maxium of twelve and a half to twenty-five years in prison.

Chapter 25

ONCE AGAIN, IT'S ON

*A*dorned in all black as they huddled in the warehouse, planning their attack on law enforcement, Latesha held front and center as the girls listened intently. "No matter what angle we look at this situation, what those cops did to Vicky is inexcusable and we're not gonna let that shit ride. Our payback to them motherfuckers is gonna be cold and calculated!" She continued, "When we get done dealing with the 75th, there's gonna be quite a few dead boys in blue left in our wake!" She assured her crew in a murderous mind state.

"Yeah!" Goldie chimed in. "And I wasn't feelin how she looked when them court officers brought her into the courtroom with her clothes ripped up n'shit with her mouth and face all swollen!"

"Riigghht!" Althea agreed, shaking her head in disbelief. "And I know she felt mad heated coming out like that too. But she tried her best to disguise her anger and discomfort just to show us that she was holding up under the circumstances."

"Yeah! But come on now!" Michelle began, "We been around each other too damn long for us not to detect when one of us is stressed. No matter how big of a fortress she tried to build around herself. She still could not hide her emotions from us, cause we all saw right through it. So with that said, whatever get back you got in mind, Latesha, I am ready to ride with you until the motherfuckin' wheels fall off!" She added with a crazed expression.

"Oh, we're most definitely gonna ride tonight. Ain't no question about that!" Latesha shot back, removing her customized ostrich skin carry-on bag from her shoulder. "Nesto blessed us with these disposable cell phones right here." She said opening the bag. "But we only need to use two tonight for our mission. Althea...you and Kacky take one. I want y'all to call the police from somewhere in the East where it's normally quiet, on some ya'-man-or-boyfriend-beat-'chu-up-type-'a-shit. If they ask if he's brandishing any type of weapon, say no! After the call take the battery out and wipe the phone down, even if you made the call with your gloves on. Then ditch them separately. Nine times out of ten they'll send just one patrol car." Latesha assured. "Do y'all thing and get back here. As for Michelle and Goldie," she said with a smirk, "y'all bitches coming with me. We gonna holla at them blue coats who's always lamping by New Lots train station at this time of the night. So everybody grip da'fuck on up and lets get some get-back for our girl, Vicky!"

* * * * *

Hit #1

After making the bogus domestic violence call to 911, Althea exited the stolen vehicle and walked the half block to the location where New York's finest would shortly show up. Entering the building, she crouched behind the ground floor staircase of the deserted hallway until she heard the crackling sounds of walkie-talkies when the two officers entered the building's foyer.

"You know, Bob...these goddam niggers just can't seem to get along with one another. Always at each other's throats." One officer said to the next as his hushed statement still managed to echo through the quiet first floor hall.

"You got that right." His partner agreed. "They should all be caged the hell up and shipped back to the jungles of Africa."

Althea smirked to herself as they headed up the

stairs knowing that her two soon to be victims were of Caucasian descent. "Oh boy," she thought, "I am gonna enjoy this." as she swiftly crept up behind them just as they approached the second landing. With her silenced weapon trained on the back of the closest officer's head, she pinched her trigger. "Pssst..." was the sound of the shot that slammed into his skull and spiraled through his dome before knocking out his two front teeth upon exiting his mouth. Quickly, Althea diverted her aim on his partner before he crumbled to the ground.

The second officer froze, momentarily paralyzed by the fear of death. He then nervously turned, looking into the eyes of the Grim Reaper who came in the form of a beautiful but deadly black woman. Frantically he attempted to remove his gun from its holster, but wasn't quick enough on the draw. Althea squeezed two well placed shots that tore into his forehead before exiting out the back of his skull and traveled through the plastered wall of the halls interior. She turned on the heels of her black Air Force One's, before the thick puddle of her victim's blood could circle around her feet, tucked her weapon into her waistband and casually strolled out of the building undetected.

Two and A Half Minutes Later . . .
Hinsdale Street · Hit #2 . . .

After laying her motorcycle down in an abandoned debris covered lot, Kacky made the call and dismantled the cell phone before tossing it's battery in a nearby sewer. Then power walked the two blocks to a dark Hinsdale Street, where most of the buildings where vacant. She sat on the stoop of the three family, Brownstone apartment building. Her appearance there would give them the assumption that she was indeed a resident of the complex. She patiently waited for them to come and investigate a frivolous altercation. "Beautiful." She said moments later under her breath. She watched the patrol car bend the corner of Glenmore Avenue and merged onto Hindsdale Street as it headed in her direction. Both officers diverting their focus left and right, while scanning the addresses, they drove ahead then came to a slow crawl when the passenger tapped his partner in acknowledgement of the alleged callers address. They then eased into a parking space on the opposite side of the street.

Adjusting their hats atop their heads, while exiting the vehicle, the driver politely said to Kacky, "Um, excuse me, Ma'am, did you call 9-1-1 for assistance?"

"No. I didn't Officer, but I'm willing to bet that it was the lady who lives in the basement apartment." She said with a slight nod towards the basement entrance. "She and her husband are constantly at each others' throats."

"Thank you Ma'am." The Officer politely said.

"You're welcome." Kacky replied, with a wide smile as they turned and headed towards the basement stairs, located beneath the set of stairs she was sitting on. Just as they were approaching the door she pulled her silenced ten millimeter from her Michael Antonio, thigh high boots, stood at the top of the stairs with her gun expertly aimed on them and repeatedly squeezed her trigger, hitting her victims in the head, neck and back. "That's for my homegirl, motherfuckers." She whispered before taking her time to collect the spent shells, then fleeing the area.

Three Minutes Later
Ashford Street - Hit #3. . .

"Yeah, just like clock work!" Latesha mumbled through gritted teeth to Goldie and Michelle, as they hopped out of the stolen Ford Taurus. Quietly they cat-stepped through the darkness of the night, crossing an otherwise busy New Lots intersection, they approached the vehicle of their prey, which was occupied by three of New Yorks Finest. With the stealth movement of their arms, the three women educed their weapons. The officers sat in the patrol cruiser van eating donuts and sipping on styrofoam cups of coffee, completely oblivious to their surroundings, until the cocking sound of automatic weapons diverted their attention towards their left. Latesha raised her firearm and the officer in the driver's seat nervously dropped his cup of coffee onto his own lap. He turned his head in the opposite direction and threw both his hands up in a defensive manner. She sent two shots into the vehicle that shattered the slightly cracked window before striking him in the neck right below his left ear lobe. **BOOM BOOM**! The second shot perforated his scalp then penetrated the cavity, producing extensive destruction of his cerebellum. Explosive grunts of pain echoed from the other occupants of the van as Michelle and Goldie firmly clutched their H.K. MP5 weapons and let loose a deadly barrage of gunfire as armor piercing hollow points ripped through their bodies until the screaming subsided.

Just as they were making their way towards the get-a-way car two transit cops came dashing down the steps of a nearby elevated train station with guns drawn and one blabbering into his handheld communicator. **BOOM, BOOM, BOOM!!!** were the sounds that barked from Latesha's ten millimeter. The slugs just barely missing its target as the officer dove over the railing and took cover behind a parked automobile and returned two shots. His partner wasn't so lucky after Michelle sent three slugs in his direction that raced through his pelvic area, severing his tail bone as he layed sprawled at the bottom of the stairs screaming in agonizing pain, before she put him to rest with a single head shot that left a gaping hole the size of a toilet paper coil.

"Go get the other one! I'm'ma hold y'all down!" Goldie yelled before sending a volley of shots into the vehicle that the cop used for cover, causing him to duck out of sight. On que, Michelle and Latesha trotted in his direction, out of Goldie's range. Once she ceased fire, the officer rasied up with the intentions of returning a barrage of his own, but was surprised before he could fully extend his arm to discharge his weapon. Nervously shaking as he stared down the nozzles of both of their firearms. The split second shock cost him his life when they dumped a fusillade of bullets into his head, face, and torso. Leaving him unidentifiable as chunks of his brain matter and globs of blood seeped from his wounds.

"Come on Gee! Let's get the fuck up outta here!" Latesha yelled while waving her comrades on as they high tailed it back to the get-a-way vehicle and disappeared into the night. The assault on Vicky at the hands of the Law had transformed the Sutter Angels into a murderous organization. One the local precinct had never seen. They left a trail of police bodies all over East New York, making sure that law enforcement had their work cut out for them.

* * * * *

Moments later, responding to a 911 call of shots fired, several squad cars descended to the scene. The first few officers on the scene would witness the horrifying sight of the deceased bodies of their colleagues sprawled about the intersection of New Lots and Ashford Street, from the result of multiple gun shots. While securing the crime scene their attention were drawn several yards away towards the windowless police van where they would stumbled upon the other three slained officers lying lifeless inside the department vehicle as their bodies continued to bleed profusely.

The homicides of nine more New York City Police Officers were splattered across the news. The incident made not only the local news stations, but it also received headlines across the country.

"NEWS FLASH"

"Good evening, this is Briana Moultrie reporting from Global Network News 82, where moments ago we've received conformation that there has been a multiple police slaying in the East New York section of Brooklyn. Unidentified thugs have launched deadly attacks against police officers, triggering raids and clashes. Authories believe that the alleged triggermen were brought in by local thugs from other parts of the city to continue the assassination of Law Enforcement Officials!"

"The Mayor have deployed an extra hundred police officers to help the 75th Precinct sweep through the East New York area in hopes of capturing those responsible for the senseless bloodshed of New York's Finest, prompting the largest mobilization of security in Brooklyn's history. Citizens are complaining that the media is only showing concern for the brutal slayings of the police and not making mention of the police brutality that has been occurring for many years. Not just in Brooklyn, but New York City as a whole, causing residents to develope a deep distrust for law enforcement. Once again, I'm Briana Moultrie, from Global Network News 82, saying… so long."

⸮

Chapter 26

KACKY & CYE xxx

After a long evening of ripping and running all over Brooklyn with the other Angels, Kacky made her way back to the comfortable confines of her home. Winding down for the evening she showered, slipped on a pair of boyshorts, and an oversized t-shirt then tied her hair down with an worn silk scarf, that seen better days, and got into her bed.

Hours later, she was in deep sleep, dreaming of her imprisoned boyfriend, Cye Green, who was due for discharge the following morning. Everyone outside of his parents respectfully referred to him as Tony Rome.

They were stark naked, laying there next to her atop of a comforter which was draped on the hard wood floor of their living room, directly in front of the 60" flat screen television. They were watching the final minutes of a porno movie. After its conclusion, Cye beamed lustfully at the swollen mound of Kacky's vagina. Then without warning he leveled his face to her pussy and began dabbing the tip of his tongue at the end of her clit while he held her vagina lips apart with his middle and index fingers. Allowing his tongue to slide up and down the avenue of her slit, enjoying the sweetness of her essence as he proceeded to please her with his talented tongue. "

"Ssss..." Kacky sighed when he encased her clit with his lips and began sucking and slurping it. Causing her love button to throb along to the beat of her heart. She cradled the sides of his head with both hands and let a light stream of her liquid essence slowly ooze from her sexual existence. Sensing she had came, Cye stuck his tongue as far as he could into the cave of her vagina and slithered it around her confines the best he knew how.

"Ooo Ooo, ssss....huhh! Oh Cye..." She moaned as his oral assault sent shockwaves in short spurts throughout her body as his tongue caressed the velvety walls of her pussy. When he began tongue fucking her vagina with the to and from movement of his head, Kacky humped her hips up and down at a slow pace, meeting him clit to nose, each time. It felt like she was having an outter body experience when she came again. Only this time it was like a mini Tsunami. Her out-flowings coated his tongue and lips as she let out a primal scream upon her release.

After her orgasm subsided she climbed on all fours, face down with her ass positioned high in the air clutching two hands full of the comforter as she anticipated his entrance. Getting behind her, he spread her left ass cheek apart with one hand and gripped his penis at the root with the other. His dick head slid along her slit, finding the entrance to her love tunnel. Cye surged forward with his pulsating shaft, causing Kacky to whimper, "Ssss...wuuuw." He pumped his dick in and out of her pussy from head to root like a seasoned porn star, grinding inside when he was completely engulfed. "Ooow, yeah baby, work that dick in me..."

He drew back until the crown of his penis peeked out of her vagina lips, gripped her tightly by the waist and thrusted up into her welcoming pussy with brutal force. "Like that baby? Uurrgh!!" He rammed again.

"OUWW!!" The second plunge caught her off guard. "Oh ye yeess, hun! Yesss..." She answered before burying her face into the comforter. He proceeded stroking into her long and deep. Her clit continued throbbing in sync with her heart beat and she knew she would cum again. "Yeah Daddy! Fuck this pussy! Long and deep! Oooh yeah, just like that. . .long and deep. Oh yes, oow...yess!" She began panting when she felt her pussy tighten around his dick as his rhythm picked up its pace. "Oooo yeah Baby, that's my...ooo shiit, that's my spot!" She cried out then began throwing her ass back at him.

Cye looked down between them in amazement as he witnessed his dick disappear and reappear in the confines of her love canal. He was so excited that he gripped a handful of her hair, pulling her head back while calling her filthy names. "Yeah, take this dick, you nasty freak bitch...take it!" He said in a deep guttural tone that didn't faze Kacky one bit. She kept throwing her back side on to his penis, meeting his every stroke as he long dicked her with abandon. A few moments later she let out a low cry, but it only incensed him more as he continued ramming away at her pussy.

Stars began to form in front of Kacky's glazed over eyes. She came hard and strong as her body shuddered, glistening his shaft with her thick cream. But he kept on pounding her pussy. She knew if this kind of pounding lasted another five minutes the next stop would be passing the hell out beneath him. Yet she wouldn't dare tell him to stop as he commenced on digging his long shaft in and out, up and in and at times in circular motion, stirring her insides. Then without warning he penetrated her asshole down to the last knuckle of his right thumb.

So much cum dripped from her plugged pussy-hole that she thought he shot off his load, but the juice was all hers as one orgasm after another rolled on. He waited for Kacky to finish her wave of climaxes before withdrawing his thumb and cum slickened dick before instructing her to turn around and administer a blow job.

Kacky never thought she was any good at deep throating, due to her gag reflex, but she really enjoyed the feeling of a big hard dick hitting the back of her throat and he was more than happy to oblige. Kacky's clit began to stir again as she felt his dick slide deeper and deeper down her throat, as she bobbed her head up and down his shaft. A short while later, she gripped his penis at the base with one hand and cupped his testicles with the other. Drawing back to the crown of his penis, Kacky lavishly licked and sucked it while massaging his ball sac. Then ran her tongue along the underside as she held it upwards against his stomach. The moment she inserted him back into her hot wet mouth, he grabbed the back of her head and used it like a human punching bag, with his dick like a fist. He rammed and jabbed it into her mouth until he could feel the pulsating motion increasing. She was no longer sucking his dick, she was now a semen receptacle. "That's it Babygirl...swallow dat dick. Ssss...yeah! Swallow dat shit!" Cye barked with a menacing growl as he bucked wildly into Kacky's face with tremendous force, causing a few tears to escape her eyes as his dick-head rapidly banged at the back wall of her throat causing saliva and pre-cum to drool from her jaws, as she gagged and fought for oxygen. Seconds later he tensed up, jerked and exploded, "Uumm. Oh shit...god damn! Uuuhh, uhh, uhh!" filling her mouth with his sexual fluids. Cum dripped from her lips, down her chin to her breasts and onto the floor. If she hadn't been so tired, she would have licked up every single drop.

Just when she thought it was over, he shoved her back onto the comforter and dicked her down in several more positions. When it was finally over and done with, Kacky thought she would die from pussy exhaustion.

The blaring sound of her cell phone startled her out of the dream she was having. That's when she realized that the crotch of her boyshorts were drenched in girly juice. Glancing at the clock that rested on her nightstand, she also noticed it read 7:57am. "Hello!"

"Yeah, it's me." Cye said, "Get your ass up and buzz me in!"

She smiled mischieviously to herself, reached down into her underwear and rubbed her moist pussy. "I'm getting' up now. Jus' gimme a few seconds." She answered, before easing into her bedroom slippers to let her man in.

Chapter 27

KEY WITNESS . . . 6 MONTHS LATER

*W*hile at a weekend Lawyer and District Attorney Gala, Vicky's attorney received information that there would be a surprise star witness by the name of Kashawn Green. The witness was scheduled to take the witness stand and positively I.D. her client as the person responsible for the arson manslaughter case that has been getting a lot of publicity since Vicky's arrest. Prior to receiving this new information, Alice was absolutely sure she had a one hundred percent chance of an acquittal and with a $25,000 bonus to get Vicky off, she could not afford to allow anything to hinder her successful reputation.

They had just come to the conclusion of the day's proceedings, which was the showing of the video tape, that didn't have enough clarity to positively identify her as the person actually committing the crime. "Listen!" Alice said as she shifted her body around in her seat to face Vicky, "The State has a key witness, but I promise you, I'm gonna bust my chops to get you off. You got my word on that," she continued "but, I need to know from you, right now, how...."

"You can't be fuckin' serious!" Vicky snapped, interrupting her legal respresentative in the middle of her spiel. Vicky studied the attorney's face as she spoke, knowing there weren't any witnesses that could I.D. her, or so she thought.

"Oh no! I am very serious, Sweetheart!" The half black and Jewish attorney stated with sincerity in her tone. "Now what can you tell me about Kashawn Green?"

"Kashawn Green?" She thought. . ."I don't know a Kashawn Green. . .wait a minute! Kashawn Green." She repeated, "He's someone I had a brief altercation with before I went on vacation a few weeks before my arrest. What da'fuck he got to do with this case?" She said in a tenacious tone...a tone that didn't go unnoticed by Latesha, Kacky, and Goldie, who where the only Angels that attended the proceedings. They watched Vicky's angry expression spread across her face and curiously wondered what was going on.

"This may sound funny," her lawyer began, "but apparently he identified you by the partial frame of your facial features from the video and the shape of your derriere."

"I don't believe this shit!" Vicky spat, shaking her head in disbelief. "Gimme ya pen for a second and a piece of paper!" After being slid the items, Vicky began jotting down a few lines:

> This bitch just told me there's gonna be a testimony, most likey tomorrow, from some nigga that can I.D. me. Just look in my car where I keep the very important things and everything will be alright. Have fun! He drives a yellow Audi.

"Here. Give this to Latesha." She commanded her representative after folding the small piece of paper. Latesha read the brief note, tore it into tiny pieces and threw it in the nearest trash can as she left out of the court building with her sister and Goldie following behind.

* * * * *

"Oh Shit!" cursed Latesha, snapping her head back the moment she laid eyes on the man's face that was on the photo identification card. "This rat ass nigga was at the grand opening of the Crystal Ball!" She added before extending the card to Goldie.

"How you know?" Goldie inquired while studying the picture.

"Cause he complimented Vicky about her legs when we were leaving the dance floor and instead of her saying thank you, the bitch straight went in on 'em! Y'all know how her dog-gone mouth is when she get weed and liquor in her damn system!"

"Yeah tell me about it." Kacky chimed in as she peered over Goldie's shoulder. "Damn!" She snapped before pointing her index finger at the bottom of the card. "1027 Arlington Avenue. That mufucka is right from the area. We can go get him right now. Do his ass real dirty before we off his ass."

"Nah Sis." Latesha said, shaking her head from side to side. "We gonna let Smurf come out here later on tonight and deal with'em. Cause I want that Sammy da'bull ass mutherfucker to suffer real fuckin' bad for what he's putting Vicky through!"

Later that night Smurf, a boogie down Bronx native, who the Angel's met a few years back, through Lil El's right hand man, B-hov, sat behind the wheel of an old Dodge van. A few yards away from the informants address, he studied the face on the I.D. card as he patiently waited for the rat to pull up in his cheese colored Audi.

Chapter 28

COURT DATE

*T*he Angels and a swarm of supporters sat calmly in the 360 Adams Street court room. Latesha made sure that everyone from the New Life Baptist Church came to show their support for Vicky. After all, the Angels would donate thousands of dollars a year for the maintenance of the House of Worship. After a successful motion for a speedy trial and almost six months spent at Riker's Island Women's House of Detention, Vicky couldn't wait to step out a free Angel. She sat next to her attorney, draped in a cream Anna Sui dress and a pair of four inch matching Charles Jourdan ankle boots, patiently waiting. Almost everyone wore thick cotton shirts that read "Free Vicky" with a five by seven photo of her from her Junior High School graduation. Latesha's mother even showed up with a herd of her Eastern Star Sisters, all wearing their uniforms.

Chewing on a fresh stick of Double Mint gum, her lawyer slid to her along with a small piece of paper that simply read, 'I'll see you at your Welcome Home Party'. Vicky smiled then spun around in her seat, with her left elbow resting on the top of the chair. Then made eye contact with Latesha before mouthing the words, 'Thank you.' Latesha cracked a sly grin, before mouthing her reply, "You're welcome, Bitch. Now turn around." waving her hand dismissively.

Vicky couldn't help allowing her eyes to briefly roam around the room and nodding to herself in appreciation at how her crew virtually brought the community together in support of her freedom. She turned around just before the Judge made his way from chambers. The A.D.A sat with his arms folded across his chest blankly staring down at a thick pile of legal documents. His forehead began to perspire so he reached into his suit jacket's left pocket for his hankerchief, before removing his spectacles and lightly dabbing the cloth around the top part of his face. Then took a big gulp of water from the plastic cup that rested on the table he sat behind.

The jury, who were previously informed of the no-show of the State's key witness, began filing out of the deliberation room, making their way back into the court room. Vicky sat nonchalantly chewing her gum and making eye contact with each one of the jurors as they took their assigned seats. The Court Clerk stood and began..."Criminal Case 4177/02; The State of New York verses Vicky Davis." He then waited for the judge to allow the attorney for the defendant and the A.D.A to state their names for the record.

"Mr. Rosenthal." The judge said giving the prosecutor the avenue to introduce himself.

"Good afternoon, Your Honor. Brian Rosenthal appearing on behalf of The State of New York!" The A.D.A. stated in a clear, loud voice as he stood.

"Ms. Kennerly!" The Judge nodded as the A.D.A. took his seat.

"Good afternoon, Your Honor." Vicky's lawyer politely greeted, brushing her loose fitting wool skirt as she stood. "Ms. Alice F. Kennerly, on behalf of the defendant, Vicky Davis, who is present here today!"

"Alright!" The Judge began after clearing his throat. "With regards to Ms. Davis, today is the day set for the prosecution witness in this matter. Is there any legal cause or reason why the court should not proceed?"

"Yes, Your Honor! May we approach the bench?" The Prosecutor requested.

"You may approach!" The Judge said, motioning for the two of them to step up to the bench for a side bar.

"Your Honor," Mr. Rosenthal began as he loosened up his silk tie, "I'm unable to locate my star witness, as you already know. However, if you could just grant me thirty minutes? I'm assuming he's on his way."

"I object, Your Honor," Ms. Kennerly interjected, "The State had an ample amount of time already for his witness to be present for testimony."

"With all due respect Your Honor, this is a Manslaughter case!" The Assistant District Attorney pleaded.

"You've got fifteen minutes to have your witness up on the stand. AND that's all I'm granting you!" The Judge barked, causing a strand of hair to fall between his eyes then brushing it back with the palm of his left hand. After informing the Jury of the witness time frame for testimony, he called a brief recess.

Fifteen minutes later, after receiving confirmation that the witness hadn't shown, the Judge instructed the Jury to reach a verdict. The jury Foreman stood up and faced the court clerk.

"As to the charge of Manslaughter in the First Degree, how do you, the Jury find the defendant?" Everyone in the crowded courtroom paid close attention as they waited for the Jury Foreman to announce the verdict.

"NOT GUILTY!" he replied. The court room erupted with cheers and tears of joy.

"Quiet in the Court!" The Judge yelled over the jubilant crowd of supporters, to no avail, while banging his gavel. Vicky, who was now six months and three weeks into her pregnancy, stood to her feet to hug her attorney, showing her appreciation for a job well done.

She then turned towards Latesha, who was leaning over the four foot banister, that separated the spectators from defendants, and thanked her with a warm embrace before leaning in for a whisper, "Y'all Bitches had a lot'a fun while I was gone." Vicky said, referring to their retaliation on law enforcement for physically abusing her at the precinct while interrogating her.

"And revenge was bitter sweet, too." Latesha replied.

"Yeah! Fa'y'all. But the mutherfuckers that beat me up in the 75th are still in existence." She whispered through gritted teeth, then added, "And I want personal revenge. Look what they did to my eye." Bringing her index finger to a scar that required four stitches.

"Ah, Bitch, stop whinning like a baby." Latesha snapped before reaching into her Issac Mizrahi, leather canteen bag for her Christian Dior sunglasses. "Here, take these and put 'em on."

As they strolled through the building's first floor lobby, the Angels and their supporters celebrated the victorious outcome of the verdict with loud chants, cheers and whistles of triumph. Just before reaching the glass revolving doors, Vicky noticed the two arresting officers who brutalized her at the station house, standing a few yards away, staring at her with gritted teeth. They both were shaking their heads in shocking disbelief, as they wondered how a Not-Guilty verdict came down with evidence of guilt being so blatant in the video tape. Little did they know they'd soon have another mind boggling homicide to solve whenever they discover the body of their lone informant. . . Kashawn Green.

The evil that The Angel possessed was now revealed in her eyes. Nothing but the darkness of her designer shades could conceal the look in her eyes, as she shot them both a villianous glare, complete with the promise of vengeance.

Exiting the courthouse, Latesha clutched Vicky's left arm as they proceeded down the wide concrete steps that lead to the curb, where Ronnie greeted her with a brief diamond infested french kiss as he held her affectionately. He then opened the front passenger door to his cream colored Range Rover to help her ease into the seat. She waved everyone goodbye and thanked them for their show of support for the umpteenth time, since the verdict. Then Ronnie got behind the wheel and pulled off, driving expertly as he weaved the luxury SUV in and out of the hectic afternoon traffic. A half hour later, they were pulling into the driveway of her house, where they would spend the remainder of the day making passionate love.

* * * * *

It would be weeks after the conclusion of Vicky's trial, when Kashawn's detached head would be discovered, and The Daily News would read as follows:

THE DAILY NEWS

A human skull found in a Brooklyn warehouse with a rodent stuffed in its mouth have been preliminarily identified as the remains of 32 year old, murder witness Keshawn Green, police said yesterday. A cleaning crew found the skull in an Igloo cooler Tuesday night while cleaning the warehouse in the East New York section of Brooklyn, said a police spokesperson, Officer William Moynihan.

During the trial, the D.A. had a tiny feeling in the back of his mind that the ending of his no-show key witness's story might not be a happy one, but he never imagined anything like this. "Who in their right mind would even think something like this would happen?" He asked no one in particular when he was informed about the discovery during an important meeting at his office.

Chapter 29

ANGEL'S PARADISE

*T*he line that was formed outside the club was almost unbelievable! Hundreds of party goers from all five of New York City's boroughs and as far away as Perth Amboy, New Jersey, showed up at the newly established *"Angel's Paradise"*, to pay homage to the recently uncaged Angel.

The Angels spent thousands of dollars to transform their warehouse into an extravagant club. The exterior's architecture was designed like a movie theatre, complete with a spacious ticket booth, where attendees would pay their twenty dollar entrance fee and have the back of their hand stamped with an invisible angel. To the right of the booth were two enormous oak wood swinging doors that led to a narrow hallway where patrons were required to place their hand under a purple fluorescent light for verification, before passing through the state of the art metal detector that was specifically invented for airport security.

Once verified, patrons are lead through another set of doors that brought them to the dance floor. The dance room of *"Angel's Paradise"* was carefully crafted with four huge fans, rotating from the completely mirrored ceiling. Hanging from above by fishing wire were eight lifesize angels that were handmade mannequins with dresses and wings crafted from feathers, chiffon and light weight tulle. The high-powered fans caused the angels to fly above the over-crowded dance floor. There were sixteen foot long bars on either side of the club where a set of three female bartenders serving topless with pasties covering their nipples, clad with a pair of milk white angel wings and matching thongs.

The VIP lounge was encased by a four inch thick, darkly tinted bullet proof glass with several glow in the dark angels, protruding along it's center. The twenty by eight foot room was draped with wall-to-wall, one and a half inch, twenty two hundred dollar almond brown Moroccan carpet and three matching cowhide sofas with contrasting ivory and brass coffee and end tables. The lounge was now occupied by a dozen male and female Angel Associates. They were clustered around the room, sipping on their drinks and conversing with one another, as they enjoyed the evening.

The exquisiteness of the club made it obvious to the previously unknown, that the Angels were handling some serious bread. Latesha and Goldie roamed throughout the venue together greeting a small portion of the twenty-five hundred patron's that flooded the club's decors.

"Hey, what's up, Playboy? I see you're really enjoying yourself." Goldie said once they approached Smurf, who had an unknown individual with him.

Smurf was adorned in a two peice, eggwhite and beige linen suit. His Yves Saint Laurent cologne permeated the air as he two-stepped in a pair of matching $1,100 custom-made alligator shoes, clutching his glass of coconut flavored vodka. His diamond infested bracelet and thumbtack sized diamond earrings gleemed off and on like a strobe light while he chilled with his Bronx comrade, Rough Sex.

Rough Sex, himself, was donned out in a peanut butter and brown Gucci suit with matching Gucci loafers, bopping his head to the sounds that blared from the system with his hand cupping his chin. On his wrist he sported a $45,000 time-piece that was embedded with enough diamonds to cause Stevie Wonder to squint his eyes. Around his neck hung a 18" platinum link chain with the initials R.S. filled with diamonds that swung left and right as he swayed to the music.

"Yes I am. I'm also feeling how y'all put this shit together!" Smurf replied to Goldie between sips of his drink. "And by the way.... " he continued with a nod of the head, "this right here is my comrade, Rough Sex!"

"Rough Sex?" Goldie repeated arrogantly.   "Yeah, but you can call me R.S if you'd like." The five foot eight, light brown skinned, slightly musculared gangsta interjected with his right hand extended.

"And I'm Goldie." She replied, shaking his hand.

"And my name is Latesha. Being Smurf's comrade makes you one of ours, as well. Welcome to the family." Latesha said before extending her own hand. At that precise moment Vicky and Ronnie strolled through the entrance.

"Daayuum! It's crowded up in this bitch!" A bo-hipped walking Vicky barked over her right shoulder as they maneuvered through the crowd. A few yards away she spotted the other Angels sitting at their custom-designed U-shaped booth.

"Eeel!" Althea began with her nose squinched up, as they approached. "Why da'fuck you walkin like that?"

"Shit! I tell you why." Kacky interjected, "Cause her dare-gon' coochie is tender!" Instead of answering, Vicky just smirked and motioned her thumb back and forth, as if hitch-hiking, at a smiling Ronnie, who was standing behind her with his arms draped around her baby bump belly.

"I don't know what's so funny, Ronnie. You need to let her relax for a few days, shit! She aint even been home seventy-two hours yet and already you digging her damn guts out like you're crazy." Michelle preached, working her head side to side the entire time she spoke.

"Yeah, well if you really knew ole'girl the way you claim to, then you'd know that she ranted and raved until I gave in to her demand to get boned."

"Then she got exactly what she was looking for fa'bein so damn hot and jumpy in da' ass."

"Right." Kacky chimed in agreement with Michelle.

"Now come sit cha' hot tail on down." She commanded while patting the empty space in the booth. After helping her ease into the seat, Ronnie took the seat next to her. Seconds later a barely dressed waitress brought over an assorted variety of fruit flavored vodka for everyone except Vicky. Ronnie stole a quick glance at her flesh, swaying ass cheeks, as she turned on her heels and headed back towards the bar.

Shortly, thereafter, the waitress returned with a pint of Tropicana orange juice and a couple of bottles of spring water for Vicky. After the waitress placed the drinks on the table and walked away, Ronnie lifted his drink for a nice swig and the opportunity for a double take when he cut his eyes in her direction as she strolled off. Vicky took notice to the disrespectful behavior and leaned into his ear and whispered, "Don't make me smack both of your eyeballs into the same socket, mufucka." He was spared further verbal abuse when D.J. Sweet Pea, the clubs premier disc jockey, sent the latest smash hit by Don Stone called "Street Legends" bleeding through the speakers. Almost the entire club went into a chant.

> ♫I'm from the same borough as Big Drac and
> Walter "Tut" Johnson/Amar, Bogart and Lil Rick
> Martin/Lil Kim, Fox - Biggie and Jigga/, Guy
> Tony, Killer Ben and Black Knowledge da'Killa/
> Red Bug, D-Nice, Kev Webb what up?
> Pappy Mason, Haitian Toby, Baby Sam.
> Yeah, ya, bread was up! ♫

"Ah man! That song reminds me of that joint 50-Cent did a while back that payed homage to all the dealers in Queens!" Kacky excitingly said after the song subsided.

"Yep, me too!" Althea agreed. "You talking 'bout Ghetto Qu'ran."

"Ar huh, exactly!" Kacky replied.

"Hummph! Exactly my damn ass. That's the mufuckin' song that almost got his dumb ass kilt. All on record singing about niggaz and their ill gotten funds, like that shit was cool or somethin'." Michelle ranted between sips of her Smirnoff raspberry flavored vodka.

* * * * *

Both Latesha and Goldie, who were facing the front of the club, as they chatted with Smurf and their new affiliate took notice over their shoulders of the two security personnel, who walked over to Beefy, the head of security detail. They watched intently as one of the men explained something to him with a confused expression on his face. Whatever he said had caused him to impulsively rubber neck his head left and right as if he were looking for someone in particular throughout the sea of party goers.

"Uuhm, Gee, would you mine checking on that for me?" Latesha asked, in a tranquil manner, nodding in their direction.

"Sure. Excuse me, y'all. I'll be back in a moment." She assured their guests, before mobilizing through the crowd. "Beefy, what's goin' on?" She inquired as the two men turned and walked off when she approached the 6'4", 260 pounder.

"Shit!" He cursed, "I was damn near breaking my motherfuckin' neck tryin'ta spot one'a y'all up in this hectic ass crowd. It's two bitches out front demanding to be let in or they gonna so-call pop off and all this other gangsta shit my boys were telling me they were barking out there." He continued, after taking a deep breath. "So I ordered my guys to politely ask them to leave the premises and if they didn't comply to drag them bum-ass bitches down the block by their damn ankles and. . ."

"Hold da'fuck up!" She snapped, cutting his spiel short, as she held her palm facing him. "Nigga you confusing da'hell outta me, right now. We don't close our doors until 1:00 am!" She paused a second and glared at her gold Rolex. "It aint even a quarter to, yet."

"Yeah, but them bitches aint tryin' to pass through the metal detector!" He interrupted.

"Oh, is that right?" Goldie asked with her lips twisted in a gnarl.

"Yup!"

At that moment the two security guards came walking back up at a frantic pace. "Excuse me Boss!" One of the men politely said, before interjecting, "But them lil bitches out there is packing heat and . . ."

"And how da'fuck you know that?" Goldie barked in an aggressive tone, before he could continue.

"Cuz, they drew'em outta their bags after I denied their request to see the owner."

"OH YEAH!" She snapped before gesturing with a wave of the hand to the other Angels, who were scrutinizing the scene from their seats a few yards away. Being extra careful not to draw any attention to themselves, the Angels got up, grabbed their clutch purses and zig zagged through the crowded dance floor in separate directions before altering their routes and headed towards the entrance. From afar, Latesha couldn't help but to admire the manner in which they dispersed, knowing how they all pride themselves on their control whenever things seem to get out of hand. To be cool headed, calm and collective in the trenches was something to really be proud of.

After convincing Vicky to remain seated against her better judgement, Ronnie eased her .380 automatic from her Gucci bag and slid it into the back pocket of his Coogi jeans before catching up to the other girls. Just before reaching the entrance, the voice of a female could be heard very loud. She was raving deliriously in a brave tone.

"Motherfucker, it aint like we tryin'ta get up in there

for free. We just ain't going for all of that security shit. All your dumb ass got to do is go get one of the owners like I said before. Case motherfuckin' close!" The female barked before the huge doors swung open.

There was complete silence for about three seconds before the loud sounds of screams erupted as the Angels embraced their childhood friends whom they had not seen in almost fifteen years. Raquel and Matilda, sisters of African and Puerto Rican descent and original Angels, who they lovingly referred to as Rocky and Moe. They spent the last decade and a half living in Bridgeport Connecticut with their parents, who thought it would be best to finish raising their then teenage daughters outside the crime infested New York. Little did they know their little girls helped contribute to the City's crime rate and moving did not solve anything. You know how the saying goes, You can take the people out of New York, but you can't take New York out of the people and no matter what location on the planet they moved to, they always remained Sutter Angels at heart.

"Look at chall, looking all Angeled out in-shit!" Goldie complimented the pair with a bright smile who were both draped in all white form fitting Vivian Tam mini dresses and matching Madeline Reba suede sandals.

"Yeah! And Raquel you done put on some weight, girl!" Kacky stated after briefly sizing up her old comrade, who obviously had blossomed over the years with delightful porportions.

"Damn sure did!" Agreed Michelle. "And I hope you aint taking none'a dem damn booty injections, either!"

"Nah girl! This is all me!" She assured while turning in a three sixty, before adding with a smile, "And the only injection goin' in this booty is semen injections!"

"Eeel, Bitch, you nasty!" Althea snapped in a defiant stance with her face contorted.

"She ain't change one damn bit!" Kacky added.

"Yeah, and her wanna be porn star behind aint gon' never change either." Her sister sharply stated while shaking her head from side to side.

"Alright!" Michelle began with her head cocked to one side, " Now that we've gotten over the initial shock of seeing y'all back in the Big Apple, which one'a y'all gon' tell us how y'all knew about the welcome home party for Vicky? Especially since none'a us had no contact number to reach . . ."

"Well, Mrs. Wanna-know-every-motherfuckin'-thing," Matilda interrupted, "for your information, Latesha reached out to us through somebody she knew at the local radio station out in Bridgeport."

"Yeah, da'bitch had da'mufuckin" D.J. puttin our damn government names all on blast over the air waves n'shit." Raquel chimed in before her sister continued her spiel.

"Anyway, we called the station and before he gave us her cell number, the nigga asking twenty-one questions! What's her sister's name? How many Angels is it! What's the block after Sutter Avenue? Like we in'a motherfuckin' 50-Cent video n'shit. Then when we get here, we gotta threaten to shoot this motherfucker up before one'a the G.I. Joe soldiers go and get 'chall so we can get in with our shit." Matilda ranted, patting her Chanel bag that concealed her .32 caliber revolver, nodding at the security guard she was screaming on just moments ago. Who was now standing next to Ronnie, getting an eyeful of Raquels physical composition.

"Ok! Now that everything is all cleared da'fuck up, lets get inside and show the crowd exactly what the Sutter Angels are made of." Goldie said before turning to lead the way.

* * * * *

Nesto, who was in the VIP lounge, being entertained by two scandidly dressed women, noticed Vicky parlaying alone in the Angel's lounge area and decided to excuse himself for a moment to personally welcome her home. A broad smile broke across her face as she watched him through calm eyes, make his way towards her. Reaching into the pocket of his Armani dress shirt, he approached and pulled out a small black jewelry box and leaned in for a peck on the cheek.

"Welcome home, Vee." He said as he extended the box to her.

"Oh my God." she warmly said in a hushed tone with her left hand held to her mouth after flipping open its top. "This is so beautiful Ness. Thank you so much!'

"You're welcome. I figured you'd like it."

"Like it!" she snapped with her head back. "Shit! I love it! As a matter-of-fact, here! Put it on for me!" Turning her back towards him. Nesto draped the diamond chain, complete with a three inch diamond and platinum praying angel with extended wings, around her neck, fastened it's clasp and warmly embraced her before returning to the VIP area.

* * * * *

"Listen, Smurf!" Latesha began, "I want you to know that we, and I'm speaking for the other girls, as well. . ." She stated before taking a long drag from her Newport cigarette then continuing, "we really appreciated the disappearing act you performed on Vicky's behalf. So we put together a few things for you to show our deep appreciation. So, before the club closes, I'll have a brick 'a dat pure white for you. And tomorrow afternoon, you could come through for the other things we have for you."

"Thanks! That's a good look. But, you know anything I do for the Angels, I do from the heart." He calmly stated with affection as he patted the left side of his chest with his right hand.

"I know, I know. And what we're doing for you is from the deep confines of our hearts, as well." She assured.

* * * * *

When several party goers recognized the two long-lost familiar faces, Raquel and Matilda had to stop a few times for brief greetings as they snaked their way through the crowd. When they finally approached the lounge Vicky's eyes widened to the size of quarters before a steady flow of tears began to stream down her face. She stood to her feet to effectionately embrace her childhood ride-or-die home girls. Ronnie decided to give them their private moment and drifted off into the audience.

"Welcome home, Bitch!" Raquel flatly said as she extended her arms, palms flat on her shoulders, "And wipe them damn tears, you'a Sutter Angel!"

"I didn't do no damn crying during the vigorous training them crackers put me through in the military. And that was four years of pure motherfuckin' hell!"

"That's right!" Her sister agreed, "Cause Angel's don't cry! We make other mufucka's families do that shit for us?"

"Yeah! Y'all right." She agreed before wiping the tears away with the back of her hands.

"And if you don't mine me asking, who's dare gon' ding-a-ling you sucked for that damn ice you rockin' around ya'neck?" Her question drew snickers as well as admiring comments from the other girls.

"Ah, Moe, please! Nesto just gave me this as a coming home present."

"Nesto? Where his fine ass at?" she asked, briefly scanning the crowd.

"He around here, somewhere. Why, you gonna suck his dick to get one'a these, too?" Vicky cracked, while twittling the emblem between her thumb and index finger, as they all broke out in laughter.

"Now that was a good come-back, I aint gon' front. You got me with that one." Moe managed to say in between laughter.

"Anyway..." Raquel began, once the humor subsided, "where da'hell Latesha at?"

"Oh, she standing down there on the left, before you get to the bar." Goldie stated as she pointed in Latesha's direction, who was intently focused in on them the moment they arrived and was waving them over.

"Vicky, you pull yourself together, cause when we come back, we gone' tear a hole through this damn dance floor." Raquel said.

"Yeah, and I hope all this extra weight don't hold you down, either." Her sister added as she rubbed Vicky's stomach.

* * * * *

"Shit! What da'hell took y'all Bitches so damn long ta'get here?"

"Why don't you go'in ask them so-called security guards y'all got out there! Them mufuckers wouldn't let us in." Matilda bitterly ranted.

"Why not?" Latesha asked, diverting her attention from one to the other, as Smurf and R.S. casually stole glances at the two well porportioned light skinned complexion sisters.

"Because!" Her sister began, while striking a defiant pose with a hand on her hip, "We got some extra weight with us and didn't wanna go through all'a dat searching bullshit!"

Latesha shook her head from side to side before responding, "I told you when I spoke to you on the phone, that I had y'all. So why y'all even bring heat?"

"Shit! I'm keeping my hammer on deck 24-7 and three mutherfuckin' sixty-five."

"Humph, me too!" agreed Matilda.

"Anyway, y'all here now, so let me introduce y'all to y'all new comrades." Latesha said before directing her attention to the fellas. "These are the two Angels y'all haven't met yet! Raquel and her sister Matilda. But, they prefer to be addressed as Rocky and Moe. Girls, this is your new comrades, Smurf and Rough Sex."

"Rough Sex!?" Raquel repeated, leaning back on her heels with her head arrogantly cocked to the side, as R.S. stood there nonchalantly for a few seconds, bobbing his head to the rhythm of the beat with a sly smirk on his face from the reaction he seemed to always get from females during an introduction.

"Yeah. That's my handle." He finally shot back, "And it is what it is!"

"Oh, is that right?" Raquel asked.

"Indeed so, Sweetness." He politely answered as he continued, swaying his upper body to the old B.I.G song, "Hypnotized".

* * * * *

Feeling extremely tipsy after spending most of the night sampling alcohol fruit drinks and hugging the bar, Vicky's attorney, who was now in the far right corner of the club in a two piece black and white pin-stripped pantsuit, that looked more like something she'd probably wear in the courtroom defending clients, was being taught the latest dance moves by Black Pat and Tameko. Her off beat movements not only made it obvious to them that she wasn't a frequent party goer, but also drew weird facial expressions and snickers from nearby patrons. When the D.J. spun on Lil Kim's old hit, "Big Momma Thing" every female in attendance took to the dance floor, where an unaccoutable amount of males immediately put their moves to the test.

Vicky, despite the babybump worked the floor with seductive gyrating moves so sexually expressive, that she drew the welcoming attention of four guys who began dancing circles around her, screaming loud chants, "Go Vicky, Go Vicky, Go-go-go-go-go-go Vicky!", which only encouraged her to work her body like never before. Her perfectly shaped ass moved around underneath her Tadashi Shoji mini dress like it had a mind of its own.

"Get 'em Girl!" Raquel yelled from a few yards away, as she worked her moves on R.S. who basically moved in step while she grinded and swayed her voluptious behind into his private parts.

The attorney, who seemed to finally have gotten into the groove of things was now sandwiched between Guy-Tony and Lil Jus, two trigger happy thugs from the neighborhood, that worked security detail for the Angels organization who were fervently grinding into her as if they were literally having a three-some on the dance floor.

A few songs later, more thirsty than winded from the vigorous dancing, Raquel and R.S. decided to have a drink. Once they reached the bar, he gestured for one of the bartenders to come down to their end where he gave his order. "Raspberry vodka with a twist of lemon." He calmly said before a short pause, "Shaken, not stirred, please!"

"And uhmm. . ." Raquel began as she viewed the variety of drinks available through squinted eyes, then ordering, I'll have two Nuvo Lemon Sorbets!"

R.S. could not help staring at Raquel's pouty lips. She had one of the most sensual mouths he had ever had the pleasure to lay his eyes on. When their drinks arrived, he took a perfectly rolled blunt from behind his ear and slid the bars ash tray up in easy reaching distance before sparking it up. They conversed and enjoyed each others company for the remainder of the night.

Money Ain't Nothing But a Thing

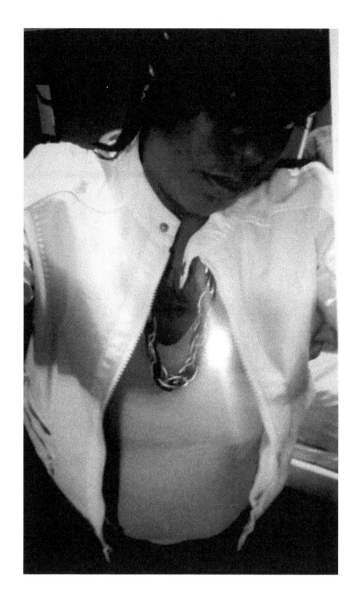

Peaches

KNOWLEDGE

Kacky

Shakira

Shannon

Latesha

Latesha & Candy

Latesha

Ant, Ivan, Big L & Ra-Son

Latesha J.

Nimatola

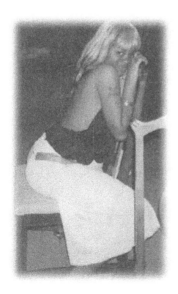

Nyasia

Aniya Kelly

Red Bug

Brittany

King Tut & Nubbz

Tameko

Peek-a-boo   *Tasha*

Soul B

Nubbz & Go

Patricia & Yolie

Rozz aka . . .

Mrs. Robinson

Shawna

Kim

O.G. Shabazz

Yafeu

Tavonia Lynda Carter

Valisa - R.I.P

Haitan Jack

Goldie & Latesha

Jimmy Henchman

Sana   *Atry & Friends*

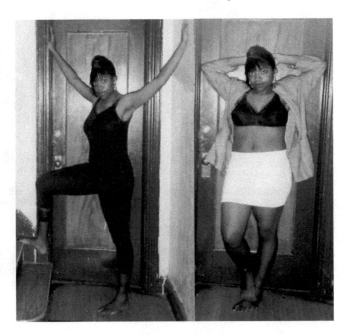

Black Pat

Susie & Ernesto

Antoinette   Valerie

Ne Ne

Meeka & Mike

Kacky & Riddick Bowe

Nicole aka Soonie

Erica

LUZ

Ty, Tracy, Brinesha,
Ondia, Vonia, Tyneeka

Chapter 30

CAN WE LIVE

After being rewarded fifty thousand dollars in cold hard cash, a brand new Matta Black Denali XLT, with smoke gray nubuck interior that sat on twenty-four inch matte black joker rims, with chrome lips and a kilo of pure cocaine for his handy work and with R.S. riding shotgun, Smurf decided to head back to his Bronx neighborhood to talk to the local king pin about the possibility of putting some work up in his East Tremont Avenue crack den, which they estimated at bringing in anywhere between sixty and seventy-five grand a week. With the constant flow of feinds the gold mine attracted. "This is all your idea, nigga, cause you know I'd rather just sell the whole brick to 'em and keep it mufuckin" movin!"

"Why do that, when we could just cook da'shit up and make more dough off it?" R.S. sharply questioned as he sat back nonchalantly. "Rocking that shit up and moving it in dimes and nickles is gonna bring back some extra big faces."

"Shit!" Smurf cursed. "Fuck all'a dat Nino Brown shit. We aint no damn drug dealers. We're grim reapers, nigga. We toe tag motherfuckers."

"Hold up, homie!" R.S. snapped back, "I just know you aint think that I was talking about us making a career outta this shit here? Cause that aint nowhere near the case, at all. This'a one time thing. That's why I made the suggestion that we cook it up to bring back more product in the crack form and holla at this nigga about lettin' us get a couple days to make some extra cream. As oppose to opening up a spot we don't plan on maintaining. Trust me..." he continued, "we're on the same page."

"A'ight! Now that you put it like that, it all make better sense to me." Smurf agreed as he eased the vehicle along the curb where Camel was posted up a few yards away, conversing with two of his soldiers, while his scandidly dressed girlfriend clutched his hand, hanging on his every word. After coming to an abrupt stop and killing the engine, Smurf slid down into his seat and sat contently.

"Ayo, Camel!" R.S. barked in a stout tone, causing Camel to divert his attention in their direction with his free hand held to his forehead in a salute, blocking the afternoon sunrays. "Let me holla at'chu for a minute home team!" He said, gesturing with his head for Camel to approach the vehicle.

"Ayo, Slug! Who da'fuck is that in that whip?" Camel asked one of his henchmen, who looked on through squinted eyes, while easing his hand towards his waistband.

"Ahh, man, that's that lil nigga, R.S.!"

"Psss!" Camel hissed before yelling, "Nigga! Why da'fuck you calling me like I owe you some mufuckin" money or something?"

"Oh, this nigga gettin' his O.G. Bobby Johnson on in front of his peoples like we sweet." R.S. stated in a hushed tone through gritted teeth before Camel approached, peeking into the vehicle.

"Man, what the fuck y'all lil niggaz want?"

"We wanna eat like you eating!" R.S. answered coldly, obviously still angered by the way the older street legend had spoken to them.

"Nigga, what!?" he snapped back defensively, "You better recognize who the hell you talking to!"

"Whoa, home team! Be easy, we aint coming at'chu on no guerilla type'a shit." Smurf calmly assured. "We respect ya gangsta and all dat. . ."

"Yeah, I should hope so!" Camel interjected with a snarl before reaching into his front left pocket of his rayon slacks for a Newport cigarette and matches.

"Maann, we're just tryin'ta get rid of a brick and . . ."

"A brick?" The greed in Camel's eyes was obvious as he cut in again, rotating his attention between the two as he lit the nicotine stick.

"Please, just hear me out, Bossman." R.S. began in a tranquil manner, "We'll plug you in with a good connect out in Brooklyn. All we're asking is that you give us three days in ya spot to move . . ."

"Nigga!" Camel interrupted for the third time before blowing a cloud of smoke into R.S.'s face. "Don't ch'all ever in your life come at me side ways again. Like y'all built like that or y'all gonna be two sorry ass motherfuckers. And that aint'a threat, nigga! It's a fact!" He cautioned while brushing imaginary dust from his shoulders as his eyes glittered dangerously.

His two goons who were scrutinizing the whole scene began strolling their way over. "Is everything a'ight here, Cee?" Slug asked his boss, once they approached.

"Yeah I'm good! These lil niggaz was just leaving."

With nothing else to talk about Smurf cranked up the ignition and eased into traffic with Independence Day on his mind.

"I guarantee him and his cronies will be there the next time we come through!" R.S. said.

"Yeah, and he's gonna pay for all'a dat disrespect too! Believe that!" Assured Smurf.

Chapter 31

BABY SHOWER xxx

Just like her coming home party, Vicky made a late appearance to her own babyshower. After easing into a parking space, she slid her Gucci sunglasses down the bridge of her nose and glanced over the frame for a clear view. She admired the unfamiliar peanut butter colored B.M.W 750 IL that was parked with several other vehicles along the horse shoe shaped driveway of Latesha's home in Beacon New York.

Exiting her automobile, dolled in a beige Basant knitted mini dress that was personally hand crafted by designer Shaunali Nanda. On her feet were matching $1,200 Chrissie Morris sandals. Vicky trekked along side the colonial style home, snapping her fingers to the rhythm of the music that blared from the two fifteen inch Bose speakers, in the backyard. Her Gucci bag swung from her forearm, while the light breeze that bounced off the nearby river blew through her freshly done, shoulder length wash n' set.

The rest of the Angel's and their closest associates were either swimming, dancing or loitering around the Olympic size swimming pool. Latesha and Althea sweated over a searing grill preparing hotdogs, barbeque chicken and turkey burgers. The moment Vicky stepped through the backyard, the sweltering crowd that awaited her arrival began whistling and applauding. Goldie, who was sitting poolside at a long foldout table conversing with Matilda, Michelle and Kacky, had began shaking her head as Vicky approached, "Aahh ahun, Bitch, that damn outfit look like it was tailor made for a professional hoe!"

"R*ii*ght!" Agreed Matilda, with her nose turned up.

"Ahh please! Y'all bitches stop hatin'!" Vicky snapped back, waving her hand dismissively before flopping into the large throne-like red velvet chair that Latesha had purchased for her, specifically for todays occasion.

"And where's Ronnie?" Kacky asked more out of concern.

"He had to make and emergency run back to Alabama."

"On the day of your dog-gon' babyshower?!" Michelle interjected, snapping her head back in disbelief.

"Yeah! And he better hurry his ass da'fuck on back, too! Shit! My damn coochie is on fiiire!" Vicky said.

"*You*!?" Matilda sharply began, "SHIIITT! Just the mere mention of a ding-a-ling a'get my kat flowing like Niagara Falls!"

"Hummph, I know what ch'all mean girl!" Michelle chimed before taking a sip from her glass of pearl coconut flavored vodka and continued, "A damn banana ain't safe around me, right now!"

"Yeah! And that nigga R.S. might not be safe around Rocky's hot lil ass right now either!" Goldie cracked, causing the small group to snicker as they stole glances at the two who were standing at the far end of the yard deep in conversation.

"Oh y'all can trust and believe," her sister began, "before the night is over with, she gon' sink her claws in that mufucker. Especially since they been burning down the minutes on each other's cell phones for the last couple'a days . . ."

"A'ight ch'all! The food is ready!" Althea interrupted.

Just as Althea yelled for everyone to line up to be fed, Gwen strolled through the gate carrying a medium sized gift wrapped box. She was draped in a brown sheer and satin Vivienne Tam mini dress that hugged her 43" ass. Her small pedicured feet were snugged in a pair of cream four inch heel, open toe Fennix alligator sandals that clicked-clacked with every stride as she gracefully strode through the yard. The scent of her Vera Wang perfume victoriously battled the aroma of barbeque and marijuana as its intoxicating smell permeated the air. All eyes fell upon the upstate goddess. The fellas gawked as they openly lusted. Dre, one of Nesto's henchmen who had just climbed out of the pool, stood there in his Ocean Pacific shorts, dripping wet with his mouth hanging open as she approached Latesha, who after taking the box from Gwen, began introducing her to all those that mattered.

"Uhm, uhm, uhm. . ." Nesto hummed in a hushed tone to one of his boys while they stood in line for their food, clocking Gwen, who was headed in their direction, with Latesha before stating, "Shorty's ass is crazy."

The moment they approached, Latesha began. "Yo Ness. I wanna introduce you to somebody. This is our new business associate, Gwen. Gwen, this is my childhood friend and life time comrade, Nesto." She stated, diverting her attention between the two as they greeted one another.

Everyone knew from the results of her sonogram test that Vicky was bearing a baby boy and purchased their gifts accordingly. So an hour after satisfying their hunger, they each grabbed their gift wrapped presents from the huge pool shed, then placed them on the long table in front of Vicky and one by one she began opening them. The first was a powder blue bassinette with an overhead merry-go-round of angels. "Aaww, this is soo cute!" Vicky fervently sighed as she examined the item, then read the to and from sticker that was pasted on the crumbled wrapping paper to I.D. its' presenter before mouthing the words, 'Thank you.' to Nesto. He was standing a few feet to her left with a warm smile gracing his face as he nodded in response.

Then a box containing ten pair of baby Jordan sneakers with matching outfits in a variety of sizes, colors and styles to last for the next three years. "Hummph, I know y'all waiting for the next mufuckin' M.J. to come along and win them bum ass Knicks a damn championship, but my son aint gon' be no dare-gon' basketball player!" She flatly stated. She continued, unwrapping the next gift which were two car seats, one atop the other with a medium sized manila envelope in its' top seat that simply said 'From Goldie'. "Now Gee, what the hell am I gonna need two car seats for? I'm only giving birth to one child!?" she questioned her comrade, who sat at the far end of the table before tearing the seal from the envelope and pulling out a custom license plate that read "Bu-D-Grl" with a single key held in the upper left corner by a strip of scotch tape.

"Well, one is for the Volvo and the other is for your new Beamer that's parked out front!" Goldie defiantly answered before her childhood friend excitedly thanked her.

For the next ten minutes she unwrapped presents. The very last gift was in a large unwrapped black leather jewelry box like casing. Believing she or the baby were being presented with something incredibly expensive in the form of precious jewels, with everyone looking on with anticipation, she excitedly pryed open the case, revealing a gold tip nine and a half inch onyx shaped penis with the words "Joy Rider" engraved in rhinestones complete with bulging veins. By the way everyone erupted in laughter, she could not determine exactly who the guilty party was. "Oh y'all got jokes, huh?" she said more of a statement than a question as she scanned the crowd through squinted eyes.

With all of the excitement surrounding Vicky, no one noticed when Raquel and R.S. slipped off into the house for a secret rendezvous. The sexual attraction between the two was at an alarming rate neither one of them could no longer ignore.

After following her into the guest room that Latesha had prepared for her, R.S. pushed the door shut with the heel of his hard bottom crocodile shoe and eased up behind her as she stood near the night stand removing her diamond name plate earrings and slipped his rugged hands beneath her Nicci Ricci blouse, caressed her breast and felt her lemon drop sized nipples stiffen underneath her sheer bra. "Huhmm!" She let out a soft moan then turned to kiss him passionately. Their tongues swam around in each other's mouth while he removed her bra with the skill of a magician, pulling it away from under her designer garment. Then reaching around her, he began unzipping the back of her Elie Saab mini skirt, allowing it to fall to the carpet. She immediately got busy working on undoing his linen slacks. Then she reached between his legs and gripped his erect penis, looking at him lustfully through glazed eyes. "Let me drive this stick!" She thirstly whinned, stepping out of her panties revealing her dicktator pussy cat, a simple strip of hair resembling Adolf Hitler's mustache. Without responding, R.S. aggressively spun her around.

Now bent over the nightstand, bracing herself on her elbows, R.S. got down on his knees, spread her voluptuous ass cheeks and ran his tongue the entire length of her moist vagina, licking and lapping up one lip and down the other a few times before concentrating on her clit. Blowing and gnawing it lightly as she shook and shivered from the unfamiliar sensation. He professionally tongue boxed her love button with flickering jabs, stiff upper cuts and over-tongued rights and lefts. *"Ssss, Mmmm...,"* was all she could muster while he vitalized her clit like no man before him. Sucking it into his mouth as the tip of his tongue brutalized and strummed the rigged button like a seasoned guitarist. *"Huuhh, Oooo. . . I-I-I'm cum, cum, cumminnn. . .*
" She warned between gasps, before the stream of love water ran down onto his welcoming tongue. The sweet taste stimulated his taste buds, heightening his thirst for more as he continued to orally service her with a crazed passion. Moments later she

tensed up, realizing she was about to cum again. He slid his right thumb inside her dripping wet pussy and began jamming it in and out. Than all of a sudden, he chomped down into her left butt cheek, a little too hard for her liking. She jerked forward before looking over her shoulder with the *"nigga-is-you-crazy"* look on her face.

"What da'fuck you jump for?" He said through gritted teeth. WHACK! Was the sound that echoed throughout the spacious room before his palm print appeared across her right ass cheek. The unexpected contact caused her orgasm to squirt out. ***"Turn ya got-damn ass back around!"*** He commanded, and just like the Angel she was, Raquel complied. Getting to his feet, R.S. entered her warm love tunnel and stroked into her for a full fifteen minutes before she took him into her mouth sucking and slurping his penis to perfection. ***"Ooowe, Ahh shit!"*** He groaned, clutching a handful of her hair while she administered an oral assault of her own on his manhood.

"Uuhhmm, uuhhmm, uhmm, uhmmm!" She moaned, with the crown of his dick at the back of her throat. The vibration caused him to let loose a heavy load. She gulped twice and kept on sucking until she was sure his erection would hold up for the grand finale. Several minutes later, they crawled onto the queen sized canopy style bed where she placed both her ankles behind her neck and welcomed the onslaught of his member as he began long-dicking her slow, deep and hard, while gnawing and sucking her protruding nipples. She moaned, groaned and sighed as she stared up into the stained glass dome ceiling through dreamy eyes and scraping her nails up and down his back.

"Ssshhiiiitt, you got some good ass pussy!" He stated with heartfelt meaning. Once her vagina began spasming around his dick and opening on the down stroke, then tightening on the up stroke, his testicles drew up indicating he was close to nutting again. He instructed her to get on top. But little did he know he would get the ride of his life. Switching positions, she mounted him with a six o'clock split, both hands flat on the mattress and eased down onto him, then slowly rose all the way back to the tip. Repeating the process over and over.

After a couple of minutes at this pace, she went for broke, bouncing every which-a-way in a frenzy, which encouraged him to hump up into her, meeting each other stroke for stroke.

"Ooww-oow-ooww-o-o-o-o-oow-oow-ohh, yyeess, yeesss. . . aahh, shiiitt!" She cursed. Frantically thrashing as she rode and ground down on his penis, enroute to ecstacy. *"Aaahh-aahhh-ahh-aahh, yess, baby, ahh, yess."* Although her room was located just above the pool area, her pleasurable moans and groans were drowned out by the blaring music.

Oh - yeah, yeah, yeah, shit! I'mma bout to buss off!" R.S. said as he thrusted up into her, *"Yeah! Mmm...me too! Ahhh!"*

She came. Her orgasm triggered his. It was so intensed he gripped her ass and shot straight up into her love cave. Ten minutes later, after washing up, they found themselves poolside amongst the others . . . sexually satisfied.

Chapter 32

VISITING B-HOV

Sitting on the opposite side of the small round knee high table in the C-74 Adolescent Reception Center's visiting room, on Riker's Island, clothed in his gray prison jumper, B-Hov everso often diverting his vision throughout the spacious room, where some prisoners could be heard intensely arguing with their spouses as small children ran amock, playing tag as they laughed hysterically, ignoring the Correction Officer that had only minutes ago asked their guardians in a tranquil manner to keep them seated at their assigned tables.

The guard who did a security round every fifteen minutes had all of a sudden disappeared after getting paged through his hand held communicator. That gave a Latin couple, who sat at the second table in the isle along the left side wall the opportunity to release some overdue-pent-up-sexual frustration. The female who was dolled in a purple and blue floral sun dress shifted her body sideways, draped one leg over the other before scooting to the edge of her seat, and lifting her dress so that the inmate who was now sitting atop the foot and a half high table, could enter her. The inmate peered left and right, frantically stroking in and out of her vagina. Just to the right of them a burly looking blonde causcsian woman was administering an impeccable blow job to an obviously younger African American male, who groaned and wailed with his head tilted back as his eyes rolled to the back of his skull.

B-hov spoke at a tone that could only be heard by his good friend, Smurf. He summoned him two days ago for an important sit down. "Listen my nigga!" He began after clearing his throat. "What I'm about to say to you might sound a lil crazy, but what I'm asking you to do for me is even crazier. But it aint something that I wouldn't do for you, if the shoe was on the other foot." He defiantly stated before pausing a second to take a deep breath as Smurf listened intently. "I just got word through my attorney, right before I called you the other day and he informed me that my case is gonna get thrown out completely, and . . ."

"Whoa! Whoa! Whoa! Home team!" Smurf interrupted B-hov's spiel with a curious expression. "What da'fuck are you saying?"

"Homie, please don't give me that side ways look your giving me right now. . .you know me better than that!" B-hov snapped before sliding further to the edge of his seat and continuing, "Now, here's the deal. The State is gonna toss out the indictment so the Alphabet Boys can pick it up and charge me with continuing a criminal enterprise, conspiracy to launder monetary instruments and that 848 shit that carry's a mandatory life without parole sentence."

"So what you got in mind?" Smirf inquired.

B-hov, looking both ways and over his shoulders before coldly answering, "I want my comrades and close affiliates to get me da'fuck up outta here on my next court date, before the bus gets to the Bronx Supreme."

The childhood buddies shared a brief moment of silence as Smurf stared into B-hov's eyes and absorbed the seriousness of his statement before asking, "When is your next court date?"

"Fifty days from today."

"Aight. Say no more." Smurf calmly said before adding, "Oh and by the way, stay tuned into the news tomorrow evening. Cause me and R.S. gon' holla at that lame ass nigga Camel for rejecting a business proposition and then trying to style on us in front of his toy mu'fuckin soldiers. So we gon' turn East Tremont Avenue into tremendous gun play." He added with a venomous snarl before preparing himself to depart the facility.

Chapter 33

BULLETS OVER THE B-X

*S*trolling down East Tremont Avenue, carefully peering left and right and sure enough just like R.S. thought, the soon to be former kingpin was mulling about in front of the Post Office chatting with a couple of his henchmen, when his eyes froze on them, the moment he glanced over the male shoulder whose back was facing the two ghetto grim reapers. R.S. and Smurf drew their weapons.

"RUN!" Camel yelled to his buddies. Then he ran south, up the avenue in the middle of the street in a forty-five degree angle through the busy Bronx traffic. R.S. ran into the street behind him but almost got hit by an old Cutlass Supreme, traveling in the same direction driven by an elderly woman who seemed more shocked at the sight of his firearm than the fact she almost killed him before slamming on her brakes. He never looked back as he continued pursuit. Camel hauled ass across the street and dashed through the carwash. R.S. let loose three shots, **"DOOM! DOOM! DOOM!"** All but one missed its target. The lead whizzed into his left upper thigh, knocking Camel to the pavement. He hurriedly got up and started trotting with a limp and crouched down a few yards away between two parked cars across from McDonald's, unaware that R.S. was focused in on his every step as R.S. made his way towards him. Camel peered around the vehicle, just as he approached and came face to face with his killer. An audible gasp escaped his mouth before he spoke in a frantic tone "Come on man! Please don't do this!" He began pleading, "I-I-I'm'a give you da'spot."

"NIGGA! How da'fuck you gonna give me what's already mines?" R.S. barked before pulling the trigger of his Smith & Wesson, double action 10 millimeter. **"BOOM!"** The slug slammed into his skull leaving the contents from his skull pouring onto the concrete.

A fusillade of different calibers diverted his attention back towards the direction he had come from. He fled at top speed to assist Smurf in the festivities at hand. Bending the corner, a woman of about thirty-five years of age with two small children screamed hysterically as she hovered over her kids to shelter them from harm as he passed them in front of the Playhouse Strip Club. That's when R.S. noticed Smurf in the middle of the block holding court, trading shots with two of Camels most loyal soldiers, with his face twisted in a murderous snarl continuously pulling the triggers on the twin Glock 21z with high capacity extended clips which held 31 rounds each. The sounds loudly echoed through the neighborhood. One of the gunmen ducked behind a parked vehicle just in time as a slug whizzed passed his head blowing a chunk of concrete from the building behind him. He then extended his gun and returned a few shots of his own, which caused Smurf to roll to the ground, coming up on one knee. He continued busting, **"BOOM BOOM BOOM!!!!"** The other gunman was a few cars away letting loose shots from a .380 over the hood of a Pathfinder. Smurf crisscrossed his weapons and fired at both men, **"BOOM BOOM!!"** Shooting the windows out of parked cars, causing their alarms to blare in unison. The second gunman was so keyed in on Smurf that he didn't notice R.S. pinching his trigger in his direction until the front windshield of the truck was blown out. Realizing the shots had come from the opposite direction meant him and his partner were sandwiched in. He took a chance and dashed in R.S.'s direction, firing as opposed to facing the twin assault that Smurf was administering. That's when Smurf struck him from the blindside causing his body to jerk back as R.S. ran full speed ahead, in the adversary's direction firing into his chest and torso, until he went crashing to the pavement at that precise moment. Then his weapon recoiled indicating the firearm was empty. He immediately reached into the back pocket of his Evisu jeans and slapped in the extra clip, viewing the direction Smurf was aiming his weapon.

R.S. followed the nose of his comrades weapons, crouched low as he maneuvered ahead along side the parked vehicles. From the lone gunman's peripherial vision he saw a figure move and diverted his aim towards R.S. Smurf took this opportunity to move in for the kill as he came to his feet with both hammers extended inches away from one another, dumping lead into the gunman when he rose up, as shell casings spilled out the side of his weapons. When he crumbled to the ground, they ran up on him and dumped a volley of shots into his face and head until it opened up like a cracked eggshell, with brain matter and thick globs of blood calmly flowing down the concrete.

Hearing the gunshots come to a conclusion, pedestrians came from their sheltered positions and began trotting and speed walking to their destinations.

"LET'S BE UP OUTTA HERE!" Smurf suggested as they tucked away their weapons and blended in with the horrified crowd until they reached the Twin Donut Eatery, an establishment owned by their long time Arabian friend, Hybeeb. When they entered the shop, Hybeeb escorted them to the basement where a secret passage lead to an underground tunnel that ended at 179th and Bronx Park Avenue, where Smurf's Denali was tucked out of obvious view in the rear of a garage directly on the corner that was owned by the Arabs uncle. Hopping in, they drove at a smooth pace, listening to Wu Tang Clan's "Wu Tang Forever" CD, as they bent a left onto Boston Road. Then came to an abrupt stop when the red light caught them at 178th Street.

Chapter 34

GIVING BIRTH PREMATURE

*T*hirty three miles away from her old East New York stomping ground, Latesha stood front and center in the dining room area of one of her two Long Island condos. Her left arm folded across her chest, dragging on a cigarette pacing the length of the table. Back and forth holding an important meeting with a few of her out-of-town employees while Dutch, her massive size red nose pitbull continuously circled the long conference table.

"Murdoch," she began to address the dealer who controlled the Willingboro section of New Jersey. "Since you're moving our product at an alarming rate, I'm gonna push you three times as much every month, so that you won't have to keep making too many unnecessary trips back here to New York for re-ups." She paused a second for another pull on her Newport and inhaled a cloud of smoke. The dealer shook his head in agreement. "And as for you, Jamel..." she said, pointing her cigarette toward the 340 pounder who controlled an entire Pennsylvania town, before exhaling the smoke from her nostrils, "Your funds aint coming up the way they should, so I'm gonna have to demote you and . . ."

"What!" Jamel snapped, banging his pudgy fist on the pine wood table, spilling his drink and causing everyone in the room to shift their focus towards him. He was obviously displeased with Latesha's decision to demote him. His eyes quickly became a crimson red, thick pulsating veins formed in his neck as he short-windedly ranted and raved. The pitbull, just a few feet away, began to growl, revealing a row of sharp teeth that looked as though they were capable of tearing a mouthful of someone's inner organs from out of them in an instant. This breed of dog was the most dangerous of all K-9's and rivaled the ferocity of a Serengetti lion. Jamel found them to be vicious and unpredictable creatures, sort of like a crazed mentally ill patient. The dog closed his snarling mouth shut only when Latesha snapped her fingers and ordered him to stand down, but it stood there viciously staring the heavy-set man down. Jamel decided to ignore the agitated dog which proved to be the best thing to do. While, he continued to plead his case as he and Latesha went back and forth.

Seated to Jamel's left was none other than Flatbush's very own crowned drug kingpin, Chucky Don. A six foot-three, light-skinned complexion, muscular built brother who bore such striking resemblance to the late great Pimp-C. Pimp-C was a member of the Texas rap duo, U.G.K (Under Ground Kings). The only difference between the two was that Chucky Don possessed the undisputed debonair, swagger of broad player, Bishop Magic Don Juan. Chucky Don emphatically had undying loyalty and the utmost respect for Latesha. He had the golden pleasure of knowing her since the Spring of 1974. The two became friends shortly after Chucky Don and his family migrated to the U.S. from the small island of Jamaica and settled in Brooklyn's notorious Vanderveer Housing Complex, where Latesha would often visit relatives.

Chucky Don casually sat back in his seat allowing a thick cloud of smoke to escape his lips after removing his favorite expensive imported cigar from his mouth. With all the endlessly back and forth between Jamel and Latesha, he decided he had clearly heard enough nonsense for one night and figured it would be best to intervene before the situation took a turn for the worst, knowing Latesha wouldn't hesitate to put Jamel's fat ass on ice.

After adjusting his 24K gold diamond and emerald choppard cuff links, he rested the lit cigar in the ashtray, cleared his throat and raised his hand abruptly silencing Jamel with a brief venomous stare and began to speak in a huss and subtle tone.

"Listen here . . .," Chucky Don said as he uncrossed his legs and continued to address Jamel without acknowledging his presence, "It's nothing personal, Homie. This'a business!" He paused to emphasize his point, "And in any business, when an employee isn't effectively or efficiently following through with their job description, it creates a very hostile work enviorment. Especially in our line of business. Cuz, here it is . . ." He said before taking a sip of Miscato and placing the glass back on it's coaster. "We are all playing our part. Knocking our shit off, three . . . four, sometimes five pounds a week. And you mean to tell us your bitch ass can't even get rid of one punk ass pound?" He paused a second then turned to face Jamel. "It's quite clear your lame ass is dead weight."

Jamel offensively sprang to his feet, fuming. "Check this out my man . . . I don't know what da'fuck you heard about me, but you ain't 'bout to be sitting up in here calling me all outta my mufuckin' name n'shit!" He firmly stated.

Chucky Don wasn't the least bit moved by Jamel's weak attempt of trying to bass up. He nonchalantly laughed in his face before saying, "I strongly suggest you sit your fat ass back down in that chair and lower that tone before I start to take your bitch ass serious and end up having to discipline ya nickel and dime ass up in this mother fucka!" Chuck warned, unholstering and cocking back the hammer of his chrome black diamond encrusted handle Colt .45 and rested it on the table out of Jamel's reach.

Watching the scene through calm eyes, Latesha reached between the two guys and extinguished the butt of her cigarette into a large glass ashtray, then spoke in a tranquil manner.

"Jamel, I'm gonna advise you not to ever do that again. That dog. . ." She said with a nod, "is professionally trained to respond to any form of a threat and will react without command when the owner, that would be me" she sarcastically said with her index finger pressed against her upper breast, "is threatened and will continue to attack until commanded to terminate. So if there's a next time..." She paused a second for effect, "which I hope not, I won't snap my finger."

Upon conclusion of her spiel her cell phone began chirping. Jamel flopped back into his seat as Latesha immediately answered the call. She listened briefly then cut the line. "Uhm, fellas, I'm gonna have to adjourn this meeting until tomorrow. Vicky just gave birth prematurely."

Chapter 35

BONED OUT OF TOWN

*S*tepping out of a clothing store on Manhattan's Madison Ave., Black Pat ran into Tee, who she's been trying to contact for the last two days to no avail. What Pat didn't know was that Tee had good reason not to be disturbed. She was on a secret rendezvous with someone she met a few weeks ago at a club she and Tameko attended out in Long Island.

"Well...aint this 'bout a bitch!" Pat began before placing her shopping bags on the ground. Then greeting her best friend with a feminine hug and a peck on the cheek. "Giirrl, I've been blowin' your phone dafuck up for two days straight. And now I bump into your stink ass on my shopping spree. I hope you know you had me worried like hell. So what's up, bitch? Where you been?" She concluded through investigating eyes. Tee knew that look all too well and knew that Pat expected an explanation for her calls being ignored.

"A'ight...you got me girl!" Tee stated in a defeated tone then added, "I was with that nigga Drip."

"Who?"

"Drip. You know that dark-skinned dude with the cornrows, I met that night at the club in East Hampton. From Rochester!"

"Where dafuck you seen him at?"

"I ran into 'em at The Coliseum out in Queens. He was about to enter the jewelry store when I spotted him. And you know I was fly as hell. I was rocking my green Chanel mini-dress with the plunging neckline. So before I stepped to him, I hoisted these 38 double D's up a few centimeters. Huh, you know these here babies were placed on women for all men's feeling and sucking pleasure!" Tee went on in her rapid-fire monalog, momentarily cupping both breasts gently as Pat stood there listening with her arms folded across her body, shaking her head.

"Anyway, the moment I approached him, his eyes almost popped out his damn head. I'm talking about mouth wide open and all'a dat. So...long story short, we went back to his place, which was in a suburb area just outside of Rochester, called Brighton. And GIIIRRRLLL!! Let me tell you!!" Tee managed to add before pausing a second to catch her breath. "The place was humongous! Six bedrooms, four baths, a pool and a mufuckin' jacuzzi, all sitting on a well manicured three acres of land!"

"Get da'fuck outta here! For real?"

"I'm dead fuckin' serious!" Tee shot back with a stoned face expression.

"Did you give'em some pussy?" Pat asked in a hushed tone after briefly looking both ways to make sure no one was in earshot.

"SOME!? *SSShhiit*, I gave'em all the damn pussy he wanted for them two days. I *even* let him bust my anal cherry, too." She let her last statement linger a few seconds. Taking Pat's ears completely hostage, causing her to immediately interject before Tameko could continue.

"Aaaahhhh, ahun. Say word!"

"WORD!"

Now staring her friend down through squinted eyes, Pat began with rapid questions without batting a lash. "So, how was it? Was it good? Did it hurt or what??"

"Nope. Not at all, girl! He relaxed me first. Sucked my pussy to perfection in the doggy-style position. Then rubbed my back, planted warm kisses on my neck and he even licked my asshole inside and out. Then after smearing that K-Y Jelly shit around in my anus...you know that stuff I told you about a while back when we were watching that porno at the spot . . . *aannyway*, after that he pulled off the condom and put a fresh one on. Then he thumb-fucked me for I don't know how long. I just know that shit felt good. Real good. Then when I least expected, he plunged his dick up my ass to the hilt. I screamed so loud that he tried to cover my damn mouth. I was about to bite his mufuckin' hand off, when suddenly, the feeling turned to pleasure. *Mmmm...*" Tee continued. "I don't know what the hell happened Pat, but I started scooting back. Trying my damn best to bury as much of his dick up in me as possible. My eyes stared off into space as we went back and forth. Meeting each other stroke for stroke. I can't front, those were *some* nights, girl! Shit! That nigga layed that pipe on a bitch like a plumber. Plus there were a few moments when I thought he was gonna literally split a bitch in half."

"Are you serious?"

"WHAT!!" Tee barked, causing a few pedestrians to divert their attention toward them. "Am I serious!? Hell yeah, I'm serious. That motherfuckaz shit was stretching me all outta proportion."

"Well that's what'cha get for trying to be like that porn chick, Pinky." Pat joked. Then continued, "So what's the 4-1-1 with him? Did you find out if he got a steady chick or what? Cause you know how these niggaz be getting down. Plus he out here ballin' too! Shit...probably got a wife hid somewhere."

"Nah, he aint married. But he did tell me that some bitch name Gina from his old hood be stalking him all crazy n' shit. But she's the least of my worries." Tee assured.

"I know dat's right girl!" Pat replied as they high-fived each other. The two chatted a few more minutes then went their separate ways.

Chapter 36

REVENGE

*I*t's been well over a month since Vicky gave birth to the five pound eight ounce Ronnie, Jr. Little Ronnie has been in Latesha's care for the last two days. And with Ronnie Sr. down in Fayette handling their Alabama operation, she had the house all to herself. But today would be the day she'd bring one of her promises of revenge to fruition. Swinging her legs over the queen sized bed and slowly getting up with her hands raised above her head, she stood on her toes and stretched the five foot, eleven inch frame before pulling her wedged boy short underwear from the crease of her ass cheeks with her thumb and index finger. After a quick shower, she draped herself in a blue loose fitting pant suit and matching two inch leather heels, grabbed her Tory Burch Tote bag that contained the items needed for her mission and hit the door.

In a little under fourty minutes, she was pulling into a parking spot two blocks from her destination, directly in front of a boys and girls club that had seen better days. Before exiting her vehicle, she flung a silk scarf over her head, tied it in a knot beneath her chin and slid on a huge oval shaped pair of sunglasses, then put on her black leather gloves. Entering the building's lobby she examined the directory on the left side of the wall, than slid her index finger down the names of occupants until she came to the name she was looking for. Proceeding through the spacious lobby that led to four elevators, two on each side, she took the first one on her left and pushed the button for the seventh floor. The elevator moved upward with ease as the soft rhythm of jazz seeped from the tiny speaker that rested overhead. At the conclusion of her ride, she stepped out of the elevator and strolled down the narrow, dimly lit hallway. She noticed an elderly Hispanic woman dressed in a maintenance uniform, exiting an apartment two doors away from her intended destination and headed in her direction.

'Oh well', Vicky thought to herself as she slid her hand down into her tote bag. When the woman came within four feet of her, with the speed of a cheetah, Vicky drew her silenced .38 caliber revolver, aiming at the womans waist, she then brought her index finger to her mouth.

"Shhh! If you scream I can guarantee your demise, but if you follow my instructions you'll live to see another day."

After giving the woman brief instructions, she nudged her down the hall to apartment 222 and stood out of view with the nozzle of her pistol trained on her. The woman did exactly what she was ordered to do and politely knocked on the door with the knuckle of her right middle finger.

"Just a minute!" Came a woman's voice from inside the apartment. Her footsteps could be heard as she strolled across the hardwood floor. The peephole slot went up and just like Vicky commanded, the elderly woman smiled broadly, then the door came ajarred.

"Good morning Marisol. What can . . . huhh . . ." The woman gasped at the sight of the gun when Vicky brought the weapon to rest between her eyes with the swiftness of a feline.

"Bitch, if you say another damn word, I'll blow your brains da'fuck out." She venomously stated through clenched teeth before shoving the Latino woman into the apartment with her.

"Who was it hun?" Her husband shouted moments later from another area of the apartment. Hearing no response, he walked into the living room where his wife and neighbor were on their knees with their hands locked in flexicuffs, behind their backs. "What the . . ." WHACK! Vicky came down across his cheek with the pistol from his blind side, causing blood and shaving cream to splash on the wall as his straight razor went sailing to the floor.

"Aaaeeii!" He screamed, holding the side of his face, looking at her wide-eyed and full of fear.

"It aint no fun when the Angel got the gun, huh?" She said with a wicked grin. "Now get 'cha bitch ass down on da'mufuckin" floor!" She cuffed him to the back with plastic restraints as well. Then stuffed a handball into his mouth. "Since you like abusing women, you should enjoy this lil show Im'a perform for you!" She stated with cold and bitter humor. Then with all the might of a professional soccer player, she kicked his wife square in the back just below her shoulder blades. As she fell forward, her head went crashing into the sharp corner of the nearby marble coffee table, knocking her unconscious. The sound of the impact caused the elder woman who was just inches away, to cringe as a stream of tears ran down her face. Her husband layed there on his stomach with his eyes pleading for his wife's mercy as blood leaked from the huge gash in her forehead.

"Uhn uhnn, bitch! Don't play that possum shit on me!" Vicky said, pulling her back by a clump of her blonde hair. WHACK-WHACK-WHACK-WHACK!!! She beat the helpless woman upside the head with the gun in a vicious rage while her husband defenselessly looked on as her lifeless body slumped to the woodgrained floor. The cracking sound caused the couple's three month old baby, who was in the adjoining room to wail uncontrollably. Turning towards the male with a smirk on her face, Vicky pointed the blood dripping weapon towards the next room, while he shook his head hysterically from side to side as tears built up in his eyes.

"My, my, my! What da'fuck do we have in there?" Vicky sarcastically asked. The Latin woman was quiet up until that point.

"Mees, please don't hurt da'baby!" She pleaded in her native accent.

Ignoring her, Vicky went into the next room. She came back cradling the infant in her left arm. She quieted the baby with the pacifier that was attached to it's bib than calmly walked up behind the woman. "Psst . . . psst . . . Mind your mufuckin' business." The two slugs slammed into the woman's head killing her instantly. Vicky then tucked her gun and placed the chubby cheeked baby girl, faceup only inches away from her tearful father. Then trekked into the kitchen and began removing the grill-like racks from the oven. She rummaged through cabinets until she found what she thought would be sufficient enough.

After tossing a stick of butter into the aluminum turkey pan, she brought it into the living room and placed the infant inside. "Revenge is best administered when there is no emotions involved." She snapped through clenched teeth with fire in her eyes, before turning on her heels. After placing the pan in the oven she turned it on a low temperature then took her pistol from her waistband and calmly walked back over to the whining man.

"Detective O'Keefe!?" She began. "I've followed you three times a week to this here building. Even on the days of my coming home party and babyshower. I prayed for this day to come and my blessing couldn't have came at a better time than now." She said, wiping a tear from his cheek. "If you can remember, I never shed one tear while you and your partner put hands and feet all on me, in that interrogation room! So why are you crying?" She asked, took a deep breath then continued, "All I could think about was revenge. So man da'fuck up, motherfucker!" She barked, pointing the gun at his head, pinching it's trigger three times. Psst...Psst...Psst, then exited the apartment. "One down. One more to go." She said under her breath as she stepped into the elevator.

Entering her vehicle, she looked down at her watch and cursed inwardly, than smacked the dashboard before pulling out her cell phone and punching in some numbers.

"Yeah! What's up?" The voice on the other end said, after answering on the second ring.

"This is Vicky, I aint gon'be able to make it to the Bronx in time, but I know y'all gon' have fun."

"Oh, we most definitely will!" Goldie assured her before cutting the line.

A half hour later, Vicky pulled along side his partner's vehicle in the precinct's parking lot, as he was killing the engine. She came to an abrupt stop and trained her silenced weapon on his head with lethal intention. The moment he pulled on the door handle, she pulled the trigger. The bullet slammed into the cop's skull, leaving him sprawled across the vehicle's front seat shaking loose his soul, as his brains seeped from the gaping hole in his cranium.

"PAYBACK IS A BITCH, MUFUCKA." She stated with a venomous snarl, before easing out of the parking lot and disappearing into the morning traffic.

Chapter 37

UNCAGED

*J*ay, a long time friend of B-hov, sat comfortably behind the wheel of his late 1980 black Chrysler New Yorker. He parked at the tip of the bridge just at the Riker's Island visitor parking.

"OK, Playboy!" He began, speaking into the disposable cell phone. "There's a whole fleet of slaveships leaving Fantasy Island, so how'n da'fuck am I suppose to know which one Kunta Kente' is on?"

"Just blink the headlights twice and when you see the surrender flag you'll know." The voice on the other end answered.

After flashing his lights twice a six inch piece of toilet paper began wagging from between the gated window.

"Aight, Playboy, he's headed . . ." was all he got out before the line went dead.

* * * * *

After hanging up the pay phone, Smurf strolled past the train station's entrance, crossed 149th Street and casually stood next to Raquel at the bus stop, directly in front of the neighborhood's post office, on the Grand Concourse. With his guitar case resting at his feet, they pretended to be waiting for public transportation, chatting during the morning rush hour as predestrians filed out from either the local 2, 4 or 5 trains before making their way to work.

A short while later, Raquel's cellular phone rang. She answered at the conclusion of the first ring, after clearing her throat. "They just got off the Major Deagan, so y'all should see them in less than two." Michelle said once the bus passed her on the bridge where she sat in her car with the hood up before disconnecting the line.

Raquel stuffed the phone in the back pocket of her form fitting Apple Bottom jeans, then signaled Smurf with her eyes that it was now showtime. He reached down for his guitar case and casually trekked away from the crowded bus stop. Diverting his attention south of 149th Street, where in near distance he saw the bus making its way towards him. Ignoring the blinking don't walk signal, he stepped into the middle lane and with a flick of the thumb the guitar case popped open. After retrieving the firearm he kicked the case towards the curb and brought the weapon shoulder length, placing the driver in its crosshairs.

"Oh Shit!" The driver yelled with a horrified expression before the single shot slammed directly into his throat, causing the bus to swerve into oncoming traffic, then coming to a crashing halt head on into a minivan. Crowds of pedestrians ran for cover as women began yelling and screaming at the top of their lungs.

Raquel trotted towards the bus entrance with her .40 cal. automatic drawn. The second Correction's Officer was lying under the dashboard blabbering into the transmitter with a terrified look on his face. **BOOM!** was the sound that shattered the glass from the frame of the door.

"Open this mu'fucker up! RIGHT NOW and keep your hands where I can see'em, too!" She demanded in a sturdy tone. Reaching up with both hands in clear view, he pulled the lever that opened the door as a small debris of glass fell to the pavement. "NOW STAND YO' PUNK ASS UP!!" Getting to his feet with his hands held above his head, he pleaded with his eyes to be spared. "Aight, now remove your gun from the holster!" She commanded. "And be sure to use your thumb and index finger!" The officer did as he was commanded and held the firearm out in front of him, gingerly. "Throw it over there!" She gestured to her left. The weapon went sailing several feet away. "OK, toss the cuff keys and go open that damn gate that separate you mu'fuckaz from the prisoners. Then I want you to take your ass to the rear of the bus."

Nervously, he unlocked the gated divider and hurried down the aisle trying his best to duck and weave the wild punches from obviously angry but joyful prisoners, as he made his way to the back where he curled himself up at the foot of the emergency exit, which could only be opened from the outside.

"Listen up Fellas," she began, after entering the bus demanding their full attention, their focus was captivated by the sandy-haired, green-eyed exotic looking female beauty, "I don't give a flying fuck if you get off or stay da'hell on this slaveship or not, but every mufuckin' body is getting their damn cuffs taken off."

After getting two eye-winking signals from B-hov, she immediately uncuffed the two individuals that were seated across from him in the front row first for obvious reasons. Then she got to working on him and the well-groomed older cat he was cuffed to. In less than two minutes all twelve prisoners were uncuffed. The sounds of police sirens could be heard approaching.

"Yo! Hurry da'fuck on up in there!" Smurf yelled, diverting his attention in every direction with his weapon firmly gripped in both hands. A few fellas began brutalizing the C.O., beating, kicking and stomping him in and out of consciousness until he would never awake again. The prisoners then dashed off of the bus behind B-hov and Raquel, running in every direction. Some ran down into the nearby train station where they lost themselves just before the police arrived. The two blue and white patrol cars descended to the scene from westbound of the Grand Concourse and the officers exited their vehicles with weapons drawn. Smurf let loose a barrage of .223 mil.

bullets from the M-16 assault rifle, causing them to retreat behind their patrol cars.

"Here, take this. I gotta go'n hold Smurf down!" Raquel said while handing B-hov the keys to one of the get-a-way cars, after trotting behind the post office, where they were stationed. "It's for the one parked in front of the three garbage cans." She yelled over her shoulder after turning on her heels to join Smurf.

From her angle, she noticed two uniformed officers running up from the subway and she took cover behind the row of nearby pay phones. She tucked her gun into the waistband of her jeans, crouched low and began running towards them screaming.

"AAAhhh! Oh my God! Oh my God!" she wailed, coming within a few feet of them.

"Miss, stay down right there!" One of them yelled, motioning with his service weapon for her to take shelter behind the fire hydrant. The second he took his eyes off her, she backed her gun out from her waist with lightening speed and blasted both men neatly and efficiently. Blood gushed from the gruesome face wounds of the men. "Stupid mother-fuckers!" she spat to herself.

A few yards away a pudgy shaped African-American officer came dashing from the rear of the college building brandishing his weapon. He headed towards Sam's Restaurant in hope of catching Smurf from the blindside, but he fell head first from a wild shot to the left buttock at the eatery's entrance. He layed there for a moment as rapid gunfire echoed throughout the morning air. RATA-TAT-TAT-TAT-TAT!! Two slugs came smashing inches away from his head into the door frame, as pedestrians who took shelter in the restaurant looked on in horror. "Shit!" he cursed, then got on his hands and knees and made a limping dash for cover behind a large mailbox.

From his rear he could hear the sound of a motorcycle accelerating, but when he turned his head in that direction, it was too late. R.S. sent a storm of bullets into his frame from the Mac-10 he had extended under Kacky's right arm between the handle bars as she gunned the Honda CBR motorcycle down the Bronx sidewalk to the other side of the street where he jumped off the bike to assist Smurf.

The two old school gansters with minor charges who opted to stay on the prison bus and who hadn't seen this much drama in a long time, watched from their seats with keen interest. "God Daayum!" One yelled from his crouched position at the center of the bus. "Niggas and Bitches is turning it up out this mu'fuckaa!" He added after the Lincoln Continetal, minus its windshield, jumped the curb on 150th Street, flying down the Grand Concourse.

Matilda came through the sunroof top of the car with a H.K. MP5 submachine gun raining slugs in the direction of the police with the help of Goldie, who was squeezing off two 9 millimeter Parabellums with her arms extended from the back right passenger side window. Althea, with her right index finger clenched around the trigger of her weapon maneuvered the vehicle with one hand while firing her Walther PPK .380 with the other over the dashboard. Bullets zipped into the plain clothed officer that had, in a matter of seconds, reached into the neck of his shirt, pulled out his badge hanging from its chain, whipped out his gun and moved towards the action. Only he never got the chance to discharge his weapon. All but two slugs entered through his protective body armor. "Aaaiiiee!" The pain was so excruciating that he could not help but scream. He turned clutching the lower part of his stomach as blood squirted between his fingers and trotted away the best he could in the opposite direction. Down the hill he stumbled and fell. His weapon slipped from his grip as he weakened from the immediate loss of too much blood. Breathing so rapidly, he was afraid he might hyperventilate and began to feel dizzy and disoriented. He thought that if he got to his feet, at this point he was sure to fall back to the pavement. Choosing to lay there on his back watching the clouds speed by through blurred vision he heard in the near distance the sound of a vehicle coming to a screeching halt. As he struggled to retrieve his weapon, a few feet from where he layed, he heard a familiar click then a voice spoke, "GA'HEAD MU'FUCKA, TOUCH IT AND I'LL FINISH YOU OFF RIGHT WHERE YOU'RE LAYING!" He noticed it was a female's voice. A voice, nonetheless, that sounded dangerous and meant every manifested word uttered. Goldie stood in a shooting stance out of his direct view.

"Pu-pu-put th-the weapon . . ." was all he managed to say, as his finger tips met with the handle of his service revolver. Goldie's eyes blazed with venom before she fired the fatal shot into his temple, ending his career on earth.

"He's gone! Let's go Bitch!" Althea yelled from the car to Goldie, who was now kicking the lifeless body of the officer.

A half a block away three cops had split up. One took cover behind a large nearby tree. Smurf sprayed a burst of shots at him that sent small chuncks of bark flying. Wood debris splattered into the cops face and a small splinter flew into his left eye causing him to squint. With his vision practically non-existant, he bagan shooting wildly in an attempt to fend off the deadly team of gangsters. But luck wasn't on his side as R.S. trotted towards him with a tight grip on his Mac-10, shooting from his hip. He and Smurf continued squeezing off, riddling the officer's body with bullets. The cop's body lifelessly slumped to the ground.

A few yards away another officer took aim and fired two shots in R.S. direction, but missed. He fired again, this time hitting him in the left bicep. Blood began to profusely gush from his wound and onto the ground. **BOOM-BOOM-BOOM-BOOM!!** Was the sound in rapid succession, as

R.S.'s short burst of fire tore into the cop. He wailed uncontrollably as he went crashing to the concrete. R.S. sent another volley, **BOOM-BOOM-BOOM-BOOM-BOOM!** The cop was hushed forever as he layed there motionless.

"Aight, lets get da'fuck up outta here before we get knocked!" Smurf warned as more police sirens wailed in the distance. R.S. adrenaline caused the blood from his wound to flow more profusely, and he grimaced from the agonizing pain as they sprinted away. "Damn! Where da'fuck is Rocky?" Smurf yelled out as they approached the get-a-way car.

"Ahh, I - I never seen'er!" R.S. managed to say through obvious pain.

"Shit! I hope she got with the other Angels." Smurf spat, entering the automobile and unlocking the door for his wounded comrade.

Crouched behind a post office vehicle, on the opposite side of the street, a lone cop took aim as R.S. was about to hop into the front passenger seat of the car. However, before he could tug at the trigger, a dying thought flashed through his mind when he felt the muzzle of cold steel pressed to the side of his head. A fraction of a second later the loud sound of a gun went **BOOM!** And whatever else he was thinking, in that short time span, began gushing out with the blood from the gaping hole as he went crashing to the ground. The loud cannon-like sound startled Smurf and R.S. causing them to reach for their weapons, which they had already tucked away.

"Don't worry Fellas, y'all know y'all got an Angel watching over y'all." Raquel said as she stood there blowing the smoke from the gun's barrel with a smirk on her face. Climbing into the vehicle, she relieved herself of the irritating wig she was wearing, extracted the contact lenses from her eyes, unfastened her 36D-cup bra and slid it through her sleeve. "Here, tie this around your arm, it'll staunch the blood flow until we get you some help." She

stated, handing R.S. the bra over the seat. Finally, they all
let out a sigh of relief as they fled from the scene.

To be continued . . .

Intelligent Allah
Author of "Lickin' License"

K. Deezy & Maneesa
(Big Meech's Daughter)

BK & Computer

D, Web, BK & Bo

Big & Lil Ox

Southern Angels

Quesha

Sable &
Albany's Finest

Trenea & Nyasia   *Gwen*

Chereda & Latesha

Crystal

Queen

Southern Angels

Nesto

Knowledge & Rozz   *Koolaid & Tammy*

Rosa & Gunz   *Tamek & Shakira*

Bar & Fatima   *LaTasha & Will*
          aka *Scar*

Bryant & Luz   *The Real "RoBo" Just
          & Friend*

Big Wise & Wifey   *Drip & Gina*

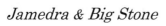

Jamedra & Big Stone   *Jose*

Shorty B

Prince & Knowledge

*Green Eyes Born
& Taheem*   *Dobbs*

Rough Sex   *Chino- BX Finest*

*Knowledge, Shorty Dip
& Just God*

-Drac & Wolf

Chucky Don

Vee

Mr. Nasty

I-Queen (center)

Skinner & Black Pat   *Gotty & Skinner*

Cleo & Tina   *Bar & Stone*

Bilah, Wadu, Shabazz, Artiste,
Scribby, Tek Won

Cool & Friends

Legendary Bogart

Gina & Friend

Justina & Amanda

*Cleopatria, Maria, Kacky
Benetta & Heather*

Bree, Autumn & Atry

Kiana

O.G. Gracie

Duwanna

Angie

Kacky & Shameek

Kacky, Michelle, Laura, Paula

Skinner

Shannon   *Kacky*

"The Sutter Angels"

Kacky & Sarita

Tameko

Eye Candy

Knowledge

Rose'

Goldie

Nett

Autumn & Atry

Joey

Kiana

Big Phife

Hot ain't the word to describe.
Porn Star "PINKY"

Sin by F. Gee Heyward

I may not have lived the glamorous life of Karrine Steffans, or any other Video Vixen for that matter, but I was just as reckless; and in some cases, I may have been even worse!

My life is no fairy tale. There have never been any white picket fences, pretty little Yorkshire Terriers or some handsome Knight in shining armor escorting me to the high school prom. To even be telling you my story now shames me in a lot of ways.

You see, I grew up in midtown Manhattan, Amsterdam Projects on 64th Street, to be exact. My mother named me Tabitha Johnson, but most people called me "Sin". Yea, of all the nicknames I've gotten, it's been Sin for most of my thirty-two years. So by the time I turned thirteen, the initials of my birth name, TJ, would be accompanied by the word HOOKER! You know, like that old television cop series.

Anyway, by then, I had already taken to the streets of New York spreading my young legs throughout the Five Boroughs and other surrounding areas. So I didn't care two-shits about what anybody called me!

My mother tried to send me away to her sisters' house in Lithonia, Georgia, at first. But that trip only lasted nine days. The moment Aunt Mary caught my full lips wrapped around her husbands' penis; Sin was on the next thing smoking.

Needless to say, the threat of sending me to a group home met serious confrontation from my step-dad, whom my mother seemed to care more about than she ever did us, me and my two younger siblings that is. But, boyyyy, if she only knew the real reason why her so-called Billy Dee Williams was helping me out, she would've probably went into cardiac arrest. Well not an actual heart attack, but I strongly doubt she could've stood to hear how my step-dads' mustache used to tickle and make me laugh whenever he stuck his tongue in my eight year old mouth. That's how old I was when it started. Or how he would make me dig for coins in his pocket until his thing moved. Or the time on my twelfth birthday when I awoke to him sucking me down there until I literally felt myself peeing in his mouth. I would later come to find out that it wasn't pee, but my very first experience at having an orgasm.

Oh I had a list of things on him, so I made him my personal defense attorney to stop my mother from sending me away. If she would even fix her mouth like she wanted to throw me into the system . . . I would immediately start crying then run to daddy. And let me tell you, although he hadn't touch me since the first time I threatened to tell someone about the sexual encounters, if he didn't stop my mother from sending me away, from time to time my step-dad would shake his head, sadly and hug me to his chest.

"Sin, you gotta stop this, No one is going to send you away, but think of the examples you're setting for your little sister and brother."

I would've actually believed he cared if each time he hadn't had a hard-on when he held me.

But I learned a lot about myself at an early age. People used to joke and say I had a Southern girl's booty, and they were right. Maybe it was the Similac milk or something because my mothers' butt, right now at 51 (the prime of her life according to her Forbes) wasn't as big as mines way back then. And to top it off, I was the only girl I knew with sprouting titties in second grade. Yep . . . by the time I was in fifth grade, most of the boys had either touched them or paid to see'em. Sin may've been moving faster than a water main-break, but Sin sure wasn't no dummy! I knew the power of my pussy like college professors knew the curriculum they were paid to teach.

Back then boys wasn't all that crazy about dark skinned sista's like me. I'm talking the early to mid-nineties, but with my advanced puberty and wantonness for sex, I was more popular than Regina, my best, best friend. A redbone who the boys jokingly called Casper the Ghost, because of her light complexion and the way she made a dick disappear in her jaws.

She and I were like black coffee and cream. Cutting school, getting piercings and tatted, building up our SUPERHEAD status on the staircases, elevators and projects roofs, wherever we went. If she would spit when she made a boy cum, I would swallow his friends' babies just to make him wish he'd chosen me to suck his dick instead.

See, Regina and me had an unwritten agreement to try to out-do the other, but to never step on the others toes while trying it. We were inseparable, going hard like twin sisters wearing identical outfits. But not anymore!

Before I go on, it's because of this book that Regina and me are no longer friends. A lot of people distanced themselves or outright . . . stopped talking to me all together as a result of this revelation . . . people who just didn't want me to release this book.

"Book?!" I would say. *"This is no book . . . this is just scraps and pieces from my journal . . . the diary I kept for as long as I could remember."*

As a result my stepfather recently copped out to a four year Sodomy and Endangering the Welfare of a Minor, but asked me if I give a damn?! Sin is not a liar! You hear that mom? Sin doesn't have a reason to lie. Since doesn't write fiction and you should know that Sin has never been good at holding her tongue! So like Regina and many others who tried to hate or stop me from telling my story, just know that hiding in your shell is for turtles. I want the world to know the truth . . . fuck it, if it makes you mad.

~~~~~

Chocolate Heat by Tameka Avant

Mya couldn't believe her divorce was final. She had worked so hard to be a faithful wife and make her marriage work, but it just wasn't meant to be. Her ex was a terrible husband, but because she was taught to honor her marriage while growing up, she stayed. She even stayed through verbal and physical abuse and heartache, but today she was officially free. Mya scheduled an appointment to have her beautiful shoulder length hair cut into a short sassy bob with some highlights. This was a new life for her because normally she was afraid of change. She was the type who kept it simple and didn't like a lot of attention, but tonight at her "Divorce Party", as her friends named it, she was going to celebrate being free and happy. She didn't even know how to date anymore. She didn't know where to go to have fun or what to wear but her friends took care of that. They took her to the mall and picked out things that Mya wouldn't dare pick for herself but she agreed.

Later that night Mya stood in the full length mirror and had to admit that she was looking hot! She decided to wear the all black ensemble with the lace shirt, leather mini, fishnet stockings and shockingly high heeled stilettos. Mya giggled. Who was this sexy dominatrix looking back at her? It was too late to turn back now. She sprayed her body with her favorite fragrance, grabbed her small clutch purse and headed to the new club Risqué that everybody was talking about. She took a deep breath. What in the world had her hoochie friends talked her into? She was too old for this mess! She should just go home. As if her friends could read her mind, her phone rang. It was Alicia.

"Where you at hoe?" Alicia was always the loud one, but she had a good heart.

"I'm outside in the parking lot and I don't want to get out," said Mya.

"Well you either get out or I'm coming to get you."

Mya hung up the phone on her friend. She knew that it was not a thing for Alicia to make a scene in public. Mya took a deep breath and got out of the car. She headed toward the long line and heard the music pumping all the way outside. She was about to go to the end of the line when she heard Alicia scream her name. She was at the door entrance waving to her to have her come to the front of the line. "Girl! I thought you changed your mind on us. We know you, scary cat!" Alicia had no idea how right she was. Mya just nodded and took Alicia's hand while she led her through the swarm of hot sweaty people dancing and drinking the night away. She felt so out of place. Alicia looked at her friend and immediately knew that she would need a drink. She took them to a table of about five more girls from work and they sat down. A waitress came over to the VIP area to take their drink orders. After saying hello and giving hugs, Mya looked around the club. It was dark with flashing lights and fake smoke. It had a lot of mirrors and just the right amount of light so that you could see what was in front of you. The music was great and everybody was happy to be out. It was an older crowd so Mya didn't feel like somebody's auntie when she looked about. A song that was a current hit came on and everybody stood up at her table to hit the dance floor. They grabbed her hand and dragged her out to the floor. She stopped to grab her drink that Alicia ordered for her and went to the floor with her friends.

~~~~~~

Gabriel looked across the dance floor from the bar at the group of girls who just stepped on it. All of them were hot! He licked his lips as he checked out each woman to see which one he would talk to.

He never had a problem getting girls. He was even known as a lady's man. He didn't do the long term thing and he made it a point to let any girl he got with know it. Three years ago he gave his heart to a woman who pretended to like him too, but then he found out she was married and had two kids on the side. He vowed that no other woman would waste his time again and he did everything in his power to keep his word. He put on his game face and was ready to head over to talk to all of them. Some were light skinned, some had long hair, some were thin and some were short. But the girl at the end of the line of girls caught his breath in his throat. She was beautiful. She was like a warm cup of hot chocolate, honey, and caramel all wrapped into one. She danced but not like the other girls she was with. She looked like she didn't have anything to prove. She closed her eyes, swayed her hips, and moved her body like she had all the time in the world.

Gabe felt a tap on his shoulder. His boy Wade caught site of the girls too. "Man, you see them broads over there? I gots to get me some of that!" Wade licked his lips and headed that way. Without looking, Gabe held out his hand to stop his friend from going over there. He wanted to make sure his friend didn't get a head start on his Ms. Chocolate over there. Gabe paused and laughed, "His chocolate?" Nah! She was sexy, but he must be tripping, he didn't even know the girl, yet. He walked ahead of Wade and led the way. He tapped Mya on the shoulder. She was so into her own zone she barely noticed him. So he grabbed her by the waist. Mya turned on her heels to give him one of her famous "back up Negro" faces and she paused. She looked up into one of the most handsome faces she had ever seen. He was about 6'3", 250 pounds of solid muscle, cinnamon brown, with a killer smile. Mya blushed and smiled back. She shook her head and took two steps back. No matter how attractive he was, she didn't know this stranger. She would've remembered if she had. Gabe whispered in her ear, "Hi beautiful. Can I dance with you?" Mya blinked out of her daze and said, "Sure." That's all she could manage to say. Gabe took her hand and led her a little further off the dance floor to an isolated corner and held her close. As if on cue the music switched to a classic slow jam and they started to sway to the music. Gabe inhaled her scent. She smelled so good. Her hair was soft as she put her hands around his neck and laid her head on his chest. Mya felt at home. Like this is where she could stay forever. He was a sweet combination of hard and soft and she smelled his masculine cologne that she couldn't get enough of.

"What's your name sweetheart?" Gabe asked her.

"Mya, what's yours?" "My name is Gabriel, like the angel. But my friends call me Gabe." Mya smiled, an angel, huh? With that sexy body and smile she could guess that he was far from an angel. Gabe grabbed her chin and tilted her head up to his and softly kissed her lips. Her lips were soft and sweet and tasted like honey and chocolate just like he imagined. He never kissed women he just met! Mya instantly felt his arousal pushing into her stomach and she felt a shiver deep in her body. This was not like her at all. Maybe it was the drinks but she wanted more. It had been way too long since she let herself go and have a good time. Tonight she wanted Gabe and she would have him.

Gabe asked her if she wanted to go to his room for the night so they could get to know each other, better. She knew that she should say no but, whatever! This was the new Mya. She wanted to have fun. She told Gabe yes. He suggested she text her friends and let them know his name and where they were going. After a short moment Alicia texted back and told her to go for it. She said to be safe and give all the details in the morning. Gabe led her to his brand new Lexus 460 LS. She was impressed. It was shiny silver with black interior. And it smelled like this sexy man. He turned on soft music and held her hand while he drove. They were at the hotel before she knew it. She was suddenly nervous. She bit her lip and wondered if she should just go home. Gabe looked at her lips and said, "Mya, are you alright? Did you change your mind? You don't have to come in if you don't feel comfortable."

The problem was that Mya was too comfortable, that's what made her worry. She looked into his light brown eyes and sighed. She took a deep breath and said, "I just want you to know that we are here to have a good time. No strings attached. I've just gotten out of a nightmare of a relationship, so I just need you to make me feel like I'm Mya again. Is that ok?" Gabe smiled. What more could a man ask for? He kissed her gently and led her up to his suite. He was going to enjoy every minute with Mya and take his time making this a special night that she would never forget.

When they entered the hotel suite Gabe closed the door behind them and looked at Mya. She was so naturally beautiful. He dimmed the lights and led her to the couch. He sat down and pulled her on his lap. He gently grasped the back of her neck and kissed her deeply putting his wet tongue inside her mouth, swirling and withdrawing, pretending it was his dick in her sweet wet pussy. Mya groaned. She could feel his thick arousal grinding between her legs and she pushed into him wanting to feel more. He knew that he could not feel her like he wanted in this position so he picked her up and carried her into the bedroom and gently laid her on his bed. Mya looked up at Gabe as he took off his shirt to reveal his sexy muscled chest and she licked her lips. When he slowly stepped out of his pants she almost died. He had the most gorgeous thickly muscled legs and thighs she had ever seen. Not to mention the enormous long erection straining against his boxers. He grinned sexily when he saw the desire in her eyes. He came over to her and took her feet into his hands and slowly took off her heels while massaging her feet. She whimpered. His hands felt so good. He continued rubbing her fish-netted legs until he reached her thighs and then slowly kissed back down her legs to her feet. She arched her back for more. Gabe flicked his tongue over her toes and said, "You like that, Mya?" She shuddered, nodded yes and opened her eyes to look at him. She could not believe this was happening.

He suddenly stood and said he'd be right back. Mya was not sure what to do. Should she undress? Should she strike a sexy pose or check her hair? She didn't have much time to think about it because Gabe was back. He held some items in his hand and Mya was curious. Gabe came to the side of the bed and said, "Mya, do you trust me?" She didn't know what to say. She didn't know him, but she somehow felt safe with him. She couldn't explain how she felt. All she knew was that she wanted him tonight. She would blame it on the alcohol later. Mya said, "Yes" very softly and his smile broadened even more. He held out a silk scarf and covered her eyes. He used another silk scarf and gently tied her arms to the four poster bed. It was not too tight but tight enough so that she could not get away. Mya started to panic. "Gabe what are you planning to do with me? I don't like this."

Gabe caressed her face and ran his fingers across her lips. "Shhhh, its ok, Mya. I would never hurt you, ok?" She reluctantly nodded her agreement. He proceeded to slowly take her clothes off until she was only in her fish net stockings, bra and panties. Mya was glad that she bought the new sexy lingerie set to go with her outfit. She would have croaked over if she' worn her granny panties.

Gabe's eyes could not protrude further out of his sockets. Oh sweet mother of pearl! She was unbelievable in her sexy underwear. She had sexy long legs, chocolate thighs and hips and the most pretty dark chocolate nipples showed through the lacy bra she wore. He wanted to taste them. He rubbed the strawberry edible lube on the top of the swells of her breasts and slowly swirled his tongue over them. She moaned with delight. He pushed the cups of her bra down and pinched each nipple until they puckered up like they wanted to be kissed. Then he bent his head and suckled and slurped on both until they glistened with moisture. Mya felt the pleasure go straight to her pussy and it throbbed aching to be filled. He poured strawberry on her and kissed her stomach then paused to open her legs to him while he pulled down her fishnet stockings. Mya lifted her hips to help him. He looked at the barely there lacy underwear and inhaled. He could smell her sweet arousal. It smelled good enough to eat and that's exactly what he planned to do. He took his thumb and placed it over her clit and bent his head and licked her from her butt hole to the folds of her pussy lips. Mya screamed out in pleasure. He ripped the panties off of her and stuck two fingers inside of her to get her ready for his thick penis. He pushed them deeper and deeper inside of her. Mya bucked against his fingers and cried out, screaming his name until she came all over his hand. She tasted like chocolate heaven. He lifted her blind fold. He wanted her to see him lick each finger clean from her juices. Mya pulled at her arm restraints. She was frustrated because she wanted to touch him and please him too. Mya panted, trying to catch her breath. "Gabe, untie me please! I need that dick inside of me!" Gabe had planned to leave her tied up a while longer but he wanted to be inside her too – Now!

He was so hard, he couldn't wait any longer. He untied her hands and she pounced on him like a tigress. She straddled his hips and kissed him hard and fast. She kissed his neck and bit his shoulder. She licked his stomach and yanked down his shorts.

Good Lord! How was that thing going to fit inside of her? She looked up at him and all he did was grin, wide. Mya got off of him and said, "Stand up and hold on the bed post." He looked confused by her dominating voice and attitude, but did what she said.

"Mya, I want…"

"Shut up Gabe!" Not a word or I won't give you your surprise!" Gabe closed his mouth. He had no idea what she was up to, but he couldn't wait to see. She took his arms and held them above his head while tying them tightly to the bed rails. She took the other scarf and told him to open his mouth while she gagged his mouth so he couldn't speak. Mya had never done anything like this before but after she had read so many erotic fantasy books she was ready to play the role. She looked over his heap of clothes and found his leather belt and smiled. His eyes widened, unsure of what she would do next. She grabbed the strawberry lube and rubbed it on his back, legs, stomach and thighs. She grabbed his hard erect dick and squeezed until she saw the drop of pre-cum on the tip of its head. She smiled and repeated what he'd asked her earlier. "You like that Gabe?" He nodded his head. She got on her knees and blew on his dick. It twitched. She crawled to the back of him and licked him up his legs all the way up his ass crack until she got all of the lube off. He tried to move away because he couldn't take the pleasure. His dick stood up straight like a rod.

"Stop moving, Gabe!" Thwack! She hit him on his ass with the belt. Gabe jerked in surprise. It stung but not enough to bruise. Thwack! Thwack! He closed his eyes tightly. She removed the gag so that he could speak. "Want some more, Gabe?" Thwack!

He yelled, "Yes, Mya baby. It hurts so good!"

"It's yes, Mistress Mya to you lover boy!"

"Yes Mistress Mya!" She stood in front of him and said, "Good boy!" She turned around and spread her legs while pushing her heart shaped ass up against his dick then slid up and down him until he moaned. He was about to come before he got inside of her pussy.

"Mya! I mean, Mistress Mya, I need to come inside of you!" Thwack!

"You can't come yet lover boy." She dropped to her knees again and grabbed his dick with both hands and rubbed lube all over it. She licked him slowly from his balls to his head until his knees buckled. "Mya, you're gonna make me come in your mouth!" Thwack! "Good lover boy. Come for mommy." He thrust himself deep into her throat. She gagged but held on to his thighs. He thrust deeper into her mouth over and over again and he almost lost his balance but he held on the bars above his head so he wouldn't fall. He couldn't wait anymore. He spewed his hot juices down her throat. She spit it back up and it dripped down her chin onto her chest. She stood up and untied his hands. He fell back onto the bed and grabbed her waist on the way down. She fell on top of him. They laid there catching their breath and Mya grabbed a tissue next to the bed to wipe her face and hands. Gabe just stared at her like she was from out of space. "Mya baby, where have you been all my life!?" She just laughed and smiled. He looked at her and smiled. "Now it's time for me to punish that pussy, Mya!" She crawled over him and put her ass in the air while looking back at him. "That's Mistress Mya to you lover boy!" He tackled her down to the bed and kissed her hard and said, "Let the games begin!"

~~~~~~

Gabe couldn't believe his luck. First he'd met a chocolate Goddess whom he thought maybe he could one day take to get a cup of coffee, but secondly he got a chance to see her naked and taste her. The icing on the cake had to be when she took all of him in her mouth and gave him the best orgasm of his life! His mind raced with what he wanted to do to her but he had to play it cool and slow things down. He wanted to make a good impression on her so he didn't want to act like an amateur horny teenage boy.

So, he paused, took a deep breath and looked down into her eyes and said, "Mya, I really would like to get to know you better. My mom raised me to be a gentleman so I have to ask... do you want to stay the night here with me? We can get room service and I promise to make it a night you'll never forget." Mya smiled and said yes. She was already having a night she would always remember and she couldn't imagine what they could do to make it even better. Gabe looked relieved. He gently took her by the hand and led her into the bathroom. She nervously raked her hands through her short bob and as she looked in the mirror she only noticed a few stray hairs out of place but nothing too bad. She smiled at her reflection. She was a new woman and she liked the sexy lingerie clad vixen that stared back at her. When she looked over to Gabe he slid her one of his sexy smiles, and guided her to the steamy hot glass shower. He kissed her gently and said, "I think maybe we should rinse some of this sticky stuff off of ourselves. I want to taste you again." Mya shivered. She had barely recovered from the first time he licked her there. He slowly slid her bra straps down her arms and unhooked the back where it fell to the tiled floor. He licked his lips as he gently pinched each nipple and she moaned. He pulled down what was left of her torn panties and Mya stepped out of them and looked down at him while he was still on his knees. She read the look of desire in his eyes. He stood up and lifted her up into the steamy shower water. He let her slowly slide down his body. He grabbed some liquid body soap and lathered her body up with it. Gabe couldn't decide who was enjoying this more because she closed her eyes and sighed while he massaged her shoulders back and breasts. Mya leaned her head back and bit her lips in ecstasy. She almost lost her balance when her knees went weak from the way he took his time to please her, but he caught her with his big muscular arms just in time. Mya giggled and he asked her if she was ok. She told him she was fine. Mya's ex husband was spoiled and selfish, so she didn't know how to react to being treated with such reverence and care. She leaned into the water to rinse while Gabe hastily soaped and rinsed himself. He didn't want to waste a minute when he could be touching her. He turned her body away from him and had her lean her arms against the tiles him so that he could see that heart shaped ass in the air. He spread her legs and went down on his knees to get better access to the sweet nectar of her pussy. He breathed in her scent again deeply as the water beat down his back. He took his fingers and spread her wide while he slowly lapped at her entrance. She almost didn't make it as she writhed and moaned his name in pleasure. When his fingers and his tongue pushed into her at the same time she clawed at the wall and tried to balance on her tip toes to let him taste her even more. He lifted her leg and speared her with his tongue while holding her thigh in place so she couldn't run away.

Mya was delirious with pleasure but she didn't want to come so fast. She wanted to enjoy this until the last drop but, she didn't know how much more she could take. Her breasts pushed against the warm tiles of the shower and she loved the way her nipples felt with the rubbing sensation against the wall every time he thrust his fingers and tongue deeper into her pussy. She was on the brink of climax when Gabe stood up, pushed her back further down then thrust his long dick deep inside of her already drenched hole. She forgot to breathe. It was a shock to feel his enormous dick stretching her wide and dipping into a place inside that her ex never could get to even if he tried. Gabe paused to give her a chance to get used to his girth. She was so wet, yet so very tight. He was about to lose control so he kissed her back and neck while he stayed very still. Gabe said, "Mya, are you ok? I didn't hurt you did I?" She answered by pushing back against him then slowly sliding up and back again until the friction felt like she would come. Gabe growled and pushed back. He reached in front of her to grab her breast and pinch her nipple while he moved his hips in a slow grinding rhythm. She screamed out "Yes! Oh yes...please Gabe, just like that!" Gabe smiled a predatory smile and took that queue to let loose. He pulled out of her turned her around and lifted her legs to wrap around his waist. He stroked his length and guided it back into her pussy letting it go as deeply inside her as he could. Mya threw her head back and sighed. The water pulsing around him, and his dick deep inside her was almost too much to take. He kept his hands gripped on her ass and he cupped her head and pulled her hair while he kissed her passionately. He could not take it anymore; he looked down at her and said, "Cum for me baby. Now!" She shook and bucked her hips and he held on to her even tighter. "Gabe! Gabe I... I'm coming!" Gabe's body shook as he came inside of her at the same time. She closed her eyes tightly and rode the wave of ecstasy all the way top and slowly came back down again. She slid down his chest until she felt her feet touch the floor then lay her head down on his chest while he wrapped her in his arms. Gabe sighed deeply, he felt weak. He let the water fall down over them and kissed the top of her head. He'd just had the best sex of his whole 32 years of life. He was a bachelor who knew how to please the ladies so, that said a lot. Something felt different with Mya and he didn't want to get into what it was yet. Mya looked up and saw the look of confusion on his face. He shook his head as if to get the serious thoughts out of his mind then pasted on a smile. He turned the now cold water off, reached outside of the shower door to get a fluffy towel. He wrapped it around her and then got one for himself. Mya stepped out of the shower and went to sit down on the bed. Gabe stood awkwardly at his dresser. He grabbed some lotion from the dresser and kneeled at her feet and started rubbing it on her feet and legs. She smiled and said, "Gabe you are so sweet, a girl could get used to this." She had no idea how much he wanted to please her. He felt like he wanted to give her anything she wanted and he didn't even know her. He stood up and sat next her on the bed. He looked at her and said "Mya, you are a beautiful lady, and you deserve to be treated like a queen. Any man who can't see that is a fool." Mya blushed, rolled her eyes and said, "Gabe you don't owe me anything, and you hardly even know me." Gabe said, "If you give me the chance I want to get to know you better." Mya blushed and said, "I would like that." He asked her if she wanted him to order room service and she agreed that after the workout they had food would be welcome. A little while later eggs, bacon and toast arrived and they ate while chatting and getting to know each other better.

When they finished eating Mya found her clothes that were thrown in various places in the room. Gabe just grabbed a robe. He walked her to the door. Gabe said, "Mya I just don't feel right letting you take a taxi. Are you sure you won't let me take you back to your car?" Mya just shook her head no. She just wanted some time to breathe and think about all of the wonderful things they'd done last night. She reached up on her tip toes to give him a shy soft kiss on the lips. She said, "Gabe, I had a wonderful time. You rocked my world. I will remember this night forever." With that she turned and headed to the exit and took the stairs to the lobby where she saw her waiting taxicab. She pulled out her phone to text and let Alicia know that she was ok. She knew it was only 8 a.m. so she probably still asleep. She leaned against the window and smiled. Even though she knew she would probably never see Gabe again she knew that today was a good day.

~~~~~~

Gabe wanted to run after her and tell her not to go yet. He really liked her, and he had to see her again. He thought she was beautiful, and sexy, plus she was very witty when they conversed over breakfast. His wide grin dropped when he realized he didn't even get her phone number...

To Be Continued . . .

Tameka Avant is a long time resident of Upstate New York where she is currently raising her two daughters, Arielle and Amari, with a little boy in the oven. When she isn't writing stories she is working on her business "Avant Entertainment" where she sings at events and writes original songs. She is an Alum of the Rochester School of the Arts where she majored in voice and dance. She enjoys reading, acting in local productions, and spending time with her children and Fiancé Eric. In her spare time she is traveling and playing with her new puppy "Mister." For more information about how to reach Tameka for events or story requests please contact her @ (585) 397-7247 or TamekaOne79@hotmail.com. She would love to hear your feedback and suggestions.

 *A Father of four, born in South Jamaica, Queens, New York and raised in Brooklyn's East New York neighborhood, F. Kalife discovered his fondness of book writing through his love of composing essays during the course of his twenty-eight years of incarceration. He's a man of great vision with goals of one day having his hard work transformed into movies. In which he hopes will be successful at the Box Office. He was heavily inspired by W "I-Khan" DeJesus, author of Gorilla Khan, to pen and have his debut novel, "Brooklyn's Own", in which DeJesus, himself is co-author, to be published. When F.K.R isn't laying the ground work for future projects, he's communicating with the love of his life, Rozz aka Sweetie, or mentoring future up and coming authors in their quest to have their work published.*

KNOWLEDGE is the foundation of all things in existence. Knowledge is also the intelligence which is gained from watching closely and listening carefully for the purpose of gaining divine intelligence.

Rosalind is most known for her sewing talents. She was introduced to it at the age of 11 by her mother. She took a liking to it and has made it a part of her life ever since, learning professionally from Fashion Institute of Technology and Parsons School of Design. While taking on various sewing jobs, she also took on the responsibility of two siblings after the death of her mother. Raising four children definitely has its challenges, but it never deterred Rosalind's mind from wanting more in her life. With thoughts of someday writing a book or two, she continued raising her children and building her business. Once she met Knowledge, fell in love and became His Mrs. Robinson, things changed up a little. Before she knew it she found herself working with him on his next novel, The Sutter Angels. Being involved in the development of writing a book has been a great learning experience and she is looking forward to publishing more novels with her husband, as well as independently.

"Never let the behavior of others destroy your inner peace."
Unknown

Also Written by F. Kalife:

Brooklyn's Own: The Notorious A-Team

To contact F. Kalife write to:

Fredrick K. Idlet, DIN# 88B2323
Washington Correctional Facility
72 Lock 11 Lane · PO Box 180
Comstock, NY 12821-0180

Thank you for purchasing and reading our book. We truly hope you enjoyed your read. Please add yourself to any of our social media pages and email list so that you will be informed of "The Sutter Angels 2" and more great street literature from Suga Puss Publishing.

Peace and Blessings,

Mr. & Mrs. Robinson

CPSIA information can be obtained
at www.ICGtesting.com
Printed in the USA
BVHW041942020119
536908BV00009B/341/P

9 781508 831754